UMBRELLA

UMBRELLA

WILL SELF

BLOOMSBURY

LONDON • NEW DELHI • NEW YORK • SYDNEY

First published in Great Britain 2012

Bloomsbury Publishing Plc
50 Bedford Square
London WC1B 3DP

www.bloomsbury.com

Bloomsbury Publishing, London, New Delhi, New York and Sydney

A CIP catalogue record for this book is available from the British Library

ISBN 9781408820148 (hardback)
10 9 8 7 6 5 4

ISBN 9781408832097 (trade paperback)
10 9 8 7 6 5

Typeset by Hewer Text UK Ltd, Edinburgh
Printed and bound by CPI Group (UK) Ltd., Croydon CR0 4YY

MIX
Paper from
responsible sources
FSC
www.fsc.org   FSC® C020471

For Deborah

A brother is as easily forgotten as an umbrella.

– James Joyce

I'm an ape man, I'm an ape-ape man . . . Along comes Zachary, along from the porter's lodge, where there's a *trannie* by the kettle and the window is cracked open so that *Muswell Hill calypso* warms the cold Friern Barnet morning, staying with him, wreathing his head with rapidly condensing *pop breath. I'm an ape man, I'm an ape-ape man, oh I'm an ape man . . .* The lawns and verges are soft with dew, his arms and his legs are stiff – a rigor he associates with last night's tense posture, when *I aborted* the fumbled beginnings of a non-committal congress. While Miriam fed the baby in their bed *hawsers and pipelines coiled away into milky, fartysteam – the enormous projectile retracted into the cradle of my belly and thighs . . . I'm an ape man, I'm an ape-ape man . . .* the Austin's steering wheel *plastic vertebrae bent double, kyphotic . . .* had pulled at his shoulders as he wrestled the car down from Highgate, then yanked it through East Finchley – knees jammed uncomfortably under the dashboard – then across the North Circular and past the blocks of flats screening the Memorial Hospital before turning right along Woodhouse Road. Under the bonnet the pistons hammered at his coccyx, the crankshaft turned his pelvis round and around, while each stop and start, each twist and turn – the very swivel of his eyeballs in their sockets – didn't ease this stress but screwed it still further into his frame: *bitindrill, chuckinlathe, poweron* . . . In his already heightened state he had looked upon the city as an inversion, seeing the parallelograms of dark woodland and dormant grass as man-made artefacts surrounded by growing brick, tarmac and concrete that *ripples away to the horizon along the furrows of suburban streets* . . . While his domestic situation is by no means quiescent, nor is it settled, and the day ahead – Ach! *A beige worm of antiseptic cream wriggles into the festering crack of a bed sore* . . . Bitterly he had considered: Is my dip' psych even relevant when it comes to this first-aiding, the sick parade of a shambling citizen militia? . . . *I'm an ape man, I'm an ape-ape man* . . . The drive into work is already automatic. — Still, it's a shock that his destination is this *folly with a Friends' Shop. Along comes Zachary* . . . Hush Puppies snaffling the gravel path that leads from the staff car park – where cooling steel ticks beside floral clocks – towards the long repetition of arched windows and arched doorways, of raised porticoes and hip-roofed turrets. *Along comes Zachary* . . . creeping noisily up on the high central dome with its flanking campaniles in which no bells have ever rung, as they are only disguised ventilation shafts designed to *suck the rotten fetor from the asylum* . . . *Along comes Zachary* . . . avoiding the unseeing eyes of the tarnished bronze statue that hides behind some forsythia – a young man *clearly hebephrenic* . . . his face immobile forever in its suffering, the folds of his clothing *plausibly heavy* . . . for he looks altogether weighed down by existence itself. *Along comes Zachary* . . . chomping beside the arched windows now, and the arched doorways, and then the arched windows *again*. He admits himself into this monumental piece of trompe l'œil not by the grand main doors – which are permanently bolted – but by an inconspicuous side one – and this is only right, as it begins the end of the delusion that he will encounter some Foscari or Pisani, whereas the reality is: a low banquette covered with *dried-egg* vinyl, and slumped upon this *a malefactor*, his face – like those of so many of the mentally ill – *a paradoxical neoplasm, the agèd features just this second formed to quail behind a defensively raised shoulder.* A hectoring voice says, You will be confined to your ward and receive no allowance this week, DO YOU UN-DER-STAND? *Oh, yes, I understand well enough* . . . which is why he continues apace, not wishing to see any more of this *routine meanness . . . Along comes Zachary – and along* a short corridor panelled with damp chipboard, then down some stairs into the lower corridor. *Along comes Zachary – and along –* he has clutched his briefcase to his chest, unfastened it, and now pulls his white coat out in *stiff little billows.* You'll be needing one, Busner, Whitcomb had said – *a jolly arsehole, his long face a fraction: eyes divided by moustache into mouth –* else the patients'll think . . . *Think what? Think what?!* But the consultant's attention span was so short he had lost interest in his own phrase and fallen to reaming the charred socket of his briar with the end of a teaspoon, the fiddly task performed inefficiently on the knobbly tops of his knock-knees. – Why were the staffroom chairs all *too low or too high? Along comes Zachary – and along . . . I'm an ape man, I'm an ape-ape-man, oh I'm an ape man*, his splayed shoes crêping along the floor, sliding across patches of lino, slapping on stone-flagged sections, their toes scraping on the ancient bitumen – wherever that was exposed. *Scrrr-aping.* He wonders: Who would dream of such a thing – to floor the corridors, even the wards, of a hospital with a road surface? Yet there is a rationale to it – *a hectoring, wheedling, savage rationale* – that explains itself via the voices that resound *inside the patients' bony-stony heads, their cerebral corridors and cortical dormitories* ... because these are roadway distances – a hundred yards, a hundred feet, a hundred more, *a North Circular of the soul.* No signs, though, *no Tally-Ho Corner* – instead: lancet windows that peer out on to the airing courts from under lids of grime, *exercise yards, really*, separated by the wings and spurs that partition the *long sunless trench* between the first and second ranges of the hospital. *Spurs budding from wings – more spurs budding from them, the whole mad bacterium growing steadily larger and more complex in the hospitable suburban substrate. Along comes Zachary* ... On the windowless side of the corridor there are doors with bossy signs on them: PORTERS, CANTEEN, MAINTENANCE DEPT CANTEEN, SYNAGOGUE, BOUTIQUE – *boutique!* then BREAD ROOM – *a room full of bread* ... and there are also ramps leading up to the wards above. *On he comes* ... and still the *deep throat gapes* in front of him, a gullet of light-stripes indented with bands of pockmarks – the original plasterers' decorative scheme – or else scattered with medallions and stone-rustic quoins seeped-upon-brown. *On he comes* ... tenderly touching the flaking veins of old gas pipes, to the bare copper of one of which has been Sellotaped a single flyer for POPULAR SWING BAND, The Rhythmaires – but, he thinks, can this be that dated, or is it that the air in here and everything else ages faster? This is at the corner where the western corridor intersects, a rounded corner *worn down by lurch-upon-lurch – No! It was designed that way to stop them killing themselves, which they will do.* And get used to it, Whitcomb had said perkily from behind his *plastic comb moustache*, because you'll have to deal with a great many more. That's just the way – how it is. A great shame – but how it is. Hanging may've been repealed by

Parliament . . . he puffed small and aromatic clouds of *cosmic faux pas* . . . but it remains the number one method of execution in here – this decade is proving quite as swinging as the last! Not that Whitcomb was being callous, it was just that that's *how he is* – like so many psychiatrists of passable competence, so accustomed had he become to speaking to the distressed and the deranged in tones bridled by concerned neutrality, and employing vocabulary purged of any upsetting words, that when set free he became laughably inappropriate – or would be *if there was anything to laugh about*. Nor had he expected his new junior to deal with the amusing suicides himself – certainly not by swabbing, or even so much as looking – *that's what nurses were for, surely!* – only that he should be prepared for how the more feisty ones, *with sprightliness fizzing in their melancholy*, would smuggle a sheet to the lavatory, tear, twine and then knot it to the crook of the pipe where it entered the cistern. *The blessing as well as the curse of this Victorian plumbing*, Busner had felt Whitcomb might well have said – it was his sort of remark – but instead he was obliged to furnish his own homily, for any death, no matter how meagre, demanded at least this consideration: *The blessing as well as the curse of this Victorian plumbing is its robustness. Kick and thrash as they might, the most ardent suicide was unable to break the pipe . . .* They sometimes manage – this from Perkins, the nastier of the charge nurses on 14, one of the two chronic wards to which Busner had been assigned – to hang themselves from the bloody chain, would you believe it! We find 'em with their bare tootsies in the kharzi . . . Busner believed it. He saw rivulets of urine and faeces running down the gutters between metatarsals, *plip-plopping into the commode while up above the cistern splutters unceasing* . . . That first suicide, which he had not only looked upon but also helped Mboya – the nice nurse – to cut down, had

5

suspended herself from the completely reliable pipe – and so in death she was wedged in the awkward gap between it and a white-painted window that had been halved lengthwise when this cubicle was partitioned into existence – *yet more evidence – if any were needed – of how the hospital altered its own cellular structure to create new morphologies for new pathologies to be diagnosed by psychiatrists accredited by new professional associations* ... while the inmates remained the same, patient only in the way she now was: inert, with no sign of her bowels having been emptied apart from ... *that smell*. Instead, her papery skin, *oh so fine*, crinkled into the flannelette of a too-big nightie. She was, Busner had thought, a dead dry moth, its cellular structure decaying inside of this far larger one.

... Apart from that smell: *faecal, certainly – but antiseptically chemical too, with a sharp tang of floor polish* — a still more intense blending of the odour that emanated from the pores, mouths and hidden vents of the inmates confined to the first psychiatric ward Busner had ever visited, more than a decade before, where he had *student-foolishly* inquired, What's that smell? And been told it was paraldehyde, a liquid sedative as limpidly brown as the state it was intended to induce ... *in Henry, in Napsbury* ... *where he still is* ... *my brother lest I forget*. Paraldehyde – how much of it had been poured down throats in asylums throughout the past half-century? *Gallons* ... *demi-johns* ... *barrels? Hosed into them, really, to put out the fire*. And now what was left – *this rain inside the building, this rusty old rain falling down from the saturated plaster to the asphalt floor*.

All this had jetted Busner forward *sea-sluggishly through the greeny-briny*, the sounds of crying, sobbing and cackling amplified by the third-of-a-mile corridor, distorted by its scores of alcoves, then spun by its rifling so that, with unerring accuracy, they strike him in one ear and revolve around his head to the other . . . *Axoid: Bold as Love.* *Along comes Zachary, my tremolo arm vibrating as I sing to my own don't-step-on-the-cracks-self . . .* past the HAIRDRESSER and the SCULP-TURE ROOM, then out from the main block of the hospital towards ART THERAPY and the REMINISCENCE ROOM – the last Whitcomb's own humane innovation. In this section of the corridor the light from the south-facing windows gives him the sensation of trundling lousily along a trench, *paraldehyde . . . paral- . . . parados!* that was the word for it – the side of the trench where they stood to *fire their machine gun, its traverse . . . the airing court, its ticcing picking off the enemy that comes bellowing across the dormant grass: madness – a banshee. Along comes Zachary . . .* Not that he has had the corridor to himself – there's been a steady stream of staff and a few purposeful patients on their way to buy pathetic sundries or attend therapy sessions. A few purposeful – but many more let out from their wards simply to wander the sprawling building. There was one platoon – or so he'd been told – who marched from the Camden Social Services office in the north-west to the Haringey Social Services office in the north-east, then headed south to the lower corridor, and tramped the entire length of it before heading north once more, and so complet-ing a mile-long circuit of the hospital's insides which they would make again and again, until ordered to halt for food by their bellies, or for rest by their feet, or for medication . . . *by their keepers.* Yes, there have been these patients in their charity cardigans soiled at the hem, thick socks sloughing from thin ankles, their eyes cartooned by the wonky frames of their National Health glasses – for whom *a corridor is a destination.* None of them is real – nor remotely credible, not compared to this: *Along comes Zachary . . . the me-voice, the voice about me, in me, that's me-ier than me . . . so real, ab-so-lute-ly, that might not self-consciousness itself be only a withering away of full-blown psychosis?* This must, Busner thinks, occur to everyone, every day, many times, whether or not they are walking along a corridor so long that it would challenge the sanity of *a once-born, a cheery Whitman. Still . . . that way madness about madness lies . . .* a madness that has already diverted his career from the mainline before it got started, sending him *rolling into the siding that connects to this laager,* with its *buttoned-up soul-doctors and Musselmen, all of them compelled to serve under the campanile, the water tower, and the chimney from the stained brickwork of which a smooch of yellow smoke licks the grey sky over North London. Along comes Zachary . . .* the corridor is narrow – ten feet at most – yet none of the human traffic thus far has detained him until now — when he is fixated by one transfixed. It is a patient – a woman, an old woman . . . *a very old woman, so bent – so kyphotic,* that upside down she faces the sagging acrylic belly of her own cardigan and *vigorously assents to it.* This is all that Busner can see: the back of her *nodding-dog* head, the whitish hair draggling away from two bald patches – one at the crown, the second a band across the rear of her cranium. At once, he thinks of twitchers he has seen on his chronic ward, screwing their heads into the angle between the headrest and the back of their allotted armchair – twitchers, wearing themselves away as opportunity hammers away at the inside of the television screen and applause comes in monotonous waves. She is at once a long way off and close enough for him to manhandle. After the eruptions – and there are many lifetimes of afterwards – it settled down on him, an understanding soft and ashy, that all the important relationships in his life – with his uncle Maurice, with Alkan, with Sikorski and the other Quantity Theorists, with his wives – definitely with his children – were like this: *fondling familiar, their breath in my nostrils caries-sweet, sugar-sour — yet also radiophonically remote, their voices bleeping and blooping across the lightyears.*

They take a long time to reach one another — the psychiatrist and the old woman patient. To see her, to *see her* properly, Busner has to wade through a Brown Windsor of assumptions about the elderly insane. — Moral aments, McConochie had called them in the subdued and amphitheatral lecture room at Heriot-Watt, neither knowing nor caring — so far as the young Zack could see — whether this malaise was born of heredity, anoxia, syphilitic spirochetes, shell shock — or some other malfunction in the meaty mechanism altogether. The dopamine hypothesis was beyond hypothetical to McConochie, *the dope*, whose favoured expository method was to get a chronic patient in from the back wards and *put them through their hobbling paces on the podium.* This, a dour travesty of Charcot's mesmerism, for it was his students who became hypnotised by their professor's monotonous description of the schizophrenic to hand, whose own illness rendered her altogether incapable of evoking the harrowing timbre of her own monotonous voices. McConochie, the worn-out pile of whose fustian mind would be bared — as he wandered from lectern to steamy radiator and back — by his inadvertent references to general paralysis of the insane, or even dementia praecox, obsolete terms that meant far less than the vernacular: loony — yet which served their purpose, inculcating his students — Busner too — with the obstinate conviction that any long-stay inpatient above a certain age was afflicted not with a defined pathology but a wholly amorphous condition. — It is this loonystuff, at once fluid and dense, that Busner wades through, and that, besides clogging up the interminable corridor, also lies in viscous puddles throughout the extensive building and its annexes. The old woman's head *vibrates beyond my*

9

reach: a component on an assembly line just this second halted by the cries of shop stewards . . . She tics, and her crooked little feet, shod in a child's fluffy bedroom slippers, kick and kick at a lip of linoleum tile that has curled away from the asphalt. *Kick and kick: micro-ambulation* that yet takes her nowhere. Busner thinks, inevitably, of a clockwork toy ratcheting on the spot, *a plastic womanikin doomed to topple over* . . . but she doesn't, and so he comes on, his thighs *heavy, aching* as he forces his way through his own clinical indifference.

Right beside her now, bent down like her so that he can peer round her palsied shoulder and into her face, which is . . . *profoundly masked: rough-bark skin within which frighteningly mobile eyes have been bored.* – Shocked, he withdraws, and the old woman is at once *far away again, shaking and ticcing, her fingers scrabbling, her arms flexing I'm an ape man I'm an ape-ape* . . . Perceptible flames of movement ignite on her left-hand side, in the middle of the densest thickets of akinesia, a paralysis not only of the muscles . . . *but of the will itself – abulia?* then flare up one arm, across the shoulders, before *exploding into ticcy sparks and so dying away* . . . *Torticollis* comes to Busner *uselessly* – and such is the parasympathetic drama he has just witnessed that he is amazed when two auxiliary staff, their black curly hair *aerated cream* in white nylon snoods, casually part to circumvent them – . . . I tellim mek a gurl an offer she'll 'preciate, their remarks volleying between him and the old woman . . . See, 'e cummup 'ere mos days . . . – before they reunite and carry on, oblivious. — *Electric woman waits for you and me* . . . with Nescafé and a marijuana cigarette *burning rubber* after the International Times event at the Roundhouse. Somewhere in the bedsit grot of Chalk Farm . . . Busner had taken the *wrinkled fang trailing venom,* his eye caught by Ronnie Laing and Jean-Paul

10

Sartre paperbacks stacked in the brick-and-board bookcase . . . *nauseating*. Her boyfriend's hair hung down lanker than the bead curtain she clicked through with the mugs. She was in velvet – the boyfriend *in a sort of hessian sack*. Was it Busner who had been time-travelled here from a past as jarringly austere as his test-card-patterned sports jacket and drip-dry tie, or, to the contrary, they who had been op-art-spiralled from a pre-industrial opium dream of foppery and squalor? *Later* . . . she frigidly anointed him with tiger balm and then they coupled on a floor cushion covered with an Indian fabric that had tiny mirrors sewn into its brocade. The boyfriend hadn't minded *gotta split, man* and Busner was split . . . *a forked thing digging its way inside her robe.* She fiddled with bone buttons at her velvety throat. His skin and hairs snagged on the mirrors, his fingers *did their best with her nipples. She looked down on me from below* . . . one of his calves lay cold on the floorboards. There was *the faint applause of pigeons* from outside the window. — His strong inclination is to touch the old woman, his touch, he thinks, might free her from this entrancement – but first: Are you all right? Can I help you? *Nothing*. The upside-down face *faces me down*, the eyes slide back and away again, but their focal point is either behind or in front of his face, never upon it. – Can you tell me which your ward . . . is? He grasps her arm – more firmly than he had intended *acute hypertonia wasted old muscles yet taut, the bones beneath acrylic sleeve, nylon sleeve, canvas skin . . . thin metal struts.* The fancy new quartz watch on his own plump wrist turns its shiny black face to his as her malaise resonates through him . . . *Along comes Zachary* . . . he wonders: Am I blurring? Ashwushushwa, she slurs. What's that? Ashuwa-ashuwa. One of her bright eyes leers at the floor. He says: Is it my shoes – my Hush Puppies? Her eye films with disappointment – then clears and leers pointedly at the floor again.

She is drooling, spit pools at the point of her cheekbone and stretches unbroken to where it doodles on the tile with a *snail's silvering*. At long last . . . *slow, stupid Zachary* bends down and presses down the lip of the tile so that the toe of the kicking slipper scoots over it. Then . . . *she's off!* Not doddering but pacing with smoothness and fluidity, her shoulders unhunching, her neck unbending and pivoting aloft her head as her arms swing free of all rigidity. – It took so long for Busner to reach her, so long for him to decide to touch her, that he's agog: she should be right in front of him not twenty yards off and *falling down the long shaft of the corridor. Except* . . . already her gait is becoming hurried then *too fast* . . . *festination*, another uncalled for Latinism, pops into his mind as the old woman is *swept away from me on the brown tide* . . . Is this, he wonders, a contradictory side-effect of her medication? The lizardish scuttle that counterpoints Largactil's leaden tread? Because, of course, it is unthinkable that she shouldn't be dosed with some form of chlorpromazine – everyone is. The drug saturates the hospital in the same way that paraldehyde formerly soaked the asylum, although a few isolated voices – Busner's muted one among them – have, while not doubting its efficacy, its . . . humanity . . . questioned its necessity. For all the good this does, because there's no damning its sepia-sweet flow, a single wave that nonetheless drowns out many, many voices. Not having seen quite so many chronic mental patients in one place for some years, Busner has been struck, since arriving at Friern, by *the chloreography*, the slow-shoe-shuffle of the chorus from which an occasional principal choric breaks free into a high-kicking and windmilling of legs and arms. Noticed this tranquillising – but also become aware of a steady background pulse of involuntary movement: tardive dyskinesia that deforms the inmates' bodies, flapping hands, twitching facial muscles, *jerking heads* . . . They are possessed, he thinks, by ancient subpersonalities, the neural building-blocks of the psyche . . . *She is gone* – or, at least, too far down the corridor to be seen any more *a human particle*. Busner, who is interested in most things, has read about linear accelerators, and so he takes a green-capped Biro from the row ranged across his breast pocket – green for his more imagistic aperçus, red for clinical observations, blue for memories, black for ideas – then writes in the notebook he has taken out and flipped open: *What will she smash into? What will happen then? All the subhuman parts of her – can they be observed?* in the long dark corridor where they play all sorts: *skippin'* and boats and *hoopla-for-chokkolits*. Mary Jane comes to *smackem*, Lookit the skirtin'! she cries. In the passage it's *allus* dark – so *dark inna coalhole*. Illumination comes only from a fanlight above the door, comes on sunny days in a single oblique beam a *Jacob's ladder* that picks out a *burnin' bush* on the floorboards that Stan and Audrey jump into and out of – Yer put yer leff hand in, yer put yer leff arm out, Shake it a little, a little, then turn yersel about, the little ones, they are, going *Loobeloo, loobeloo*, but Bert just laughs at them: You're rag-arses, you aynt got no proper cloves, juss smocks, and he swings open the front door and goes out on the step to play with his marbles . . . his *wunner* . . . *his fiver an' sixer inall.* He has them all neatly wrapped up in one of their father's noserags, wrapped up and tied in a little bindle. He sits on the front step and gets them out and places them in a row. Audrey peeks from behind the door and sees *claybrown, marblewhirl, glasstripe* with *sunrays* shining through it *so pretty* she cannot resist it when he goes down the four steps to sit at the kerb and twist fallen straw – but *grabs it* and darts back inside. Stan's eyes are wide, Yul catchit, he says, yul catchit. They stand in the *burnin' bush* looking at the striped marble glowing in Audrey's palm and neither of them can move – Yer put yer leff leg in, yer put yer leff leg out, yer put yer leff leg out, *yer put yer leff leg out* . . . but it won't go *no ferver*, it is stuck there kicking and kicking against an invisible barrier, while, terrorised by the imagining of what Bert *will do to me*, Audrey's head shakes, *Yer put yer noddle in, yer put yer noddle out* . . . The door crashes back on its hinges and there he is: Where's me stripey! He howls, then charges for her, *Yer put yer whole self in, yer put yer whole self out* . . . He grabs her wrist so hard she feels the bones grating together inside it, then twists it so that the fist opens helplessly. A'wah-wa-wa! A'wah-wa-wa! she blubs. Audrey's big brother's starting eyes are fixed on his beloved marble – but hers, hers, are equally held by the peculiar bracelet he wears, its golden segments *fiery* in the *burnin' bush*, and on the back of it a huge black jewel *Mother's jet beads*. Audrey staggers, almost falls, bends double to escape the *hurt* and is caught there feeling the long *Vulcanised* strip of tension that loops round her middle and stretches in either direction the length of the passage *an inner tube pulled tight round the rim of a bicycle wheel*.

Stuck in the present's flesh are the looking-glass fragments of a devastating explosion: a time bomb was primed in the future and planted in the past. The debris includes the row of houses along Novello Street towards Eel Brook Common, their top two storeys weatherboarded and bowing over the roadway under widows' peaks of rumpled tiling. There's the fat-bellied kiln of the pottery in the crook of the King's Road and the ragged patterning of the yews in the misty grounds of Carnwath House. Old Father Thames sucking on weedy-greasy piles stuck in the mud all along the riverside from the bridge to the station. Her own father sucking on a hazel twig he's cut and whittled with his pocket knife to slide in and out of his

14

muddy mouth, in between his remaining weedy-greasy teeth. — Audrey's father, Sam Death: not De'Ath, not lar-de-dar, not like some uz thinks they're better than they should be. Namely, Sam's brother Henry, who styles himself like that and resides in a new villa somewhere called Muswell Hill. They have their own general, the De'Aths. Audrey has heard this said so many times that even now, a big girl of ten, she cannot forestall this vision: a rotund man in a scarlet jacket hung all over with gold braid, and sitting on a kitchen chair in a scullery. His white mutton chops creamy on the rim of his high collar, his red cheek pressed against the limewashed wall. Not that Audrey's mother speaks of the De'Aths' general enviously – there has always been a niceness to this understanding: while the Deaths are not the sort to have servants, neither are they those *what serve.* And while the Deaths are no better than they should be, neither are they worse than they might. Whispering in the parlour before the new bracket was put in, before the cottage piano arrived – whisperings when Mary Jane put a solar lamp on the table at dusk and it rounded off the corners of the room with its golden globe of light. Guttersnipes, they hissed, urchins, street arabs – different ones came on several occasions to say, If it please you, sir, ma'am, I bin by the line-up fer the Lambeth spike, anna bloke wot wuz innit said if'n I wuz to cummover west an' tell iz people there'd be a tanner innit. But Sam Death is not the whispering sort: A tanner! A tanner for a windy nag stuffed with skilly! You'll count yerself bloody lucky t'cummaway frummeer wiv a thru'pence – now fuck off, or I'll call fer the blue boys! The arabs aren't down – thru'pence is *a good dip,* so they skip from the avenue into the Fulham Road, tossing their caps up as Audrey's father buttons the long skirts of his rabbit-skin coat, saying, There's one as won't be dining wiv Duke 'Umphrey t'night.

15

Audrey never sees *ve windy nag*, knows only of her father's other brother from these evening sallies – Sam heading off to head him off, muttering that: It's a crying shame Honest John Phelps the ferryman is no more, so cannot take him across to the Surrey side. So, James Death the pauper uncle becomes all paupers for Audrey – when she's sent to fetch her father from the Rose & Crown for his tea *Jim's* is the shadow that capers beside the trapdoor dancers. In the flare of a naptha lamp, she sees him, grovelling beneath one of the coster's stalls in Monmouth Street market – cowering there, picking up orange peel and *pressin' its smile to 'is ol' man's mouf* . . . Then there's the screever kneeling on the pavement outside the ironmonger's on King Street, where Audrey waits while her mother goes in to buy a tin of Zebra grate polish. This rat-man scratches a gibbet on the granite with charcoal, not chalk – a fraying hank of marks from which hangs Uncle Jim, who sings: *Je-sus' blood ne-ver failed me ye-et* . . . his cap in hand.

Stanley, his blazer hung from the privy's latch, feeds the chalky inner tubing into the steel groove – *Gilbert, Gilbert Cook* . . . does something similar so that Audrey *bites my lip* –. But not yet – before then, when Albert sits at the kitchen table, his shirtsleeves cinched by *fascinating* bands, their parents are already styling themselves Deeth, to rhyme with teeth Sam picks, his face *swellin' beet-red*. You'll have an apoplexy, guv'nor, says Albert, dipping his nib and filling in Olive's line of the census form with quick, clever, cursive, clerkish writing. Don't guv'nor me, you jack-gentleman, Sam growls, what matter if we change an a to an e? Whose business but our own? Albert has his father's hand-me-down face, which would be handsome enough *onna a fat man*, although it appears queer on their tapered heads – the smooth flesh *bunching up* at their brows

16

and along their jawlines. It'd be the Ministry's business, I'd say, t'would be better if you left off – and as he speaks Albert continues to write, Death, Violet May, daughter, —, — — — —, — —, Secondary, his pen *morsing* from box to box, the dashes indicating further shared characteristics – 'til at least I've gone into rooms, I've no wish to speak for the others ... who, despite having grown up with Albert always before them, are still agog when he does two things at once, *both perfectly*: piano playing and reading the evening paper, timing an egg while totting up the household accounts – no alternation between hand and foot, or coordination between eye and hand faults him, no variability of scales confounds him. 'E's twins inna single skin, said a local wag, seeing Bert unerringly volley a football even as he was marking possibles for the guv'nor in the Pink 'Un with a stub of pencil – this when father and son were still close, down at Craven Cottage, the playing field all round kicked and stamped into a happily tortured morass. Audrey thought: if we're Death, then Uncle James must be dearth – this a word gleaned from Bible and Bunyan at school, for the Deaths are not regular attendees, let alone communicants.

When four out of the five Death children had left the house on Waldemar Avenue, Death, Samuel A. Theodore, 51, married, 31 years, Night Garage Inspector, Omnibus Coy, Worker, was still known, familiarly, as Rothschild Death, on account of the flutters and the rabbit-skin coat, and the *arf and arfs* he downed in pubs and penny gaffs from King Street to Parsons Green and Mortlake beyond, ales that imparted a jovial gloss to his coating of bombast. Familiarly, *yes*, for *those sort won't be told*, but formally it was Deeth, and when the three Deeths transplanted themselves from the London clay to the red Devon loam, with Albert's assistance taking up residence in a cottage at Cheriton Bishop – where Mary Jane had been raised – they became known locally as the Deers. — Sam Deer totters around the small garden, Olive Deer watches him. She has seen pictures in the illustrated weekly and read the accompanying text. The pictures are obscure – the words surpassing allusive. Olive, who knows nothing of adult bodies besides her own, still wonders how it is that they get food into the women in Holloway Prison who won't eat . . . who keep their jaws clamped shut. She wonders what it might be like to tell someone that a twisting rivulet of ants has leaked into the cottage from the rain-washed garden. Got in, flowed up the stairs, sopped up the grooves of the candlewick and, not unpleasantly, are infesting *me merry bit* . . .

Stanley mends the inner tube, feeding it through the water in the wooden pail, the *kinked eel* sends a *piddle* of bubbles to the surface. He pulls it out, mops it, marks its *gills* with the chalk. Caught in the *kink*, the corridor stretching away in front of her . . . *longer than time*, Audrey *burns with covetousness* for that safety bicycle, convinced she can ride it better than him – fix it quicker. *Neat as a pin* in the tailor-made she's bought with her first week's wages from Ince's, she covets it – and resents him. It was one thing to be still soaping Bert's collars – from when they were nippers his primacy was taken so much for granted that there was no more need to speak of it than *what you got upter in the privy*. But Stanley – her *baby*, her *bumps-a-daisy*, that he should have this and not her, well, she was reft, the suspicion creeping into her that he's never *given a fig* for her. Playing out, playing Queenie – and *I was Queenie*, and the Wiggins boys all *mocking me* . . . and that lousy boy, who come up from Sands End – the one Mother said az the stink of gas onnis togs – picks up the ball and dips it inna puddle, then rolls it in some horse shit, and when I turn

18

round he throws it at me so 'ard the string busts and all the soggy, shitty paper wraps round my face and spatters my pinny, an' Stan leaps on 'im, thumpinim proper, defendin' his big sis, and the Sands End kid ad vese big obnail boots, no stockings, juss vese boots . . . coming down on Stan's face . . . a yelp! The Wiggins boys screamin', turnin' tail. There mustabin a nail come loose – there was that much blood. When Bert come out of the house and dragimoff, the Sands End kid was spittin', Garn! Piss up yer leg an play wiv ve steam! Still . . . maybe . . . maybe even then *it was all a bloody show* . . .

Cold meat, mutton pies, Tell me when your mother dies . . . November in *Foulham*, the streets greasily damp – the colour of rotten logs. Bad air from the river, bad air from the Works, rotten malt gusting from the Lamb brewery over Chiswick way. In the back bedroom Audrey rubs the soot-stained muslin curtain against her cheek and peers down in the near-darkness at the backyards of their terrace and those of the terraces behind, fret-worked by walls and fences into separate territories, each with its own upright hut . . . *a command post – Ladysmith relieved. Come inter the ga-arden, Maude!* And see the raspberry canes *scattered spilikins*, the humpback of an abandoned cask, a pile of bricks, a birdcage *shaped like the Crystal Palace* that *them two doors down adfer a myna*, which had croaked back at the cat's-meat-man: *Ca-a-at's me-eat!* Until *p'raps a cat gotit*. Audrey! *Or-dree! Cummun get yer tea! Cat meat, mutton pies, Tell me when your mother dies* . . . She should have been down there with her sisters, fetching yesterday's leg of mutton down from the meat safe, peeling and boiling potatoes, scraping dripping from the pale blue enamel basin. *Or-dree!* She can't be *doin' wivvit.* Time enough for tasks later – her soda-scraped hands *bloaters* floating in the *scummy* water. Besides, she cannot abide her mother just now – Mary Jane who stinks of chlorodyne, and slumps narcotised on the horsehair chaise her sons dragged in from the parlour when it split. Her *Ladysmith*, a bell tent of grey woollen shawl and black bombazine, her tired auburn hair down *rusting* on her big shoulders. I can't be bovvered wiv me stays, she says, not when me mulleygrubs comes upon me. Audrey is repelled by her – disgusted that her mother vouchsafes her *women's ailment* to her alone – the *sly thing, Or-dree!* – where they jumble together in the sewn-in pockets of time swung apart from the *general shindy* of Death family life.

She comes clattering down the bare stairs – the runner in the hall has yet to reach them, it trails behind the Death's measured tread as they mount from floor to floor of No. 18 Waldemar Avenue. When they had arrived, the house – barely twenty years old – had just suffered its first demotion: sold on by the family who had bought it from its spec' builder to one Emmanuel Silver, who had sliced it into three residences. The Deaths – Samuel, Mary Jane and the three older children, who were then very small – had the ground floor, a proper kitchen range and a *spankin' new geyser*, although they and the other families still had to share the old bucket privy in the backyard. The Poultneys had the rooms on the first floor for a while, until Abraham Poultney was laid off from his job as a fitter with Ellis Tramways, a happenstance that coincided – or may have been caused by – the death of their younger daughter, Rose, from diphtheria. She wuz not the right sort, Mary Jane said of Missus Poultney. Not that she wuzzn respectable – but she 'ad no backbone, poor soul. I didn't see little Rose for, ooh, on toppuv a week – you remarked onnit, Ordree – so I goes up there and finds they'd put her on toppuv the wardrobe in the back bedroom. The whiffuvit – terrible, it wuz. The merciful Deaths had paid for the funeral – including the toy casket, knocked up from deal, *cheap but decent*. At about the same time, Samuel had secured his own position as Deputy General Manager of the London General's Fulham garage – this, after long service as a driver, and latterly a conductor. *'E was a blackleg in the strikes*, said Stanley, years later, *so they give iz nibs iz dibs*. Audrey never thought this the whole story – she had seen how her father was with horses *bussing and petting 'em* . . . She had been with him one time when he stooped down in the road after another hearse had passed by and said, See 'ere, girl, 'ere's shit an' straw both. What they eats an' what they lets fall at the far end. Straw's 'ere to muffle it up when they carts us away. When they've planted us in the ground, we'll turn inter 'urf – which is only by wayuv sayin' another sorta droppin'. It was an uncharacteristically lengthy speech for her father to have made – at least, in the presence of a member of his own family. — Parked outside the Cock & Magpie with a jujube to suck – or not, Audrey heard not Father, Samuel or Sam, but Rothschild Death holding forth in the public bar: on the follies of the turf, the moonstruck fancies of the new women and the socialistic madness of the Progressives. An occasional late hansom or growler might bowl along King Street – straw bristles plaited in its horses' tails, followed by a 'bus rattle-chinking towards her father's garage. A swell got up in Ulster and homburg might elbow a tinker woman away from the pub door, *bloody jade*, giving a keyhole warbler the chance to slide in to the *goldensmoky* mirrored cacophony on his coat-tails. Once ensconced she might yowl out, Well if you fink my dress is a littulbit, juss a littulbit – not too muchuvit! While hiking up her petticoats, such as they were, until overwhelmed by cries of outrage: Flip 'er a tinker, Rothschild! Gerriduv ve drab! Her father's face hanging mottled from the shiny platter of his topper's brim, the hiss of the jets in the outsized glass lamp that hung above the double doors. Up there, in the elemental radiance, floated a softly moulded figure in a dainty print gown. Up there, where *speechless Thought abides, Still her sweet spirit dwells, That knew no world besides* . . .

Audrey had seen her father with horses – and she had seen him with men, a stallion among them, his commerce easy enough – yet fraught with sufficient danger to give him authority, *Gentlemen, I have dived into Romano's, and now* . . . his *sausage seegar sizzles innis face . . . my tissues are refreshed!* He's a study, Rothschild, a quick turn, who hooks his thick neck in the crook of his bamboo cane and hoiks himself offstage. He had *so they said* once thrashed a navvy to *wivvi-naninch,* not that you would divine these *fistic manoeuvres* from the way he plotted his course home down the Fulham Palace Road, his flame-haired *slippuv a dorter* clipping along in front of him, lighting the way through the particular to *anuvver meat tea* . . .

Albert and Stanley sit, both with books held open by the lips of their plates, both with collars unbuttoned, their tea cups cradled in their hands for warmth as much as refreshment. Vi and Olive gawp, pasty faces pinched by pointed shoulders, each with a slice of bread and dripping in their hand as they behold this virile spectacle: the man and the boys taking turns to hack at the leg of mutton, then put meat in their too-similar faces. Albert's glassy paperweight eyes, Welsh-slate blue, scan up and then down the narrow columns of Rous's Trigonometric Tables – not consigning cosines, sines and tangents to memory, only confirming the tight joins of the granite setts already laid out along the rule-straight roadways of his metropolitan mind. And Stanley – his complexion cooler, his brows finer than those of his older brother – he sighs, ahuh, shuffling fingertips from one page to the next of a Free Library book. His eyelids flicker and his fringe bobs, the whirring mechanism of Bakelite and crystal rods, propelled by scores of flywheels, squeezes his very atoms into the kinetomic beam in a number of abrupt spasms that, while they bend him back so far his just-stropped neck touches his rear, are not in the slightest discomforting – and all the essence of Stanley is then discharged from the elevated muzzle of the contraption, shooting a streak of light between the spokes of the Great Wheel at Earls Court. Up and up above the city it goes – dolorous hoots from the steamers anchored at Tilbury, gas-mantle-ssssh! in the upper atmosphere – and higher still, the clouds flickering far below. In one aperture pickelhaube-helmeted Junkers slash each other's cheeks to ribbons, in another the Tsarina kisses an egg set with rubies and garnets. The beam is so high now that Stanley's atoms sweep into orbit, girdling the earth once, twice, thrice! Before tending down and down into the viridian heart of Africa, where, in a jungle clearing, awaits *Fortescue, my mechanic*, cranking the handle of an apparatus that sucks the beam into its celluloid funnel. Stanley is an apparition that swiftly solidifies, panting in a patented woollen Jaeger bicycling suit. He and Fortescue shake hands vigorously. Capital shot, old bean! the mechanic says, as a nigger chief steps forward from the trees, his honour guard of naked warriors dropping their tribute of tusks *at the feet of the scientific adventurer* . . .

. . . *Olive*, Olive! Oh, I dunno, there's summat wrong wiv you, girlie, carncher see yer father's wantin' izale? Olive turns back to the scullery, limping on the toes of her too-tight boots – she almost lays a hand on the ruddy range to steady herself. Audrey agrees *there's summat wrong wiv that girlie*, and moreover: *They're in cahoots*, they want her to be like this, lost, confused, *a top spinnin' round 'em*. Sam plucks the beaded cloth from the jug and pours a draught into his moustache cup, and there are *beads* of sweat on Mary Jane Death's forehead. Above her in the cabbage-steam-fug hangs a sampler Audrey sewed at school. — *One, two, three, four, girrrls. One: needle in the right hand. Two: thread in the left. Three: Through the eye. Then four: loop and knot. Now, thimble drill* . . . Audrey's hands, not suited to this fine work, twitched and shook in an ague that she felt incapable of mastering, or even to be a part of her at all, but something that snowed down poisonously from the arsenical-green ceiling . . . *Thimbles on yer thumbs, one-two, thim-thumbs, thimthums, tee-to-tum* . . . — Out of the eater, she says, came forth meat and out of the strong came forth – Burrrurp! Really, Samuel, Mary Jane says, laughing, mussyer? *They're in cahoots*, together *they've made five now an' loss none.* Stanley laughs at his father's eructation and says, Judges, Chapter 14, Verse 14 – thass evens, guv'nor. Albert, without looking up, grimaces and Audrey can hear what he hears: the echo of one brother inside the other's bony cave. I'm inbertween 'em – I'm a prism or a lens. Beams of Stanley, beams of Albert, playing, each on the other brother's *blank face* . . .

The curious *round-'ousing* of a big man pulling himself together with his braces – his moustache is *wet wiv beer* and tobacco-stained above his hidden lip. Hard to imagine that there is a lip beneath it, because Samuel Death's hair is so fleshy in tone, and, if it weren't for the reddening of his cheeks, you would think the *tache wuzziz lip*, while there are waxy skin strands plastered at the back of his bare domed head: Bedlam engraved in the Illustrated London News. — A large worthy-looking body walking along the quayside of a Mediterranean port, a basket of laundry dumped on her head. Four sailors dice in front of a tangle of ropes and spars while gazing at her behind. None of the Deaths know where this racy print has come from – it simply cropped up on the wall, hiding the wallpaper with its criss-cross pattern of violets and pansies, wallpaper that is steam-slackened, torn into strips, and certainly antedates the Deaths, for, when Audrey was a littler girl, she was convinced her baby sister had been named after it. — Violet now clambers on to the chair her father has risen from, and, smuts on her cheeks, reaches up to fasten his collar stud. All of them have been dragooned into his toilet: Stanley sent to fetch the showy coat from the hook in the passage, Olive buckles his gaiters, Audrey and her mother mix tea and gin into his flask. Only Albert remains at table, his eyes triangulating a realm of purer forms, his fork negligently *sccccrrrraping* gravy shapes. Samuel cries, Get the Coniston's! A hair tonic he madly applies to the front and back of his dome, as he places first one profile, then the other, before the oval of looking-glass chained up by the door – this, a motion that shows off to its fullest effect the sharp isosceles that, together with his love of swank, has earned him his moniker. Not, Audrey muses, that he's like the landlord, Silver, who comes attired soberly in bowler, wing collar, impeccably shined and elastic-sided boots – but whose face is sallow, handsome, the features somehow exaggerated, *outlined wiv charcoal.* The Deaths are plaster mouldings, Romish swags and vine trails pressed into their whiteness. They are pink and blond, brown and blonder, all save Audrey, whose flaming glory and cake-crumb-scattered cheeks betoken ... *wot? Or-dree, Or-dree, Ordree's mammy gorrersel knocked up by a navvy!* Howsoever the taint was acquired, these are no distinguishing marks – leastways not up towards the Munster Road, where the houses are all *knocked abaht* and there's a family of Irish – or two – in every room, and the *ginger nuts* are everywhere in the streets. Still, *Comes the Jew-boy, Comes the Yid, Comes the Jew-boy for iz gelt* ... is sung with gusto on

Thursday evening, with whichever of the two little girls is to hand, grabbed and bounced on his knee. Samuel breaks off only when he hears the *sccccrrrreeeching* of the front gate, then he goes to the door to watch, derisively, as Silver undoes his trouser clips, pulls off his gloves and courteously doffs his hat. From the Horeb heights of the doorstep Audrey's father hands down a tosheroon, then a second, which is followed – after an insulting interval – by a sixpence. He places the coins in the dapper man's palm, *paying t'be fucking crucified*, before, sucking on his own gall, he retreats to the Golgotha of the parlour so that Silver may trot upstairs and do the same to the other tenants.

The odd panting and heaving that accompanies a tall and corpulent man working his way into a full-length overcoat. *Oof-oof.* The rabbit fur lies slick and rough in the gaslight, the Coniston is sweating *offuvim stink up the privyole.* Over her father's shoulder Audrey sees Stanley's impish expression: a valet, preparing to *cuttim dahn t'size,* by saying, *I say, Pater, that's a wewwy extwavagant costume for an hexplorer-chappie who ain't heggzackerly headin' up the Wivver Congo, only dahn to the 'bus garage by Putney Bridge* – say it, that is, if *'e wuz mad.* Samuel Death takes a further dekko around the room, then makes a final imposition of paternal discipline: Wozzat?! He snatches the flick-book Violet has just that moment snatched from dozy Olive – Audrey knows which one, it was given away with the Daily Mail on the occasion of the old Queen's final birthday parade, stiff cards sewn so they could be riffled and *By Jingo!* The horsemen fresh back from *bashin' the Boer* soundlessly jingle across Horse Guards Parade, their mounts breasting the staccato dust-puffs. Samuel peers at it, lets it fall to the painted floor, *extwavagantly* unbuttons the just-buttoned skirts of his coat. Parts them and reaches in his waistcoat pocket for his watch. Well, pshaw! – the skin curtain billows – You're welcome to vese guttersnipes, Mary, me old Dutch – she simpers on the chaise – if'en I don't look lively . . . All eyes are on his fumbling fingers, all except Albert's. Samuel Death holds the timepiece up by its gold-plated bracelet, its face a lozenge of jet eclipsing the present that flows behind and in front of it. He pinches the tiny buttons either side of the casing and peers at the red illumined figures, 08.54, each digit composed with straight bars, bevelled at their ends. *Gaol numbers . . . I'm in gaol . . . in the spike – the booby-hatch, ha-ha-hooo – help me, helpme, hellellellellpme, Stan, Bert's torturin' me! Ashuwa-ashuwa . . .* — The long rubberised strip of tension loops round her middle and stretches in either direction along the corridor, pulling from the past to the future, lashing her to the moment – her belly *bulges so bad*, she feels *queer, like I might . . . I dunno.* Before she came down to tea she took the piece of calico she had folded into an *'Arrington Square* and put it down the front of her bloomers, although not really grasping why *every lady should know the greatest invention of the age for women's comfort . . .* Stanley releases the semi-inflated tube and it snaps into the bicycle wheel and *off I go! Leaping like a pea onna griddle . . . the pink 'un in Holywell Street . . . stuckinim – stuckinerr . . . We only start the generator for the electric from time to time, Miss De'Ath, wouldn't you agree that candlelight is more aestheti- cally pleasing?* Cables swagging the length of the workshop *sheeee-ung-chung-chung-chung!* Her lathe-bed ratchets back and Audrey loosens the chuck, switches the bit – a fuse rattles down on top of the others. Then they are streaming out from No. 1 Gate, *Where are the girls of the Arsenal? Working night and day, Wearing the roses off our cheeks, For precious little pay . . .* red-and-green flags come from nowhere and are waving on the tops of 'buses thronging

Beresford Square. *Shoulders back! Necks straight! Arms swing! We are the munitionettes, the suffragettes, the wild revolutionary girls!*

What can it mean, this sudden shift from paralysis to movement? Busner is left rooted, all the sour rot from the hospital's miles of intestinal corridor blowing into his puzzled face. This must be, he intuits, something – some definable pathology . . . *surely? The marked counterpoint between akinesia and festi-festi-na-shun, D-E-C-I-M-A-L-I-ZAYSHUN. DECIMALIZAYSHUN. Soon it's gonna change the money round, Soon it's gonna change the money rou-rou-round!* Easier, Busner thinks, to conceive of the Friern corridor as an endless conveyor belt, running around and around, bringing towards him patient after patient pari passu, so that if he can maintain concentration he'll have ample time to make the appropriate diagnosis of neurosis, dipsomania, dementia praecox, generalised paralysis of the insane, syphilis, addiction to socialism, schizophrenia, shell shock – the diseases historically synchronised and so entirely arbitrary, the moral ament becoming, on his next go-round, the mentally deficient, on his third, retarded, fourth, mentally handicapped. *Rou-rou-round. Soon it's gonna change the money round* . . . The hospital's fantasia on the theme of the Italianate belies, he thinks, its real purpose as a *human museum* within which have been preserved intact these *specimens, crushed and mangled round-rou-round, I'm an ape-man, I'm an ape, ape – Enough!* He must seize upon an action with which to fracture this reverie, exactly as the pressed-down tile allowed the elderly woman's foot to scoot forward. He finds it in the *automatism* of consulting his watch, an involved process since his wife – overreacting to an interest in gadgets Busner once feigned – gave him a new quartz model, the first to be affordable, for his thirty-first birthday. So: he flips the heavy gold-plated bracelet from beneath his shirt and jacket cuffs, he brings the little black face up to his own, then pinches the small buttons either side of its casing so that the digits are illuminated *redly, futuristically: 08.54 ... late already for the ward rou-rou-* he at once sees and feels himself to be a colossal white canister spinning slowly end over end and sharply illumined against the infinity of blackness ... *I am late ... already, must pinch ... harder, I can't ... see ... the time!*

He awakens to discover himself an old man who lies pinching the slack flesh on the back of his left wrist with the fingers of his right hand, fingers that prickle with arthritis. He awakens to the *pity of it all,* for *I was up only ...* he struggles on to his other side so he can check the clock radio on the bedside table ... *three quarters of an hour ago,* when he stood in the musty toilet, his sweaty forehead pressed against the mildewed wall, *dropsical – late-onset hydrocephalus?* and stared stupidly at the *splutters unceasing, a plip here, a plash there ...* then at the *ecclesiastical* window with its opacity of *wormy smears – out there breaks the blank day –* then at a toilet roll once dampened, now dried, its lumpy multi-ply reminiscent of *epidermal corruption* not seen since student days – *keratitis, rhagades, the stigmata of congenital syphilis* – and then only as plates in textbooks. On the lino, by the El Greco of his old feet, there was a pile of old proceedings, *peedewed, to be read at stool,* and so the memory's overlay peels back to reveal the exact same vignettes – wall, toilet roll, medical journals – and Busner realises that *I have returned!* A triumphalism he acknowledges to be inappropriate for a sleepy walk even as he looks to the window and *vermiculated quoins* comes from somewhere – *but where?* Then, as he turns, not bothering to flush, and shuffles back towards bed, it occurs to him that he troubled to ask someone he knew then, someone who had specialist knowledge, because they were so ugly, those worm-riddled blocks set into the gateposts of the hospital – *but which hospital?* There had been so many – *Twenty? Thirty?* – up until his retirement the year before, after *hanging on at Heath far longer than I should've . . . and why?* Almost certainly to postpone this present mode of life, one his children viewed as pathological, a senile depression – possibly the forerunner of dementia – that had been kept at bay by his pottering, his peculiar job-reductivism, consulted as he had been mostly by other consultants. Busner knows better: this is the re-emergence of an essential self, long since *buried and worm-eaten . . .* The passage from the toilet to his bedroom is narrow and angles around a portion of the adjoining and more modern office building, an insurance company which, in the process of construction, somehow managed to exact a few cubic feet from this end-terrace Victorian property of no distinction, a brick and masonry *cell like all the rest* — A burst of clickety-clack from the keyboards of the brokers who factor risk within inches of his sloped shoulder almost derails him. John! he hears one call, quite distinctly: John! Female, fifty-three, ten years no-claims – one for John at Aviva? *They're all called John,* while *here am I, a prophet in the wilderness . . .* There is no soft Persian runner beneath his feet, as there would be at Redington Road, only coarse and colourless carpet offcuts that he himself had pulled from a wheelie-bin in back of the discount furniture store in Cricklewood, *Slumberland!,* where he had picked up the few sticks needed to prop up this domestic scene, this *granddad flat. Granddad! Granddad! You're lov-ley, Granddad! Granddad! We lo-ove you!* It's a curse and a blessing, this, as he shuffles through the doorway and spies, clasped by April morning sunshine, the bars of his bedstead, with clumps of his damp *straitjacket* wadded between them. To incontinently recall these, the lyrical

leftovers and junked jingles of seven decades, would be an affliction ... *timeitus*, he smirks ... had Busner not come to appreciate,
since his retreat here to the first-floor flat on Fortess Road, that
within the patterns made by their effervescing in the pool of his
consciousness are encoded wider meanings – he balks at truths –
ones not surveyed or even guessed at by the mental mapmakers with
whom he has spent his working life, notwithstanding the elegance of
their modelling – theoretical, neurological – or the crassness of their
professionalism. The unyielding mattress calls forth only this: a tired
acknowledgement of his own flabbiness. Walks have been resolved
upon and not taken, meals are spooned from tins and forked from
plastic containers, or else spread on bread – lots of it. This particular
Busner kneads soft stuff into a pillow-shape and puts his swollen
head on to it while cavorting with all the svelte fugitive selves that
have spun away from him in this ... *dizzy dance, Granddad, Granddad,
we love you!* And he loves them too, but after he and Caroline parted
it seemed superfluous to do it all again, acquire a fourth wife who
would demand the application of yet another decorative scheme to
the walls that had contained him, on and off, since he was ... *what,
ten or eleven?* He remembers his uncle, Maurice, leading him by the
hand through the wintry chambers of the house on Redington Road,
his tight-fitting overcoat so long and black that when he stooped
he ... *was a drainpipe ... stiffness ... rigidity ... hypertonia* –. It
would be superfluous and *besides the point* – if he wished to go that
way ... *Well*, he had considered getting back together with Miriam
– whom he viewed with *genuine affection* when they met at grand-
children-centred events, and with whom, of course, he still had to
deal when it came to Mark. If not with her – and, after all, he had no
idea of how Miriam felt about him – there might be the possibility

of tying up *the loose ends of relationships still more unravelled* ... But no: the real point being that in *some place or other one of me and one of them are already united in the bicker of minor ailments, cemented by the mucus of passion spent* ... So, whatever the anxieties of his children – two of whom are mental health professionals with all that this implies – Busner had thought it better to simply *walk away*, will the house to them while he was living and *walk away, not quite a sannyasin* ... gingerly he rasps the underside of a jowl – although at long last committed, after decades of dependency, to once more *caring for myself.* 09.01. – When he had stopped wearing ties that was when *I stopped fidgeting with them, obviously* ... *the pill-rolling tremor we called it: tremor at rest, the patient's gaze forced upwards, the hands held out in front, the index fingers rubbing the pads of the thumbs – and the shrink?* He sat there watching them, rolling the end of his tie up and down: *tremor at rest.* Nothing, Busner thinks, comes of nothing – although, LCD digits come of pinching. He had been dreaming of a hospital and got up to pee, then gone back to bed and returned to another hospital – or was it the first again, only in a different era? The plaster strings around the cornices torn away, and the plaster laurels dressing the windows and doors pulverised, the gaps concreted in, then pebble-dashed. Was this the same hospital – or a smaller one? One equipped with a few acute wards, some offices, and a workshop for occupational therapy – *which he had liked* ... Busner had visited them all as he careered through his professional life – Hanwell, Napsbury, Claybury, Shenfield, the 'Bec. Visited them all while organising trials or conducting studies or working as a clinician. He thought now, wistfully, of the long minutes spent watching the cutlass shadows slashed by a pot plant on geometrically patterned wallpaper during an interminable group therapy session ... *No!* It had been a visit – it was a visit that he dreamed of. A visit – and *the smell was on him* . . . the smell of sweat, Largactil sweat. There were greeny linctus beads on his spotty forehead and a filthy mark on the inside of his lumberjack-shirt collar. He liked to look at the redwood, he said, which he could see from the window of his ward. Surely, Busner had thought, it isn't beyond their ability simply to keep him clean – although he, far better than most, knew that it was. Surely, he had almost screamed into the mustiness of the day-room, they can stop his legs from kicking! For if this wasn't pathetic enough, Henry Busner – my brother – had whimpered: *I – I can't con-con-control them, I can't* . . .

. . . *control mine, now.* Sleep is an impossibility – and there's no hospital for him to be admitted to any longer. He has retired: there beneath the breeze-billowed brown curtain, probed by the April morning sunlight, are stacked orange boxes printed with the name La Cadenga and filled with the coprolites he has cleared from his office at Heath Hospital, transferred briefly to Redington Road, then carted on to here. *I – I can't con-con-control them – the fossilised shits.* Propped against the boxes is a brolly he has no recollection of having bought, borrowed or taken up. But that, he thinks, is the way of it: umbrellas are never contracted for, only mysteriously acquired, to be fleetingly useful, then annoying and cumbersome before even-tually being lost. And this losing is itself unrecalled, so that what usually impinges is only the umbrella-shaped hole where one used to be. 09.10. *Ten again.* As he pinches the slack flesh on the back of his left wrist with the fingers of his right hand, it comes *in an old mannish drizzle*: D— E- C- I-M-A-L-I-ZAYSHUN, then *a gush*: *DECIMALIZAYSHUN! Soon it's gonna change the money round, Soon it's gonna change the money rou-rou-round!* — Old age is, it occurs to

Busner as he lies stranded on his side staring at the clock radio, a form of institutionalisation – it deprives you of your identity and supplies another, simpler one, it takes away your clothing and issues you with a uniform of slack-waisted trousers, threadbare jackets and moth-eaten cardigans, togs that are either coming from or going to charity shops. This done, it commits you to a realm at once confined and unbounded, an atrophying circuit of corridors that connect strip-lit and overheated rooms where you fade away your days reading day-old newspapers and specialist magazines – albeit not ones relating to the specialty that awaits you. Old age takes your food and purées it, takes your drink and reverses its distillation, takes – *No! changes the money rou-rou-round!* He knows that this is all too soon, that he is a mere freshman when it comes to such higher forgetting – that when he was first at the Royal Infirmary he had still been fleet, so that, lunging for the ovoid ball, he grasped a teammate's shoulder to *grope my way into a lowering sky . . .* — anywhere, so long as it wasn't the shambles of the ground, any leather so long as it wasn't the *ruptured buckler of a corpse's thorax I'd cackhandedly dissected . . .* Later, he had been compelled, he felt, *to serve beneath the chimney . . .* or the campanile, not that any bells ever rang there, for it was only a disguised ventilation shaft through which the noisome stenches of the hospital *rose up to the heavens . . .*

The staff bore had told him upon his arrival that formerly new patients had been brought in by special trains that halted at New Southgate under cover of darkness. The platform was at the bottom of a steep cutting and could be accessed by zeds of cast-iron stairway – although the patients were taken along a foot-tunnel that angled up through the chalky earth to the easternmost tip of the hospital. This meant that they didn't surface at all – in their committal was their interment – but instead found themselves being marched dazedly down the long, semi-subterranean corridor to the different stages of their induction: deloused in a tiled trough, subjected to a questionnaire and an intrusive medical examination, shaved, cropped, then issued with rough ticken tunics before being allocated to a ward and given their supper: a tin mug of beef tea and an arrowroot biscuit. The clickety-clack of the brokers' keyboards drills through the wall — *the bubbles are popping now*, each one leaving behind a few *dribs of recall* . . . the vermiculated quoins were, Busner remembers, only on the gateposts of that eastern wing – which was a later addition to the building. 09.15. He wonders: What rumours would those new patients have heard about the booby-hatch? In a way it hardly mattered, when there was so much worse inside their own heads. He feels the weight of his ageing face, its exhausted eyelids collapsing into their sockets *glow orange*, and through a slit he sees the white bars at the end of the bed and thinks, I once looked through bars like those and pinched time – that Casio. He is, he senses, *almost there*, but first a necessary interlude: Moog music, the Mekon revolving on his Tungsten dinner plate through the open French windows of the dining room and ricocheting off the sideboard, the grandfather clock, the teak drinks cabinet . . . *rou-rou-round*. Did we, he muses, really measure drugs in grammes – surely decimalisation went in waves? Wouldn't it've been in grains, and fractions of grains? He peers through the white bars and sees his thinner, younger self peering back – smooth-cheeked and with a full head of reddish-brown hair. He has an old-fashioned sphygmomanometer looped around his neck, the thick rubberised cuff dangles at his breast, the heavy steel casing of the gauge knocks against the bedstead ting-tong, ting-tong. His stubby, nimble fingers roll and unroll the frayed end of his dun

35

woollen tie, then idly pump the black rubber bulb of the sphygmomanometer, back to the tie, back to the bulb. A face looms at
Young Busner's shoulder, *Mboya? I don't wanna die in a nuclear war, I
wanna sail away to a distant shore and make like an ape man, La-la-la-
la-la-la-la! La-la-la-la-la-la-la! Steel drumming, wood-on-steel,
steel-on-steel, ting-tong* ... Mboya's face is a teak whorl with deep,
yellowy creases spreading out from full pink lips. The whites of his
eyes are yellowy, his anthracite hair is shaped in an almost-Afro, and
he generates calm, which Busner somehow associates with the cross
he wears on a chain around his neck, a cross the psychiatrist cannot
actually see, but which he senses poking between the buttons of
Mboya's pale-blue nylon tunic. The cross, Busner knows, is one with
a circle around the join of crossbar and upright ... *Coptic? Celtic?* He
would like to ask Mboya for ... *help?* What stops him is not professional pride, only the shameful awareness that the charge nurse has
given him so much help already. Her eyes? Busner begins by way of
an observation. Mboya is judicious: Ye-es ... So Busner asks, Rolled
up like that – are they always? Following this sally, and for want of
anything more constructive to do, he moves to the side of the bed,
removes the pins and lets down the sidebars so that he can lean in
over the old woman. Her posture is ... *bizarre*, the spine curved and
rigid – *give her a push and she'd rock.* Her pinched face is not a face but
a mask of greasy seborrhoeic skin, her lips are stretched rubber bands
that pull away from crumbled gums set with two or three stray teeth.
Busner looks around for a bedside table or locker upon which there
might be a beaker with her dentures in it, but there's no such thing
— her bed stands in the centre of the dormitory together with ten or
twelve others *guano-dashed rocks in a sea of speckled-tan linoleum* that
have been arranged head to toe, a leftover measure from the time

when they might have *coughed TB in each other's faces* ... Not all of these beds are barred, but it's clear that those who've been allocated them lack the status needed to earn them one with its head against a wall and a locker beside it. No one on Ward 14 has anything as homely as a lamp – but at least these beds partake of the wall-mounted disc, a moon that slips through the long, dark nights. Mboya, who has been at the hospital since the late fifties, has spoken to Busner of trough beds and water beds, and other kinds of medieval restraint – although *this* ... *this cage* seems quite bad enough. Is she always ... He has leant down far enough to look into the eyes, which are not eyes but rounded wedges neatly torn in her mask by – *ring-pulls*, which only last weekend he had experienced for the first time: two cans of Coca-Cola from the sweetshop on Holly Hill, snapped open and placed beside the boys on the bench, he leant down laughingly with them to peer into the holes that *sweetly misted* ... By no means – Mboya speaks with colonially educated precision, answering the question Busner has forgotten he posed – these seizures ... or episodes, they happen with great regularity, Doctor, once every sixteen days, and last for ... oh, well, I should say at least five or six hours. And sometimes she will be in this state when I leave for the day, and still be like this when I come back on shift the following morning. Paaa-ha! A sudden expiration of gingivitis breath, then, a-h'h'herrrrrr, she draws it in again – but the mask remains fixed, the eyeholes showing only off-kilter sclera – no pupils. You see – Mboya has a clipboard sheaved with notes he refers to from habit, not necessity – mostly she can feed herself, get along to the day-room, but ve-ery slowly. Then, at other times, it's as if all this time she has been being wound up, because some little thing – I don't know what – will set her off, and man, how she goes, her little legs –.

37

The nurse stops, *but why? Has he perhaps stepped over an internal line of his own by revealing how he views them?* Busner wonders: How does he cope? Does he see them as sprites, as possessed – or are they automata? Then again, there is a certain obscenity in referring to those *little legs*, which, arrested in the mid-writhe of torticollis and exhibiting marked hypertonia, cannot be covered up. Her Winceyette nightie is bunched up around her waist and neither man is prepared to risk his clinical detachment by yanking it down over *those mutton shanks.* — It is only as he grasps her arm, preparatory to applying the cuff that Busner remembers: I've seen her before. Mboya lifts his clipboard. Oh ... yes? Busner says, No, no – not on the ward round, I've seen her in the lower corridor – she was catatonic, jammed up like this but standing with her foot caught by a loose floor tile. When I freed it she went off like a rocket on her, he laughs, little legs. Mboya grins. Ye-es, that's typical of Miss Dearth, ve-ery typical. She's unusual in that respect – the others are mostly one thing or the other, jammed up like this or all shaky, rushing ... Busner has ceased to hear him ... *Do I somehow partake of her shakiness, when I touch her do I begin to blur?* For in the extreme rigidity of her forearm, which she holds at a sharp angle in front of her chest, with the fingers seemingly curled about an immaterial lever, he can sense a terrible compression, thousands upon thousands of repetitive and involuntary actions that are *struggling to get out.* This is, he thinks, not a paralysis as it's commonly understood but an extreme form of oscillation: her muscles are whirling around bony axles, her bones are shuttling back and forth on cartilaginous treadles, her cartilage is itself *cogged ... it appears still until you touch it, and then it goes haywire, the wire coiling around you, dragging you down ...* The old woman hasn't gone haywire, though: *her tragic mask confronts my comic one, I'll never be taken seriously with these flabby cheeks and froggy lips* ... He looks away, flustered, and sees cold light dumped by a transom on to a *writhing caterpillar* that resolves into another old thing, who, presumably *overdosed on Largactil*, thrashes about in a bed beside the double doors that lead to the main area of the ward. He looks back to see an early bluebottle – the hospital is plagued by flies – orbit Mboya's *woolly globe*, and pictures a toy frog one of the boys has, if you *squeeze a little rubber bulb* ... his fingers find the bulb of the sphygmomanometer ... an *obscene tongue of rubber unrolls* underneath the plastic amphibian, flipping it forward. All, he thinks, these agitations – some of which must be connected causally. The right-hand swing door pushes inwards, a face looms spectrally in the small window, the amplitude of its pathology *plotted by the wire graph* – then is gone. All these agitations – the arrow on the FIRE ESCAPE sign is more mobile than this face confronting his, which has no eyebrows or lashes worthy of the name, two – no, three – hag hairs on the chin, that chin sharp, the cheekbones sharper, the skin a cracked glaze beneath which ancient freckles have run together into liver spots. He has leant down so far that the crystal of the gauge lies cold against her giblet neck. Paaa-ha! a shudder of the sunken chest. *It's not food – it's faecal. The others are mostly one thing or the other* ... — In the submarine hospital all is agitation, the fin-flip along corridor after corridor after corridor, flowing in and out of recesses and embrasures, swirling around buttresses and foaming down the salmon runs of the staircases, at the bottoms of which it dissolves in a spray of tics and jerks and grimaces. Even so, Busner has noticed these others, caught sight of them with the eternal evanescence with which the eyes *capture a shape in water* – and on finer days he has seen them outside, caught treading water in the airing courts between

39

the first and second ranges of the hospital, or else thrashing further afield, in the grounds, where other patients merely sidle the tendency of the ornamental beds. And in the day-room of his other chronic ward, where the inmates are restrained in easy chairs by too-tightly-tucked rugs, pinioned in front of televisions that show *capable hands shaping clay* – in that drear row he has seen *an other*. Then again: passing by the doors of the main hall, where the cupola is obscured by a cantilevered mezzanine, Busner has been pulled up short by this halting exchange: Nothing, my lord . . . Nothing! Nothing . . . Nothing can come of nothing, speak again – and upon entering found *a dim hurly-burly*, a stage hung about with dusty swags of blackout cloth and scudding between them *a fool* in a black turtleneck pullover playing a play-within-a-play, his players a hyperactive Cordelia and a comatose Lear who droned to a pool of patients that had eddied in from the surrounding wards to lap against the stage. In all this agitation a single ripple stirred the psychiatrist's attention – and, without knowing how to classify him, Busner still knew that this too was another of the others of whom Mboya now spoke.

The others, who were mostly *one thing or the other*: either like this old woman – whose humming arm he held – whirled into a twisted immobility, or else unwound *spastic, hypotonic* . . . these others of the others he had seen considerate nurses prop against walls, only for the patient to drip down once their backs were turned. Both kinds, Busner has noticed, share this uncanny capability: that they render those around them either too sharply focused or too blurred. The somnolent and akinesic ones were so very still that they partook of the hospital's very fabric – Busner stood, captivated, watching them standing, thin, rigid and bent beside the old lancet windows, while those passing them by smeared a photon trail across his retinas. By contrast the ticcy, antic ones were impelled forward – goaded by some neural whip, they skipped, taking hundreds upon thousands of tiny steps. They are, he thought, the ones who couldn't keep still for the long seconds when the plate was exposed, and so they marked the present with a ghostly impression even as their bodies faded into the future. Time, he thought, it has to do with time. The psychotics, for all their extravagant claims of having been sent *sliding back down the shiny curve from the future to warn us of the Victory of the Machines*, are rooted in Now. Their stagy delusions are well dressed with the technologies of the present: transistors, assembly lines and answer-phones – while their persecutors are just as frenziedly up to date: Black September infiltrating grey March, or the Irish social worker responsible for the Islington patients on Busner's acute ward whom at least six of them believed to be an IRA gunwoman, *devilish Bernadette*. As for the brain-damaged, the spastic and the otherwise touched – their faces have no expression at all, but instead the features rise and then set as their bodies respond to *circadian Rhythmaires*. Then there are the leucotomised – for they are here as well, their hair crinkled or their scalps bare where clamp tightened, saw grated and drill bit. Busner has marked them, the pre-frontals – they are trapped in a very exact layer in the hospital's stony strata, being all of an age – mid-forties – to have been interfered with twenty years earlier, when such things were the fashion. Be that as it may, their wayward-ness is constantly being updated, as witnessed by the anguish in their eyes, which are forced inwards by the raw mechanics of their loss of control: I can't help it, Doctor, the one on Ward 20 said, I can't help it, I can't help it, Doctor, I can't . . . Doctor, I can't, I-I-I-I-I . . . But *these others*, they are both of this time and escaping from it, *of now and then* . . . And this particular old woman, who alternates between

41

being one kind and the other, has alerted him to their existence *as a group* – a status that Mboya, with his vastly greater experience, has now confirmed.

Is she –? the psychiatrist asks. No, the nurse replies, there's no need – except from time to time to help her sleep. For Busner, these past few weeks have been mostly this: a tallying of drug charts, the sounding of sunken chests, the winding on and the stripping off of the sphygmomanometer's heavy cuff, the listening in the hush of the ward for the rush of arterial blood. Entering the damp pits of their beds he has gone potholing in the fistulous sores that extend inside these hollow patients. It is, he knows, impossible to write a prescription of this form: Constant and sympathetic assistance towards effective mobility is to be taken ALL DAY – and so he only tiredly scrawls tetracycline in a fixed cycle. Whitcomb has allocated Busner two chronic wards, 14 and 20, and as a sop to his clinical expertise he is also allowed a part in the decision-making on Ward 11, over in the separate Halliwick unit, where the acute admissions are held apart from the main body of the hospital for assessment. Hence all this *promenading* – a ward round that provides him with *a mile-long constitutional*... He wonders, a bit, if Whitcomb, the shit, has done this deliberately to exercise his tubby junior – then reflects as he collects his keys from the Admin Office that the organisation of rosters recently ceased – or so he has been told – to be a decision made by clinicians, because *the bureaucrats have taken over the asylum*, which is only fitting given that in the absence of anything resembling a cure the medical staff have for years – decades probably – operated as patient-pushers, stacking, hole-punching, binding and ultimately filing away their workload in this tray, that drawer or some other neglected pigeonhole. In the nether regions of the hospital,

Busner supposes, there must be the analogues to all this: the *histrion-ics*, the *kerfuffle*, the *seems agitated*, the *150mg Stelazine intra musc*, all of it scrawled on preprinted forms churned out by the relevant department, then *stuffed in buff* and laid on metal shelves to gather the finest of dust. The Records ... *a map of a map* that is in itself ... *a map*, or at least a diagrammatic representation of the hospital, which is a self-sufficient realm – *Shumacher would approve* – what with its metal workshop, its pottery, its bakery and its kitchen garden where *bulb-headed inmates cultivated a few onions* ... While Friern Hospital is no panopticon – even an all-seeing eye could never squint along these telescopic corridors – nevertheless, to move about the sprawl-ing buildings is to be incorporated into this mapping as a live element: a *blinking light travelling through its circuitry*. The endless reflexive states implied by these *maps of maps of maps*, in his more thoughtful black-Biro moments, recall to Busner's mind Cantor's infinite sets and transfinite ordinals – but mostly he experiences the insight as *dizzying*, the 1,884 feet and six inches of the lower corridor rearing up to become its own perpendicular axis, the entire gloomy institution *enacting its own axonometric projec-tion* ... Hurrying now from Admin past the doors of Nursing Admin and Voluntary Services, he is out of breath, having already trotted the five hundred yards from Ward 14. There are a further three hundred to go — *and for what?* So he may be met at the doors by Perkins, who will unlock them with a show of efficiency before Busner has got his key in, an action that confirms his *control*, thus forestalling Busner's inclination to say, There's no need to keep these doors locked, it's no longer hospital policy, now is it? Perkins, whose martial bearing tells the psychiatrist *I didn't miss out on National Service after all*, and who is the perfect type of the NCO despite his white nylon tunic and brown suit trousers, Perkins, with his *shoe-shining-brush* moustache and *rain-dashed radiator-grille* mouth, Perkins, with his *iron hair corroded by its parting*, Perkins, who understands full well how to treat a junior officer, how to manipulate him, let him see only what he wants him to see. It is too soon yet for Busner to have found out the extent to which the other staff are complaisant or merely coerced by Perkins, but that one or other is the case he has no doubt, for they have been drilled into marching up and down the fractured parade ground of the ward, hauling the meds trolley into place, unlimbering its fake-wood-veneer lid, firing the gelatine shells, then moving on. On the ward rounds they do together Perkins is assiduous – making it seem that the subaltern has arrived at decisions alone, while prodding him towards them with rhetorical questions: Wouldn't you think . . . Doesn't it seem best if . . . Haven't you found in cases such as this that . . . Not that any doctoral dispensation is needed to *funnel the tranks* into the patients – under the campanile all 'scrips are repeats and it is, quite simply, *more medicine that helps the medicine go down . . .!* A patient's medication card is only an aide-mémoire for these busy pushers to remind them of the dosage. In point of fact, these index cards are never filed, and if a qualified busybody wishes to discover who's glugged what since mind out of time, he must visit Records and grope through the fuller notes deciphering his predecessors' handwriting, which, Busner has often thought, is illegible not by accident but design.

Be still! This is not why he has come to Friern – *yes, yes*, he will do his Hippocratic duty, neither doing any conscious harm nor allowing any to be done, but for now he is through with *boat-rocking*. *Leave it to the Grocer!* He is done too with elaborations of theory, the multiple threads of which, mind-spun, elaborate and then over-elaborate airy yet substantial models that *fools such as me took for the phenomena they only loosely represented* . . . He will, in particular, resist the urge to ask Perkins why it is his *dee-lightful wa-ay!* to give higher doses of chlorpromazine to female patients – resist, because he knows. The charge nurse says of one who lies shaking in a barred cot, She's ever so fractious, Doctor, aren't you worried that she may harm herself? Of a second female patient, who, for the third day running has been confined to the quiet room – a deranging euphemism for a padded cell – the charge nurse contends: We really want her to be happy, Doctor, but when she's allowed the run of the ward she pilfers from the others, then accuses them of taking her things, and before you know it there's a right barney going on. I mean, you wouldn't dream it to look at her . . . And indeed, you wouldn't, because what sits on this *blancmange slab* is but a *shrivelled raisin* of humanity who shivers in a midi canvas tunic, a uniform, Busner thinks, appropriate only for a slave labourer . . . but she grabbed a fork an 'adda go at putting it in Bettany's eye, and y'know, if I wasn't on hand I think she would've – now that isn't good, is it, Doctor? The whole purpose of this speech being – Busner realised hours later, after having administered the injection himself – to introduce subliminally the words good and doctor into his own mind. But surely, if he is a good doctor, Busner should do something about the bad nurse he has seen, together with his cronies, cackling over a spread in the Sun showing women's libbers in Afghan coats holding aloft a dressmaker's form lashed to a cross. I'd crucify those bitches, he thought he heard Perkins say – yet he couldn't be certain, the ward office was so full of rattling tea mugs, cigarette smoke, smouldering tin ashtrays and clanking filing cabinets, so squeezed between the dirty panes of two permanently shut sash windows. — Perkins and Bettany, caught at it, gave him the approved glare for new boys – or recruits – who have been gazetted for bullying. Bettany had a chubby, kind countenance full of light-hearted dimples, yet Busner suspected him still more than Perkins – he knew the type, slow-witted, malleable and big. Bettany would be the one to administer the thump therapy, that's what they called it, Busner knew – he'd been told all about it by a refugee from the asylums, Dave Catterall, who arrived at the Concept House in Willesden ranting about being beaten by psychiatric orderlies and having water-soaked towels held over his mouth – tales Busner, whose own asylum experience had been brief and circumscribed, had assumed were exaggerated until they were confirmed, to the letter, by other residents. *So what if we were?* the nurses' adult faces lisped childishly and Busner burned with indignation. Yet *how could they know?* that he hadn't been a new boy for decades – only a *left-behind one* watching the Rileys and Rovers crunch away down the drive, hearing the last call for the bus to the station. *Left behind* to wander the voided corridors and deserted classrooms, left behind for so long and so often, that on several terrifying occasions he had to spend the night alone in dormitories empty of everything but their *unwashed-boy-smell and the pitifully snivelling ghost of the twelve-year-old that was me – and, of course, the other left-behind one.*

Is she able –? the psychiatrist asks, and Mboya waves the clip-board wearily. Obviously, he says, it's impossible for us to get her up on the off-chance – there's many more like this and we're short-staffed as it is, but luckily Miss Dearth has her ways . . . *Miss Dearth? Can I have heard him rightly?* wears a bulky nappy held in place by plastic bloomers. It is these the two men have avoided looking at – nakedness would be less obscene. Mboya continues: I cannot be altogether sure, but I think she may be our longest-term patient

– and she does indeed have her ways. The nurse, who is a head and a-half taller than his colleague, now does a wholly unexpected thing by squatting down neatly on his haunches. Busner goes more awkwardly after him, and then they are looking at a great oddity, a phenomenon so unaccountable that, until Mboya starts to explain it, he cannot properly see what it is that's before him. She gets hold of all sorts of things, Mboya says. There's old shoes she's found on the bottom layer, on top of them maybe some soap dishes she takes from the bathroom recess – yes, and on top of those saucers . . . I think she has a special liking for the saucers, some years – if she can get enough she'll use just them. But this year you can see she's brought some stones in from the grounds – flat stones, and there's bits of roof slate she's put on top of those . . . The result was roughly conical and about two feet high, its apex almost meeting the coiled springs of the bed. The two men peer – one from the foot, the other from the side – at this *what? Shrine – or grotto?* Beside Busner's splayed fingers sandy soil scatter-trails to where the roots, stems and heads of two or three shredded daffodils lie in an opening neatly contrived in the structure. There is also a nightlight, the tiny flame of which kindles a homely glow on a pile of crumpled paper inside the arch. Oh, he says, is that –? I mean . . . Mboya is conciliatory: It does no harm, Doctor, we make sure of that, and, like I say, Miss Dearth – Audrey – she's been here . . . well, when I started she'd already been here many, many years . . . Mistaking Busner's silence for disapproval, when it's only that he finds the scene surpassing strange, Mboya hurries on: She's a sort of institution, you see, and her little spring shrine is, well, other patients – staff as well – they like to . . . He points and Busner now notices coins lying among the *quick green fuses*, shiny new nickel-alloy five- and ten-pence pieces, together with a few tarnished tanners and chunky thruppenny bits, *how soon they've come to seem of another age* . . . He reaches for one of little dodecahedrons and presses it hard between his fingers, so hard that when he parts them it sticks to his forefinger and he sees the portcullis impressed in the pad of his thumb. He lifts it to his nostrils and smells its cold taint of old blood. For quite a while Busner takes the little voice *Pliz remembah ve gro'o, onlee wunce a year* for thought – *a colleague?* recalled droning on in a case meeting. *Pliz remembah ve gro'o, onlee wunce* – next he thinks it comes from the over-tranquillised patient on the far side of the ward – *a year, Farver's gonter sea,* Muvver's gonter bringim back . . . finally he realises it is right in his ear, *but micro-phonic,* and, straightening up, he leans back in to hear this: the utterances of some still smaller and more warped old woman vibrating in the larynx of this one. He tunes in to the friction of the parched lips: A penny won't urtyer, a ha'penny won't brayk yer, A farving won't putyer in ve work'uss . . . Now the cold dial of his sphygmomanometer lies cold against her neck and smells still *fishy* – she had found it together with plenty of others underneath the fishmonger's cart and there were more in the gutter in front of the Leg of Lamb, *a mean little gaff,* her father said of it, *a grog shop for the navvies and shonks,* but Audrey thought the low weatherboard building – little more than a shack – had a *romantic air,* not that she altogether understood what this was, saving that sometimes when Mother left her and her sisters with Missus Worth she would put the three small girls in a row, admonish them to be still and, opening the lid of her cottage piano, send silvery sound bubbles floating up in the stuffy parlour to kiss their reflections in the mirror, then die. When Missus Worth shut the lid, she said, Girls, that is a very romantic air what I have played you. – Then is it that same romantic air that hovers around the Leg of Lamb, or

48

is it the carolling blue tit come down for a milk churn? Audrey is a little feart of the dark outline left on the old boards by a mulberry tree that her mother said used to grow there – maybe that too has a romantic air? The oyster shells smell fishy and they've got weedy beards, but there's a horse trough by the pub and Audrey scrubs them until *vey cummup luvlee* and Bert comes by with Mother, who cuffs her while Bert laughs: You don't do no grottoing 'til July, Or-dree, an you does it wiv fresh shells, not manky ones. Alluv ve uvver girls is doin' spring gardens now, you ain't gotta be different. She does have to be different, though, so she bundles the shells up in her pinny and Mary Jane drags her back to Waldemar Avenue, where Audrey makes her grotto by the front railings, ordering Vi and Olive to get pebbles *like vese – not vose*, and boxing their ears in turn. Three or four Sally Army oafs come by, just loafing, not marching, one lugging a big bass drum, the others *larkin' abaht* with their horns, squelching and parping. They're pulled up short by the unseasonable grotto – and by Vi, who's cried so much she has smutty rings round her eyes. They give the little girls a penny and Audrey sends Vi to get a candle from Curtis's on the corner, then she sneaks it alight from the range and afterwards is content to sit at the kerbside holding the toes of her boots *warm puppies*, what with it being a fine evening and the sunset catching the *swags 'n' roses* so sharp, the swags and roses Mary Jane pointed to proudly, *See, proper stukko* . . . and the balustrades that ran along the first floor of the terrace, their pillars plump and squared off. In the gathering darkness Audrey croons the rhyme: *Pliz remembah ve gro'o, onlee wunce a year*, or possibly only thinks she does in the hope that it will ward off Strewel Peter, whose cloud of orange hair rises above the *chimblies* opposite. How could her mother say that? When all the swags 'n' roses were the same, all the houses were the same? How can anything be beautiful or noble or romantic when it's the same? Farver's gonter sea, Muvver's gonter bringim back — She's beef to the heels, that one! cries Arnold Collins, who works on the 'buses with Audrey's father – *eez iz conductah* – and who comes along the road fulfilling the same role after hours, because Sam Death looks *quite tight*. The two men are carrying their work satchels and Rothschild still has his gauntlets on – he tousles her hair with his sweated-leather-and-horse smell, then cups her cheek to pull her other one up to his *wet scrubbing brush*. As her father bends over, his waistcoat bunches up, and his watch flops from its pocket, so that for an instant it lies *cold* against her clenched face. Collins stands a few feet away, thumbs in his own waistcoat pockets, cap at a jaunty angle. 'E finks isself a reg'lar masher,'e duzz, Audrey has heard her father tell her mother, the two of them taking their ease over a glass of port wine. – There's a marshyuness over 'Ammersmiff, a shop girl up in ve Bush. He belches, laughs, wipes his moustache. I dunno, some chap is gonna givim a pasting one of vese days – all of this said with indulgence bordering on respect. But Audrey never likes the way that Arnold Collins looks at her, his hard black eyes rolling over her hair, her chest, her ankles. Getting ready for bed in the front bedroom with the little girls, Audrey still feels those black marbles upon her – and, as the boys join them and all five Death children kneel to murmur perfunctorily, Godless Muvver, Godless Farver, Collins's eyes are on her yet. In bed, she huddles up against Violet to avoid them while concentrating on the lantern show behind her own eyelids: dark processional shapes moving through riverside mist that are at once *the marshyuness, the shop girl* and also stately ladies with extravagant bonnets, bustles and parasols that transform into Just So elephants, *how-dee-how-dahs* waggling on their backs to a brass-band accompaniment, *Oo-rum-pum-pah! Oo-rum-pum-pah!* magically transmitted from the bandstand in South Park, *goldschein*, the world sucked gurgling into the *fiery trumpet*, then blown out again, *when all it was, when all it was* . . . was a line of cows being herded by a farmer's boy across the scrublands of Barnes Common on that *ripping day* when Bert played truant and took her with him over to the Surrey Side – *'Ow we caught it!* – Singaht, girl, singaht! His watch is cold against her cheek, his leather fingers twist her chin. – Singaht! Singaht! She quavers . . . A penny won't urtyer, A ha'penny won't braykyer, A farving won't putyer in ve work'uss . . . and Sam Death exults: Ahh, gerron! She's a precious little goose, ain't she, Arnold? She must avvit. He pulls the other man to him by the lip of his satchel, then sifts through the pouch, selecting, then tossing one coin after the other into the opening of Audrey's grotto. – There's a penny anna ha'penny anna farving – an yer know what, girlie, it won't break me never, coz I'm the fellow az once divvied up a shilling – a whole shilling, mind – to set wiv the Tichborne claimant over at Leadenhall Market. Did I ever tellya that, Arnold . . . Did I not? And the two men are up the front steps and into the house, from where Audrey hears her father calling mockingly, Mary Jane, you'll av some fine gal-an-tine for Mister Collins, willyer not?

Scant light from Waldemar Avenue's newly planted lamps casts the shadow of the balustrade into iron *Bedlam bars* that fall across the two beds and clash with the bars of Olive's cot. Violet has kicked the coverlet away – her skinny legs lash about *beef to the heels. Spring-heeled Arnold* is poised on the window ledge and Audrey thinks: *I'll never ever sleep, I'll never ever sleep* . . . that she'll go mad with not sleeping, mad with the *pissmist* from the potty in her nostrils, mad from the counting up of her two pennies, her ha'penny and her farthing, then dividing this sum into eleven farthings, then adding them together again. Coins on the blackboard, coins on the slates, fingers in the inkwells, *Two-times-six-is-twelve, three-times-six-is-ay-teen, four-times-six-is-twenny-four,* an entire classroom of Audreys and Stans in their drab clothes and their cracked boots, their plaintive treble voices plaiting, then unravelling into two sound-streams that flow out through GIRLS and BOYS into afternoon streets to twine once more – dirty boys' hands grabbing pigtails to *straitjacket* the girls in the *booby-hatch,* until someone comes to release them, *D'you wanter claht in ve jaw! Coz you never did touch my ed, so there . . .* the Wiggins boys dancing round her – then little Stan caught as well and flung in there with her, howling, his shirt torn. — No wonder we called the game Bedlam, thinks Audrey, a big girl of fourteen now, walking back from Shorrold's Road Baths on a Saturday afternoon and seeing a load of kids mafficking. We called it that – not that we knew what Bedlam was. It had been mixed up in Audrey's six-year-old mind with the Cyprian Orphanage and the Gunnersbury Isolation Hospital – places to which children were *removed,* leaving a hurting gap behind for days or weeks that soon enough their siblings grew into. She turns the corner into the Fulham Road thinking that cherry blossom is frogspawn in the pond-green sky, and looking forward to the slow stroll past Anderson's Tea Rooms, savouring the cakes surrounded by fancies, until she sees her father with his foot up on a shoeblack's box and wishes she hadn't — because nowadays Audrey believes that if she sees him he can spy her *at once.* He has become *a stage magician,* the smoke from *the seegar stuck in 'is face lime-lit green an' fleein' to reveal . . .* Arnold Collins. *Go which way you will, you will run up against them,* and it makes it worse that, as her father swaps feet, Collins doffs his hat and says: She's gainin' flesh, guv'nor, an' it ain't all rare meat neevah. Sam grunts, Well, why shouldn't she? She's not some bantin' flapper! Now, Or-dree, I've a co-mission that Mister Collins 'ere az hentrusted me wiv –. He breaks off to snap at the boots: Givvit some elbow-grease, boy! Then resumes, We'll be headin' up West, you and I, time a farver showed iz dotter ve runuv ve place, ain't it so, Arnold? Collins only twitches his tight lips, fiddles with the brim of his boater, pats the lush brown wings of his pomaded hair. Audrey feels the dampness of her shift at the backs of her thighs and sighs. – But, Father, Mother'll be wantin' –. A chop of the smoky hand: Yer mother's always wantin', Audrey – allus will be. He fiddles out a coin and drops it on the paving stone – anticipating this, the boots is there, grubby face ruffed with white-blond curls pushing up from beneath his corduroy cap, a single tooth questing from his bottom lip. Givovah, yer worship, he says scrabbling for his penny. Dob uss two more like vat an I can make me passage fer Noo Yawk. Death's sardonic smile snips him a pair of jowls he wags at the boots. They ain't letting your sort in juss now, he says, you're best off sticking it out 'ere on ha'pence a boot! Uneasily, Audrey takes in piece by piece how Collins dresses *much snappier* than he did when he was with London General: a swallow collar clips his plump neck, his boater has a blue-and-purple-striped ribbon, his patent-leather boots have cunning suede darting, his tongue darts from side to side in his mouth each time he opens it to speak: And, ah, the, ah, goods, guv'nor? Death slowly transfers his contempt from the boy to the man: Whatever you say, Arnold – shall I cable to you at your a-part-ments to arrange our ren-dez-vous, or have they by any chance a telephone appliance at that sixpenny ding-dong of yours over Marylebone way? After all, this is a new century now, ain't it – no need to wait any more is there? Time, distance . . .

53

our wizard mechanical contrivances have them altogether ee-lim-ee-nated. Collins is *throttled*, his cheeks flush. Ah, he says, ah-ah, his tongue *darting* until Death relieves him: Givovah, Fred, I'll see you at the Magpie like always, and now – good-byee! Taking Audrey by the arm, he propels her ahead of him off along the road at *such a lick* that for the first hundred paces she has the disturbing image of herself *hooping-the-hoop*, her skirts flaring, then falling to expose her bloomers. She looks back just the once to see Arnold Collins arranging his boater on his springy hair, the boots still supplicant at his feet.

Manners got yer tongue, Missus Ward? Since when has her father's every second utterance become a puzzle she feels it may be dangerous to solve? For how long has she been this tremulous in his presence? And, liking the fluttery sensation of the word in her mind, Audrey rolls it around, *trem-u-lous, trrr-em-u-lous*, this, surely, is one of *the finer feelings felt by advanced young ladies as they stroll among the hollyhocks* –. I said, manners got yer tongue? His *cleaver* nose, glanced side-on, *slashes* through bricks and hedge and shop awnings. They turn into Parsons Green Road – There goes Roffschild an' iz dotter, says a white-aproned butcher with a calligraphic moustache, the words in their wake, but surely . . . *mennabe heard?* Audrey teeters between shame and pride while her father – *the personage* – seems oblivious, *ramrod-straight* he promenades, the ferrule of his umbrella striking hard every fourth paving stone. Rotten egg, he mutters, exuding not malice but Coniston's hair tonic, which, blown from his shiny face, whitewashes the walls of the dingy courts and alleyways around the railway bridge. When they reach the New King's Road there is a cream-and-brown 'bus clopping in towards the kerb, a *lode-stone* drawing people to it, and Audrey too feels the *static thrill*, as once when Stan rubbed a celluloid dickey on a scrap of velveteen and held it to her neck and the hairs at her nape *prickled*. – Hi! Fentiman. Her father raises his umbrella and, thrusting her in front of him, they cut through the gaggle. Mister Death, the conductor says, tipping his hat, and they squeeze up the stairs and make their way to the front seat. *Finest penny to be spent on the London stage*, her father has said often enough, and he also says, *A wide window on a widening world.* Sitting, Audrey is aware of the hard slats pushing her sweat-damp petticoat between her thighs, while her hands lie useless and freckled on top of them – she thinks of the Westray's Whitening Powder she covets above all things and how it would give her the porcelain complexion of Miss Gabrielle Ray ... Father is speaking of *Bert's benefactor* as *whip-smack and harness-jingle* the 'bus mingles with carts, hansoms and the occasional fly. – Why, Audrey, d'you imagine that Mister Phillips takes such a generous interest in our Albert? Some might think it a little queer, paying for one not your own ... At least this remark is straightforward enough – besides, Audrey senses she isn't expected to answer, only bear witness to. – There's some as might rebuff 'im out of pride alone. The 'bus swings wide to avoid a young lady, her weighted skirts caught up in the chain of her safety bicycle, her leg-o'-mutton sleeves frisking. Oh! Audrey cries, then flushes. Her Oh! hangs in the sudden soundlessness, for the 'bus's wheels have been shushed by wood paving. *A well-set-up woman of pedigree* in an old-fashioned coal-scuttle bonnet sits on the other side of the aisle, staring and staring and staring *like she ain't never seen a girl before.* Audrey wishes her navy dress weren't so shabby, wishes her red hair didn't flare from her head, wishes the cables strung from the multiple crosstrees of the rooftop electrical conductor were the rigging of a fleet clipper slipping anchor and sliding on the ebb tide down *t'wards Gravesend and freedom ... And yet ...* this unexpected excursion is . . . *a treat*. Formerly, Rothschild would often take one or other of his children for a ride, but since he became the deputy manager she cannot have been on the 'bus more than a handful of times – the trip to Windsor Park last summer, that was by brake, but apart from this she has walked from home to school to market to Sunday school to the baths, and very occasionally to watch Bert and Stan play footer, while their Sunday afternoon entertainment is itself a promenade in the park they walk to. Now, the animalistic swing of the 'bus, the bell-ring of spring, the syringas in the front gardens and the flap of the shop awnings – all of it fills Audrey *wiv soda bubbles*. The tangy pitch from the navvies' crucible in front of St Mark's College is blended with the soot-fall from the Lots Road Power Station – and still the pair down below strain on, their broad backs rising glossy, their hoofs cleaving the chestnuts of their own drop-pings. Fentiman has come up *fer a natter* with Rothschild, who's *addenuff* of fresh air, struck a match on his boot and is puffing benig-nant cigar smoke, while studiedly ignoring the boring of the coal-scuttle woman's eyes. — They speak of Sir David Barbour and wily John Pound and *blinkin' Balfour*, of whom only the last is known to Audrey. From time to time Fentiman pivots away along the seat-backs to issue more tickets, then returns to bemoan the tramlines' encroachment. Sam Death is sanguine. Those white-livered nabobs'll never have the front, he says, to sweep awlviss away. 'Lectric trams wiv all their cabling and their track'll awluss be too cumbersome for the middle of town. Fentiman listens respectfully, *donkey-faced* and *sweaty* in his black work suit as the guv'nor expatiates: No-no, change ass t'come – no gainsaying that – and change is always a friend to some and an enemy to others. Now, see, there's the tuppenny tube an' the padded cell, an' now they've their shield appa-ra-tus there'll be

56

no stopping 'em from nibblin' froo the underbits like mites in cheese. No, change is upon us – but it ain't the 'bus'll be sluiced down the gutter, mark my words . . . It ain't us should worry – it's them.

The slow thrumming of a player-piano eases in – the one Audrey had heard in the Aeolian Showroom the last time she had been up West, with Mary Jane, who, in a capricious mood, had said: *Juss coz we ain't quality don't mean we ain't allowed to avva gander.* Then, when the counter-jumper parted his coat-tails to sit at the instrument, she couldn't *'old 'er tongue an' warbled on,* a portly nightingale who forced her accent through some imagined mangle of respectability. – Ooh, yairs, isn't it luvverly, such fine mahoggerny – while the fellow's knees rose and fell as he trod in the melody, Doo-d'doo, doo d'doo, doo-d'-dooo, doo-d'-dooo, triplets of notes going up and down. Audrey straightened up, lost her *hoydenish* hunch – seeing that she took a *genuine interest*, as he continued to march on the spot, the demonstrator spoke of *Brarms, 'is intermetso,* and how this was a very high-class roll for the *conny-sewer.* Listening closely to the trills and coos, her stiff fingers freed themselves from the back of her dress, her chin stilled. The easy motion of the young man's thighs, the invisible digits pressuring the ivory skin, the so-fa-la! rising up to the ceiling, the exposed roll revolving while around it the world turned – this was beauty, this was what Miss Conway at school meant by *harmon-ee –.* A bang, followed by a whip-like crack, the shock of it seizes every passenger on the top deck of the 'bus as the pair shy and a trap horse coming from Sloane Square rears in its shafts. Through a curtain of blue smoke that rumples up into almond blossom, the spectators see this freak: the wheels and chassis of a new-fangled motor car with the upright black body of a hansom fixed on top. A-ha! Ha-ha! Sam Death chortles as the 'bus driver wrestles his horses past the vehicle, which rests at an uncomfortable angle with one set of wheels up on the kerb. – Oh-ho my, what a sainted palaver! The motorist and his mechanic are flapping their tweedy wings over the open engine compartment, which still belches, and Sam says: Must've come from the other side – *meanin' Vauxhall, not 'Ades* – and, while it may seem unlikely, Fentiman, that 'Arry Tate an 'is pals'll do away with our equine friends . . . The conductor regards Audrey's father respectfully as he speaks, as do the other passengers, surmising that the big man has a professional bent – but Audrey recoils from his *portmanteau* eyes and the *Stilton veins* that marble his *fine pro-bo-siss*. While the 'bus continues past the gardens of Eaton Square and the Fulham garage manager speaks of machines, she dreams of terrible chimeras, men with wheels in place of legs, their bellies a dreadful contrivance of rods, gears and flywheels, smoke venting from their iron buttocks. She envisions horses whose hindquarters are *'Oxton whizzers*, while steering columns have been speared between their shoulders so that their riders, sat astride their red-hot withers, may twist them this way and that, neighing, screaming . . . A horse's scream is a fearful thing that Audrey didn't know she knew, coming as it does from a part of her mind that she didn't know she had. It comes from underneath the mattress where things fester and cog-buttons are bug-toothed. Stan's stories came from that place – the leopard man and the dog man, their screams in the night when their flesh was sliced and stretched. The beasts howled beyond the stockade, while Vi and Olive pulled at Audrey's nightdress, hiding their faces, baring her shoulders. The three of them gaoled by the bedstead as their brother's dark mouth *swallers the nightlight* . . . The vehicle, madam, says Sam Death, has been engineered by taking the body of yer normal 'orse 'bus and securing it to the chassis and wheels of a

Daimler petrol motor 'bus ... Her father believes he has won over the coal-scuttle with his informed disquisition. From their elevated position, as the 'bus rumbles from Buckingham Palace Road and on to the forecourt of the station, they are well placed to make a survey: Over there, madam, you may espy a Thornycroft 'bus, the motivation for which is supplied by steam from a coke-fired boiler, heggzackerly the same as a locomotive. Yonder, by the portico of the Apollo, that there is the Fischer 'bus, an innovation of the Americans, it employs both electrical and petrol engines in furtherance of increased reliability. Be that as it may wery well be ... he continues as they inch their way down the curved stairway behind her heavy silk train ... I doubt wery much its utility, indeed, I foresee the futility –. However, she has no wish to be lectured further, and so cuts Death off with a tilt of her bonnet and a twist of her parasol's handle. And a good day to you too, madam! he says with the utmost repugnance and, raising his umbrella to salute Fentiman, he allows its ferrule to travel on, tracing the pilasters and wrought-iron balconies that cover the station's façade. We 'ave reached the terminus, he says, and, taking her arm, guides her between vehicles jockeying for passengers, then past an advertisement for Germolene so large its letters loop across the end wall of an entire four-storey block, the *l* encircling an open window from which a slavey in a mob-cap stares frowsily down on the crowded street. Urchins scamper into the road to grab harnesses, then pirouette for a flung copper, as the stand-pipes of toppers somehow join in Audrey's mind with the droppings underfoot and the gulley-slops in the gutters. Here, more than in Foulham, the city is beset by its own contrariety: the smooth and stony Portland faces of the buildings along Victoria Street are streaked with smutty tears, the alleys that crack the mirroring windows of the smart shops are choked with costers' carts piled with *fruit an' veg' already on the turn*. Flies dash damp in her face – faces all round are pastier than *those on my manor* ... They are *deeper dahn an' ahtuv ve light* ... He points out to her the yellow-brick bulk of Queen Anne's Mansions rising above the rooftops in the direction of St James's, its mansard roof festooned with cabling. He speaks of the hydraulic lifts that raise the well-to-do tenants up fourteen storeys, and of the piping that supplies the pumps burrowing beneath the streets. — He conjures in Audrey's mind a vision of the city as all connected up by streams of invisible power: the telegraph cables coursing with letters and figures, the electricity zipping through gutta-percha sleeves – her own vision *skronks* so that the beaver skin of a passing homburg conceals ... *an eye*, a girl's pretty face splits lengthwise, *sideways* ... She wishes she could turn aside to enjoy the steamer trunks, fishing rods and pith helmets carefully arranged in the window of the Army & Navy Stores, she wishes she could *get in there wiv 'em* ... but her father will not slacken his pace. For the first time on this peculiar excursion Audrey feels the frigid probing fingers of anxiety: he is so intent, his moustache spit-damp, his high forehead shiny with *perspiration* ... on they go, his umbrella marking the time for their marching feet, tap-tap, tap-tap, *tap-tap* ... Her uncovered head falls back, *my crownin' glory* swishes between her shoulder blades. A great purple-grey quilt is falling over it all, cloudy clumps trapping the scurrying bedbugs in their own poisonous fumigation. The air darkens and darkens: a smutstorm in lurid yellow suspension from out of which swim the castellated battlements of the Westminster Hospital, supported by VOLUNTARY CONTRIBUTIONS – beyond this the rigid skirts of the Abbey fall perpendicular from its stony stays.

An impression of the *bashed boiled-egg* face of the big clock, and of

the gentlemen petrified on their plinths – Audrey sees the pipe organ
of Parliament, hearkens to its maddening fugue . . . She looks down
at her freckled hands, lying once more in the lap of her shabby dress,
'ow they shake with palsy. Her father tenderly places a bag between
them, the rumpled paper, cloth-soft. She withdraws a bonbon reeking
of acetone and presses it to her bloodless lips – then tastes the pear
essence as it bashes her teeth. – You 'ad a little turn there, m'dear. His
solicitude is more troubling than his contempt. They are on a motor
'bus that shudders up Whitehall – a leather hanging strap tap-taps
against his bowler, he pats her hands, the action as involuntary as
hers. He speaks of the 'bus and its route from Victoria to the Bank,
but Audrey cannot hear him that well for her hands have twisted
into claws that scrabble on the mounds of her thighs, back and forth,
over and over, in a pattern that cannot really be a pattern – since it is
never repeated. The unstoppable movement towards the city's central
lodestone is affecting, Audrey notices, her father's elocution: aligning
the wayward consonants, repelling the colloquialisms. – As I was
saying before, Audrey, Mister Phillips is now making a fuller commitment to Albert – he's to board at Woodford. Mister Phillips has
arranged it all with the Drapers, while he himself will pay for his
books . . . his sporting equipment and suchlike. Well –? This is not,
she realises, a question – it's more akin to a chairman's patter between
turns, and so begs the question, What's coming next? She sees Albert
as Mister Phillips must have, spottin' 'im in Anderson's, the tall youth's
bulging grey eyes running down the column of figures scrawled on a
bill – tu'pence for this, ha'pence for that, thru'pence for the Eccles
cake – his severe mouth pronouncing the total instantly. His family
are, of necessity, familiar with Albert's prodigious calculating ability,
his pals too: they call him Datas, after the music-hall mental

prestidigitator. Just as his father has his moniker shouted after him in the street, so Datas Death has his own salute, *Am I right, sir?* Although unlike the genial Datas on stage, there's no jocularity to Albert's correctitude. He is *rigid in all things*, disdaining brawling, yet looks *fit to kill* if he's accused of having *funked it* by failing to answer a question or complete a computation. Now the days are balmier he strips to the waist in the hugger-mugger of the backyard – having obtained a copy of Sandow's Magazine, he performs the exercises it describes using Indian clubs he has made by sawing up old railway sleepers. — Datas is not Stanley's hero, but *Enigmarelle, the Man of Steel* – he desires to be *a mechanical man* with an engine *hammerin'* in his belly and smoke *spurtin' from 'is mouf an' nose* . . . I've never been up on a motor before! is Audrey's answer, shouted over the *rattle-bash* that reverberates through the saloon. Her eyes skitter to the back platform, fall from it to the pattern of crushed droppings-on-tarmac that unrolls there. Try as she might, she cannot will the grunting 'bus aloft, up from the congeries of cabs that mesh into a *millipede* inching its way from Whitehall into Trafalgar Square. Audrey cannot – *yet Stan flies* whenever he wants: he positions her beside him in front of their mother's new cheval glass and tips it back to fling them *suddenly, silver, skywards* . . . Stan says: In twenty years' time everyone will be an aeronaut, Colonel Cody will perfect his war kite and there'll be gazetted aeroplane services connectin' all the cities of the Empire. Airships'll carry the heavy freight that goes now by sea: pig iron, coal, Canadian wheat. They'll anchor up above the Pool of London and the air will be fick with their hawsers – the stevedores'll operate movin' beltways high as cranes. See! Up we go, Aud! And again he tips the glass so the flame-haired girl and the bat-eared boy lift off, *suddenly, silver, skywards* . . .

Getting down at Charing Cross, still sucking her pear drop, Audrey turns from the *sooty black drainpipe* of Nelson's Column to be put upon by PHOSPHERINE THE REMEDY OF KINGS and PLAYER'S NAVY CUT, momentarily *sandwiched* between two sandwich men, and once freed engulfed by the hubbub of the afternoon crowds – clerks and shop-walkers released for their half-day dodge and jig across the road. One *snappy chappie* pops under the very shafts of a growler – the cabbie flicks his whip, but the three ladies behind *chandeliers wrapped in muslin* disdain to notice. Bloody oaf! Her father's oath rises above the charivari as he upbraids a ragamuffin the worse for drink who cavorts about an organ-grinder. A few paces on Audrey looks back at this man's pillbox hat, his torn and filthy scarlet tunic – he is an old soldier, who hops on an ashplant, the empty leg of his trousers flapping — but Sam Death won't be caught napping, he weaves through the throng along the Strand, then wheels Audrey round to join a queue who are taking their turn to peer in the eyepiece of a kinetosocope plunked down beside the foyer doors of the Old Tivoli. Her head ducked into this commedia, she sees a pretty Colombine pirouette around a capering ape – *Might I escape?* – her gyration not smooth but jerking forward, then back, the double-exposure of the film depicting a meeting with her transparent double. The title card slots in: *Miss Lottie Farquhar, Appearing Nightly in 'Darker Delights', Stalls Seats for a Limited Period, 5/6d., Fully Electrified, fssschk-chk-fssschk-chk* . . . His *paw* on her again. P'raps it'd be agreeable to you if we were to take the back way? Audrey wonders what errand can it be that her father runs for Arnold Collins, his inferior – one he has always treated with amused contempt? The tip of his umbrella fingers the joins between the cobbles as they cross the corner of Covent Garden, ignoring the leather-aproned porters lounging against the empty crates, ignoring the rotten fruit under-foot and the arabs scrabbling for it – the dusk is massing in the corners of the square, *lyin' in wait*. Little Dublin, he remarks casually as they cross Drury Lane. Every third store-front is boarded up with heavy planks, some scrawled with *crim' sigils*, although *why? There's nuffink 'ere to avaway*. The narrow entries to the godforsaken courts are blocked off with timber bulwarks, and through a gap in one Audrey sees the limewashed ghost of a dwelling, some of the condemned tenants standing in front of it, their faces and clothing creased with dirt – they are, she understands, too weak *wivunger* to be dangerous. One boy her own age who lolls in a doorway wears no trousers – *no pockets . . . no pockets t'pick* – his man-sized shirt torn up past his hips, an idiot grin slitting his *potato head*. The final shard of the boiled sweet snaps between Audrey's teeth. They simper, the *three little maids . . .* Women of the unfortunate class, Death chews this phrase over before spitting it out more coarsely: Wimminuv ve un-for-tun-ate class, they'll sell their selves for thru'pence, tu'pence or a loaf of stale bread . . . One makes as if adjusting something in her bodice: *a corsage that's invisible*. Audrey feels her *bubbies* prickle and the sweat-damp shift still wadded between her thighs. *I don't need no Snowdrop Bands, I need the double-you-see* – there are no words to say this, a year or so ago, yes, but not now. Beyond the pub hatch where the whores have gathered the street ends in another timber bulwark – this one two storeys high and plastered with the pink cheeks, golden curls and frothing white suds of HUDSON'S SOAP. To the right of the hoarding a cranny leads into a long, narrow lane, the carriageway barely wide enough for a cart, the shop-fronts to either side antiquated, their many-paned and thick-mullioned windows plastered *wiv 'udson's dirt*, as are their horizontal shutters, some of

64

which have been let down to form the basis of stalls. Up above are more wooden bafflers tilting out obliquely from the buildings — Audrey breaks step. – Those? Death is amused by what's pricked her curiosity. Those're mirrors, Audrey, t'catch a slice of the 'eavens and chuck it in the winder. 'Course, anyone peeping down from on top could see a body steppin' inter 'er smalls . . . *Who is he, my father?* As they go on, the hush she had not been aware of deepens, the never-ending snarl of the city streets tails away into a single bark tossed from jaws to jaws: a solo motor horn yelping.

The alleyway scores deeper into the damp clay. Halting, her father takes a small leather-bound volume from the stack of books on a stall – and, as he lifts it to his face, the cover falls open to expose marbled endpapers, then drops off altogether, along with several leaves that *swipe* their way to the ground. At once a white head pops up from behind the stall, *the Mad Mullah!* turns out to be a mousy man, his turban wound out of an Indian shawl, and when he's hauled up his pince-nez from the length of its black ribbon and clipped his *nubbin innit* he sees Death clearly. Oh, it's you, Rothschild, he wheezes *wordy notes* – he has swallowed the consumptive's *harmonium.* Audrey's father gestures with the broken book. – I shall, of course, recompense you for any loss, Mister Fellowes. The mousy man plays a *mournful chord*: Why bother, eh? This'n – he gestures in turn – all done for now an' gone, done up proper, done up prop— and there's another *pump on the pedals, he oughtn't to run on so, 'e ain't got the breff.* Mister Fellowes is tieless, his collar unfastened, his Turkey throat *gobbles*, in the dark recesses of the shop a caged bird *fluttercheeps.* — Death utters this: As the papers have it, there's substantial com-pen-say-shun available along the way for those who've longer leasehold . . . and freehold, naturally. For the first time

Audrey notices her father's ponderousness when he *speaks proper*. She blushes – and to hide her confusion takes a book from the pile on the stall, Sermons of the late Reverend Simon Le Coeur, D.D. A little friend o'yourn, is she –? She has attracted the bookseller's leer. Samuel barks, Yes, a special little friend! He grabs her shoulder and twists her upright, pulling everything *tight*. Tell me – his grip *tightens* – has Mister Beauregard ceased trading yet? The mousy man runs his fever-pink eyes the length of Audrey, *from top to toe*, before answering disdainfully: Beauregard won't cease 'til the wreckers' ball drops on that fucking garret – not that 'e ain't made his 'rangements, fixed up premises with some shonks on the Mile End Road. Death lifts the beetle carapace of his bowler, runs a hand over his damp pate. In that case, he says, I will ascend – he has some, ah, merchandise for Brother Collins –. Mister Fellowes coughs, retches, spits derision: While you've some fer 'im inall! This is a statement of fact, accompanied by the retrieval of a waxed paper, its unfolding, the savage poking of a pinch of snuff into his nostril. Hm . . . Death mutters . . . mebbe. He hooks his umbrella over his left arm and gropes deep in his trouser pocket. Audrey stands *wrung out* and abandoned. 'Ere – he presses a thru'pence into her palm, *hard* – you'll find a coffee shop along aways. Sit tight wiv a cuppa anna slice, I'll come after yer inna bit. The mousy man's sneeze follows her down the road, heff-heff-heff-p'shawww! – she turns back once but her father has already disappeared.

A cake sits on a tin stand in the window of the coffee shop, which otherwise is indistinguishable from the rundown book dealers flanking it. Audrey looks at the cake *black as coke* on its dirty paper doily. A sign beside it contends TEN OUNCE CHOPS 6d., CUTLET 5d., FRIED ONION 1d. That's all. A man comes from within to stand in the doorway – wound tightly into his apron, he's *the same shape* as the milk churn he sets down. He has thick black curly side-whiskers and below his red cheek a *redder* goitre rests on his Gladstone collar. A barefoot piker boy comes limping along the lane, his cap pulled right down, the sleeves of his man's jacket rolled right up – his arms are *all striped lining*. In one hand he holds a skinned rabbit by its ears and, stopping by the coffee shop man, he raises it *bloody socket where its guts were* but says nothing. The man shakes his head: Inna pig's arse. The boy limps on. Cummin an' eat befaw we boaf starve . . . It's a while before Audrey realises he's addressing her, and then she complies. There's nothing much to the coffee shop – four pew seats, two rickety tables – everything is coated with the brownish patina of tobacco smoke, grease and ingrained dirt. The gaslight and the geyser are confused in one another's piping – both are lit. The man asks Audrey what she wishes for, and while he is absent in the back the geyser heats up and begins to steam – droplets condense on the ceiling, then fall, one *hissing* on the gas-mantle. *It's raining inside* . . . She opens her hand: the thru'pence has impressed a portcullis on her palm. The man comes back with a mug of tea and two slices of bread and marge, sliced diagonally. I dunno why I does vat, he says, looking at the droplets swell and fall, but I allus do. He turns the key in the pipe and the geyser pops off. Could I –? Is there –? There can be no mistaking *surely* the reason for her discomfort . . . He points offhandedly and says: Jakes is out back. She goes and finds a lean-to against the kitchen wall, beyond it another section of the two-storey-high timber bulwark, and beyond this the wreckers' ball hangs in the foggy dusk, a *black moon*. When she returns, he's lit the geyser again, and, as she nibbles the slices and sips the tea, he stands erect by the matchboard counter, head up, massaging the goitre while doggily listening to its rising notes . . . *there's no 'arm innim.* All that's left are crumbs, smears, *dregs* . . . still her father does not come. Abruptly, Audrey rises from the pew – the man gives her a penny and two farthings change, which she holds so tightly as she walks back up the road that the metal discs replace her knuckles, *Enigmarelle, the Man of Steel.* There's no one about except a *tall gent inna topper* who reminds her of an illustration she's seen of Bransby Williams *the 'personator,* so cross-hatched is he by shadow. Fellowes's shop is shuttered — tapping fearfully on the door, she is relieved when it swings open, so scurries in to the smell of mouse droppings, cat's piss and the ammoniacal residue of birds. Inside there is no illumination at all – only different strengths of darkness, the *black bat night* brushing against her. She mounts the stairs to the accompaniment of a concerto of creaks – one flight, a second, a third and a fourth – then peeks along a landing at eye-level, to where bright white light leaks from beneath a closed door. She hears – in there – a sharp intake of breath, h'heurgh! and a *piggish grunt.* Her belly seethes with *glow worms* — last month Mary Jane *fixed me up* with cotton pads and an itchy belt sewn from hemming tape. When Audrey pointed out to her the advertisement in the back of a Free Library book – *Sanitary, Absorbent, Antiseptic, Available from All Drapers* – her mother snapped: What d'you fink we are? but not unkindly. A cord that stretches taut from her tummy-button along the landing and under the door draws her in with each h'heurgh! every *piggish grunt.* She barges the door with her shoulder and collapses into a room lit brilliantly by clear bulbs under shades of frosted glass. In front of a floor-length nankeen drapes an aspidistra in a hammered-bronze pot, beside this a chaise-longue covered in green velvet, on this the skinned rabbit *what the piker 'ad* its glistening dead legs sticking up from a *mess of petticoats*. Standing with his back to Audrey, a *bare-arsed* man does something to the rabbit's belly, *guttin' it –?*

– No, no, no! That won't do! A florid man with pomaded hair, in his shirtsleeves and a fancy embroidered waistcoat, comes out from behind a kinematographic apparatus set up in the tapering corner of the attic. No, no, no! he cries again – his expression is mad and guile-less – this 'ere girlie's torn it –! Mister Beauregard? Audrey ventures, but the red-faced man ignores her, his regard is fixed. — When Audrey turns back there's no coney, only a girl a little older than her who sits on the chaise buttoning her *bubbies* into her bodice. The girl's hair is up apart from a few stray locks, and atop its nondescript mass sits a lady's toque complete with magenta-dyed ostrich feath-ers. There's no bare-arsed man either, only Audrey's father, who's standing there in his long rabbit-skin coat and buttoning up gloves *I've never see before.* He doesn't acknowledge his daughter but raises his bowler to Mister Beauregard, says, O-vwar, m'dear, to the girl and, retrieving his umbrella and a brown paper parcel from behind the drapes, conducts Audrey unceremoniously from the room. They are borne down the stairs on the *wave* of electric light – its *crest breaks on the blank street.* There is no sign of Fellowes – only his name fading across the tops of the shutters. – All this – Samuel Death strikes with his umbrella at the complicated dinginess of the Jacobean frontage – will be gone wivvin weeks . . . He sounds neither regretful nor cheered by the prospect. *I do not know 'im* who leads her on through streets *shuttered* by the massive timber bulwarks, working their way through the condemned rookery to the purlieu of Waterloo Bridge, where, through a gap, they can see the workings: navvies' picks thrust handle-first in grave-fill, beside this *Calvary* a *slough of despond wellin' over* with night-time and the *drowned-corpse smell of the river.* Why, Audrey longs to ask him, have they stuck bills on the insides of the hoardings? For surely navvies aren't likely customers for Beecham's Powders or a GUARANTEED 7 HOUR PASSAGE from Tilbury to Cherbourg. There will be, Samuel says, a grand booleyvard runnin' norf t'Olborn, the newest street in Lunnun town, with the nobs pacin' up an' pacin' down . . . an' there'll be a tunnel connectin' to the bridge for the trams runnin' under a twenny-storey buildin' that'll 'ave business premises, an arcade of posh shops, theatres . . . This, Audrey realises as they go through the Saturday evening drowse of Lincoln's Inn, is his gift: this tour of the city about to be swept away, and this portrait of an orderly city of the future. – At Chancery Lane the boys are crying Bulgarian Massacre! and there's a feverishness to the tipsy clerks gathered round a sandwich stall. Finally, it is night. The *wreckers' ball has turned and dropped, the air fills with dust, fog, smuts* . . . thickening with *dark droplets, I dunno why I does vat – but I allus do* . . . as the passengers rise up from the Underground station *dewy mushrooms sprout* alongside the old timber house fronts of High Holborn. — This, I recall, Audrey says: the glacé silk and the oiled cotton of the covers, so many of them – and t'were only a little drizzle . . . It ish, Gilbert Cook says sententiously, to the petit-ourgeoishie of London what a fetisssh is to an African primitive – he manipulatessh it, speaksh to it, forgetsh it at hish peril, for, should the shky godsh choosh to show their dishpleasure, he will be losht without hish portable shelter. Conshider thish, Audrey, when Crushoe – that quinteshenshial petit-bourgeois – is cashtaway, the firsht implement that he makesh for himshelf ish an umbrella! This speech would be hard to tolerate were Gilbert not *bare-arsed* – he has *no shame,* and this is more satisfying to Audrey than anything they do to each other: his insouciance, standing there rinsing out the prophylactic device in the rose-patterned bowl, pulling it between the *mangle rollers* of his chubby little fingers so that the water *spurts*. It reminds her that it was instruction that formed the greater part of his seduction: he described how she should insert the pessary beforehand – and then after use the syringe to sluice herself out while squatting above a different bowl. Audrey had admired Gilbert Cook for this commitment to the technical aspects of free love, far more than his written advocacy thereupon. – Admired him for this – and for his abjuration of all *jealous sentiments*. I tell you, m'dear – he said on that first occasion, as he curled his hand to simulate her vagina and spoke of how to exterminate *the troubleshome spermatozoa* – not sholely sho that I may enjoy your delightsh without, um, complicationsh – although I do fervently wish to enjoy them, and on thoshe termsh preshishely – but in order that you may enjoy shimilar, or in all probability far greater onesh, with whomshoever you choose. His teacherly approach to the exercise of deflowering her had been *what I needed*, the hot suffusions of shame and guilt coming first, and then, in response to his instruction, she found herself left free to enjoy – that first time as well – his demonstration. Yet, despite the vigour with which he impressed upon her his vision – that *the shex relashion ish all about ush, if diffushed*, and that *we do not do it, either like pershonsh or animalsh*, but attract it, *like lightning-conductorsh* – Audrey was appalled to discover herself after their second liaison exhibiting all the symptoms of a *love-struck moon calf*, some *diaphanous Daphne* or *vapid Venetia*, who cared nothing for the *New Dawn* of womankind, but only the old and poetical ones. Now, setting the *slug* down, he comes to sit beside her and says, Tell me, why d'you shpeak of thish inshident now – of your father'sh conshorting with proshtitutes and their pornographersh – ish it becaushe we have jusht . . . fucked? Audrey strokes the green damask of Venetia Stanley's chaise-longue and runs a finger around one button, then a second. No, she says eventually, no, Gilbert, it's not that . . . it's . . . How she *loathes* Venetia Stanley without ever so much as having *clapped eyes on her*. Try as she might to prevent herself, Audrey has asked him whether their relation is physical – although he disdains the idea: Venetia? M'dear, she's a baby, she's shwaddled in the eternal childish-nessh of wealth, shponged and pampered by her nurshing maids and wet nurshed at houshe parties . . . That may be so, yet for Audrey the closeness between the society lady and the socialist is *insupportable*, especially here, where a portrait photograph of her attired as Diana the Huntress stares down from a nearby whatnot . . . it's the umbrel-las. Aha, the umbrellash, the fruitsh of your laboursh. He *mussav a way of fixin' 'em* – his dentures – because holding forth in drawing rooms or public meetings his tone is full and *loud as sounding brass*, while at such times as these, at his ease, divested of his clothing, his hair dishevelled, comes this endearing *lishp*. She counters: I don't make umbrellas, Gilbert, or brollies, or garden tents, or portable pavilions for the bloomin' beach – I'm a typewriter, I make words. *Such words*: Dear Sir, in respect of your order of the 15th instant, I regret to inform you that we are unable to supply the precise numbers of the Peerless and the Paragon models that you requested due to Fox's tardiness in fulfilling our own order for their patented Aegis frames. As I know you appreciate, all Ince & Coy umbrellas are finished to the highest standards and employ the Aegis frame as a matter of course due to their superior quality and efficiency. We are consigning by carrier a gross of the Peerless pro tempore, together with an hundred of the Paragon, and will endeavour to complete your order at Fox's earliest convenience. I remain your obedient servant, A. De'Ath, Expediting Clerk, on behalf of Thos. Ince. An initial will suffice, Miss De'Ath – so said Appleby, the crabbed and querulous senior clerk – some of our customers may not be so tolerant when it comes to the matter of female employment . . . *More tolerant than you, I'd wager!* Appleby is senior only to Audrey, the two occupying the garret above the Bishopsgate premises, he seated on his stool at an old-fashioned high desk under the dormer, while she is thrust under the attic's slope, up against the *mouse-gnawed* wainscot. Her Sholes is mounted on its small table, and each time she returns its carriage with the inbuilt treadle mechanism she is forcibly *kerchunggg!* reminded that this is women's work: *sweated, menial, repetitive.* Although the truth is that her actual responsibilities exceed his – Appleby, in his grisly old suit and soured linen collar, is *a makeweight*, kept on by Ince's out of gratitude for service tendered long since. He scratches at the accounts, wages and inventory books. Each Friday he totters to the bank accompanied by a sturdy boy armed with a cudgel — and he conveys to Audrey only the faintest outline of the matters to hand, leaving her to endow them with the necessary materiality. All the letters, all the memoranda, all the advertisement copy – *such words* her hands make, inverted into claws that scrabble about on the keys of the Sholes, over and over, in a pattern that *cannot really be a pattern since it is never repeated.*

– No, I didn't mean thoshe wordsh either, Audrey . . . For a man who supposes himself in thrall to the progress of the labouring classes, Gilbert has a most *extreme aversion* to work itself, in all its forms, except for the production of his own words . . . I meant the wordsh you have sent forth in that frail barque, the Ardent, on to the world'sh watersh. In the shadows of his shirt his penis *hunches* ringed by rolled skin-folds *bamboo stuck in you.* At the Ince workshop, in

73

back of Old Commercial Street, the piece workers, *Jews and Jewesses mostly*, cut the silk and gingham, oil it, stretch it, sew the finicky loops and sleeves, then feed in the ribs and attach the handle – *Vwar-la!* another Peerless or Paragon or elegant ladies' walking umbrella. Over and over they do it, their strange and sallow faces also *oiled and stretching* – hands *chapped and chafed*, covered with bunions in winter – summer brings the stench from the fish stalls in Black Lion Yard, but always there is the high reek of *poultry*.

It is a paltry thing, Gilbert, she says, rising to pull up her petticoats and roll up her stockings. Snap! goes one garter. A paltry thing, and taken only by those that assent to its contents already, read, I believe, not even by them. Snap! There is a silver tray with cut-glass decanter and soda siphon. Audrey lightly touches the fluted neck, the cool grooves – she picks up a pin and begins to fold strand upon strand of her *red raffia-work*. The window is masked by a heavy drape, but beyond it she knows stand the high-gabled houses with their triplets of *artistic* windows, while beyond them lie the embankment and the river *sweating its noxious vapours* – she pictures the lurid swirl of tannery waste caught in its sluggish flow. – I shall have to go. – Musht you? – Yes, *yes* – back to Missus Phelps in De Beauvoir Town, back to tinned Gong soup heated up on the oil stove, back to the airy sensation of falling to sleep without the *deadweight of Father, Mary Jane, and the rest* . . . She steps into the *respectable* embrace of her shirtwaist, buttons it, moves to the drapes, parts them. Down below a motor-taxi rattles by the kerb, Venetia Stanley – *it can be no other* – stands withdrawing coins from the beady security of her purse. She has come from tea at the Dorchester, Audrey imagines, or a piano recital at the Bechstein Hall – and she has no cares beyond *the troublesome proliferation of her purple plumes upon the hats of her inferiors* ... Turning, Audrey says decisively, I should like to hurl a brickbat through her dear friend's window – through all his bloody windows! Gilbert has taken upon himself flannel underwear *none too clean.* She will not venture, he says, to dishturb us, but jusht in case ... He uncrooks the arm of the Victrola with one hand, while expertly winding it with the other. His face swells *monstrous* in the beaten tin horn as the melody sings though the hiss. Thought is a melody, Audrey thinks, while the body is an inert mechanism of *cogs, springs, chains and ratchets* ... His hands are on her neck, her fingers are hooked in her bootlaces ... – No, really, Gilbert, I must go. He claps his hands to his thighs. Ha! Well! Sho may it be, he says, and looks about for the *exasperation* of his trousers. Shall I shee you on Thurshday at the meeting? I believe Shtanley will alsho be attending ... He knows of their *disagreement* – a word too flimsy to contain the violence of their falling-out. Didddle-di-diddle-di-diddle-di-di-di! The pretty trills from the phonograph scatter before her rage, *resurrected*: Stanley, who, despite his waywardness, will, she knows, be martyred. Stanley, his lissom arms outstretched, his palms pierced by the tips of the steel ribs, his ankles *bound to the umbrella post by an India-rubber ring*. So to Cook, Audrey is emphatic: Stanley comes not for George Lansbury, or the car-men, or any principle 'soever. He is in thrall to that fine lady and her pimp – my brother has no position, he's all but disowned by our father –. She stops, hearing the shh-ching of the drapes being drawn in the drawing room below – the Victrola, which went off *half cocked*, has *diddled* to a halt. Her lover views Audrey appraisingly throughout the awkward business of buttoning himself up. He completes his costume with a cigarette – he smokes a brand called Logic, *one shilling for a box of twenty-five!* You love him, Cook says amazed. You love him more than any other

75

– more than your shuffaragette friensh, more than our schocialisht comradesh, more than –. He is a shapeless *tweed bag with a smoky drawstring* ... Suddenly, she grabs him and pushes him backwards, thrusting her hot face against his bare neck. She feels the cold trickle of her love between her clenched thighs. I love you, Gilbert, she pants, I love you. Audrey knows this is no *romantic felicity*, or *brazen fortitude*, but *revolutionary: And all around the slaves do dwell, Who are called to labour by a bell* ... – And you love me, Gilbert, don't you – she shakes him – you love me too! His shoulder has snagged the copper teat of the light switch and they look up at the electrolier curling over their heads, look up and are *smitten by the incandescing clapper in its frosted bell.* Beyond this lamp there is another, and beyond that one a third – and so on, a great profligacy of illumination that draws Audrey's eye along the curved roof. Sam Death explains how the electricity is *jenny-rated* way over west in Wood Lane, and how there are *substayshuns* all along the route of the railway, where this strange fluid is subjected to still more mysterious refinement before being piped down into the tunnels to feed the lamps and the middle rail at their feet, which, unlike the *evilly gleaming sisters* that flank it, is *dull* and neglected. Audrey cannot *stay wivvim* – she knows this doesn't matter. — Her father speaks of the Greathead shield not on her behalf but on behalf of an absent other ... *Am I right, sir?* The air crackles ozone *a celluloid dickey rubbed on velveteen* ... at her feet are others' feet: *spattered* spats and high-heeled boots *dainty as cake decorations.* Audrey tries hard not to stare at the lady and gentleman: she with her hands lost in her muff and a fever spot on each painted cheek, he, lifting his watch by its chain, tapping the platform with his cane, pushing up the brim of his topper. Then the same again: mechanical, unthinking. Stan *only 'ad the one lead soldier*, a pith-helmeted bugler in scarlet tunic and tartan trews, he lifted up his battered bugle to his chipped lips, tooted, *lifted 'is battered bugle to 'is chipped lips an' tootled.* There was a big bolt through each of his shoulders and there was Stan's little big finger *makin' 'im do it.* The train is coming, straining up the incline shaped by the underside of the Fleet's irrelevant banks. Rothschild Death raises his voice to shout about planned extensions and a turning circuit buried beneath the Uxbridge Road. He sounds proprietary enough to be an investor in – A southern extension, 'owsabout that, Or-dree, then we'd be tunnelin' our 'ole way 'ome, snug as –. The engine explodes from its *'ole, a shell fired by a dreadnought* that cruises far below in the *brown earthsea*. Its lamps send *deffrays* lancing along the tiles, while Audrey hears the *paddin'* between her own ears as she listens to the roar of its trajectory. Although she knows it cannot hit them, she grabs the arm from which the parcel destined for Arnold Collins hangs by its loop of twine. – Fine companion you are! Her father exults in her fear, draws her near – from under his furry arm Audrey watches, appalled, as the platform with its cargo of buckram and boaters and nodding plumes slides away behind the row of yellow-lit windows. Seated beside her father, she sees not the advertisement card REDFERN'S RUBBER MATS FOR THE OFFICE, above the rushing darkness into which the carriage sinks, then rises to another crest at British Museum Station, then sinks once more. Her hands are back in her lap and they tap-tap-tap with the clack of wheel on steel – but Audrey remains detached, bobbing in her seat as the train surfaces at Tottenham Court Road, at Bond Street, at Marble Arch, where, her head clamped in the *eyepiece* of the window, she is compelled to see through her own diaphanous self to the electrified fssschk-chk-fssschk-chk as the platform pulls away again, this time its display more various: *tailors' dummies* hung about with Ulsters and macintoshes *shared by two*, the full skirts hiding *Little Titch* on *a pantomime horse* ... in between are arranged *in no particular order* an oil stove, a steamer trunk, pearl-handled Colt revolvers in an open display case, a selection of travelling rugs, a hat stand hung about with moabs, a writing desk with a stuffed raven set upon it, a toy train set that is this very underground railway made *awfully small*, a hassock embroidered with the Prince of Wales's crest, a pianola, an indicator board ringing for service *in every room*, a probang, an electroplated punch bowl, Malacca canes fanned out on a Mackinaw, a regimental table piece in the shape of a sepoy shooting a tiger, a toaster, an electric lamp, a fondue set, a patented 'Galvanic' weight-reduction belt, an electric blanket, a stereo cassette deck – *whatever that may be.* Audrey can hear the disembodied voice – sweetly covetous – naming these things as they are shuffled before her, but the kinetoscope is difficult to focus on when she is *so constrained* ... a barbecue! His and hers dressing gowns and a cuddly toy! The voice finishes on a triumphant note, synthetic sounds swell to make the shape of music, and an invisible audience shapes its hands to make applause ... *this fiendishness will be Albert's doing: a brace* adjusted so as to force her to stare up at the ceiling, its screws *threaded in the bone* to either side of her eyes. *This ... kinema film his doing as well: a means of torture.* The brace presses Audrey's face into a *muzzle* that smells of old sweat – her legs are bound *in a single leg of some tartan trews*, her hands must *loosen the chuck, switch the bit and turn the wheel* by touch alone – she feels the fuse cap *drop into my lap* ... the lines in between the ceiling tiles converge sickeningly *but it's not so bad* ... she isn't like Gracie, who's been in the Danger Buildings *too long – poor Gracie*, who shared a cubicle with her in the Plumstead hostel and who also received *Cristobel's message to join in the war effort and once the workers were with them to rise in the reddy dawn. Poor Gracie, who doesn't know me, who's demented, whose skin is still canary-yellow – are they putting Trotyl in her food?* In the early years Audrey had been happy to assist – to coo, bill and generally calm them before their *psychoetheric reordering*, before they were made to *desire the images*, if not the *Ding an sich*: atoasterafonduesetanelectricblanket – the words chew together now in avaricious haste, astereocassettedeckabarbecue!'isnerrsdressin' gownsannacuddlytoy –! Off. Clicked *off.* The aerial sits *alien antennae* on the old set, which is warm and smells of *singed dust*. Busner straightens up, turns – the silence in the day-room of Ward 14 is slowly infiltrated by moans, mutterings, then: Wotcher do that for? Mister Garvey – mid-sixties, hypomanic, recent transfer – protests: That's my favourite bloody programme, that is. Busner lifts an emollient hand and *strokes* the air. Please, he says, please . . . it'll only be for a few minutes, I just want to ask Miss Dearth a couple of things . . . He waves the clipboard he holds in his other hand, and the papers stir up *powdered milk, dried urine*. The high-backed and upright armchairs face him in two shallow crescents, and are far more accusatory than the bundles dumped in them. Awkwardly, Busner manoeuvres between the rows, jostling past knees covered up with rugs and others frighteningly exposed: *Oof, look at that contusion . . . a Waterloo sunset.* The day-room's ill-fitting sash windows are buffeted by the wind, strafed by raindrops, and so he is reminded *It's April*, as he drops himself into the seat beside her. Her poor old face is crammed into the angle of the headrest, her scrawny legs are rigid and the torsion of her upper body is painful to behold – yet, despite this, her hands move methodically, deftly, pulling upon an invisible lever, twirling an immaterial flywheel with such assurance that the

79

psychiatrist does see *steel basted with oil, the fireside glow of bronze*. Miss Dearth, he begins, I have your original admission form from . . . together with the notes made by medical officers during your first few years here. — It has taken him over a month to beg, cajole and wheedle these from Records, they see no point to it any more than Whitcomb does. – There're plenty of fancies floating around this place, Busner, that's why you're better off confining yourself to facts, to routines . . . It is pointless to observe to his nominal superior, or to Missus Jarvis, the *hideous old dragon* who crouches on the *nest of paper and card breathing bureaucratic fire* at him, that these records are precisely that: facts, and facts about routines. De'Ath, Audrey, Admitted 26th September 1922, Born Fulham, 1890 (age 32), Spinst. 5'2", 7st. 8lbs., Address Flat G, 309 Clapham Road, Stockwell, London SW, had been subjected to a medical examination, so it was noted that: she showed no signs of tuberculosis, rheumatic fever, smallpox, being postpartum or having had any confinements. De'Ath, Audrey, had been admitted – it was cramped into the preprinted boxes of the form – as a rate-aided person, exhibiting symptoms of catatonia that led Doctor M. H. Hood, Medical Superintendent, unhesitatingly to diagnose Primary Dementia *whatever that was*. A year later Doctor Ventor concurred in respect of one Death, Audrey, but a note written by a Doctor Hayman, dated a scant three years later, just as definitively – the Latin tag underlined thrice in purple ink – characterised one Deeth, Audrey, same other details, as suffering from Dementia Praecox. As he had laid out the ancient sheets and file cards on a sticky-ringed coffee table in the staff room, Busner found himself moved to consider the evolution *in symbiosis* of these names. For, as the Mental Health Act of 1930 modified Colney Hatch Asylum to Colney Hatch Mental Hospital, so Deeth, Audrey, mutated into Deerth, Audrey, who was given – courtesy, he imagined, of the slow absorption of Bleuler's terminology into the fabric of English psychiatry – an equally authoritative diagnosis of schizophrenia. It would have been next to impossible to have tracked this pseudonymous patient down through the decades within an institution that remained in a continuing identity crisis, were it not that Miss De'Ath, AKA Miss Death, AKA Miss Deeth, AKA Miss Deerth, remained in *exactly the same place, a moth – not dead but hibernating and growing more and more desiccated with the years –* despite the subsidence of entire spurs, the constant renovations called for by the shoddy workmanship of its original contractors, the fires and the wartime bomb damage, the admission and departure, by death or discharge, of thousands of the mentally distressed. In the late 1930s, when the hospital saw fit to reinvent itself as Friern Mental Hospital, relegating – *or so they hoped* – the echo of the booby-hatch to the chants of children, Miss Deerth, Busner assumed through yet another error of transcription, became Miss Dearth. And so she stopped on Ward 14, an incurable schizophrenic whose profound catatonia was her most enduringly remarked upon characteristic, now that the decades had worn away all contingencies of sex, age, class and name. Her catatonia ... and her dyskinesias and dystonias of all kinds, her muscles crimped, then cramped, her hands vamping and vibrating in the vice of her malady – so that, come the 1960s, when the hospital adopted the modishly informal nickname Friern, and the surf of chlorpromazine was up, old Miss Dearth's symptomatic consistency was noticed by a not-yet-jaded junior neurologist temporarily attached to the staff — a certain Doctor Mohan Ramachandra, who must, like Busner after him, have bothered to read at least some of her notes and seen that, while she had been subjected to one round of insulin coma therapy in the late thirties and a single *experimental jolt* of ECT a decade later, she had mostly *stepped over the high-tension cabling that snaked through brains for the next twenty years.* He so concluded that, far from her twisting, ticcing and transfixed gazing being the consequence of too liberal dosage with major tranquillisers – since as yet she had been prescribed none – there might – *just might* – be a physiological explanation for her forty-odd years of torpor, a hypothesis that led to his jotting down *very tentatively, in pencil*, a single word, Parkinsonian, on the final page of those notes, followed by a ? that absolutely guaranteed there would be no follow-up

until now. *Well, she's never in the way, Always something nice to say, Oh what a blessing. I can leave her on her own, Knowing she's okay alone, and there's no messing. She's a lady, Whoa, whoa, she's a lady!* I presume that you and, um, these others – Miss Deerth, Miss Deeth, Miss Death and, er, Miss De'Ath – that you are . . . one and the same? Busner leans into the headrest as far as he dare, entangling his hair with hers – there's nothing to hear beyond the *pigeon burble* of fluid respiration. He tries another tack: On your notes . . . Miss Dearth . . . You were seen by various doctors over the years . . . Do you recall Doctor Hood? *Nothing.* Or maybe Doctor Hayman? *Nothing again.* A trolley comes wheedling along stacked with aluminium-lidded plates, the sulphurous stench of overcooked Brussels sprouts rolls over the trench where he hunches – other patients rise to fetch trays and there is a modest cacophony. Frustrated, Busner rears up. Mboya has gone – there are only orderlies in blue-and-green-cheque nylon housecoats passing out the featherweight cutlery, handing over the scratched-opaque plastic beakers. *Oh what a blessing – there's no messing* . . . He tries again:

How about Doctor Cummins – or Doctor Marcus? This last name is his trump card, surely it will elicit a response, *surely?* Sjoo-shjoob. I'm sorry? He tucks his ear in still further – her cheek is deeply creased, she has been sleeping *on sheets of disordered time.* Sjhoo-shoob. *Or is it jujube?* His ear brushes her purse lips, Please, he says, please Miss Dearth *or whatever your fucking name is,* please try again . . . the wishbone jaw articulates, releasing foul breath and two pellets of sense: Jew-boy. For a moment Busner imagines she has roused only to insult him, then two more pellets follow: he . . . was, before she falls silent. *Of course!* It is not in Busner's nature or deportment to become a whirl of activity, yet this, he thinks, is what I am. His springing up releases her flywheel – and so her hands *go to it* again: the right rotating, the left adjusting, while he grips his clipboard and plunges straight through the row of chairs. Oi! Garvey leers at him *dying Pakistani* a cuspid of mash in his otherwise toothless mouth – Busner sheds sorries as he sees that someone has switched the television back on, although *it like me lacks vertical hold:* jagged compartments going up and up, a Brucie in every one. He slaps the set's wood veneer cheek once, twice, *hard* and Fanks, Doc, follows him and his stinging palm – but he doesn't look back. It's the Saturday evening before Easter Sunday, he should be *at home with my wife and kids,* with Miriam, Mark, Daniel and the baby – not here, where in the intensifying gloom the Austin's headlights sweep across the trompe-l'œil façade of the hospital, *It's a fake,* because, while it looks like a hospital on this holiday weekend, there won't be a single doctor in the entire asylum, the three thousand or so lunatics prevented from taking it over only by their own institutionalised inertia. — The vulnerable prey of his own soaring enthusiasm, Busner wrestles the car around the ornamental flowerbed, past the lodge and turns left on to Friern

83

Barnet Road. Settling down into the cold, damp vinyl odour of the car, merging *my own foam rubber with its,* he sets course for St John's Wood through another spring squall. He had telephoned again from the nurses' station to confirm that he was coming and Marcus's voice – clipped, bored and nasal – said: I thought I made it clear to you when we spoke yesterday evening, Doctor Busner, come whenever you like – there's nothing else to do. And to Busner, despite Miriam's censure, it also feels that *there's nothing else to do . . .* An ultimatum had been set when they quit the Concept House the previous year: No more enthusiasm – *enthusiasm almost got you bloody struck off!* Now it has him in its talons again, gripping him as tightly as he grips the *kyphotic* steering wheel and directs the Austin's blunt nose to part the rainy spangles that trail across the carriageway. Last night Miriam had taken the children to Seder at her parents' without him – it was the first time this had happened since she *laid down the law.* He remained poring over Audrey Dearth's notes at the kneehole desk he had installed in the corner of their bedroom, having failed in his attempt to enthuse her too by showing Miriam the entries made by Doctor A. Marcus that began in 1931 with him effectively dissenting from his colleague's diagnosis of schizophrenia, and ended in 1941 when, Busner assumed, he had been called up. You see – he had grasped her elbow – here he's written Enc. Leth. And here he expands on this: I consider it likely this patient may in fact be suffering from the somnolent-ophthalmologic form of encephalitis lethargica. Then here . . . he riffled . . . here, here, here and here! Every time he sees her over the next decade he's moved to write something – he scrawls across her drug card when she's been given paraldehyde Not Required. He writes next to another doctor's observation that her oculogyric crises – whatever they may be – are functional: Nonsense. See, see!

84

Miriam, who has a dip' psych. of her own, *wouldn't see*, she only echoed the baby's full-throated protest from the next-door room: See what? She pulled away from him and said, What is this encephalitis lethargica anyway? Believing he had her hooked, Busner had begun hauling on the cuff of her cardigan, dragging her towards the entry in the musty Britannica he had inherited from Maurice: There – he'd glossed it – end of the First War . . . Came before the Spanish Flu epidemic – maybe a precursor? Thing is, onset Parkinsonian – fevers, night sweats, swoons – but then paradoxical: some lapse into comas, others the reverse, suffering sleeplessness to the point of agrypnia! Maybe a third of 'em died, another third recovered completely, and a further third seemed to get better, but then a year, three – perhaps as many as five later they relap—. She took back her arm, saying, Zack, the baby is crying, she can't sleep right now. Miriam's freshly sculpted bob was *polished ebony* in the sharp light of the Anglepoise, Mary Cunt, he thought, then said: Don't you see? This patient of mine at Friern, she's just one of scores in the hospital I've identified – there must be hundreds more still scattered throughout the big asylums, possibly thousands. Don't you see, there's nothing at all wrong with them psychologically – or at least there wasn't to begin with, now . . . who knows – this was a virus that attacked the brain stem. Miriam had been arrested in the open doorway, her fingers rubbing her own shaven nape *in sympathy?* her hip *still boyish* nudging the wicker laundry basket from which *dripped* a pair of his own underpants *piping hot*. I tell you what I see, she said. I see the same sort of pathetic reductionism at work here that was operating when you fell under your pal Ronnie's influence . . . *that voice banishes my concentration* . . . Then there was no mental illness to speak of, only different ways of looking at the world. Different – she spat individual syllabic seeds – ex-i-sten-tial phe-nom-en-olo-gies. And now, again, there's no mental illness – hey presto! All gone! All better! And in its place this encepho-thing. I wonder, Zack – really, I wonder when it'll occur to you . . . this had been her parting shot, and he *the dumb dog sat there obediently waiting for it* . . . that simply wishing madness away won't make anyone regain their sanity – nobody at all. Soon enough the baby's crying shuddered to a halt, stoppered by a bottle. He could hear Miriam calling to the boys to get their coats – then car keys jangled, the front door slammed, the starter motor of the Austin coughed and whined, coughed and whined again. He sat there worried she would return to upbraid him some more until, eventually, he heard the car accelerate away – then he began to worry she would never return at all. Now, the same engine fulminating by the lights at Henley's Corner, Busner sits waiting in the clammy day that Henry carefully removed all the polythene from their uncle's dry-cleaned suits, then, taking the wire coat hangers, bent them to form the framework upon which the filmy stuff could be stretched. These strange *blooms of the future* were finished off with large amounts of Sellotape before being planted in between the delphiniums in the – at that time – sterile and ordered front garden of the Redington Road house. *He was always good with his hands – still is.* Zack already knew better than to interfere, although it can only have been a few weeks since Henry had returned unexpectedly, mid-term, from Cambridge, filthy, unshaven, his knuckles scabbed, and told his younger brother that the Authorities had concealed an intercontinental ballistic missile silo beneath the quadrangle of his college. His plastic flowers planted, Henry got out the hose and stood there drenching the same spot for an hour, then a second, then a third. He drenched it until the earth liquefied and flowed down the path, out

86

the gate and down the road, bearing privet leaves, twigs and blades of cut grass on its thick and sinuous back. He drenched it until their uncle returned home to find him standing there, his *kaleidoscope eyes on the marmalade sky*, his trousers soaked and mud-spotted. Then Henry began to water Maurice. Soon enough there was a clangorous police Rover – soon after that an ambulance. Uncle Maurice, with his interest in the Elstree Studios and his brittle-coiffed friends, had *had a flare for dramatics — although to be fair* he had tried persuasion before, many times.

Marcus's address in 1941 had been given up grudgingly by Missus Jarvis of Records. There was still a Doctor A. Marcus listed in St John's Wood, yet Busner hadn't been convinced he had the right man until, upon apologising for calling on the evening of Good Friday, the pre-war voice on the end of the line said: We Jews also celebrate the death of Christ y'know – an outrageous statement, presumably intended to drive away callers, but which in this instance had the opposite effect. Busner had the unnerving sensation – so clearly did he hear the other man's voice inside his head – that they were only two hemispheres of the same brain, yoked together by the citywide stretching of the corpus callosum phone line. He's the one, Busner had thought, and now, having been buzzed in to the mansion block on Abbey Road, he climbs the wide and shallow treads of the stairs to see *a Jew with a military bearing – he's definitely the one*. Of course I remember Miss Deerth, Marcus says before anything else. He stands: a tall, stooped figure *Stravinsky ugly* with a pot-belly and a large nose with a broad, flat tip *duck-billed*, his bifocals pushed up high on a balding cranium. I saw her at least monthly, if not more often, for getting on for ten years, why shouldn't I remember her? There're members of my immediate family I've seen less of – and found less, ah, congenial. In the *twitch of the bill* towards a mousy wife who stands in the tenebrous corridor, there is a nasty implication, one confirmed when Marcus ushers Busner on without making an introduction and she withdraws, presumably to a kitchen. They breast smelly vapours of chopped liver and frying potatoes, their feet crackling on a plastic strip laid over the carpet, before entering a *weird chamber.* Can I offer you a sherry? Marcus asks, as he points to one of a pair of club chairs of thirties vintage with burled walnut sides *like the dashboard of the Austin* that face one another over a nest of red lacquered tables. The sherry is Cypriot – *incredibly sweet.* Marcus un-nests one table, a second and then a third to accommodate all of the case notes Busner withdraws from his briefcase. A frosted bulb of high wattage is exposed in a *perverted* way by the scalloped edge of its paper shade and the mean white light strikes Marcus's face – a face that, as is so often the case with the *ageing male,* has been inefficiently shaved, leaving bristly crests on either cheekbone and along the line of the *resolute* jaw. You have to understand, he says, that it was all too common in the first wave of the epidemic to have one patient correctly diagnosed with encephalitis lethargica and sent to a fever hospital, but for his as it were twin in every symptomatic respect to be diagnosed with dementia praecox and sent to a mental one. This … *he dips for his sherry* … happened all the time – and it went on into the twenties, when the second wave of the epidemic felled many more of those who it'd been thought had fully recovered. Still, to be fair to the doctors of that era –. Marcus interrupts himself: But why? Why be fair to 'em! Sherry *spittles on my precious notes!* Some of 'em were outright bloody pervs – it's a fact. Marcus shudders. Feelin' up the patients – having intercourse with 'em if they were biddable, or sedated with opium, hyoscine – henbane even. They gave sex hormones to schizophrenics – I expect they were swallowing them as well! There were sadists too – but then I daresay there still are. Those who take sheer bloody delight in applying restraints – or ordering it done –. The outburst suddenly stops: *Is he guilty himself – or sly?* Of course, Marcus runs on dismissively: these were the exceptions, the bad apples . . . *Or simply touched?* . . . the vast majority of the staff were as responsible as they could be in the circumstances – if a trifle, um, unempathetic –. She creeps in from the soundlessly opened door, one shoulder raised, *To ward off his blows?* with an oblong blue Tupperware platter upon which are lined up *shield bosses* Ritz crackers, each meticulously coated with chopped liver. She un-nests a still littler red lacquered table, sets down the platter and retreats under the cover of her rigid perm' *is it a wig?* At once there is an avalanche of crumbs that scatters between the cable-knit ridges of the old man's cardigan as his lips purse about a cracker, his dentures *fiddling in their skin bag.* Help yourself, he says a little grudgingly – then: You cannot be so wet behind the ears that you don't know that diagnostics were in their infancy. Besides, you can have no idea of the caseload and what a bloody caseload! Even in the early thirties there were still plenty of inmates at the Hatch with TB – and fresh cases coming in every week. They all had to wear a caution card on a ribbon round their necks – yellow for TB, red for diph-theria, green for . . . something else, I forget. I said help yourself. Busner does *mm . . . crunchy, creamy, salty – surprisingly . . . tasty.* We considered pulmonary TB to be the twin of insanity, so closely were they associated. In my time there I had plenty of colleagues who, I knew for a fact, still believed that one caused the other, although not altogether certain – euch, euch! – which. Marcus makes a conduc-tor's gesture, the long fingers of both hands spatulate, *duck-billed* and raised up – if he could see himself, Busner thinks, he'd diagnose acute chorea – then brought down once, twice and a third time, so that cracker crumbs and pâté blobs are left *in suspension*, flickering in the bright light – a *meteor shower* the *old alienist* thrusts himself through to spit: I doubt you've ever seen a case of lupis vulgaris outside of a textbook . . . and Busner, confronted by nostrils eaten away at by sharp shadows, thinks, I could be looking at one right now, but only confirms: You're right there. Marcus next asks, More sherry? although this inquiry post-dates the unscrewing, the pouring and the re-sealing of the bottle. Last December, Marcus continues, when we had candles in here and got out the old Tilley lamp, it made me think of my first years at the Hatch – those endless bloody corridors, a gas-bracket only every thirty yards or so. D'you know, there was a neurologist who came up a few times from Queen Square to do some encephalograms with one of the first portable machines – and that was before they'd fully installed electrical light in that mausoleum, so he could scarcely see well enough to take the readings of the electri-cal activity in the patients' brains! Marcus has fallen back once more, but now he comes once again *unto the light*: What I'm driving at here is that we'd patients with diphtheria, who'd had typhoid – with dia-bloody-betes, not forgetting . . . *a duckbill speared into the air* . . . ones poisoned by lead or arsenic or alcohol. All of 'em would exhibit peripheral neuropathy so all of 'em would be given the catch-all: hysteric. Busner says nothing, *Say nothing*, for as it is to the patient, so it is to the physician: if you want them to talk *say nothing* . . . Look – *at what, your bill, those crumbs?* – the enkies were merely another group of patients for whom there was neither the conceptual appa-ratus nor the resources to disentangle the physiological from the psychological. With the enkies one neurologist's catalepsy was another psychiatrist's catatonia – but, anyway, it's progress that's the real delusion. You, young man, might like to believe that there's no turning back – the Wasserman test and so forth . . . the replacement of diseased types by disease processes . . . but really this is utter bosh, because, after all, what've you got now with your so-called personality disorders – it's only types all over again, denigrating the poor bloody patient by saying he's got a bad character. That reminds me of something . . . Marcus pours himself another sherry to aid the process of recall, this time forgetting to impose a refill on his guest . . . there used to be a statue in the grounds, ragged-arsed Victorian kid, the Hatch's own Madness and Melancholy – y'know, the Bedlam statues – he had a plaque on his plinth that read, Monument to the Unknown Pauper Lunatic. Still there is he, in the shrubbery by the big villa off Eastern Avenue? Busner thinks for a moment, and for some reason decides to spare Marcus the ugly truth. No, he says, no, I believe he was, um, discharged a couple of years ago. I understand the feeling was at the Health Authority that he sent a rather negative message to the patients . . . and Marcus crows, See, see! They got rid of him because he represented the truth: that the patients are poor, and they're mad – and indeed that many of 'em are mad precisely because they're poor. That's the reality all their borderline-this and histrionic-that balderdash covers up! Busner, however, doesn't wish to pursue this line, no matter the extent to which *it speaks to my condition.* Instead: Enkies? he queries. They had a nickname? Marcus snorts, Naturally! After all, they were simply another feature of the post-war scene – along with limbless ex-servicemen and economic stagnation. I remember as a young man going to the cinema and seeing newsreels of enkies – quite a lot was made of 'em in their hyperkinetic phase, and you could understand why because they had a strange sort of physical genius, able to make sudden moves that were deft – but zany and prankish, y'know, juggling lots of balls, chucking stuff, leaping and skipping. Marcus, in attempting to illustrate this physical genius, makes a wild sweep of his arm, knocking another table out of the nest and scattering the notes, he juggles *none of them*. He is dismayed by his own clumsiness: I don't know ... I daresay you wouldn't be able to spot it if you saw those films now – I mean, in films from that era everyone looks like a Chaplin or a Buster Keaton – even Lloyd George – something to do with way they hand-cranked the cameras, I s'pose. The *liverish pucks* are all gone – a lot of the sherry too. Busner says, And what of Miss Dearth – as she is now? Marcus spends a while surveying the room, squinting at the *spreading behind* of his young colleague, who, as he gathers the scattered sheets from the carpet, takes in the bookcases densely packed with decades-old professional journals and Roneographed papers that *he'll probably never pick up again, let alone read*. Well ... he drawls at last ... what of her? Busner persists: I mean, you thought it worthwhile putting things in her notes, making your own tentative diagnosis ... Marcus shrugs. – It was a jape, I s'pose – I mean, it was clear to me that she was post-encephalitic, and I wrote it down partly to twit my colleagues, partly simply to show that I knew ... perhaps, pah! for posterity ... perhaps to fish you from the future – I hardly know any more, it was a long time ago. I can tell you one thing, though ... The notes are all reassembled on one of the red lacquered tables and Marcus cants forward to leaf through them, stopping from time to time to bring one up to his face so he may examine his younger self's handwriting with lenses clawed down from his forehead ... It certainly wasn't with any intention of helping her – there was no cure, she'd no one to look after her that we were aware of. It mattered not one jot which sort of institution she was confined to, given how profoundly ill she was – and you say still is? Busner assents, then outlines the condition of his patient: her long periods of catatonia interspersed by manic episodes and still stranger phases when – he screws his features into an approximation of Audrey Dearth's crises of *fixed regard* – She has her attention, her gaze . . . compelled by some invisible object up above her and to the left. Marcus is himself compelled. – Yes, yes . . . His watery eyes fix on a threadbare pelmet, its flaking brocade indistinguishable from smears of cobweb . . . this is entirely typical of post-encephalitics. Still – he snaps out of it – I'm surprised she's still with us, she must be very elderly by now. You might've thought the enkies would've been altogether worn down by their illness, plenty died in all the usual ways, of course, but I also recognised that there were these others – like her – who were almost preserved by the sleepy-sickness, as if it were a kind of suspended animation. Sometimes . . . but this is fanciful! Busner almost shouts: No, no! It's not fanciful at all – how could anything connected with these astonishing patients be fanciful? So please – please give full rein to your thoughts! He has, he realises, succumbed to the old man's very *lack of charm*, Marcus's abruptness, a stop-and-start that recalls the paradoxical condition of *those others* with their *veined, dry-leaf skin . . . who blow in drifts along the endless corridor, for the end of time has come . . . and the campanile has collapsed . . . rain falls through the broken ceiling of the pharmacy . . . blue-and-yellow capsules swirl in a clear glass bowl, schizophrenics bob for them – dipping birds . . . —* They must have reached *some sort of conclusion*, risen from their *burled walnut caskets* and got out *from under that harsh white light*, for here they are: the old man standing erect in the hallway, Busner already outside the heavy front door and

93

embarrassed for the Marcuses, whose *Jewfoody stench* can still be detected a floor down from their flat, and which seems to him to sully the deep-piled purple carpets and smirch the brass nameplate of the mansion block. Busner cannot contain his thoughts — they fly to be with *squatters sitting grouped on tea chests*, one of whom *licks a Rizla and attaches it to two others* . . . and in *another place there are disco lights making thighs blood-red* . . . *the horror*, the horror is that this, of all the possible times and places, feels willed. His hand ivy on the doorjamb, his carpet slippers mossy on the mat, Marcus says: I enlisted as a general physician, but when they discovered I was a psychiatrist I was seconded at once to the field hospitals set up in the beachhead immediately after the landings. It was very abrupt – one week the dark corridors of Colney Hatch, the next these equally oppressive Normandy hedgerows, and pitched right beside them army canvas tents . . . When I'd first been at the Hatch inmates who repeatedly soiled themselves, or those put in the padded cells, were forced into canvas tunics . . . Every time there was a show more and more boys were brought into the tents, white as . . . white as . . . They'd never seen action before – their training had consisted only of robotic drills. They'd soiled themselves – plenty had thrown away their rifles . . . by far the majority hadn't fired a shot. They sat in their own mess ticcing, and we shrinks joked – gallows humour, d'you see – that it was a busman's holiday. Chap I knew – before the war he'd been at Napsbury – he went over with the Yanks and they did some sort of a study, very hush-hush. Turned out only one in ten of their infantry ever shot with lethal intent and I can't imagine it was any different with our boys. *Where's he going on his busman's holiday?* Odd, isn't it, to think of all that mayhem, all that killing – now too in Pakistan – and yet the vast bulk of it is perpetrated by a mere handful of psychopathic personalities, the rest being there to, euch-euch, make up the numbers. They have been standing like this for so long that it would seem appropriate for Marcus to invite Busner back in, but instead he looks critically at the younger man's fat knot of woolly tie and the plump hand that fidgets with it, and says, I've enjoyed talking at you – will you come again? Busner laughs, I'd like to – and I'd like to come with news of a . . . positive nature. I mean to say, if this is Parkinsonian . . . well, there're terrific strides being made just now with chemical therapies, I've read an article in the Lancet –. The Lancet! the old man yelps, How very quaint!

Busner thinks: I'm disarmed by the feint and lunge of his repartee. He tries another tack: Did you . . . had you at any point considered if – well, it seems to me, having observed Miss Dearth, that her higher functions may be . . . intact – that she may be quite conscious of what goes on around her, although powerless to . . . intervene. He falls silent, wondering how it is possible to be regarded simultaneously with affection and derision. Marcus *quacks* more ruminatively: Forty years ago those were my own fanciful thoughts precisely, we are all too conscious – he pokes an admonitory finger up to where *Hot Love gushes* from some parental stereo system *turned up far too loudly!* – of what goes on around here, but quite without the means to intervene. Busner wonders, Is it an indulgence to feel his padded-out hips with my hands? Is it flirting with psychosis – as in the mad, bad old days – to relax inside Marcus's tinged old skin and peer down over the furred curve of his belly at the polished brass boot-scraper *and my own feet? . . . and there's no messing.*

He does not discover himself in the blowy street, nor recover himself in rhyme, *Rain, rain go away, come again another day.* The consideration that *Lords is over there* evades him, as will the coming cricket season. He doesn't clamber into the Austin's metal belly and drive up Abbey Road — he remains there, curled in the old man's caul and waiting for his own senescence to come of age, which it does after a protracted labour, long-drawn-out clenchings of that fulcrum, the prostate, upon which the ageing man tries to balance, inclining one way for a dull ache, *the other for relief* . . . Outside there is the musical whine, the quasi-rhythmic bash – all the airy clangour of scaffolding being taken down, while below on the pavement stands a conductor in a leather apron. *La Cadenga* is the name of an African woman, her hips gripped by . . . *batik?* a calabash jumbled with fruit set on her stately head. He must have rolled over in his sleep, for now Busner lies on his back, his bladder puddling and these orange boxes full of his office things clearly in view. 10.22. He has slept for another full hour and now he really must rise and to prevent himself from heading back to bed plunges instead towards the kitchenette – *Whoa! How did that happen, that tuck in time?* Although Busner is by no means a valetudinarian, it is still due to little incidents of this kind that he learns he must correctly calculate all trajectories in advance, as course adjustments are no longer possible – even in domestic space. Until touched-down by a dusty heap of muesli, his brain floats inside his skull, cutting capers for his camera I. Sitting at a counter inset with earth-toned tiles, he pours the milk, plants his spoon in the heap and paddles through the cereal — to all the desolation of station hotels, where films of milky slurry mask haddock. His uncle Maurice sits opposite, over his shoulder *in a glass darkly* a china figurine of a Foo dog, of which Busner learns, much later, that they can eat as much as they like without ever shitting . . . *like the English upper middle classes*. Maurice has the long, carefully rolled baton of

Reynolds News tucked under the edge of his plate, *where could we have been going on a weekend?* He knew. Now, Maurice says, after the visit, have you any other plans for the day? He dabs at his moustache with his napkin, drops it to the table and slaps his thigh with an attempt at merriment so desperately at odds with his discreet character – *writing cases inside hatboxes inside portmanteaus inside steamer trunks –* that they both laugh, and Zack thinks then of *James Robertson Justice* and now: When did I first know Maurice was homosexual? *Always*. His uncle: discreet, clever, careful, meticulous – but mostly clever, in a way that Jews of his generation might *try to hide*, although for Maurice this was unnecessary since he passed in all respects as an Englishman, who, if not heterosexual, was certainly nothing else. *There were more like that then, to appear neutered was socially acceptable – enjoined, almost. Hymens hardening into old age, prepuces never pulled, we are speaking of the deathly respectable here, not anyone . . . alive.* Maurice had been too clever to need to pretend to anything he didn't feel – too clever and *too kind*. An interest in music *but no passion,* some golf – always powerful and impressive cars such as Bristols, Rovers and Rolls-Royces. A little fly-fishing – *I went with him once, somewhere in Scotland . . . rhododendrons everywhere, the sea a fallen sky. Some shooting . . .* there was a gun cabinet at Redington Road – *gone before Henry got ill.* But never too much of any one thing – just as in his portfolio there was some of Cunard, a little of Trusthouse Forte – *did he know Rocco?* – and Imperial Chemicals, quite a lot of Gainsborough Studios because this was an investment that amused him, that Maurice took an active interest in – in as much as such a state of mind could ever be detected, his brownish moustache twitching, two beautifully manicured fingers rotating his signet ring, which was set with a bevelled green stone – an emerald? Hopelessly sclerotic, of course, *his heart fit to burst – and did!* The Ministry of Defence have confirmed ... *At least there was none of that pillar-of-the-community shit at the funeral* ... Sergeant Brian Culcross of the Second Battalion Royal Marines ... *That actress who read, what was her name? Minna? Minna ... Standish? It was about thrushes, certainly, and spring rain – Browning?* ... an improvised explosive device ... *But this is purest invention!* After forty-five years only the rubber stamps on their circular stand beside the blotter have any real substance. The blotter on the kneehole desk and the share certificates in its bottom drawers, tied in bundles with different-coloured ribbons like lawyers' briefs, together with his will in triplicate and an accounts book preprinted for double-entry. How apt! Leapfrogging back another forty-five years, the entries were a comprehensive listing of cocks and arseholes, their sizes, their appearance and those attributes of the men they had belonged to. In the widest column, neatly and legibly, Maurice had set down the facts of what was done, where and with whom – although there were no names, only numbers. From this presumably comprehensive tabulation Maurice's nephew could deduce very little. Zachary could not say whether his uncle had been a happy bugger or a driven, persecuted and paranoid erotomane – all he could tell was that his uncle had observed the same principle in his sexual practice as he had in his life generally: never too much of any one thing. That Maurice had been cosmopolitan Zachary had always known – but not *this* cosmopolitan, with a predilection, or so it seemed, *for all ages, races and classes of men* ... And now Jenni Murray with Woman's Hour ... as he had sat leafing through the accounts book, Zack began to understand exactly why it – along with the house and a pleasant but not excessive private income – had been entailed to him: it was the most effective riposte. Sitting at the breakfast bar of his shabby rental flat, old enough now to be *the uncle to my uncle*, Busner thinks back . . . and back . . . almost enjoying the very feminine blush of shame he feels mounting from his neck to his face, while also considering that no elapsing of time could ever be sufficient, whether biologic – the marching of entire orders and phyla into extinction – or geologic – the shuffling of plates thrusting up mountain ranges – to annul this shameful image: *Me, full of myself* at another breakfast table and *grinding away at my uncle* . . . believing it clever as well as kind to employ my *newly machined analytic tools* on the basis that *repression could be reduced to fine filings of the perverse and so blown away. Preposterous!* to interrogate him concerning his relationship with his mother – and to continue doing so, refusing to take no answer for *a no*. Yet he was so gracious about it – *playful, really*, refolding the Times, tucking it back under the edge of his plate, and warning me of Missus Mac's proximity by the slightest arching of his *beautifully trimmed eyebrows, while wryly observing, Have you read Bernard Levin's column this morning? There's something in what he says, I think, that we can both agree on* . . . — Some oat flake must have flown off and so provided the necessary bearing, Busner's hand saunters unthinkingly after it and turns off the radio, so that: Cameron Macintosh's new –. Silence. And then from the street below rises the unmistakable rattling bash of a flatbed truck's tailgate being closed, followed by its diesel engine revving, *a deep and throaty fugue. The scaffolding is down* . . . and what was the cultivation of memory – through solitude, through reverie – if not the erection of a scaffolding in order to facilitate *the construction of current behaviours.* Yes, that was it: a behavioural aid, such as the holding and then the letting fall of ping-pong balls so as to stimulate movement, or the wearing of a loudly ticking watch so as to supply a tempo by which to recalibrate the complex motor sequences needed to stand up, that should be automatic, but that needed to be *relearned . . . every time.*

Busner stands up. For a while he had thought that when he had more leisure he might do something with Maurice's homolog, which was surely a sexual self-interrogation to rival the broader surveys of Havelock-Ellis and Kinsey. He supposed it might be in one of the orange boxes under the window, or in the attic at Redington Road – wherever it was, it would be together with tea chests full of the rotting correspondence of the parents Busner had never known, their serrated postcards, their now blotched but once creamy notepaper folded into thick envelopes that had been extravagantly franked and stamped. All of it he had foreseen himself unpacking, unsheathing and unfolding, so that the pressed flowers bloomed into dust as he read the missives for the first time since their long-gone recipients set the sheets to one side. It was not – he considers as he raises the candy-striped canvas blind to discover decals of outsized and grinning pizza-eaters being leant against by real people who are grimy in the surprising sunlight that shines on the far side of Fortess Road – the unexamined life that was worthless, but the one *un-re-examined by the properly qualified.* And at once he resolves to *throw all that stuff away.* To have it all picked over by the next generation, or in the declension below that, by an amateur genealogist avid for his roots would result in a further demerit, rendering his parents' lives, Maurice's, his own, worthless minus one. – And what of Sergeant Culcross? Busner says aloud, speaking to the hip-high fridge, the enamelled BREAD BIN and the electric jug, in a vain attempt to rouse them from their complacent inanimation. *What of him?* Busner sees the young man lying on the bleak roadside, his legs torn off by the blast, and wonders: did they pick the nuts and bolts out of him before 'coptering him back to base? Was he right now sedated in a hospital bed, waiting to be told ... *like Ronald Reagan that he had nothing down below?* They might well reassure him all they could, they would probably rub talcum powder on his stumps, sheathe them in silk stockings and the leather sockets of the prostheses. No doubt capable nurses would lift him on either side, then put him on a walking machine – but that's only another kind of treadmill, because in the end a phantom limb or two would be a blessing compared to this waking, walking nightmare with the half of you that's been turned on a lathe now turned on another one ... *and what might that feel like?* In the future, Busner didn't doubt, microprocessors would be implanted in the brain and attached to sensors inserted between the relevant vertebrae – then this feeling might be examined, but for now it remained an enigma-r-elle est une vraie beauté, m'sieur! The queer little Frenchman has used the slow shoving of the tightly packed crowd to press Audrey against the railings surrounding the green. Right away Stanley suspects him of *making free* with his hands, so struggles to raise his own while spluttering, I know summuv yer lingo you – you muggins! Not much of a jibe, Audrey thinks – besides, she doesn't mind the attentions of the Frenchman, whose lavender silk waistcoat and gay straw boater are flowers in the bed of black-and-blue serge which urges in the shadow of the Empire. May I av ze plezzure to –? He frees his hand enough to raise his hat but it's ... *too late!* She cannot forbear from laughing delightedly as the gallant fellow is borne off by a flying column of florid young men in football jerseys, who, singing, Wider still and wider shall thy bounds be set, God –! carry all before them across *one fifth of the world's land, with its populations of theosophical Hindoos, jolly Hottentots, lazy Lascars, sullen Malays and woolly headed blackamoors all four hundred million of 'em!* But how many ... Audrey wonders ... Empires are there in the Empire? Bert would know ... The stretched domes and finials of this one fall on the heads of the crowd, *the ash of Vesuvius.* In the sunlight beyond there is the jig of bunting and the glare of a band limbering up – with an oom-p'poom-poom a staccato march begins and the white glove of the conductor waves the smell of frying potatoes ... *straight to me.* Next a gratified spasm passes through the crowd, See – Stan is beside her – iss a two-cylinder Siddeley they've got ... He's said this several times already, yet Audrey knows that it isn't the motor car that interests him, it's the *ortommoton* that will conduct it from Shepherd's Bush Green to Temple Bar, *its clockwork muss be woun' up right tight.* The motor car is enclosed by ropes and a rope gangway leads to it from the doors of the Empire, doors that waver on their brass hinges, then swing open to reveal, Enig-ma-relle! Not so much a shout as a wave, Enigmanigmanigmar'r'rellle, that ripples across their *jelly faces* – and at once Audrey is *plungèd into egrimony.* True, the Man of Steel does his best to move in a mechani-cal fashion, cranking up right arm and right leg, then winching them down to the step below, but, much as the flesh-and-blood spectators push and pull at Audrey, so she remotely senses the muscles and tendons pushing and pulling inside the *shiny tubing* of his suit. Besides, *who could be fooled* by that metal visor, below which an irres-olute chin is plastered with thick stage paint. A section of the crowd is bawling counter to the band, All the girls loved Ber-tie when 'e adda motor car! as Enigmarelle stilt-walks along the gangway to his waiting conveyance. That's the man what invenned it! Stan bellows in her ear: Fred Ireland! Ireland is clean-shaven with spectacles that *'e fancies make 'im look scientifical.* He prods Enigmarelle between his shoulder blades, causing the Man of Steel to unlatch the motor car's door, then climb jerkily up on to its dickey. Acknowledging the Huzzah! of the crowd with an exaggerated bow, Ireland takes his seat behind his clockwork chauffeur. 'Ow d'you fink 'e works, Ordree? Stan brightly delights – *how can he believe this fakery?* The Ireland chap pantomimically fiddling between the mechanical man's shoulder blades, Enigmarelle extending his stiff arms to the steering wheel, the mechanic in the Norfolk jacket yanking the hand-crank *ta-ra-ra*-round and *ta-ra-ra*-round and *ta-ra-ra*-boom-*de-ay –!* The sharp crack of the engine firing flutters hankies and sends shopgirls swooning, and their sweethearts seize the opportunity to *snatch a feel.* The Man of Steel tilts at the waist, pulls one lever up and pushes a second down. Oh my . . . Oh my! Close beside Audrey a *chit of a girl* is allowing *such liberties* that looking down she sees her dingy underthings, *Lottie Collins 'as no draw-ers, Will yer kindly lend 'er your-ers* . . . Boots stomp to the oom-pah-pah! The organ-grinder has done his job and his instrument is alive with its own music, its pistons drumming, its steel-shod clogs hoofing it. Self-important stewards swagger away the ropes as the mechanic lopes up beside the inventor – the crowd parts as the motor car starts, and, sceptical as she may be, Audrey cannot deny that it's a *bang-up-to-date show*, what with the band on its stand all done up with swags and streamers having achieved its own *infernal combustion – Men of Brass whose red necks . . . bull-frogs . . . red and gold frogging*. Stan, already a head taller than his elder sister, still cannot bear his poor vantage – he leaps, he pirouettes, he leans into the railings and, grasping a spear point in each hand, hops tentatively until Audrey says, Don't be daft, you'll get one up yer jacksie! Still, he's beside himself, D-don't yer see, 'e's drivin' it, 'e's truly drivin' it! Audrey sees nothing of the sort, she sees Ireland the showman throw a handful of farthings and barley sugar to the crowd, she sees the automaton wrestle very bodily with the steering wheel as the Siddeley accelerates round the green and proceeds east, flickering behind the railings, trailing pelting boys and swelling smoke. P'raps, Audrey thinks, there's no need fer deceivin' at such a speed. *P'raps*, Ireland cares nothing for the good opinion of heather sellers or railway navvies in soiled dungarees, *p'raps* he thinks he can't be seen shouting in *Enigma-wotsit's tin ear* from where she stands in the shadow of the Empire, *p'raps* — but, *Hush now! These things are far too sure that you should dream, lest they appear as things that seem* . . . Such as, the Man of Steel turned on her very own lathe. She discovered it *all set up* that morning to do the job: six operations for each of his limbs. Engage the shaft, wheel in the cutter, cut the threads – internal and external – cut the recesses. Six operations for each of his limbs – *yet I only get to see his right arm.* Others get the left arm, still further along the line of lathes there are more expert girls who braze the legs with oxyacetylene torches in a blaze of flame, and beyond them are the munitionettes who operate turret lathes, lowering the headstock down carefully until it bores into the block with a ferocious whine, then raising it up again to the point where the mechanism ejects a new canister, *empty and oily*, and awaiting a brain – *we never see these, any more than we see his privates* . . . These, Audrey believes, must be machined in a secret workshop concealed in one of the Danger Buildings – *p'raps No. 4* – where men too old or too lame for the front pride themselves on the steel pintles they turn on their lathes, each one screeeeeeeeeeeeeeching into existence with ready-made hair of swarf. When Audrey is at her lathe, she gauges every fifth right arm and turns it upside down *so's he can be checked* – checked as she was on her first day: sent down from the Labour Exchange at Plumstead, having signed on for *three years or the duration.* Coming

through Beresford Square with all that *carry-on*, the *blackamoors an'*
wogs flogging scarves an' such offa the ground, an' cockatoos in cages, an'
all manner of pies, an' whelk stalls, an' other eats, an' the 'buses pulling up
with men dangling right offa the stair rails in bunches. — That first day
Audrey and Gracie come straight in by No. 1 Gate, under the indifferent gaze of gunners cast in iron – one of the police sentries . . . *'e*
only takes my green ticket and salutes me! What larks! A male-bloody-
biped kowtowing to me! Not so the Lady Superintendent *a Vesta*
Victoria – *to put it mildly*, with a *Unionist glint* in her *'ow-now-brown-*
cow eyes and probably a *Man of Steel* somewhere inside of her. There
are photographs of the burly munitions workers *she'd like us all to be*
on the distempered walls of her office in the gatehouse, while in the
corner sits a typewriter *ticing* away, and looking mousy in horrid
sky-blue poplin *like pox-blebs*. The LS hooks the earpiece back on the
stand and barks: Age? Previous calling? I give Ince's and when she
says there's no vacancies excepting the Danger Buildings, I say, Oh,
I've experience as a turner – I've worked a lathe, done the posts for
umbrellas – Peerless, Paragon – you've one there in the corner, ma'am,
might be one I done . . . *Not strictly true of course but Lord knows I've*
seen enough done – and I'm a quick learner. Poor Gracie isn't, though
– she looks altogether fagged out, spot on her nose – must have her
monthlies – and her loosestrife hair twisting out of its pins. She
starts when Gracie barks again: I've no vacancies excepting the
Danger Buildings, then Gracie nods meekly and dab-dabs her
temples with a shaky hand. – Are you willing to enter and work with
mercury? says the LS. Are you willing to work in yellow powder and
tri-nitro-toluene? Poor Gracie sits there looking shifty – who does
she think this body is, Melchior the Mind-Reader? The LS don't give
a monkey's whether we're listening to that swine Asquith, or

fanny-about-Fawcett, or the traitor Dacre Fox – all she cares about is packing more shells. Well? the LS says, and meekly Gracie nods. The typewriter gets up to hand us our chits, then the LS sends us straight out back to join the other sixteen in our draft. There's a row of cubicles there – and in we clatter. They're plain deal with lots of knotholes – cheap privy style. The order comes from another body to: Undress completely! Then put on your coats and shoes and form a line ready for your medical exam! She's a bluestocking all right, but hiding it well under a khaki overall with divided skirts – no, trousers! Plain deal with splintering knotholes . . . *impossible to resist!* The *rollicking* of a heavy breast, its *lush, long beating teat* . . . Are you going to take all day in there? says the bluestocking, and I call back: No, no . . . but it's almost as hard not to be *inshooshiant*, that's what Gilbert would say: Be inshooshiant, m'dear, it's all you can be in the ugly face of hypocrishy – and so I am, peeling off my stockings, letting down my bloomers, and smelling the resin in the wood and the coal smoke from the Arsenal. The war to end all warsh, Gilbert said, the electric light shining through bubbles and bumper and swirling on his hand as we sat in a private room downstairs at the Criterion for our special treat before he beat his retreat back to Woking . . . – I say again: Are you going to be all day in there? Emerging blinking and *wanton* in the daylight – then, as the others had been done and dispersed, I go straight in through long white muslin curtains to where an enamelled kidney dish sits on a washstand *a baby's bassinet awaiting what dark afterbirth* . . . The clack of weights as the platform tilts beneath my bare feet. Seven stones and eight, she says. You're slight . . . nevertheless you have a very athletic physique . . . Only now does Audrey examine the hazel eyes that are examining her through round and thick-rimmed eyeglasses. They are alone – although she can hear the clatter of metal instruments from behind the muslin curtains. You lie, Audrey thinks, I am bow-legged – I didn't get enough oats when I was a pony, the goodly portion all went to my brothers ... and my father. Then she thinks: How is it that her hands are still so cold after handling the other fifteen? Cold too her stethoscope imposed above one breast. The lady doctor listens, then applies it above the other, Cough, she says, and Audrey *stirs up* the cold air around the two of them. The lady doctor moves behind and her chill fingers *sound me*. Breathe in, she commands – and ... out, slowly. Good. Crouching in front of Audrey, her *virile* face *within inches*, the same fingers *part* and *re-part*. Don't be alarmed, she says, her breath *stirring my quiff*, I'm simply ascertaining whether there is any infestation, or ... she continues sotto voce ... venereal infection. Audrey would like to tell the lady doctor that she is far from outraged – that this is how she imagines *the future* for womankind: such *impersonal* tenderness and *scientific* concern, and to restrain herself from *blabbing* she concentrates on the cold hand on her hip and the *rabbit's skin* parting on the top of the lady doctor's bare head. That all seems to be in order, she says, rising, going to seat herself at the card table that acts as her desk, and, taking up a pen, she dips, then inquires: Measles? Whooping cough? Diphtheria? Smallpox? Tuberculosis – you, or any other family member? Then scratches the replies in a ledger, *but she don't ask about the mulleygrubs.* Audrey wonders: Can she tell? When she and Gilbert first became lovers, Audrey had been moved to look *down there*, assuming that any part of her that gave them both such pleasure must be *pink taffeta, jonquil leaves, a champlevé* of nerve endings *seared into my core* – not this *snub cleft in furze*, which was so unlike Gilbert's *puppetry*. Your swazzle, she'd called it. It's Punch-nosed in its silky glove, then up it rears! No, he laughed, it needsh no name, it ish what it ish, Ding an sich . . . No, Audrey thinks now, thing-in-me, *thing-in-myself* . . . Aha, exclaims the lady doctor, Miss . . . Miss – she examines Audrey's docket from the Labour Exchange – Death, is it? Unusual name, ye-es . . . well, it seems you've been altogether fortunate – it is no mean feat to've reached womanhood, in London, in – if I may so – one of its less salubrious districts, without contracting any of these scourges, many of which would've been eradicated by now were simple hygiene measures univer—. Breaking off, she rises and goes to the washstand, pours some water from the jug into the enamelled dish and wreathes her capable hands in suds from a coal-tar bar. Over her busy shoulder she calls: I'm sorry, you may, of course, put back on your coat – your shoes. Yet Audrey has become quite blithe about her nakedness – her hip jutting, a foot poised – and enjoyed the other woman's assessment. – Miss Death . . . As Audrey robes she admires the way the lady doctor sits with her legs forthrightly parted in her plain fawn-wool skirt, her white-sheathed arms laid in her lap, the starched pleats of a cambric blouse in the exposed vee of her coat, a cameo at her full throat . . . – I hardly know, that is to say – up she gets and comes across, her hand held out *manfully* – my name is Doctor – that is to say, Hilda – Doctor Hilda Trevelyan. I believe I've seen you before at WSPU meetings perhaps? And certainly at the Opera House last September when Miss Pankhurst dropped her, ah, bomb-shell . . . *She's not certain – cannot, mustn't be* . . . Audrey is not looking any more for debate, or amity – although this she sees in Doctor Trevelyan's tired eyes and thick lips. — *I am weary too, and how can I explain this*: Samuel Death had journeyed for a full fourteen-hour day by branch lines from Devon to Andover, where he put up at a pub for the night – a circumstance *he never minded*. All that *clackety-clack* simply in order to give his younger son a *slap* in front of his new comrades, then show him off around the town in his buff coat and odd little cap *like a Turkish kepi but still in civilian trousers: riding breeches* – or so Father had written – *and gaiters*, which Audrey supposed he would've had either from Feydeau or the cuckold, and were probably the only things of real utility they had ever bequeathed *my poor little brother. Poor Stanley!* Compelled to go a'crawling with Rothschild up and down the High Street and then back to the mess at the camp, where the beer was *atrocious*, although it cost only *a ha'penny a pint.* It wasn't Rothschild who had to do jankers the following greydawn or go out to clod-hop on the sodden plain — it wasn't him, or Gilbert Cook, or Doctor Trevelyan for that matter, who would have to fight *the war to end all . . .* – I dunno, ma'am – the cockney rises up, brackish and broken – I ain't ever been at no meetin' savin' the Church Army, an' vat wuzz oanlee fer a cup an' slyces . . . Doctor Trevelyan stands looking at Audrey for longer than is acceptable for any *reasonable intercourse – am I scuppered?* Audrey listens to the burring of breath in the older woman's nostrils, smells the coal tar from her hands – she looks not at Audrey's face *but my hair – so distinctive, a flare* of Phillips's Lucifer as he pauses on the rich, Burgundy-red carpeting of the stairs, his hair still glossy and *shellacked* to his round head, although in the huge expanse of mirror that opposes them Albert can see that his benefactor's face is sickly *with fatigue . . . or worse?* You still won't? Phillips asks, ladling fresh greenish smoke with the cigar in question. No, Albert sighs, and never will, sir . . . For fear of his own face reddening and his becoming, quite literally, Rothschild – he knows some German, he knows *a lot of things . . .* but he has taken a glass of Hock with the Dover sole and he regrets even this small impairment of his faculties, faculties he assesses by calculating the number of tiles on the hall floor, the number of crystals in the chandelier, and multiplying them together as they descend. Phillips kicks spat out from under spat, until he stands *too big a piece* on the chequer-work of the hall *and listing*. A club servant comes from a door *swinging soundless*, a ribbon of tickertape in his hand that he pins to the bundle already on the baize-covered board. There are fires lit at either end of the immense and shadowy space: sea coal laid with such care that it forms two glowing pyramids, while up above there are *four thousand, three hundred and eighteen shards arrested at the point of explosion*. Phillips says, Not many around this evening, Fulton, and the servant replies chirpily, They'll be hanging up their holly and suchlike, sir. Phillips grimaces. That, he says emphatically, I very much doubt – d'you mind, Death? – he has lifted a hank of the tickertape – I forgot my spectacles in my rooms. Albert takes the bundle and unravels it carefully so as not to detach any strand from the board. He knows his benefactor will enjoy this demonstration as evidence of his own *foresight and sagacity*. At dinner, as he sawed wearily through his cutlet, Phillips spoke of how *utterly fagged out* he was with his committee work, and how he had *half a mind to abandon it all to the upstart jobbers*. Albert, scanning six of the tapes at once, announces: Cotton three per cents dearer on the Bourse than in Berlin, and the London Exchange closed four per cents dearer still . . . As he had observed the flesh-coloured mole under Phillips's lip and sipped his own glass of the thin Rhenish wine, Albert mused, What precisely do I owe him? Now, Phillips says: Can it bally-well be countenanced . . . his is a voice *pleased with its own enunciation* . . . that they will . . . will, what? I mean what conceivable methods are at their disposal? Albert clears his throat, er-hem, then goes on: They – that is to say the mill owners, sir – may consider their interests better served by putting a stop to all manufacture, reasoning that by such a demonstration of what yet lies within their control they may bring the weavers to their senses. *He paid for me initially, certainly* ... although once Albert was at Bancroft's he was quickly awarded a bursary – and then won a scholarship. Phillips says, Come – and soon enough they are in the library, sunk in armchairs so deep that *intimacy* should be easier than *imposture*. Phillips has known me, Albert thinks, since I was a boy – will he always smell the Foulham on my clothes? Will he always look at me and see clotheslines, chimneypots, tu'penny Eccles cakes? As it is, while Albert's coat may be comme il faut for the Second Division – well cut by a tailor in Swallow Street – the cuffs of his trousers *are a long way off* on the rug, *and fraying*, something probably seen plainly enough by the grandees who peer down from the library walls with *soon-to-be-cashiered* eyes. The grandees lean on marmoreal pillars, ignoring open tomes and laughing their Harrovian laughs, *A–ho–ho! A–ho–ho!* at *the upstart*. Phillips must have rung the bell because here comes another retainer, moving from pool to pool of candlelight – no gas in the library, the hiss disturbs readers and sleepers – the facings of his jacket gilded and then not, a salver with decanter and port glasses trembling in his agèd hands. Yes, yes, put it down there ... Phillips says brusquely, then *takes the sting off* with a florin. They have a glass, another and a third, Albert wishes *I could loosen this damn knot* ... meaning all his old ties. This démarche ... Phillips's affected jargon demands the right sort of rejoinder ... – D'you imagine it'll –? This is the fourth of their annual quartet of club suppers and by tradition it *passes in review* the old year, which is what Albert does, delivering pithy reports on Agadir, Stolypin, Pu Yi and Tripoli in turn, dispatches put together out of snippets of gossip, newspaper

III

reports and some of his own methodical analysis. But what say you, Phillips *tees me up*, to the déjeuner sur l'Afrique? And Albert comes back gamely: It's rather amusing to think of their funk when, eventually, they qui vive in the jungle . . . This Phillips enjoys a great deal: he guffaws, he *hee-haws – he must be tight!* Albert, phlegmatic, not inclined to introspection, nonetheless understands this: the cross-threading of their sensibilities, as, over time, he has been turned on his benefactor's lathe, a machine that was fully functioning at the time of *the retreat from Kabul.* An upright Victorian, Phillips *cannot be known by me – or anyone,* he is an established quantity that over the years has remained the same mixture of the furtive and the brazen. Sitting in the far corner of Anderson's tea rooms day after day and watching. Swapping the Morning Leader for the Daily Telegraph – but always with a paper of some sort, which, when he came in, would be a tightly rolled umbrella. At the exact point where he becomes repelled by his father's bogusness – Sam's beery sweats and horsy high spirits – so Albert is drawn into Mister Phillips's *orbit,* which, because it can be *foretold,* encourages the exercise of his ward's unusual capacity for calculation – his adding of bills with a single sweep of his bulgy grey eyes, his inability to ever neglect an order, and his capability of performing two, three . . . as many as six tasks at once. Albert's iron grip on detail has ensured this: a meteoric rise at the Ministry, where the lofty ideals of ceilings edged with plaster laurels are belied by coal fires . . . *dirtier than these* and the schoolroom atmosphere, the clerks and computers pelting each other with bent old nibs, dried-out inkwells, chalk dusters – in short, anything to hand. In the Under-Secretary's rooms, to which he obediently repairs, Albert may gain a little peace, spend a while looking out on the bodies of the elms – lain dormant since the heat wave – and the sago of ice that's forming on the ornamental lakes, and the Palace newly faced in the distance. Then he must *square my shoulders* to receive more files: jute statistics from Bengal, the remarks of that *asinine* White Rajah, Nyasaland's Border Commission – the minutes thereof. The Empire – to one burdened by its minutiae – presents *a paradoxical case, its extremities are vigorous and kicking out, while its heart is as congested as the old King's,* what with its ports blockaded, gunboats on the Mersey ... and the Irish, *always the Irish –!* We had some of 'em in here ... Phillips says, breaking in, his cigar ash having fallen and *lies prettily* in a fold of his waistcoat. Right here in the library! One three-parts-gone harpy takes me on, pokin' me – pokin' me! – with a wooden spear. I say, who the Devil're you meant to be? She says, Boadicea, and you're the Roman oppressor! I say, you're no such thing – you're Cecily Gutteridge and I know your mother! Bloody funny, took a while for the peelers to get 'em all out. What I'm trying to say ... Phillips leans forward and Albert worries that he's *forgotten himself* and is about to become *intrusive.* In which eventuality: *am I scuppered?* Because no more does Albert speak of his people than Phillips of his. — Once there was a call paid to the villa by the river in Mortlake, and Albert, aged sixteen, declaimed at great length: Nor force nor fraud shall sunder us! Oh ye who north or south, on east or western land, Native to noble sounds ... folding his *cloth ear* to the fact that the least sounds appeared to trouble Missus Phillips excessively, for in the box window she writhed decorously. She wore long white gloves and petted a Persian blue the entire time – years later Phillips vouchsafed that it was altogether absurd, because the creatures *gypped her badly.* Tacitly, the visit was not deemed a success – by either party. This business of moving the old folk and Olive to Cheriton Bishop Phillips does know of and approve. Of *the others*, however, Albert remains silent – and so has Phillips, at least *until now?* — But it's nothing to do with that.

. . . is that with Churchill at the War Office it may be the opportune time for you to consider a transfer, not that I'm in a position to know whether such a move can be readily effected . . . I do know Sir Clemens, man-of-the-hour . . . all that. He, I believe, has tremendous sway at the Admiralty . . . Albert swallows heavily and feels his Adam's apple rasp against his collar, *So*, and, in Euclidean terms: *exactly so.* Now he can see the *precise parabolas*, and he can *call down the speaking tube* and order them to *train the big guns* on Phillips's commercial target. To ask for a more precise identification – details of ensigns flown, manning, etc. – would've been *crass* as well as *impertinent.* Still, Albert knows this much: that Phillips's dabbling with the Mercers' Company is pretty much that: *a blind.* He had had a wholesaler from his own pater – but more or less *run it down.* There are investments here and others there – he alludes to visits to Armstrong at Jesmond Dene, and to his role – in a purely non-executive capacity – as one to be relied on to make up the numbers for foreign buyers. There is a special lodge, set apart in the woods . . . a delightful situation, with its wide windows facing out across a leafy ravine . . . *Lohengrin's horn* sounds *wistful* in the *gloaming: too-too-tooraa-boom-de-ay! Risqué* young ladies in *merveilleuse dresses* kick their legs, *showing the boys much more than they've ever seen before . . . Cliquot! Cliquot!* cries Sir William, his *gull-wing* moustaches *soaring* about above the upturned bowl of the electrolier, for this is a showroom for his products. The *foreign wallahs* admire the table decoration wrought from the casing of a 22-pounder, and the rifle-cartridge cruets – an experimental machine gun fires bread pills, while from the dumb waiter the silent ones *decant soup* . . . Y'know,

Phillips says, and Albert finds such *pathetic awkwardness* in the right-angling of their chairs as he struggles up towards asking about his benefactor's lumbago – but Phillips trumps him: I am most gratified by your rapid advance, you have more than justified my faith in you . . . His hand sets down his ruby of port, then ascends in arithmetical gestures . . . ten times more – twenty! Albert, unused to drinking this much, wonders if Rutherford's elementary particles of light have slowed, because he sees *ten* or *twenty* distinct hands – or are they ghosts of hands no longer existent? He raises his knee to where it would need to be were the leading hand to descend upon it – if, that is, there were the remotest possibility of them ever, *ever touching*, instead of *circling and circling and circling . . . whirligogs*, which isn't tactful, he thinks, besides what is it, Scots dialect? Golliwogs, on the other hand, must be just as offensive and yet they're commonplace – there's one on Daniel's bed, *its woolly black face stifled by the white pillow* . . . – I say. *I say?!!* – Mboya . . . I can't go on. I mean, we're working together so closely, we – I. He stops, the noise about them in the canteen is terrific, the clashing of scores of knives on plates, forks on knives, the grinding of so many robotic mandibles all linked to the same chain that loops down from the low ceiling driving them on through sausage, chips and beans. From the slim paperback tucked in the pocket of Busner's white coat floats this conundrum: *I respect Jack because he does not respect me* . . . and he sighs, ahhh, and thinks, What kind of idiocy is this? Ronnie . . . Ronnie – you've gone to bloody pieces! From a gaping serving hatch the dinner ladies labour hard to supply this *industry of mouths*, but why, why must they bash-bash-bash with their ladles so? Why – why're we all so ravenous, the patients too? Whitcomb told me he'd an obsessive who wouldn't say boo. Looked in his hamster cheeks,

115

found paperclips, screws, bulldog clips . . . Sent him down to Gower Street, they X-rayed him, then cut him open, found thruppenny bits, syringes – with needles! – several teaspoons, fondue forks, a yard of garden hose – with the squirty thing . . . Why? A comforter, without doubt – also a schizophrenic incorporation that betokened an inability to see the object as . . . the other. And us? Busner looks around him at the ravening mouths . . . We would like to *eat* the hospital. *Take the Hatch from the serving hatch and put it down the hatch* . . . He grimaces and Mboya cannot tell if this is directed at him or at Busner's forkful of mash with its pebble-dashing of beans. He says, Doctor Busner? And Busner cries, That's it! That's what I wanted to say. Mboya, can't we call each other by our first names? Mine is . . . He sets down his cutlery . . . Zachary, but mostly I'm Zack. Mboya takes the hand, his own is *dry, amazingly dry* in contrast with his face, which today looks *pulpy, that's a truly dreadful shaving rash.* Feeling the *hardwood* of Mboya's hand, Busner thinks, Surely this is the wrong way round? We should've been introduced with surnames and handshakes, this further intimacy demands . . . what, a kiss? Mboya smiles. Enoch, he says, and Busner laughs. Yes, Mboya says, shaking his head ruefully, like Enoch Powell. No, Busner counters, I was thinking that we're both biblical prophets. Mboya ends the clasp and begins to intone: In those days it shall come to pass that ten men shall take hold of all the languages of the nations, even shall take hold of the skirt of him that is a Jew, saying, We will go with you: for we have heard that God is with you. The psychiatric nurse and the psychiatrist sit in silent contemplation for a moment, then: Zechariah, Chapter 8, Verse 23. Busner is appalled by it all, and cannot take his eyes off the cross *Coptic?* that hangs around Mboya's neck, but Mboya laughs a laugh *I haven't heard before,* one that's *warm, companionable,* and says, Don't worry, Zack, the churchgoing is pretty much done with now, I got the cross because Hendrix was wearing one on the cover of one of his albums. Still, you can take the boy out of the mission school. He stuffs the cliché with a mouthful of sandwich, and Busner is momentarily silenced by egg and cress being tumbled in the *pink cement mixer*, before expostulating, You don't mean to say you know the entire bloody thing off by heart? Mboya shrugs, No, 'course not – but a good portion, I'm blessed with a pretty near photographic memory. Busner would like to ask Mboya *all about himself*, there's much that's intriguing: his almost accentless English, his air of *containment*, which is familiar *because I share it*. Also, he has been at Friern for over a decade, he must *know a lot* . . . Instead Busner says: I want to photograph the post-encephalitic patients, will you help me? And Mboya drops one heavy eyelid over a blood-shot white. He's tired, Busner thinks, we're all tired – like we're all ravenous. Mboya sucks his cheek, chk-chk, *shutter clucks*. – D'you want me to use my memory, Zack, because I do remember most of them –. No, no, Busner begins in all seriousness. I have a 35-milli-metre and a Bolex for cine films . . . then he realises: You're teasing me! And this is the most pleasingly intimate thing that has happened to him in a long time, to be teased. Teasing him is what Miriam did when they were first together, and this gentle ridicule somehow annulled all the grosser abuse he had suffered at boarding school – the anti-Semitic taunts, his underpants torn from him in the changing room, *Henry quite powerless to intervene* . . . She doesn't tease him any more, though – she has modulated her critique into *humiliation*. Busner pushes his plate to one side, he begins to roll and then unroll the end of his tie *once Maurice's*, which is heavy, knitted silk, *one of the few left*.

Mboya says, Zack, it would make sense if you're going to photograph them to have them all in the one place – on the same ward. Busner nods. – Yes, yes, my thoughts exactly – and now there's no reason why we shouldn't do this . . . — For throughout the asylum system *a cultural revolution has taken place*: mixed wards, and together with these *soixante-neufards!* He had discovered *two feisty young things* arranged exactly thus and in full view on his acute ward over at the Halliwick, and thought, Good luck to 'em, and would've discharged them right away purely on the basis of this healthy sexual function, were it not that once the head had withdrawn from the tight pocket of the covers its eyes were extremely dilated – *even by psychotic standards* – while the ungummed mouth said: I put my ear innit annit toll me you wuz cumin wiv yer dyman eyes YOU KILLED THE COSMONAUTS! Then the nurses came running and *that was that.* Already Busner suspected that the acute staff were aware of his diagnostic legerdemain, for, try as he might, the speciousness of it all overwhelmed him. So, confronted by hysterical misery, he simply imposed on it his own commonplace unhappiness: On mornings when he was low Busner diagnosed depression, on those when he was low but had also drunk too much coffee, manic depression. And on mornings when he gripped the sides of the sink and saw staring back at him from the mirror a tousle-haired Ancient Mariner whose eyes could not meet his own, and whose temples rang with the rhymes of myriad surrealistic voyages, he shaved, got dressed, drove the Austin to Friern Barnet and diagnosed the first patient he saw either as schizophrenic or as hypomanic, depending on the toss of a coin, confident that whichever one it is . . . *it'll all come out in the wash.* — Mboya says, There're a couple on 45, three on 34, one very poorly old fellow on 31 . . . He counts them off on his *teak* fingers.

Despite his amazement at this cataloguing, Busner doesn't want to interrupt his flow, so simply removes a Woolworth's shilling jotter from his jacket pocket, notes these down with the red Biro, then adds the one he saw on 14, and four they had both seen who *ticced in time* to the noise of the injection-moulding machinery in the Industrial Therapy Workshop, which was clearly audible through the walls of 26. Mboya is well ahead of him, though, for not only has he ranged the entire escarpment of the hospital – from the Fellowship Resocialisation Unit in the east to the Medium Secure Unit in the west – but he also has *a hunter's eye for the others*, picking them out unerringly from the human morass. When he is done the whereabouts of twenty-two enkies have been established. – Twenty-two for definite, Zack, there're another four or five I can't be absolutely sure about . . . Busner bridles internally *prickly pride of the isolate* at how frequently Mboya is using the just-tendered first name, *his new toy* . . . and so says doubtfully, How do you know, Enoch? How can you tell them apart? The nurse speaks forensically: Like people with Tourette's, the post-encephalitic patients exhibit all sorts of hyperkinetic behaviour. You've seen it for yourself: they yawn, they sniff, they gasp and pant like worn-out dogs, then hold their breath 'til fit to burst . . . Busner holds his own breath as he stares at this *prodigy*, who remarks, Yes, staring, they do a lot of that too – I should've thought any psychiatrist worth his salt would've noticed that their fixation is so different to the way schizophrenics' eyes wobble about. Then there's their bellowing and their cursing – such cursing! Zack, I swear, I've heard gutter talk coming out of these little old ladies – your Miss Dearth too. Busner has an urge to interrupt – B-b-b- – that's forestalled by Mboya's *traffic policeman* hand, and – Yes, urges, that's what they have: uncontrollable urges. Y'know, when I went to the

Newspaper Library over in Colindale and looked up first-hand accounts of the epidemic *You did that?* I read how they were labelled as moral aments, *McConochie's poor shades*, even juvenile psychopaths. There was one ward right here that was dedicated to keeping these patients under lock and key – poor souls! Think of it, Zack, they didn't know why they were coming out with such . . . such obsceni- ties, or why they had to grab and to touch, but you can imagine how such behaviour was dealt with in the twenties . . . Busner feeling himself *enslaved* by this onrush of the factual, struggles to assert . . . *mastery*. Erethisms, he says, by which I mean an uncontrol- lable sexual arousal – and he hopes *I don't sound patronising*. But Mboya only ducks his head to accede and continues: It's astonishing, Zack, the more you look it into it, the more you discover that the post-encephalitics have borne the brunt of every successive wave of psychiatric opinion. To give only one example, you'll've noticed how Mister Ostereich on 14 sticks out his tongue at anyone who comes near him – and it stays that way. In the literature this is called flycatcher tongue, but in the thirties, when Bleuler's ideas gained purchase here, it was decided that this was consciously willed by the patient – and aimed at the psychiatrist! They are alone now in the canteen apart from a pimply girl in a snood who mops the tea puddle beneath the incontinent urn. Far off in the bowels of the hospital there are whistles and yelps fractured by the whooshclack of swing doors. Busner pinches the buttons on his *snazzy* digital watch – it isn't that he has things to do, it's more that he feels *overpowered: in Leicester Square, where black bags are heaped, flies buzzing around them, and so I stick my tongue between sloppily tied rabbit's ears to seek out the shape of the bits of my parents discorporated by the Luftwaffe, then discarded . . .* – I'm not keeping you, Zack, am I? – No, no, please ... Enoch, it's only that I'm overpowered by your – I don't what to call it – your diligence? Enthusiasm? Mboya has been using a banana with which to indicate moral aments and their negativism, and now he tries to peel it, but the overripe skin buckles, so he slits it deftly with a thumbnail, saying, I'm not a prophet, Zack. Busner starts. – What? *Events are taking a sinister turn* ... but Mboya chews on. – I'm not a prophet, Zack – you said that we're both prophets, but in the Bible Enoch wasn't a prophet, he foretold no rivers of blood, nor did he circle the walls of this asylum blowing his trumpet to bring them down ... *the banana skin fingers his* ... He was the son of Jared and the great-grandfather of Noah and Methuselah's father – in Hebrew the name means initiated, disciplined ... dedicated. *That you are, my friend, but why?* Mboya leans forward across the table and Busner twitches shamefacedly. — Miss Down does the music-therapy session on Tuesday afternoons in the room above the chapel – I've taken Mister Ostereich and Miss Yudkin, who's on 20. She plays that Scott Joplin rag – the one in the film – the whole time, and our pair respond terribly to it, all their tics get much, much worse – the music jerks them about, da-da-da-dadda-da-dum-da-dum! If Miss Down plays a military march it's even worse – but the other day she played this piece and it was very slow, stately, I'd call it, and they both began to dance, swaying this way and that so fluently – these patients who're catatonic most of the time, dancing about ... I was so struck by it when she'd finished I asked Miss Down what the piece was and she said it was by Brahms, one of his six pieces for piano, opus something-or-other, so I went and got an LP with it on, Doo-d'doo, doo d'doo, doo-d'-dooo, doo-d'-dooo ... Busner is nonplussed by Mboya's complete lack of self-consciousness, humming away in the staff canteen ... Well, you get the picture – not my sort of thing, but I sort of got what it was they were responding to, the slowness, the gentle swing . . . If you wanted, I could make a cassette of it and bring it in – I bet it'd work on them if you played it to other post-encephalitics. — It was a long speech, and now it was done Mboya seemed a little embarrassed, which was, Busner thought, understandable, for while there was diligence here there was also a great deal of passion. Passion the *stately Kikuyu* takes away with him as he turns west out of the canteen doors and heads for Ward 14, his *almost-Afro spinning down the rifled corridor* — west, because it makes no sense to speak of left or right at Friern, *any more than it does in politics*, which is the sort of thing Whitcomb might say at a wine-and-cheese party in the Hampstead Garden Suburb, where he stands with a beaker *full of the wine merchant's contempt and perving some peanuts*, while his partner in intercourse asks him above jerks and spasms of middle-class hilarity, *But what do you think, Doctor Whitcomb – do you believe Lord Longford may actually have a point?* An inquiry initiated not because he is a psychiatrist, and thus should be expected to have an opinion on the criminality or otherwise of the insane, but inspired solely by the close resemblance he bears *hairy topiary, skin lawn* to *Packenham, Frank that was.* That, Busner thinks contemptuously, is how it is with Whitcomb. They sit low and more or less opposite one another in their armless Danish Modern easy chairs: soft, oblong slabs joined in at obtuse angles. Over Whitcomb's shoulder clambers an examination couch covered in black vinyl. There's a *brown button* in the notch behind his carefully shaved jawbone, and when Busner looks away to suppress the urge to lean forward and press it, all at once he cannot remember what Whitcomb *so much as looks like.* The consultant says with uncharacteristic bluntness, Why? And Busner says, It seems to me there's a genuine opportunity to be grasped here – both a therapeutic one, and possibly a research one as well. Whitcomb murmurs, A genuine opportunity . . . *He compulsively repeats your words – it's a tic!* Nowadays, Busner notices these everywhere . . . well, I appreciate that, Busner, but I confess I'm surprised, it's been – what? – only six months since you came to us and then you were definite about no longer wishing to pursue your research work after the, um, debacle of your, ah, therapeutic community. Whitcomb isn't so hidebound that he doesn't conduct his own therapy groups – Busner has sat in on one of these milieus, as the consultant calls them, and found it to be a miserable business, the patients pressured by him into confessing to relationships and other – in all likelihood – non-existent errors, then subjected to all sorts of criticism by their brow-beaten peers. Whitcomb sitting there, *Red-Guarding it over them, his collar getting rounder, and higher: the cadre responsible for this suburban Erewhon, where the sick are punished and their criminal persecutors sympathised with* . . . I'm not saying the Board's offer of the position was conditional on your not doing research, but I think we both know it was assumed that you would . . . *need an aerial photograph for reconnaissance.* The one on Whitcomb's wall shows the hospital from *around five thousand feet?* its façade picked out by the full glare of a summer day, the oaks, London plains and mulberries massy along the front wall and main drive, *the lawns striped* . . . Presumably it came with the office and was taken by some flyboy shrink, who, after the war, got his RAF pals to do a sortie from Hendon armed with a camera. But why, Busner muses, would anyone want such a thing? The only way to cope with Friern is to lose yourself in it so the hospital becomes a world entire – this comforting prospect of a vast country house, sited on the bluffs of North London, is not the real hospital at all. The truth demands no elevation – but a plan: the fuselage of the central block, the outstretched wings – the bomber droning over the city, *ready to release its psychotic payload*... — The war had been, Marcus had told him, *a nadir among low points* – the patients weren't on the ration, they got only job lots of whatever was available. There had been a cargo of corn flour, so that's what they were given: cornbread, three times a day, until ulcers appeared on stick legs, hair fell from swollen heads and some bright spark realised they had pellagra! A deficiency disease illustrated in the literature by *pictures of poor Negroes in the Deep South*. The doctors and nurses went to the war – and the only ones left to *serve beneath the campanile* were the patients, who were mostly Jews, for the Hatch had become the laager for any Jew in the LCC area who showed symptoms of mental illness – a thousand of them, who clustered there and waited, as the Victorian buildings, so cheery from the air, sopped up mould from the damp ground. The lavatories blocked up with their dysenteric diarrhoea, the bacon-curing plant fell doubly redundant, the shoe and upholstery workshops lay idle, the brewery and the bakery too – the entire Samuel Smiles pride of the place declined into self-helplessness as the war came to it, stray bombs obliterating three of the villas used to isolate tubercular patients, and another rogue one shattering all the windows at the back of the second range on the women's side. The war came to the hospital and eventually the patients fled. Busner doubted the existence of spontaneous remission in wartime – it was more likely, he thinks, that the scream of ordnance became *louder than the voices*, so they fled for the safety of the deep-level tube platforms where their miserable faces were indistinguishable from those of the other humped figures. They fled – yet there were always more to take their place: the shattered, the traumatised and the abandoned,

124

vulnerable enough to be preyed upon by the building itself, sucked down into its century-old swamp, where their mouths filled with barbiturates and paraldehyde – for these weren't rationed either. Outside in the mizzle stood the Unknown Pauper Lunatic, *verdigris in his eyes, so what could he see?* Surely not the world-in-a-droplet at the end of a needle that, plunging down from above, injected glucose into the hospital's grey hide and so awakened it to the daymare of now – from which it is *impossible to . . . desist.* Busner maintains *my cool.* — Well, as I say, the research aspect is only a possibility – and I absolutely appreciate the Board's position. It's much more that I think I can do something for these post-encephalitic patients if I can get them in one place. Just now, he smiles, I spend quite a lot of my day running from one end of the hospital to the other –. As soon as the words are out he wishes he could *snaffle 'em back up.* Whitcomb smells . . . *Brutal – he must be sporty, so slaps it all over to mask the sweat acquired behind the chain links . . . thwock! Oh, well played –!* The consultant says tersely: Others of our colleagues seem to manage perfectly well, this is a very, ah, extensive hospital – you knew this when you joined us . . . Busner waits to be certain this is all Whitcomb has to say, *he's loopy enough to believe in insubordination,* then makes a cleverer gambit: There are costs to consider. I mean, I can't guarantee anything, but I think that concentrating the post-encephalitics will both make caring for them easier – and therefore cheaper – and also allow us to look into the possibility of discharging some of them –. – Discharging some! Whitcomb flings up his hands and says, Well, good luck to you there! Busner presses what he hopes is his *Advantage Busner*: We've had one death on 20 this week already and there's a second patient who isn't thriving. I'm not expecting to do this all at once, just piecemeal . . . Up go the hands again, it is, Busner realises,

Whitcomb's *minstrelsy* – Lordy-lordy! You've worn me down, man, but one thing, don't expect me to deal with Admin over this, let alone the medical staff – this is your baby, Busner, you deal with it.

A ticcing baby, a drooling baby, a baby neutered and decerebrised . . . It sits on the ward floor, its eyes *fixated on nothing.* The nurses aren't interested in it, *nor are they bothered by me, un farfelu* – of which there are *more than enough* at Friern, remember: it isn't only the lunatics who're confined to the asylum. It – she – has lost control of everything, but specifically her bowels. She sits on her shit cushion and a cleaner has mopped around her a shiny disc of urine and bleach. This, he thinks not for the first time, must be what sewers smell like: a mélange of detergent and excreta, the sacred and profane confined together in airless tunnels. *Akinesia, apathy, autonomic disturbances* – she sweats, she salivates, Busner senses the *acid churn* in her engorged spleen, he envisions *ulceration.* To counteract these stark facts *I have jargon* – for he has been doing his reading. It is far easier to look upon her *Unknown Pauper Lunatic face* if he puts it in these terms: *profound facial masking.* It is far less uncanny to describe these half-shuttered and unseeing eyes as exhibiting *lid clonus.* Her face is a child's one, the features clear, unblemished – but sunk deep within a *pimpled wimple* of flesh. It – she – *is aphonic.* – Missus Gross? Missus Gross? Missus Gross? He pressures her to no avail, for *ve haff no vays of making her talk.* Busner enlists a reluctant nurse and together they heave the woman-mountain upright. While she exhibits diminished flexion of her trunk in addition to dangerous obesity, once she has her legs gathered beneath her she does her bit willingly enough. The trouble is that she cannot retain her standing posture – even in her tarpaulin dress with its bold rectangular pattern she is *no Centre Point*: she lists – and would topple over, were it not for this unprecedented two-to-one staff-to-patient ratio. The nurse sneers: I can't stand 'ere all afternoon. In point of fact she's been assisting Busner for five minutes at most. She whines: I've the meds to do, Doctor, there's plenty of others as needs me. Which is a lie: *No one needs you.* So Busner cleans her up himself. In the shit-packed crannies of her *Michelin* thighs he discovers not professional detachment but a deeper engagement, for this is simply *changing a nappy*, something he has done – although not often – to bolster his feminist credentials. The patient lies beached across her specially reinforced catafalque of a bed, and as he sponges around her pudenda she groans a'herrra! and grinds her teeth while her bare feet patter on his shoulders – several flies settle close to her *very bits*, but none of this matters. *She's mine now, my Twiggy . . . grown Redwood.* A bed sore in the region of her hip dressed, that dressing sheathed in underwear chivvied from reluctant staff, Busner fetches his tripod and Bolex camera. He is operating intuitively – there is no clear idea. In Willesden and before, he used photography to present objective images to the deluded with which to counter their disordered ones. To the same end he employed a tape recorder after injecting them with sodium pentothal. Sometimes he guided them on LSD trips – all of it, as he now admits, had only variable results. This is different, however: Leticia Gross is wholly inert, holed up deep inside her voluminous fat, and moving images of her colossal inanition seem entirely besides the point. *And yet . . . And yet . . .* he has a hunch. As with Audrey Dearth, he senses singing within her a crazy polyphony of exaggerated tics, a picking-itupandpickingitupandpickingitup, a hairflickinghairflickinghairflicking, a scratching and a reaching, and a perseverating. He sets up the camera and she fills the viewfinder: a Matterhorn, her eyes arêtes, her cheeks ice flows. The light is drab, yet he presses the button *and waits . . . and waits . . .* — Eventually, Busner tells Jonathan Lesley, I got one of the nurses to find me a bulldog clip and some rubber bands and I managed to jerry-rig it to film continuously. This reel is only twenty minutes but these other three are an hour apiece. Lesley wears a leather headband and leather wristbands and leather trousers and nothing else. He has pimples on his shoulders . . . *the spitting image of* hers. He sits over the Steenbeck twisting the heavy Bakelite knobs – it is hot in this hutch, the wooden superstructure of an old train shed alongside the mainline into Euston. A mote-filled beam of light infiltrates the blackout cloth pinned over the window, the spools whir faster and faster, while on the editing machine's screen Leticia Gross's inscrutability shivers *wind over a pool of flesh*, the very edge of her babyish lip smirks infinitesimally as some whitish thing swells in the bottom-left-hand corner – Ratatatatatat! flaps the film's tail. La Gio-fuckin'-conda, Lesley says, and that's twenty minutes of her screen test. Expertly he feeds the next reel on to the spools – it is, Busner thinks, his only expertise. At the Concept House in Willesden, where Lesley flaunted the grand title of Multimedia Coordinator, he expertly *fed himself* into the patients, who weren't called that. It was this abuse, quite as much as the shit-daubed walls, the broken window panes and the ambulance calls, that led Busner to tire of the whole botched experiment in community therapeutics. Whirrrrr! Leticia's lip resumes smirking as the whitish thing blooms into a hand that travels halfway to her face before ratatatatatat! That's the fastest forward this thing'll go with 16-mil, says Lesley, and Busner, who is leaning with hands on the back of the swivel chair the self-styled guerrilla filmmaker hunches in, wonders if it is because Lesley sweats sexual incontinence *through every pore* that he is experiencing an impulse to *stroke down* from his shoulder to his nipple while *kissing*

128

behind his filthy ear? Things at home aren't good – tense, *Miriam eyeing me more and more coldly even as the summer builds* – whirrrrr, the hand continues its *moon shot*, the mouth crinkles, shadows move across the *cratered face*, shadows Busner now realises must be those of staff and other patients passing between Leticia Gross and the window. If, he thinks, if . . . old photographs were so slowly exposed that they captured entire minutes of the past, imprisoning the purely contingent smears of passers-by, and the grimaces of sitters bitten by whalebone and pinched by celluloid on glassy cells coated with silver nitrate, then what can be said of these films? Surely this: that they take the hours we so lackadaisically lose and gather them back up into a permanent and enduring Now. Ratatatatatat! But before this a vision that both men saw: a simpering moue appearing on Leticia Gross's face while her fingers play with stray hair. Blimey, says Lesley, I think she was flirting with you, Zack. Yes, Busner thinks, a flirta-tious gesture that it took her two hours and twenty minutes to make, while moreover – this he speaks aloud – I wasn't there. Lesley pays no attention and Busner thinks: he will always be in cooperatives, and that's profoundly wrong because there isn't a particle of coopera-tiveness in him, all is savage barter. These sessions on the Steenbeck have had to be traded off against a repeat prescription for Valium . . . *which is ill advised.* Lesley's current cooperative is the London Film one, but Busner can imagine him pushing Maccabees to suicide, or Communards to the barricades – *Enoch would know which one of the disciples he'd be . . .* — The *tinfoil* new currency makes a muffled jingle in Busner's pocket as he strides along. Up here there is neither the abrasive bitumen and pretentious plasterwork of the lower corridor, nor the tacky refurbishment, which, beginning in the central block, is spreading throughout the first range of the hospital, *a plywood virus* self-replicating in the form of strip-lights, painted partitions inset with wire-gridded glass, boxed-in seating units and aggressively neutral linoleum. On one of these padded benches, outside the Patients Affairs Office, Busner sees, as he passes, three middle-aged men who, without their hectoring internal voices, would probably be *chronic complainers.* In their shiny old Burton suits – blue, brown and browner – they appear to have been recently discharged from one army, only to find themselves in this: one that shambles rather than marches, arms permanently sloped. With their cruelly knotted nylon ties and waistcoats of many buttons . . . *they are already out of joint* – the future is arriving *open-collared and with a zzzzip!* Not that it can be seen coming from up here: the first-floor corridor Busner walks along would be considered painfully long in any other establishment, but here it is a mere connective . . . *linking madness to melancholy.* Past the doors to wards 24, 25, 26 and – confusingly – 54 he strides. At the far end the corridor he turns right and from here Busner has a view down on to a cylindrical aviary in which a clutch of budgies and parakeets strum at the wire. *Such cruel constraint!* the bridling of all instinct into *peck-peck-peck, flightless wing-beats and a head-down clawing across the roof of their world . . .* He must go on, conscious that only now that he has internalised the hospital's layout can he properly apprehend its fabric: the metrical repetition of lancet window, buttress and embrasure, covered uniformly by a cracked salt-pan of off-white paint. Which is worse? he wonders. The lavish boredom of applying it or the ennui of its neglect? On he goes with a steady slap-slap-slap *along this sap* towards the Medium Secure Unit at the far end. Behind its steel door he can hear faint cries and raucous singing: Je-sus blood ne-ver failed me yet! And he wonders if in there are boys *with spirit,* or if it is only the usual gurning and head-banging – *the bottom of the pops*. Still, better perhaps than the chronic wards, which have *a totalitarian lack of imagination*, being as they are *rectangles within rectangles within rectangles*, whose inmates are subjected to the rectilinear punishment of having their cigarette packets and matchboxes taken from them. Pausing by another window as he turns the final corner into the forty-yard stretch leading to Ward 20, Busner glances across the *cane-stitching* and the tarpaper roofs of the Gardening Department. Beyond this there's an orchard of stunted apple trees – a month previously he had gone to walk in their shade, only to discover that none was higher than his shoulder. A truck parked on the road alongside the orchard is being disburdened of crates full of Corona, and after this there are only a few more annexes and auxiliary buildings before the wall that separates the hospital's grounds from its sloping *netherworld of sewage farms and shitty little fields* that patchwork down to the North Circular. After that an *excremental trudge* across a golf course and up streets lined with semis to the next escarpment, where stands *Ally-Pally: a gothic pile of shit twinned with Schloss Weltschmerz* ... Perhaps, he thinks, the patients should be taken there for an outing? He can see his new cohort *ticcing in time* as they circle a drained boating pond studded with the crumbling concrete daises that once supported ack-ack. What would they find inside the cavernous Palace itself? Nothing: teetering stacks of gilt-painted chairs piled up after wedding receptions and the ghost of the first television signal howling in its barrel vaulting. Tucked under Busner's arm are buff cardboard folders stuffed with the photographs he has taken of the post-encephalitics – the wheedling of them into place is well under way, with Audrey Dearth the first to be moved. All those boarding schools at least taught him this much: how to wheedle, how to cut the totalising corners, and, as he turns the last one into the ward, he sees them all arrayed, a multitution, the redbrick gymnasium of St Cuthbert's mortared to the concrete science block at Highdown, which in turn is cemented to the pink granite of the chapel at Clermont, the eaves of whose roof project over the fives courts of Charterhouse, a series of open-topped boxes that decline in height until they become *the bike sheds of Heriot-Watt, thrust deep down in the wynds of the old town . . .* — This reverie would have continued, had the doors not swung open on the spitting, biting, screeching *chaos of a saloon-bar brawl between cadavers.* Busner's first thought is: Oh, shit! it's Enoch's day off – because no further explanation is necessary for why it should be that two elderly women patients are fighting right beside the glassed-in nurses' station, one of whom has her teeth sunk in the thick fold of flesh beneath the other's chin, and so *worries her* – already the parquet is blood-spotted. A *black-bag-mountain* of a slack-faced woman with hay hair that at first he only recognises as a newly corralled and precious *enkie! Gnasher's teeth* sunk so deep that the other patient is able to jerk her pinhead back and forth –. Busner's second thought is: My files! For he has involuntarily flapped his arms and so they have flown – jettisoning photographs, papers and the enlargements of single cine film frames. *Bloody hell!* This stuff represents months of work, the careful mapping of all the moves necessary to ease this patient from that ward to this after making a space for them by discarding another to the hospital's own crematorium, to the outer world or, on some occasions, simply by swapping them over, but in all cases thereby *advancing the game* – which is how Busner conceives off it: a game of draughts played out on the eighty-yard-long squares of the hospital's wards. Patients are draughts – staff as well: Mboya has leapt over Perkins to join the enkies on 20 . . . *if only Perkins could be sent to the crematorium.* What's this?! he bellows at a nurse called Inglis, who flings herself at the mêlée, What's this?! she bellows right back. You can see what it is, Doctor! Reluctantly he hugs Leticia Gross's *Ally-Pally* shoulders – reluctantly, because despite the flecks of blood and saliva, and the *squealereaming* of the two women, he grasps that it is impossible to free her without loosening the other's jaws. Inglis gasps: Get the um-brella, Doctor! Get the umbrella! Which is a euphemism he knows to be widespread among the staff, and which he abhors. – Eeeerarrr'rrra'rrra –! – Doctor, please! Inglis, Busner intuits, is not much liked by Mboya, although he himself has found her to be competent enough – more importantly, she shows an interest in what he's trying to achieve. He can only surmise that it's some African-West Indian antipathy, the roots of which he can have no ken – but he wishes they wouldn't, he needs allies. Slipping in the paper slew, he levers himself up *too slow* – another nurse has arrived, umbrella in hand, a sedative bead swelling at the end of its . . . *ferrule.* This nurse, Vail, whose white face is flushed, says, Doctor – will you? And he cries: No, no! above the Rarrr'rrra'rrra –! You be my guest! then turns away from *sad cracked heels stamping as needle jabs into scrawny thigh* to gather up the images of the others, *besides it'll be me* who stitches and dresses Leticia's wound – apart from Mboya, he still doesn't trust the nurses with *my property.* Later, Busner sees the attacker in a quiet room, through the Judas – she is pathetic in the extreme as she slumps, stuporous, meditating upon a plastic potty. She's no bigger than a child, her cheeks caved in: *they've taken her plate.* In the stubble – *lice?* – covering her small head he sees the distinctive scars of a prefrontal lobotomy. Inglis had already *told you so*: What you 'spectin', Doc-tor, if'n you bring new patients on to a ward? You know what

133

dese folk're like – dey can't be doing wid change, dey hate it. Dis one, she be out of sorts ever since the fat woman come up from 24, she bin goadin' her an' ridin' her an' goadin' her some more ... All of which is understandable, Leticia Gross's very bulk inviting an assault *simply because it's there.* Although there are others of the others who should prove more irritating to the common-or-garden inmates of Ward 20 – the scatty schizoids and once-rebellious girls, whose bastard babies have long since abandoned them to the madhouse so that they may go to seek a better life. It is, Busner thinks, like any other war zone, what with its higher attrition rates for men – twenty per cent of them dead every year in the mid-forties – while their womenfolk, their menstruation suppressed by the drugs, are left behind to become this *swelling embolism of the geriatric* ... Weaned off their useless – and indeed contra-indicated – medications, Busner's emergent cohort has been spread the length of the ward, but, while amphetamine withdrawal has plunged the somnolent post-encephalitics – such as Leticia Gross – into still more extreme torpor, the hyperkinetics, now that they are no longer sheltered by the umbrella of chlorpromazine, have emerged into a downpour of tics, spasms and jerks, lightning-strike actions so forceful and precipitate as to appear virtually instantaneous. For the sleepy enkies their carers have devised certain strategies – simply to *get them moving.* There are musical sessions with Miss Down, and more mechanistic measures still: the holding and then the letting fall of ping-pong balls, or the wearing of loudly ticking watches to provide them with a tempo that can be used to recalibrate the complex series of motions they must relearn, every time, in order that they may ... *stand up.* But with the wakeful enkies – these *dark starlets* – it is only by giving them a screen test, then slow-ing down the resulting films, that Busner is able to resolve their akathistic whirr into its component parts, so identifying – in Helene Yudkin's case, to take just one – no fewer than eighty-seven different tics, among them: hair-patting, nose-tweaking, neck-flexing, bra-strap-snapping, ankle-rotating, foot-tapping, knee-lapping, copper-bracelet-rotating, tongue-darting, earlobe-pulling, neckline-adjusting, leg-crossing-then-uncrossing, inside-of-cheek-chewing, saliva-swallowing, brow-furrowing, shoulder-hunching, breath-holding-then-expelling, finger-wiggling, skirt-hem-yanking, etcetera. Which is to say nothing of what cannot be captured by the lens, namely her verbig-verbig-verbig-verbig-verbigeration: the unending repetition of words of words of words, or of phrases of phrases of phrases, that often seems to operate in counterpoint to her ticcing, *one conducting the other*. Yudkin, a petite, dark, near-perfect Sephardic princess, whose planed face appears both time-locked in girlhood and supernaturally unaffected by the monsoon of move-ment that sweeps across it again and again and again, is Busner's most compelling photographic subject. His films of her, when run through Lesley's Steenbeck sixteen frames per second, are an incom-prehensible whirl of movement, but slowed to eight, then four, then two frames, the Nouvelle Vague stares him in the face: it is only their orchestration that makes her actions appear outlandish, discretely they are all within the normal gestural repertoire – their orchestra-tion and their syncopation — for, as Busner spends more and more of his time examining the films, he begins to discern a complex rela-tionship between the tics involving phased alternations between the small and virtuosic cuticle-flicks and hair-end-splittings, and those sealion yawns and gorilla-chest-beatings that have *an operatic gran-deur*. It has taken weeks for him to capture one of these transiliences with his camera, so abrupt are they, but, having witnessed one in slow-motion, he can now also see it *from una corda to sostenuto* during live performance, just as he can spot the gathering wildness and fracturing arrhythmia to Yudkin's ticcing that is often – although by no means always – the prelude to an equally abrupt transition from hyper- to aki-, from up to way on dooown, from Jacques Tati slapstick to the one stuck frame, in which she will then remain with all that baroque musicality reduced once more to *a single, monotonously sustained note* . . . Helene Yudkin may confront Busner with the most extreme form of this syndrome, yet he remains more strongly attached to Audrey Dearth – her primacy will, he thinks, always ensure her primacy. And at times such as these, as he walks by a bay of three beds in the men's dormitory, occupied by *three studies for figures at the base of a crucifixion* Messrs Ostereich, Voss and McNeil, each different in physique yet contorted by the same hypotonic lack of posture, he wonders: Am I surrounding her by quaffers of nepenthe, while she remains in constant psychic pain? The bed she sits on is tightly made but at least unbarred, and *she has her own locker*. Her posture reminds him of the prefrontal in the quiet room: her tiny bent body is *on strike*, her cerebral cortex has *withdrawn its labour*, her facial masking is *beyond profound* – it is *a tragic rictus*, so inert that a fly alights and takes *a leisurely stroll* along her top lip. *What can she be thinking?* For he is sure that she is: from small hints – snatches of vocalised thought – heard fumbling from the enkies' mouths, Busner has become convinced that whatever the damage to their diencephalons, their hypothalamuses and their substantia nigras, these derelict brains are still inhabited. In the upper storeys of these rundown minds true sentience remains – although surely ferociously disturbed by its decades of imprisonment in *a jail within a jail*. He places his reconstituted files on Audrey's bed and from one of them removes a sheaf of photographs that he fans out, black and white on the grey institutional blanket. See, he says pointlessly, when I filmed you the other day, Miss Dearth – Audrey – I was, um, struck by something ... She makes no acknowledgement of his presence – why would she? You do not acknowledge *a ghost* that goes on: Same as before, you were making these motions that I've seen you make many times ... His soft hands patty-cake the air, rotating invisible wheels, pulling upon immaterial levers. It is, he knows, a poor imitation. When she does it, she is both precise and consistent, and the actions – so obviously the operation of machinery – partake of its solidity, its power, the rhythm of its engine without its being there! Eighty-one years old and still beavering away – but at what? ... exactly like this, and I wonder, can you tell me what it is you're working at? Busner's question leads leaden-footedly, because already he believes he knows. At the Film Coop, when they were snipping up the 16-millimetre negatives and developing them, some smarty-pants drifted through the dark room to scrounge a pellet of hash off Lesley, and, seeing the prints pegged up to dry in the hellish light, he said, Freaky, that old biddy's working an invisible turret lathe – then expatiated: See, she's turning a flywheel with that hand, plain as – it's the one that moves the lathe bed – and that's gotta be her yanking on the lever that shifts the turret up and down ... and see here, here she's pulling on another lever, the one that opens the chuck up to release the finished piece. Yeah ... the smarty-pants was inordinately pleased with himself ... it's a turret lathe, deffo. Busner asked: But what is it she's making? And the hash-head reverted to truculent type: How the fuck should I know? I mean, I juss did a summer job in a metal basher's up in Wolverhampton – those lathes're used for any bit of metal needs turning. Besides, he snorted *smug wraith*

137

in rotten cheesecloth, it's invisible, ain't it. Now Busner leans in to that *Bovril* mouth to hear, We're'erebecausewe're'ere because e're'ere because we're'ere, the same palilalia he gets from many others of the others. One by one he brings the enlargements up to her face – but whatever it is that so transfixes her, it isn't what's immediately before her eyes. She drones on, becausewe're'erebecausewe're'ere, and he's enraged – for an instant he is prepared to strike her. She is Miriam and all other recalcitrant women to him . . . Then a slippery strip detaches itself from the last print and spins to the floor, *What's this?* a second negative of the film *Lesley must've done two* that he unthinkingly holds up between thumb and forefinger to the window . . . *I wonder what the hot dish'll be in the canteen today –?* Two of the frames are *out of synch*: in one her right hand pulls the invisible lever, her left turns the transparent flywheel, but in the next her left hand operates the lever *the chuck?* while her right remains idle. Busner looks to the third frame and finds that it is sequential with the first! The front wheels of the shitty and shit-coloured Austin hit the edge of a massive pothole on Winnington Road and the entire car *lifts off its axle Fosbury-flopping inside the chassis: I'm driving on the moon, what can it mean?* When the enkies tic they do it at great speed – hence the filming, hence the frame-by-frame analysis: he wants to see individual tics siphoned off from the seemingly incontinent spray of movements – but this . . . this is incomprehensible, this intercutting of time. He runs his laser gaze along the rest of the strip, *Am I transcriptase?* And discovers five frames at the beginning of the sequence to which this errant frame belongs, but: what can this mean? He has no difficulty in finding it credible that, at a neuronal level, she has succeeded in jumping from one sequence to the other and then back – it's at a cerebral one that he experiences

138

bamboozlement: *her brain . . . is outside of time . . . so far away . . . in another place . . . in another* phase of development, Willis said when they all pitched up that morning – the varsity men, one or two others from the discussion club, and Stanley, whom they all regarded with *a queer sort of respect*, especially after Cod Drummond arrived with a handcart piled high with picks, shovels and all else necessary for the undertaking. And Stanley, while in nowise wishing *to swank*, did take up a pick and give it a few experimental swings with a view to conveying that he was altogether at his ease with such work, just as he was at his ease with another phase of development, a phrase he liked and that kept running through his head as the work progressed and the sun rose above their hot heads. Another phase of development sounded like one of Willis's pamphlets on political economy – which Stanley had done his level best to get through, though he feared he must be *frightfully dense*, for, try as he might, pretty soon after he began reading sleep would be the next phase of development. The varsity men were *bloomin' daft* to look at – they'd all come in bags, sporting collars and cricketing pullovers. Their notion of navvying meant buckling on the gaiters they probably wore for *a little rough shootin'* in the country. For the first hour or two, while they hammered away at the cobbled roadway that ran up from the High Street, their spirits continued to rise – then their lack of experience began to tell. In truth, Stanley had no more familiarity with manual labour than these beefy chaps – some of whose faces were aflame – yet what he did understand was that all work has a rhythm appropriate to its duration, one that should be nicely judged to *preserve vim*. The varsity men nattered on – clearly, whatever their belief in Willis's brand of socialism, this was still a *tremendous jape* for them: and, since they had never, ever worked, work was their *day trip*. They took cobblestones and, using picks for mallets, tried out croquet shots. Drummond did his best to *keep 'em in line*, strutting this way and that in the roadway, telling one chap to pound down the earth, a second to cart off the debris, a third to go to the Coach & Horses and fetch some ginger beer. – Ginger, mind. He was an ape of a man, Drummond, his head *big as two rugger balls*, but, for all his stamping around and bellowing, the varsity men only laughed, then, if he persisted, *ragged him*, which was easy enough to do. – Oh, I say, Cod ol' man, have you been to visit the ape in the zoo? No – why not? She's been bally well fetched all the way from darkest Africa to visit with you, you ought to show her some courtesy – some fellow feeling! Tha-at's right, Cod, show some fellow feeling – they've dolled her all up for you, or is it that you aren't partial to African ladies of your – sorry, I mean the species? This way and that Drummond stamped, the white dust covering his moleskin trousers – his face was purple, the handkerchief he'd tucked under the rim of his hat a transparent veil through which the folds of his fat neck could be seen quite clearly *one-two-three, he is me*: not at ease, never will be, with these types, despite my . . . conjunction with Adeline, a liaison that made of Stanley a man in the fullest sense, quite unlike these inexperienced . . . *virgins the lot of 'em*, unless, that is, you entered on their account the sort of beastliness she had told him went on at their schools and colleges, and which Stan could well believe, not being an innocent and having seen exquisites strolling about the 'Dilly and certain seedy sorts who favoured Guardsmen and who frequented the pubs by Scots Gate . . . hands, backs . . . necks – a martial bearing down . . . *beastliness*. The work proceeded throughout the long, hot August morning – they would dig up the old cobblestones and level the roadway, although Willis had arranged for proper contractors to come and lay the new macadam surface, because this was patently no work for *raggle-taggle boys playing at being working men*. The cricket pullovers lay in a mound on the verge. The varsity men joshed Drummond, whose misfortune it was to have a *fish tail* too big for his mouth, it *flapped about* on his lower lip, foam-flecked – hence, Stanley supposed, Cod. The men from the discussion group – Addison, Poole – travailed with greater diligence, yet equally ineffectually, while Willis, whose show this was, took it upon himself to explain matters to passers-by, at first city-bound gentlemen on their way to Hampstead Underground Station, then grocers' and butchers' boys, and eventually a van of ladies who came promenading under parasols, followed by nursemaids pushing perambulators, each distinct echelon equipped with rugs and hampers and all the other impedimenta required for a constitutional and a sit-down on the grass at somewhere called the Vale of Health, which Stanley had never heard of before – although Willis told him, portentously, that it had been the haunt of *poetical types, that Johnnie Keats and 'is ilk*. To his credit, Willis demonstrated his own socialistic convictions by making no distinction – he would waylay anyone, regardless of whether they were respectable or not. He would treat an insolent telegram boy to a lecture on the dignity of labour and a bemused carter – who clearly wished he had one – to a sermon on the ugliness of the machine. He would placate irate householders, explaining that the small curve of roadway and its embankment were, in the letter of the law, private property – his own – and that, while no permission was needed from the Borough, he had in point of fact signalled his intent with comprehensive plans posted for all to see at the town hall in Belsize Park. — Willis stands now, his beard hooking to his breast, his specially tailored Jaeger cycling suit very close-fitting, his stockings equally so

– *a Spy cartoon*, altogether a brilliant man, Adeline said, what with his pamphleteering and his lecturing for the extramural departments of the University. – You haven't an idea in your head . . . she coiled on top of Stanley, hissing, one leg between his, the other athwart them, her face on his belly, her *breath on my John Thomas* . . . They swapped their roles all the time, *she-be-me, me-be-her*, no other he believed, devoutly, could ever understand Adeline, sobbing in green chenille for the loss of him . . . *My little Pierrot!* And Stanley tripping quite as tearfully along the rutted track from Norr to Carshalton, passing Rose and Grace and Tully the footman, coming from the station, back from their afternoon off, who went on up the hill without a backward glance at the fair young man – they recognised him not, while he had spied on them all from their lady's boudoir, and from the lane hidden by lime hedging – inside and out, spying on these others . . . *another kind of servant, maybe?* Certainly, *in service* and moving along concealed passages and back stairs of his and his mistress's devising. Cod Drummond would, Stan considers as he drops a cobblestone with a dull chink, always be in service as well: *Omdurman, Krugersdorp, Lhasa . . . Hampstead High Street* . . . a soapy tang rises on the hot air from down there, where a laundry must be . . . in the sultry noonday heat Stanley throws back his head, a single *cloudy bolster* lies on the divan of the sky – he thinks of standing, awed, inside the belly of a Zeppelin, and looking down its bellying nave. He thinks of Colonel Cody's *sycamore seed plunge* – Adeline had promised him a combined ticket, he would fly the figure-eight course at Hendon, then she would join him to see the War in the Air at the Hippodrome in Golders Green: the spidery models of aircraft creeping above the audience's heads on invisible wires. He would not speak of this to Willis, despite his being a strange sort of confidant: he knew of their relation, yet was blinded to its carnal essence by his own peculiarities – a bachelor rising forty who brought bouquets to the West End stage doors not with any motive, unless it be to discover leading ladies unchaperoned in their dressing rooms and lead them unto the kindly light of a socialism, which implies *no loss for anyone, only gains all round . . .* It is my pyorrhoea, he had explained to Stanley with the frankness he believed exemplary of the New Man. Stanley laughed: Pardon? My pyorrhoea, Willis said again, baring his inflamed gums in their reddish and hairy net. It makes it next to impossible for me to . . . ahem, become intimate with a woman . . . Stanley did not altogether believe this, thinking it more likely that, while a bicycle saddle between female thighs might kindle passion, the brutal leather would only bear down still more on what little manhood the apostle of free love possessed.

Sprawling on the grassy bank, Willis's workforce drinks its Batey's ginger beer, then presses the cool earthenware to their burning cheeks. No matter what their egalitarian guv'nor said, it is difficult for them to escape the conclusion that this is serfdom – albeit of an unusual stamp. Willis was a nob of sorts, although a second son – and there was his manorial property at the top of the rise – of modest proportions, true, but a pretty enough flat-fronted little house in old honeycomb-coloured brick, with newer chimneypots *just so*, and a shining colophon of a knocker *just so*. The garden fell away so steeply to the High Street that the canes implanted to train runner beans, tomatoes and peas made a *stockade lashed together with edible rope.* Willis was a vegetarian: I graze my own garden, he said the day he took Stanley with him to the garden party at Norr — the day Stanley met Adeline and it all began under her husband's complaisant wolf-yellow eyes. *I drift, I float, I loop-the-loop* – yet, like Pegoud performing the stunt at Brooklands, I feel as at ease as if I were sat on a settle poking a cosy fire. They were all hugely amused by his pash for the aeronauts and their machines – an old yokel coming past stopped and set down his trug simply to laugh with them. Stanley thought that, notwithstanding how the flying men soared up and up, still they remained far below these bluestockings and their foppish gentlemen friends. Willis had lent him a blazer, a boater and cut him a button-hole with his own strange hands. There had been a fly waiting for them at Carshalton Station – only then, under the withering gaze of a gamekeeper's boy in a suit of cheap broadcloth, did Stanley appreciate that he passed muster – true, the boy saw him for what he was, yet still *I passed muster*. The young ladies who gathered round him, screening out the downs with their pretty gowns, asked after his people, and, as naturally as *h*'s, *r*'s and *t*'s rose up from the close-cropped lawn to mesh with his careful elocutions, the lies fell from his lips: They stopped at Dulwich, his father was in the City. The young ladies laughed, and Stanley laughed with them, grasping in that moment the poisonous quicksilver of their prejudices: that for them this was far, far below, down with the aeronauts and still more sublunary creatures – people in trade and the like. Between raised and brick-lined beds of syringas, hydrangeas and hellebore, Turkish rugs and gold-embroidered cushions with tassels had been carefully arranged, while in garden pavilions he recognised as Ince's the servants were setting out the buffet: big bloody bowls of rhubarb syllabub, meats quivering in aspic, a naked salmon laid out on its *cucumber petticoats*. He was offered champagne – but knew better than to accept. They gave him sarsaparilla flavoured with cloves instead, so he took pleasure in this and also the small woolly dogs that got under the ladies' skirts, then were reborn, yelping. He loitered, listening to the hushed amazement with which the outrages in the West Country were being discussed – some of the young ladies expressed a muted sympathy, the martyrdom of Davison was invoked. Had he been honestly himself, Stanley might have had something to add – but he was not, so did not. He hung about, caught up in the crisp curves of the maids' white caps and the neat pleats of their snowy aprons. – Later, when *cunning panther* padding he went in search of the conveniences, he found himself on an upper storey, stuck in beeswax and staring into a linen cupboard through a door half ajar at wicker trays of frilled and freshly laundered linen – pure white linen, under-clothes threaded with *white, white* ribbon, petticoats, shifts, chemises, shirts and still flimsier things. Lavender wafted across these small white meadows, and the desire to romp on them, to bury his sunburned face in those sweetly flowery furrows, was . . . resisted. He found the WC and drained himself – a *horsey* splatter, the cistern squealed and clanked and gushed and groaned. Adeline asked him about his situation – Willis had introduced her as Missus Adeline Cameron, *empee*, and she had laughed, Not yet, Fey! which Stanley knew was short for Feydeau, Willis's nonsensical nickname. Stanley said smiling: I have none. If he had but known it, it was this clumsily done approximation of charm that drew her in, her neck so long and white stretching up to him, with its tresses of dark, dark hair either side of a face . . . *some men might've found too strong*. Come, she said – not unkindly, although it was clear *she meant business* – let us be frank with one another. And so he was. She heard him out about his dismissal from Ince's, and before that the Post Office. – My old man . . . he hesitated . . . was with the London General. She quizzed

145

him: A doctor? while knowing full well what he meant. Stanley came clean: No, the 'bus company – but 'e's left there now, leff London inall. My bruvver found 'em a place down in Devon, where me muvver's lot're from. Sincerity had chipped away at his imposture – she affected not to notice. They had somehow managed to set a course away from the other guests, and looking back he saw them all grouped on the stone-flagged terraces that sat below the spreading eaves of the new house. The guests – of whom there were not that many – had, by some application of the *laws of motion*, loosely arranged themselves into *two orbits*, one around an *elderly body* in a bath chair, the other intent on a small boy who was showing them the finer points of his model biplane. Willis touched a wing – Stanley turned back to his hostess, then went where she was looking: beyond the sudden falling away of the lawn to a *melting chessboard*, cows lying *enamelled* in the centre of a field-square lashed their tails at flies, clouds dappled the flanks of the downs and on top rain drew a discreet *hatching* between earth and sky. Boots stamped across Stanley's recently filled grave – he shivered, also, there was some *forcemeat and two cold, cooked potatoes in a deal box on the window-sill . . . off by now.* His rent was far beyond being in arrears and they knew he had nothing left to pawn – they might sell the debt on *to the boys . . .* a second shiver, hair pricking thighs inside *these flannel trousers, too hot* – yet he was frigid. He dismissed the thought of Arnold Collins and the ways in which he would be beholden if he asked for *a little leg-up.* There were poppies nodding above the long grass and large dock leaves cast still deeper shadows in the hedges' shadow, and for Stanley there was a great falling away of the substance from everything – a pair of linnets hung on a bramble that trailed from the hedge, *the arms of oaks embraced . . .* Then how do you sustain

146

yourself? she asked. He mentioned a modest sum due to him for minuting the proceedings of the discussion group – of his sister and how she had obtained this position for him, as she had the last, he said nothing. Merely to say her name, *Or-dree*, was to evoke all her energy and so confirm his own moody fatigue. Stanley looked down at his shined brogans spreading on the lawn *cow pats*, and said: Also . . . I make things – fabricate them. She put her *ebonised* eyes on him and saw a well-made young man, who, despite the obvious unravelling of reduced circumstances – she could not bring herself to think poverty – nonetheless appeared *clean, with a clear complexion and an expression perfectly manly, without slyness* . . . Oh, she said, what sort of things? He recovered his other self and said: That would be difficult to explain, it's easier for me to say what I make them out of – now it's dowelling and rice paper or butcher's paper, because these are easy to come by . . . When I was with the umbrella-makers there were always damaged frames and plenty of material offcuts – oiled cottons, art silks, that sort of thing – Oh, and fish glue, but that you can always get . . . None troubled to come across to them, some cried out as they turned towards her house. The maids and menservants hurried to gather up the cushions and roll up the rugs. Adeline remained scrutinising Stanley. Are they like gazeekas or billikens, Mister De'Ath? she asked, and so he realised that, for all her cleverness and aplomb, there were few years between them, for she too had desired these daft toys. He laughed. – No, much bigger than them – when kids see them they want to play with them. I won't allow it. My models are delicate and airy things, their struts snap, their coverings tear . . . so . . . I won't allow it . . . She was hatless, and, as the rain swept over them, his first instinct was to hand her his borrowed boater – before he could do so he became enthralled by the exaltation he saw there, her strong features dissolving in the warm droplets. No words were spoken as the carefully arranged folds of white muslin at her neck greyed into transparency and her clavicle filled *a loving cup*. Over her drenched shoulder a cattle trough boiled with perfect bubbles – and still they stood. We have, she said amidst all this tumult, an apartment at the Albany. I go up to town from time to time – fairly often, in fact – not simply to visit Selfridge's and the other bazaars, but also for lectures and committee meetings. You might consider all of this frivolous – a leisured woman's profligacy with time –. Stanley mewled with the effort of finding the right register of dissent. She paid this no mind: I should be delighted if you would call on me there – say, this coming Tuesday . . . Her dress was saturated, the fabric clinging to her breasts, her belly . . . *her thighs*. Stanley could not forbear from noticing that there were *no stays or lets or hindrances* . . . at teatime, by which I mean four thirty. Only then did she put up her parasol. He offered her his arm and under this *glossy shell* they at last made for the house, slithering over the wet lawn. In Cameron the empee's own dressing room, Stanley hid behind a screen in his dank shirt. When he peeked out he saw an entire costume had been provided for him: the jacket and trousers mounted on a sort of stand, while some of the snowy linen he had admired was arranged in the shape of a man on a chaise-longue. Stripping naked, he dried himself with a hand towel, thinking of how she must be doing the same between her legs and he spasmed picturing *her cunny* – there need be no bashfulness for them, not now: she was his own little sister, caught by the rain while playing out, then *rubbed down an' set before the range*. Dressing, Stanley saw on top of the chest of drawers soft beige leather gloves, a carved wooden box full of gold and silver cufflinks, some golf tees and silver-backed brushes with their bristles in a clinch. Stanley eyed his own avaricious face warily in a pier glass, for circling the box, tilting the golf tees, lying in the palms of the gloves, were sovereigns and half-sovereigns – for *a chap short o' sugar nuff silverware* to provide the wherewithal for a month or more's diligent *loafing* – steak and kidney pie, cutlets, white seeded rolls. His mouth filled with his juices, he regretted the *brute force* of his other hunger: there had been trifle. From below there floated piano notes and the soft beating of the rain on artfully stained panes. The suit was of tweed, heavy and musty with moth-balling – yet it fitted him well enough, belonging as it did, he supposed, to a younger and more meagre empee. In the drawing room, where one of the young ladies continued to play *without mercy* while the gentlemen hubbubed over premature pegs and the Kaiser's five million men-in-arms, Stanley was chagrined, despite understanding *full well* why Adeline was so changed in atti-tude as well as raiment – she wore an evening gown of vivid purple with an à la mode rounded collar, almost chaste, and she remained closeted in a corner with Willis and the old man in the bath chair, who had, he now saw, *the shaking palsy*, and who, he deduced – with-out any evidence – was her father. Stanley had not been introduced to anyone else – he was untutored in the craft of dovetailing into well-established joinery – and so he looked about the room at the Sussex corner chairs and the long refectory tables upon which sat a multitude of vases crowded with a multitude of flowers. Cheerfully, he despised what he saw: the three-quarter-ceiling-height wood-panelling with jut-jawed heroines and heroes buckled into shining armour painted on its individual squares, and above these roughened plaster decorated with *still more bloomin' flowers*. So as not to appear *Wallie, Wallie, Wall-flowers, Growing up so high – All these young ladies,*

Will all have to die, he went to stand by the window. They spoke of Bulgaria and certain alliances, and the Irish – it was always, he thought, the fucking Irish. — Land ironclads came rumbling on enormous wheels along the neat vee of a downland valley that cut through the escarpment opposite the house. The rifles poking out from their portholes traversed, dipped, traversed again, then fired. The Maxim at the prow puttered merrily and the bullets whizzed and struck *jaunty*. More mechanical cavalry came over the brow of the hills, the leading motor cars swivelling about on the muddy ground and hitting, from time to time, small craters in the chalk that sent them temporarily airborne. Beside the drivers in their bluebottle goggles sat the technical assistants all in white, the muzzles of their electrical guns fulminated and a lightning bolt bangcrackled over the lawn, the cypress avenue and the kitchen garden, before capturing the maid with the boil on her chin in its burning tentacles. She jack-knifed, then collapsed *stone dead*, her skirts up around her waist *showin' all she's got –*. — One day, Stan said to Willis as they mounted the waiting fly, there'll be sorta air-car that'll be as easy to drive as this horse – an' as intelligent. The gamekeeper's boy sniggered and Willis made a rare quip: Who'll be in the shafts then, Pegasus? Down the wide flagged steps came the maid with the boil on her chin, resurrected, and with a parcel, dangling from its string, held out in front of her. Your things, sir, she said grudgingly. Stanley thanked her with still less grace, the boy cried nonsense: Heygeddleperway! and the fly swung off along the drive. Stanley swayed to the beat of his predictions: *There will be man-made plagues . . . And voyaging to other planets – the scientists will unlock the power of the atom . . .* The fly's wheels slid, then splashed, into the ruts, they held on to it with one hand, to their hats with the other . . . *a canal joins Europe to Asia, why not a tunnel linking England with France?* The three ducked as one to escape the drenched under-storey of the oaks that tilted in – the sun was out, still puissant enough to raise will-o'-the wisps from the flowery meadows they clopped beside. Willis kept his counsel and Stanley saw human manufactories like the one for motor cars in Philadelphia: a vulcanised belt stretched to a great length, to either side dronish workers taking parts from great zinc buckets, a leg, an arm, another leg and a breast, and another breast and a cunny, as they put together one Adeline, then the next, the female portions twitching in their hardened touch. Stanley had a thru'pence in his borrowed trouser pocket *together with?* How will it come to pass, he said turning to Willis and finding it difficult to impose any harmony on the top notes of his anger, that that sort'll be content with so much less? That they'll give it up, voluntary like, their land, their 'ouses . . . their servants too? The gamekeeper's boy flicked the horse's withers with the snake-tongue of leather on the end of his crop and the fly clambered, one wheel after the other, up on to the high road. Willis, who had been fiddling with the end of his tie – neckwear that was irksome to him, favouring as he mostly did a workmanlike neckerchief – turned his beady little eyes on his protégé and took a time to answer. The fly clopped up behind a wagon being pulled by a traction engine, and until it turned aside into a field they were all lost in its chuntering din and bothered by spears of straw flung back in their faces. Presently, Willis said, This business with the Lords and all the reforms of this administration and his previous one – lamentable as it is that they went no further, they are nevertheless a part of a general tendency – another phase of development, if you will. It may not be a, uh, well . . . a flagrant form of expropriation, still, a graduated tax on capital accumulation is precisely that all the same – slowly, one might almost say stealthily, it will carry off their Burne-Joneses and their Japanese fire screens, leaving them, in, uh, vacant possession of their architect-designed houses. You've made hnf'-h' – You've made hmn-h' – Willis whinnied up the scale *so-fa-la* as he neared an unprecedented second witticism, and Stanley wondered if he was *tight* – You've made a start by re-distrib-utin' that suit of tweed about your own proletarian person! Hotly, Stanley retorted: I will be returnin' it at the earliest hopportunity! How could Willis say such things in front of *the blabber-boy?* All right, all right, Willis said, patting Stanley's hand, simmer down young man, it's merely my jest. The best thing about Willis, Stanley reflected as the fly rattled up the cobbled slope towards the station, was that there was no malice or humbug in him – his convictions might be childlike, but he believed in them with a child's sincere fervour. Their appointed train was already at the platform, hooting to them through its steamy beard. Seated in the second-class compartment, Willis withdrew some long sheets from the portfolio that accompanied him everywhere and explained, It cannot be helped, I must correct these infernal galleys . . . The somniferous compartment could not be helped either – no one got in and there was no connecting corridor. They were as alone as they'd ever been. It wasn't until they were jolting along the long straight from East Croydon to Balham that Stanley's hands came to their senses lying in his itchy lap, *Jack the Ripper stole a kipper, Jack the Ripper stole a kipper* . . . and trembled about there for a while typewriting the cadence of the bogies *ch-k' ch-kunk ch-k' ch-kunk ch-k'* before one crawled away to a side pocket of his borrowed trousers, where it felt the precise oblong of a visiting card. A crust of dead bugs rimmed the inside of the lampshade above Willis's nodding head and Stanley applied the methods of a consulting detective to the smudges on the antimacassars – these were *cranial impressions*, each one instancing a unique pattern of hair tonic or pomade. If only they could be deciphered they would lead him, snuffling, to the culprit: Rothschild! his arm *Bill Sikes* upraised to another dog – or a dog *spliced with a child* that howls, then coughs, the *Coniston's* catching in its throat, before loping off along an alleyway past a stinking shambles where there are staved-in casks, a shed-on-stilts, and beneath this a pyramid made from horse's skulls, some flayed entirely except for their *twitching ears*. The dog-child gives a last despairing hooooooooooooooooowl and is gone into the August-evening quiet of the city that lies splayed there under the dirty orange of its senescent sky.

At Balham, Stanley is awakened by the ragged fusillade of carriage doors slamming – *sparrows're the same as the crumbs they peck at on the platform: they've been brushed off by the sky*. Willis is snoring fitfully – he is an engine with no traction on the present, no means of drawing it into the future. With a start the train pulls out, with a second start Stanley realises he has been clutching the card in Cameron's trouser pocket all this time, and at last he withdraws it so he may read what is written there in the warm waves of sunset breaking against the grimy window. The very patterning of the inky droplets where Adeline's nib caught against the engraving of her name and address suggests a *wantonness* confirmed by, Four thirty, Tuesday next – be sure not to forget your pills, this said again and again by some daughter-in-law or other with that patronising grimace that is the forte of the *Janus-faced middle aged, who look down on old and young alike*. Busner savours the slight pleasure of wilfully forgetting her name: at any rate it was the same daughter-in-law who got him the days-of-the-week compartmentalised pill box which lies – this, he can remember – beside the egg timer on the shelf above the BREAD BIN. Winching up his tracksuit bottoms and snapping their elasticised waistband around his paunch, Busner meditates on pills and forgetting. Really, he could do with a still larger compartmentalised box, divided into four, within which to place his weekly boxes. Twelve of these might then be housed in an annual box, a certain number of which could reside in a small crate, optimistically provided with sections for the years 2011 until, say, 2025, and labelled: *The Rest of My Life*. He remembers this – the *scrag-end, the residuum* – even as he recalls his own hands fumbling up the little lid and tipping out the white pill for his raised cholesterol, the speckled capsule for his elevated blood pressure and the big orange Smartie that remedies some deficiency or other about which he cannot be arsed to ask his GP, although he thinks it might be to do with his gall bladder. No, he is not insensible to ironies big and small: these are not the sweeties of the elderly, any more than pharmacies are our confectioners – we do not stand on the dark floorboards, thruppenny bits held so tightly in our hands that they stamp pink portcullises, and point to this jar or that, requesting a quarter of lemon bon-bons and then thrilling as she tips the big jar so they tumble into the scoop of the scales in a puff of sweet powder. No, the molecular structure of HMG-CoA reductase inhibitors is the scaffolding with which we build Our Father's many mansions out over the void, well beyond our allotted plot of three score by ten – *we need them to survive, but they could probably go on without us . . . There!* He has swallowed them together with a mouthful of tepid water slung back from a plastic beaker decorated with diagonal lines of other pills. He leans with a hand either side of the sink: fat old man's hands spattered with melanomas and implanted with shocks of hairs . . . *What a peculiar thing to happen to a little boy* ... Busner flicks the tiny lid of the compartment that is Thursday up and down. How many pills, he considers, did I actually prescribe in a working lifetime behind the sweetshop's counter, tipping the jar so that barbiturates, tranquillisers, hypnotics, sedatives, anti-psychotics, antidepressants and all the rest of the harlequinade tumbled out? Certainly, he had prided himself on his sensitivity – and abhorred those colleagues *not worthy of the name who were too free with the medication* ... And there'd been years outside of the system when *I rejected it altogether* ... Yet, in the end, *I tipped the jar* ... *I tipped the jar* ... Would his old office up at Heath Hospital be big enough to contain this entire poisonous jumble? *No! Not the ward either!* There were times, he knew, when he'd got hold of lots of powder to be encapsulated, or mixed up in a lab beaker so it could be slung back, or else injected intramuscularly with very large syringes – *It hurts* ... *it hurts, Doctor, it hurts* ... He finds himself once more in the bedroom and discovers one leg slung across the knee of the other. He has a sock rolled up and the *old yellow dog scratches to get in* – but where to, where should he go? All my working life, Busner thinks, I've looked out on to woodland, or grassy meadows. It had always been economics as well as part of the cure to touchdown the dark starships of the asylums in the claustrophobic countryside of southern England. The final thirty years of *my careering*, these too had included long static periods spent staring through the fly-spattered windows of his office on to the Heath, which rose up, massy, oak upon oak – here the juicy splodge of a mulberry, there the *Tuscan taunt of a Lombardy poplar* ... And enclosed as these vistas may've been – smallish clearings in the ever-encroaching forest of brick – still he had longed to get out, to drop his routines *constricting like trousers* and clip-clop away into ferny dells, an unlikely satyr *seeking out the naiads of the duck ponds, blue-green algae in their hair* ... And now? He realises he had been wrong, sort of. That there was precious little outside of that constraint: *the body ... the mind ... it all falls apart. You find yourself free to settle this new-found-land: sleeping on a flattened cardboard box 'mid the dank and rubbishy shrubbery of a traffic island – a Ben Gunn in the community,* around whom the world turns, and turns. So what? He was dressed now in the oldster togs his youngsters despise: the relaxed fit of tracksuit bottoms, a sweatshirt with Santa Fe 1997 International Experimental Psychology Conference on its saggy blue breast, a smelly old Donegal tweed jacket and cheap training shoes *nothing else besides looks ... dirtier.* He was dressed now and therefore he must go out. First, though, the tense prowl from room to room of the flat, eyes sweeping surfaces for keys, wallet and the deliciously apt Freedom Pass – and also a tan hat with a wide brim made of some synthetic stuff not stiff enough to prevent its creasing. He knows not whence this ugly headgear came, only that he's fond of it: it feels appropriate, this coronet of his own old sweat tight around his temples. He decides against taking a book: for it is so very tiring now, to winch up disbelief in the energetic doings of characters so much younger than oneself – and as for academic literature, he had forsworn it – and as for philosophy, this he did all the time. I shall pick up a newspaper, he thought, and, catching a glimpse of his rather hippy-ish form in a mirror, he wonders at this atavism of apparel, is it an *inversion of foetal ontogeny,* in which the phenotype passes through previous fashion stages? *Soon there will be gaiters and gloves ...* I will probably die, he thinks, clad in animal skins. *Hairy dags* are caught in the thick pile of the fitted carpet that runs down the stairs and along the *dusty ravine* of the hallway, under the *rectangular sun of the* transom, to where the letterbox *pukes leaflets.* Too late, he sees with superfluous clarity the telescopic umbrella lying on top of the boxes beneath his bedroom window: its black nylon sleeve and black leather-effect handle. When ... he pauses, musing ... did the umbrella first become an article to be routinely forgotten rather than assiduously remembered? Surely, to begin with, they would've been expensive items, invested with strong affect and not to be casually abandoned ... as nowadays, given their cheapness and ubiquity – Busner's attention has blipped to his unmoved bowels, and so he self-remonstrates: *do not fear them* as he finds himself in the street and at the bus stop a few yards from his front door, waiting, because that's what you do at a bus stop, and pleased by his own aimlessness – a lack of planning that, sadly, then becomes its complete opposite by reason of being observed. Also in grey tracksuit bottoms – although these are flared and have a silvery stripe down them – an alcoholic puts a lot of *effort* into his own *imposture.* When the bus comes he will sidle on by the back door, together with his can of *tsk, tsk* ... Tyskie – a Polish lager, presumably. The drinker has a thick green puffa jacket and a thin nose spidery with one big broken blood vessel. He makes conversational stabs at the old *probably my age* woman *wrapped up* beside him, Luvverly day fer April, 'ow long you bin waitin'? who clutches a Yorkshire terrier to her chest, one stiff little leg scratching the air. *La puce à l'oreille.* The alcoholic isn't, Busner judges, drunk enough to be this disinhibited, instead he diagnoses ... what? A few years ago he would've marked the man down simply as a self-medicating schizophrenic, sousing his voices in lager – but now? Well, the dead weight of that pathology is decomposing – here be psychosis, certainly, but also a personality disorder, developmentally ingrained, that makes the man unable to grasp how inappropriate his sallies are, 'E's a cute wee doggie, can I 'old 'im? let alone capable of registering the fear that uglies her face. It is a lovely day – there's no need of an umbrella, any more than there is of another era of epithetic psychiatry, for it's the *same diff': a personality disorder is only a hysteric or a melancholic by another name* . . . The spider is within biting range, Wot's 'is name? and at last Busner feels he must intervene, put a stop to his compulsive soul-doctoring, so he turns away from the playlet yet is still reluctant to abandon the bus stop because the idea of a bus ride remains appealing: an avuncular conductor unwinding the ticket from his metal belly, the subdued cheque of the moquette, the *world held gently respiring beyond the dirt-speckled window at a safe distance* . . . He wishes he had a paper printed with the world to *wrap this one in* – but doesn't want to miss a bus by crossing the road to the newsagent. Still, the traffic heading towards Archway is dense enough, a constipation of lorries, vans and cars of such bulk that *Maurice wouldn't have been ashamed to be seen driving one* . . . *The traffic grinds so* . . . *it snarls out fumes* . . . *I am vulnerable!* He staggers – an old man coughing on stinking reflux – and rights himself with the stanchion of the bus stop *emery-rough* to his fingertips. The wooziness dispels and there it is: *the shield I seek* held by a squire so intent that his cotton surcoat has been twisted out of shape by the strap of his heavy leather shoulder bag . . . *always the bags.* Busner hefts the memory of bags long since abandoned: gas-mask ones from army surplus, woollen ethnic pouches with tasselled hems, and canvas rucksacks with leather straps. He's not so out of touch that he doesn't realise what it is he's looking at – but it takes a while, during which he sees only the spirituous twist from a bottle-neck point into an iridescent panel that stretches, yaws, then furls away into nothing. He sees only this and the digits that flick and dabble against the screen, index finger and thumb pinching, then parting, pinching then parting again. What is this ticcing? Busner wonders, for, if he abstracts the shield of light with which the boy fends off the flaking stucco of the terrace across the road, he sees only this: one arm and its dependent hand held rigidly extended, the other arm crooked, its hand fidgeting – what did we call that? For this he need not struggle: *pill-rolling* comes unbidden. Pill-rolling, while the boy's fixation on his tablet computer – the eyes at once keenly focused and utterly vacant – is that not a form of *oculogyric crisis?* If so, it's one Busner joins in: this is the world to wrap the world in that he'd sought, a palimpsest worked up out of nothing, sliding away from nothing, panels over- and underlying one another, *A crucial component of any incoming government's policy will be to avert the industrial action that is widely expected, should public-sector cuts be as deep as anticipated* ousted in an eye-blink by a *smirking Osborne,* who in turn is annihilated by the *floret* of a single virion that floats in a space at once endless and measurable in microns. *The H2N5 Virus has proved far less infectious that initially supposed, an inquiry by the WHO has established that transmission rates be* – Gone, supplanted by the *bullying concertina* of the bus's door. The squire, having sheathed his shield, mounts ahead of Busner, who follows on behind, *swipeeping* his Freedom Pass under the indifferent ear of the driver: there is no jolly conductor, only this morose single-operator, his eyes fixed on the distant horizon of the terminus. The boy swings himself up on to the stairs and Busner follows stiffly after him. On the top deck there is the lobby Muzak of electric-blue seat covers and dulzure moulded plastic. The bus humps into the slow-moving traffic stream and the boy collapses oof! into one seat, the retired psychiatrist oof! into the one behind. Go slow, Busner thinks, that's what they called it back then – and they were called council workers, dustbin men and hospital porters – or ancillary staff: he has the notion that public-sector workers was yet to be coined, besides, the public sector was still growing then and gobbling up shipbuilders, electronics companies – and there was *British-bloody-Leyland! The horse-lipped posh one with the lisp – a pipe-smoker*, some thought we'd all *end up as good little Soviets. Bit of a cunt, really, him and Wilson both. All pipe-smokers are cunts!* He barks and the boy's fringe yanks his lashless eyes around *Baby Blue . . .* The shield is fending off the world, its emblematic flu virion quests for *anywhere to bind . . .* Busner covers his mouth and heaves his bark into a simulated cough, the boy pill-rolls the virion into a Mercator projection with a rash of spots upon which numbers of infected and beneath these of fatalities are picked out twice: ACTUAL and PREDICTED. It strikes Busner, who never fancied himself as any kind of epidemiologist, that there's a noteworthy reversal going on here, namely: the communication of the statistics moving faster than the disease itself, whereas, how far would you need to go back in order to reach an epidemic that outstripped its own news? Not the Asian flu of the seventies, but possibly the post-First World War flu pandemic and its more peculiar prequel? He looks upon the map, its virions – and thinks of how the boy's ticcing links macro- and micro-quanta . . . I – we – were interested in the way these tiny repetitive motions were abruptly magnified into operatic gestures *Co-mmend-a-tore!* A production where? Almost certainly Covent Garden – which wife? Whichever . . . she sat purse-lipped in the stalls as a Commendatore two storeys high, his back cloak indistinguishable from the backcloth, carried off the Don. She was unmoved by the stagecraft, *desirous only that I be carried off with him.* He smirks: to take a libretto personally, that requires a formidable suspension of disbelief –! Then checks himself: yet I cannot remember which wife it was . . . and so admits: this goes beyond mere solecism towards *a fundamental lack of feeling.* The bus wrangles some cyclists across the intersection by Tufnell Park tube, then caroms on along Junction Road. To either side are convenience stores, estate agents, more estate agents: the city digesting its own substance and so adding more *shitty value* to what once must've been solidly middle-class homes, front gardens *full of hollyhocks tended by Pooters,* their stems swaying in the breeze of a passing *horse-drawn omnibus . . . fertiliser for 'em close to hand.* Now those gardens *all gone,* all dug up and replaced by a single storey of retail hutches tacked on to the terrace behind. What did they have then? Bicycle parades, Alexandra Day parades, *Jubilee parades . . .* What did they bequeath us? *Shopping ones.* The bus has achieved Archway and the *scummy-black tower* stacked with social services that *sucks up in swirls the drunk, the deranged, the poor . . .* Busner is not surprised to see the man from the bus stop alight here, Tsykie still in hand, and together with a tiny whirlwind of leaves and plastic bags down-draughted by the Tower, he waltzes north across the three lanes of tarmac towards the Whittington. It's a direction Busner fervently wills the bus not to take – on this bright day, this day of early-spring freedom, the last thing he wishes to do is to revisit any of these secret compartments in which the insane *slosh about.* In those days, on short-term locums, or simply in pursuit of patients lost in the vortex of the system, he couldn't afford the time necessary for the wonderment these scenes demanded: the *tiled pool* of the locked ward at the Whittington, the wall of psychosis that hit you in the face as the lift doors parted – the taste of it catching at the back of the throat, *urine in carbolic,* the unremitting low susurrus of distress from out of which came the occasional yell of full-blown anguish.

Then . . . then . . . there was no gainsaying the necessity for categorisation, for generalisation – a diagnostic framework was . . . *a life-preserver.* He sees himself as he was: bobbing among the drowned and the saved, although distinguishing one from the other was *as futile as naming a wave . . .* Now, though, one does break over him: a young man, his just-issued hospital gown split up past his hips, *exposing the split of his buttocks* – not that Busner hadn't seen thousands like him, *peak after trough*, running away nauseously under neon to the artificial horizon – it was only that this one had been so overdosed with Haloperidol that he flowed, dripping in mandrops, off his bucket seat and on to the scummy floor. Doshtor, he slushed, Doshtor, can you help me? And so this one recollection takes the place of all the forgotten ones, *all the others I couldn't help either . . .* Bitterly, Busner now prays that the bus won't go up Highgate Hill, he bows down, pressing his head on to the top of the seat in front, and gravely he concedes: It was always the individual who should've mattered, never the category, *for was I not my brother's keeper?* The boy with the haircut and the iPad has gone – he is alone on the top deck as the bus heels round the bend and on to the steep acclivity of the Archway Road. Through wide windows the sun *cooks up rubber and vinyl stew* – but still the flesh is cold and old and the mind that believes *without any evidence* that it's inside a head gropes for warmth in the embraces of the past, *which're all that remain to me now . . . doddery that I am.* Busner thinks first of teenage kisses – so momentous at the time, *a gastrocnemius swelling above a white ankle sock* – then of all the rest of it: the goose-pimply fumbling that had been separated by a handful of autumns from the mummy cuddles he couldn't remember, and so – more for him than for most – was a substitute for them. He winces to think of his *penisumbilicus*, winces

162

still more as he returns to his current crumpled condition, *cells popping like bubble wrap* . . . the slow withdrawal from touch and be-touched, now, a kiss would be truly momentous, the lips of another *drawing back and back and back – a skull's rictus.* There had been – not five months since – a humiliatingly failed

coupling at a conference on affective disorders. Her packaging had been corrugated cardboard – although *that wasn't it.* Conferences, *ah!* always his favoured arena of seduction: there was something undeniably arousing, was there not, in the juxtaposition of the rigid squaring of the carpet tiles in the conference suite of a former poly-technic and the rippling pliancy of flesh? Between the expansive tedium of the plenary session and the bolting down of Lambrusco minutes later? Between the buttoned-up formality of introductions and the she-be-lying across the blue-and-bluer-striped duvet of a student study-bedroom? Cheerily looking his limpness in the eye, she'd said, Why not try Viagra? And he, struggling to insert the *old yellow dog* into the noose of his underpants, said doomily, No, I rather think not. For what on earth would that be like: his chemically engorged rocket blasting off across Stevenage or Solihull, dragging behind it the payload of his sagging body? No. It would be better to accept things the way they were: impotence as *the rhythmic introjec-tions of desire*: a steadily growing column of inadequacy working its way up inside him and sending out *little thrills of numbness.* No, better to accept gulls mobbing along the freshly painted white lines of a playing field, and when people remark, *Where've all the sparrows gone?* simply observe, *The gulls have eaten them.* Besides, it wasn't only the bare facts recalled that had grown so vivid – nowadays there was also retouch, resmell and rehear – the whole sensorium geared up to revisit *all that fucking*, licit and otherwise, but now *shorn of guilt.*

— When he had been at it, each disco dip had cancelled out the one before while violently enjoining the next – *sex was like that*. Moreover, when you were in its gooey clutches, repetitive actions sustained equally repetitive reveries: out of all those subtly different hip-thrusts, lip-slurps and neck-caresses only the one was seized upon and returned to again and again to serve for self-stimulus. The bus stops, leaning into the high kerb beyond the Jackson's Lane Community Centre, engine-gasp smokes the window of a fried-chicken takeaway, Busner's forehead vibrates against the toughened glass: he sees diamonds of mirror set in mirrored batons, he sees the *Mandelbrot set* of the Formica they reflect, he sees himself, trousers and pants *at half-mast*, shirt-tails flapping against tautened buttocks as he canters across North London from one site of special psychotherapeutic interest to the next – from Heath Hospital to the Whittington, from there to St Mungo's, from that rundown pile to the Tavistock, and from there to the Bowlby Centre in the east, in the environs of which he trips and *falls headlong!* He regains consciousness to find he's *digging into a soft plot of fertile ground* – a nutritionist or an occupational therapist, a nurse or a fellow doctor. These had not, he now thought, been affairs – with all the sophistication the term seems to imply – but rather coital sight-gags, complete with white-faced clowns, their mouths thickly smeared with lust's greasepaint. Obviously, with such choreographed pratfalls, *nobody really got hurt* – or so he'd liked to imagine. But since his manumission he could examine his libidinous enslavement from every angle – physical, emotional . . . *gulp! moral* – and it had to be admitted *Last night I saw my mama singin' a song* that as sex begets in the first instance more sex, so *Woke up this morning and my mama was gone* bad behaviour sets the gold standard for more of the same: *infidelity at fixed rates*.

The bus lows pitifully as it passes by the Bald Faced Stag in East Finchley, and Busner, penitent, applies the lash: I always had an eye for those who were inclined to stray – but what is this? In a world so plagued by catchy tunes that it resembles *a burr* this was one of the catchiest: *Last night I heard my mama singin' a song, Ooh* . . . That first time they did it they had undoubtedly been *a little bit tipsy* despite its being the middle of the day. He had resolved not to go to the pub at lunchtime – what was it, a valedictory drink for a colleague? Anyway . . . she'd been there, and when he went back with her to see about the batch she'd locked the door decisively behind them. *I thought, what's this? A few shandies for the lady, now a hand-shandy from her?* The pharmacy was hidden in the warren of rooms that surrounded the main stores – many of them long disused, *full of the queerest stuff:* old school desks, coat trees, the abandoned instrument cases of the disbanded asylum band. Matrons or shrinks came to pick up drugs from a hatch *like a canteen servery* that they reached along a dead-end corridor, *ooh-eee,* but we'd already been doing *secret things* in her small lab in back of that, *ooh-eee chirpy-chirpy cheep-cheep* –. That was it! It was everywhere that summer, a cloud of dopaminergic dust that puffed up floury under the green bowl of the lampshade. He stands watching Mimi Hanson operate the device and thinks of Missus Fitz, his uncle's cook, turning the mincer's handle so that *meat worms squirmed.* Mimi finishes tipping the powder into the hopper, replaces the measuring beaker on the bench, and, *thro' these faint smokes curling whitely* as she clips the empty capsule into its runnel and deftly depresses the lever to *marry* this tiny vessel with the funnel's tip, he notes the diamond solitaire on her finger. *Grind away, moisten and mash up thy paste, Pound at thy powder, – I am not in haste!* Some springloaded shuttle is released by her *chipped-red-varnished* nails, a paten revolves, the capped capsule comes on its little tray, Mimi picks it up and turns to face him, staggering ever so slightly under her neuropharmacological load. Two grammes, she says, her voice *kazooing prettily* through her cotton mask. I can adjust it to do one and three but halves are more diff –. He is on her, his angle so finely calculated that his pelvis pots her buttocks into the pockets of his hands, while his thigh is between hers and his mouth *partakes of the same filter*, their tongues nuzzling at either side of the mask, their teeth nipping it aside. She oofs a shandy burp as they cooperate poorly in the *three-legged race* to the floor. Busner's hands yank apart her laboratory coat, pull up the hem of her dress, pull down her exasperating net of tights and panties – she smells sweetly acerbic – *sherbet lemons?* Her tightly curly hair is near white-blonde – *a fleece*. They must've knocked over a glass vessel on their way down, for, as she grapples with his belt buckle and zip, he can hear the gently grinding noise of this rocking to a rest. Futilely now – for she is *a bare and forked thing* before him and there's no stopping this – he hopes this wasn't the eighty ounces of L-dihidroxyphenylalanine, costing *two thousand pounds!* that arrived only this morning from Sandoz in Switzerland. The lino presses prosaically on the heels of hands, his knees – it catches at his toenails, while he contorts into the *sacred pomp* of entering her, and Mimi, with her head and her breast and her arms *should drop dead!* In these times allocated for abandonment Busner is at his most professional, haaaa-haaa-ha, she exhales as, at last, he unmasks her: a kidnap victim who it would seem wishes only to be ravished by her captor, for she pulls him into her with *those nails* and for a few seconds at least there is nothing present to him but *sherbet lemons* intensifying into a *high coital sweat* . . . He frees her breast from its enclosure – the aureole is far larger and paler than he expects, the nipple is recessed and so he hunches to feed upon it. Ha'ha'hnnn! She bites his ear and he diagnoses her *mobile spasm* as *athetosis*, her *jerking* as *myoclonic*. To beat off these medical terms he looks at her face, only to find her bright blue eyes compelled by something behind and to the left of her – *an oculogyric crisis!* In Mimi's open mouth he chances upon the *wet glint* of her fillings – her shivery curls sweep the precious dustfall. He feels the beginning of detumescence and to stiffen his resolve calls upon *Miriam's face smeared sideways across the familiar pillows*: the image of conjugal right assists wonderfully in the committal of professional wrong, and, as the encephalitic on the floor *bends backwards clutching at my sides*, he wonders: Does she do the same, am I her fee-fee-fee-aaahn-say?! He pulls out suddenly and the spatter of his sperm on her skin, her clothes and the lino alerts them both to *the insanity of what we've done*. There will be more intimacy enforced, he thinks, by my mopping this up than there was in the cause of it – first times are necessarily social, *small genital talk* . . . From hers in the pub, and before when he explained the highly experimental nature of what they would be doing, Busner gathered that for all the girlishness of her ribbed white tights and daisy-patterned summer minidress, Mimi was entirely serious. *An infanta, she was, returning from the pub* . . . in the sedan chair of her transparent plastic umbrella. He had laughed at her in the spring squall, and she said: *I don't want to get my hair wet* . . . hobbled by his own garments he kneels awkwardly – there must be a cloth of some sort in the sink sunk into the lab bench. In esters of musk her face is blank – tendons are threaded through the dewlap below her chin – she shivers awake, her hands reach up and draw his *blockhead* back down to her belly. In the wooden trench far below the sheltering skylight, *the flushed bodies resume their battle* – by a thin loop the mask retains its hold on one of her lobeless ears, and from this there radiates out, along the dingy corridors, through the swing doors, across the stifling airing courts and down the wailing wards, a *widening whorl* of perturbation that courses through all the human flesh it encounters, amplifying hysterical misery into nerve-tingling pleasure – through flesh, and through walls that wobble and pulse. Through walls and in *electrostatic rings* that travel down all 1,884 feet and six inches of the hospital's central corridor, constricting and dilating its cold old plasterwork. Cracks appear in the patients – they are *fragmented with joy*, doctors and charge nurses come running, their sedative-tipped *bayonets already fixed* ... yet they cannot prevent the patients from hammering their heads against the floor *bump-bump-bump!* or sweeping up the drifts of spilled L-DOPA – Busner labours and sweat wells from the sticking plaster he had wound round the handle of the club, a mashie niblick picked up from a market stall in Beresford Square when he went for a dekko. Albert smiles down at his own feet planted lumpily in their woollen stockings on the bare floorboards of the changing room. He smiles, and thinks of how it is that an awareness of a splinter is always a posteriori – he can hear Mayhew and Arbuthnot moving around behind him, screened by the jackets that hang from the pegs set above the benches. There is the distinctive tang of deeply penetrated dried perspiration – sweat produced, equally identifiably, he feels, by useless exertion – mixed up with *liniment, linseed oil and gutta-percha* ... then comes the sharp scrape of a cleated boot, the soft slap-flap as trews are belted – but he has no specialist clothing to don or equipment to prepare, instead he wears the trousers from his third-best office suit, a light flannel shirt and his old Bancroft's cricketing pullover. Albert smiles again: he will, he thinks, tuck the trouser cuffs into his stockings – this will give him greater freedom in his stroke as well as provide the semblance of plus-twos. — When he was shown in to the Principal Overseer's office, the man hadn't known what to make of the golf club tucked under Albert's arm – or else he hadn't noticed it. Either way, Albert forbore from mentioning it and they went on to inspect the Danger Buildings, the foundries and the machine shops, with the club still in his hand. At one point he employed its handle – then unbandaged, its worn leather grip open-pored – to poke into the bronze cap of a shell casing lying on a workbench, so that he could lift it up and examine its polishing in the *sateen* sunlight that *swagged* down from the high windows. What had the PO thought? Presumably that this was some novel type of swagger stick, since, although he was also a civilian, he seemed terribly flustered by having to deal with another one – one who was also, potentially, in such a senior position. On one or two occasions he had said sir to Albert and sketched a salute. The PO was a much older man in a wing-poke collar and coat of nineties cut, with a complexion – which Albert guessed was normally ruddy – that had been leached by nerves. It could have been Albert's ramrod-straight bearing that confused the man – not that this was for show, being an entirely legitimate product of *all that footer and cricket*, and, latterly, now that Mister Wilton had had his way, *late evenings purloined on the links*. He moved, he knew, with an athlete's unconscious grace – and, although his superiors depended upon Albert for his exceptional brain power, his reasoning and his recall, while *stiffening their resolve* with his *unimpeachable probity*, he, in turn, relied on his body . . . *long-stemmed, palest green and unearthly . . . rhubarb*, grown on composting dung heaps in the kitchen gardens of Surrey. Rhubarb in last night's pie set before her lodgers by Missus Hedges, her cheap stays clicking, her bulldog face pouchy with pleasure. If he were to be *accepted by Fair Rosalind . . . by her people . . .* there would be an end to this domestic simplicity, instead: new furniture, accouchement sets – all the fussing necessitated by baby linen and the *paying therefore*. She might, he thought, bring with her *seven or eight hundred a year . . .* But this was *idle fancy*, so far was he from wooing her – he had only seen her once or twice, tipped his hat as she and her illustrious uncle passed down the Ministry stairs. To think of it was *utter folly!* Although, did he not deserve her, or some thing like her? Had he not kept himself *clean*, affixed his eye to the nail through Our Saviour's hand, not permitting it to stray to a *loosely pinned bodice?* Sitting there, Sunday after Sunday, digging up coin for the velveteen sack poked along the pew, listening with a connoisseur's ear to the *bronchial moan* of St Jude's unrestored organ, Albert views the catechism in the same light as the Annual Statistical Table compiled by His Majesty's Stationery Office: he knows them both by heart, and both ensure the maintenance of his Faith in the Trinity of the King, Kitchener and the Welsh Wizard –.

De'Ath – De'Ath? This sally Albert does not hear, it is not until – I say, De'Ath, if we don't look lively we'll get caught behind that four – which comes together with an unprecedented hand on his shoulder, that he grasps these two syllables apply to him personally, as much as legally. Mayhew, *lopsided* by his full bag, smiles down at Albert, dimples eat the neat ends of his *burnt-cork moustache*. As they leave the changing room and cross in front of the grandly named clubhouse towards the 1st tee, Albert assesses Mayhew's *lurcher gait* – he may be too meagre to carry his own bag, yet this hardly matters: urchins come trotting from the tattered shadows of the crack willows along the brook, desperate to lug it for him for thru'pence or less.

Moreover, on the train to Hanwell, Mayhew admitted to a handicap in single figures. No virtue or skill of my own, he'd flannelled – apparently the Mayhew family home had backed on to a course. There had been seaside summers messing about on sand dunes and on the links near Rustington – then a half-blue at the varsity. As the stopper pottered alongside the Great Western line through Royal Oak, Acton and Ealing, Albert's immediate superior indulged his own modesty. Albert was grateful for Arbuthnot, whom Mayhew had introduced as *doin' something jolly tedious at the Bank*, but who was *spiffed up as flashily as a Jew stock-jobber*, what with his lavender spats, silk hatband and buttonhole *big enough for bumble bees*. Arbuthnot seemed only to have been waiting for the train to chug away from Paddington before he got out his flask and offered it round, saying, To spite His Majesty I've taken it up for the duration. And when it came to Mayhew's *humbug* he did not mince his words: Give it a rest, Mayhew, ol' man. To hear you talk you'd think you didn't so much as enter into the swing, physically speaking – that the Holy Spirit did it all for you! Arbuthnot, his carnal countenance blue and red blended *mutton turned*, laughed loud – laughed longest. Now, wiping his full and saturnine lips with a snowy pocket kerchief and passing his also well-stocked bag to one of the caddies, Arbuthnot notices that Albert is still carrying only the two clubs he had with him on the train – the mashie niblick and an equally ancient spoon – takes this in, and absorbs also the désordonné of the younger man's costume, which, in the clear May daylight, presents a brutal contrast with his own natty golfing togs: elasticated tartan stockings, pale green plus-twos that flatter his heavy thighs, and a matching windbreaker covered with an assortment of belts and straps. He says, Are those your only clubs? And when Albert admits to this, the banker goes on,

Well, you're welcome to the use of whichever of mine you please – damn it, you might rather prefer to leave those behind and simply share the bag. One does not ascend so far and so fast in the Service by taking offence – not that one becomes incapable of perceiving those utterances that, whether intentionally or not, should occasion such – but the banker means exactly what he says, and this is of a piece with his whole manner, with its easy and unforced egalitarianism, so unlike that of Mayhew, who, hearing their exchange, hastens to chip in: Why, De'Ath, I should've offered before – of course, you must feel free. And when Albert demurs, Thank you, sir, and thank you, Mister Arbuthnot, I'd as soon stick with these, I'm familiar with their, ah . . . peculiarities, and to be frank I welcome the challenge, Mayhew presses uncomfortably: Come-come, De'Ath, I think no such formalities on the course – here we're all golfers first and only secondly . . . before becoming confused, so uncomfortable is he with saying gentlemen. Albert has some sympathy, as he appreciates the brilliance of his own personation: by no means affecting to be what he is not, while his flat, neutral accents and perfect diction no longer give any clue to the Foulham boy he once was. *Don't av any more, Missus Moore, Don't av any more, Missus Moore* . . . Not so: there will be thousands more of his stamp *recruited in the halls by the White-Eyed Kaffir* . . . Albert understands far better than his companions that war is always an opportunity. At last Mayhew manages to force out: . . . civil servants, then bends to place his tee, straightens, waggles, sights to where the fairway doglegs between stately oaks, dips a knee prettily as the club's head comes up, then swipes and digs. His ball bounces once, twice, and disappears into the rough – from wherever Mayhew's handicap derives, Albert muses, it cannot be his drive. — Walking down the drowsy avenue from Hanwell Station, past two new villas and an old rectory of a piece with its ancient yew and oily crows, Arbuthnot and Mayhew had discussed the deposition of the national reserves, the sack after sack of gold sovereigns that had been loaded into the Bank – so many, Arbuthnot had contended, that the City constabulary had held up all the traffic on King William Street so that the motor vans, motor cars – and even drays taken on by a few of the larger local branches – might form an orderly queue. A housemaid who had been punishing a carpet in the front garden of one of the villas left off and blushed prettily as the three men strolled past. Albert saw over on the far side of the railway line the black chapel spire, redbrick chimneystacks and umber masonry towers of the County Asylum. The lunatics were probably brought in by rail or road – but why not by the Grand Junction Canal? He heard their cries *lapping at the coal wharves . . . lunatic women . . .* they were being classified now in terms of their usefulness for the effort – why not children, then, imbeciles, perhaps? After all, they'd serve quite as well as . . . *machine-gun fodder.* The difference a year made – where would they be in three? *He, Hi, gave 'er a knock, Which made the old woman go hipertihop, He, Hi, hipertihop . . .* Now, having observed the tussock that hides Mayhew's ball for a decent while, Arbuthnot bends to poke in his own tee, saying, I've waited until now to propose my wager. The two caddies who have been taken on snigger – and the four who were not, and who sit ankles crossed in a row a few yards off, snigger also . . . *the sycophants of sycophants.* Arbuthnot's behind presents a billowy expanse . . . *barges tacking downriver under full sail . . .* but when he straightens he brings with him one of the new ten-shilling notes, taut between his fingers with Bradbury's signature floating in the sky and framed by *high, wispy cirrus . . .* I'll either award this to the best of my companions' rounds, he says, or pocket it for good. Mayhew makes another blunder . . . *he flounders, the Lusitania sucks him down* . . . – Don'tcha think that's a little steep, old chap? and compounds this with a nod of the club in the direction of Albert, who quickly says, Not at all. Indeed, if you'll oblige me, Mister Arbuthnot, may I double you? And he takes a pound note from his pocket book. – You see I have one of these new instruments of my own *shrewdly withdrawn in anticipation of precisely this eventuality* . . . Arbuthnot vigorously assents – and Mayhew has no option but to add a pound of his own to the kitty. Arbuthnot takes up his stance, which is *brutally compact.* He manages the difficult feat, for such a heavyset man, of raising up his arms to the perpendicular. Albert thinks there is too much force in the drive, although club meets ball with a clean crack! so that it ascends, whistling faintly, in a steep *Minniewerfer parabola*, which, long before it reaches its zenith, Albert calculates will overshoot its target. A two-hundred-and-sixty-yard par 4, pinched into an hourglass by the oaks, firing over these risked *the ordnance falling into a mine crater at the back of Fosse 8* – which is what happens to Arbuthnot's ball. The safer course is to *lay down covering fire* in the *no-man's-land* in front of the trees, then employ a mid-range iron to *target* the green – which is what Albert does, despite lacking both driver and suitable iron. He understands every nick and bump in his spoon, knows to several decimal points the angle of its face: once his swing has been *calibrated* he needs must exert no effort, only allow *firing pin* to meet *cartridge* unimpeded so that the ball *hipertihops* to a halt twenty yards short of the trees. Mayhew requires two strokes to clear the rough, Arbuthnot three to blast out of the bunker, the sand spraying from his *hoggish delving.* Advancing to his perfect lie, Albert swaps clubs, leans back into his downswing and lofts his ball over the embroidery of the oaks. A cleanly cut divot falls back to the earth and he takes his time tamping this down before waving the victorious mashie niblick over-head as he makes for the green, calling out, Sorry about that ... The two older men look on in silence as, using the flat back of the gripped-down spoon, Albert sinks the seven-yard putt. With the evidence of his companions' frailties afforded by the 1st hole – and no more knowledge of the further seventeen other than their length and par, as detailed by the notice in the clubhouse – Albert has already played ahead. He will, he thinks, almost certainly win by thirteen strokes – fourteen if there is some radically unforeseen circumstance. En route to the 2nd tee Arbuthnot pauses to light his pipe and indicates with the match that Albert should *tarry with him.* Are you, he asks, his *carp*'s mouth blowing *smoky bubbles*, one of Sam Montagu's men or Lloyd George's? His heavy-lidded eyes have lost the glazed hilarity they had in the train – his gaze is not cold but appraising. Albert replies, I hardly think I'm a personage of sufficient stature for either of those gentlemen to've noticed me ... His own eyes drift across to the tee, where Mayhew is performing curious knee-bends. I hardly think, Arbuthnot says caustically, that Mister Mayhew would be of sufficient stature for these gentlemen to notice him, were he not supplied with such an able Number Two. Some Ahrensmeyer, or Datas, with shrewd acuity must be seated inside this *barrel of a man,* who now pokes his matchbox between *two staves.* Albert says, What, if you don't mind my asking, Mister Arbuthnot, precisely is your position at the Bank? – Oh, p-pooh-pooh, Mister De'Ath, I believe you can do better than that, but since you ask ... there are *smoky pennants streaming overhead, a dandelion head is crushed down below* ... I make certain there are sufficient funds available for your new Ministry to be able to settle its bills on presentation – when will

175

you be starting at the Arsenal? He turns away and moves through the *white star* haze towards the 2nd tee. Running for more than four hundred yards in a long lazy *s* down to the Uxbridge Road, and skirting the obvious hazard of a millpond, the hole favours those able to *marshal their forces for a rapid advance.* Mayhew's caddy stoops to place his tee, Mayhew stoops to place his ball – he waggles his club and his shoulders, settles his stance, then again *waggle, settle*, and again *waggle, settle.* Albert's own shoulders squirm in sympathy – the last thing he wishes is for his chief to *lose face!* The drive is an adequate one, although Arbuthnot tops it by at least fifty yards. Both men play efficiently up to the green, while Albert lags judiciously before mercilessly wielding the niblick to sink a twenty-five-yard chip-and-run. And so the three men divide the hole at three strokes apiece, 1 over par. The next four, which take the golfers towards the village of Southall before their flank is turned by a lane and they retreat east back to the River Brent, are *plain sailing*: broad fairways, complacent bunkers and mundane hillocks. Albert doesn't have to try too hard to persuade Mayhew that his skill is *in the ascendant.* Arbuthnot, however, looks Albert in the eye queerly at regular intervals. We could, he says, as they stand observing a puffed Mayhew undertake more knee-bends, have played the Brent Valley course, I have membership there as well. So do several Jews, Mayhew adds apropos of the new cabinet, and I understand they've need of a motor-charabanc to take them round the nine such is their laziness –. And parsimony! Arbuthnot adds, then all three laugh – he himself laughing the longest. On the 9th tee Albert realises he is drained of energy by the effort of keeping his swing in check: his back is *galvanised* by tension, a stress that *winds* about his arms, *pricking and ripping* at his nerves and ligaments with sharp *barbs.* The hole is the most interesting thus far: running for a hundred and thirty yards down a gentle slope, to where a screen of alders hides the point at which the fairway hooks round. Through the *shivergreen* of leaves, high up on the far bank, Albert sees the pin piercing the kidney of cropped grass – it is only good sportsmanship to point out to his companions that the river is *merely a blind*. Really? Mayhew queries, pressing the turf with the toe of his shoe, *feeling for mines*. Bolstered by his subordinate's hidden directives, he has begun to play the part of a *magnanimous victor*. Albert says, I rather think that it's here the course's architect has lavished all the invention of which the holes thus far have been deprived – I wager that behind the trees there is a water feature right beside the river. Mayhew bleats again: Really? When bedevilled by hectoring telegrams from the Front *conceit is a mask Mayhew oft dons* – it is this that Albert sees obscuring his features, and through *holes cut* in it his *moist and unmanly* eyes scan the mid-distance. *Fool! Your country needs not you* ... For Mayhew has called for a 3 iron, where any save the most expert would play short, accepting two shots to the green as the price for a safe par 3. There's nothing now that Albert can do to save him – nor all the *whey-faced younger brothers in an ague of terror* who have been chucked away on this *desperate manoeuvre*. So sunk is Albert in this contumely that he neglects to observe the girlish jink of Mayhew's knees – is aware only of the repugnant slowness of the ball, towed upwards through the deceptively irenic air by *steam pinnaces that whistle towards Constantinoples of cloud*. They buzz, the machine-gun bullets – or so Albert has heard officers on leave remark: buzz as they make serrate soft things – *flesh, cloth, brain matter* ... So it proves with Mayhew's ball, which, gaining insufficient height, fatally pauses, is sheered by the buzzing wind, then plummets. Uncharacteristically, Albert pictures this: the tear in the bilious slime, the dimpled moonface bobbing up in the bloody and stagnant water. The caddy will, he thinks, be prevailed upon to wallow in and retrieve it – no willingness to it, only *a dull-witted and hungry compliance*. Suddenly he licks the metallic nib of his anger *I gave him every opportunity!* It is a transformation *that clever crapaud* registers at once, despite his being more than *half blotto*, and Albert giving, he is certain, no indication other than the exaggerated deference with which he waves Arbuthnot up before him on to the mound. The banker plays safe, his ball *hipertihopping* down the incline to lie exactly as it ought for a long chip to the green. There is a point in one's construction of a golf swing – or so Albert believes – when the player achieves that state of mind described by the Hindoo holy men: with the yogic assumption of the stance – arms up and away, the whole length of the torso *twisted precisely on the bipod* – force becomes inimical to the meditative calculation of angles: the arc the club's head will describe and that of the once-smitten ball. *All has been decided* – the stroke is a ghostly conclusion, *void and without form*. Moreover, the conflict is not with his ostensible opponents – who are feeble creatures, their features *poorly moulded in soft lead* – but with the course, this wholly arbitrary strip of land, the tangled dells and ungrazed-upon meadows of which have been invested with a terrible and futile significance. The course is not blameless – it has *drawn this fire down* on itself by reason of its very marginality. Its manifest features, streams, copses, isolated and venerable elms, mean nothing any longer, indeed, they are only there at all to provide bearings from which the combatants can get their range. Albert's long body unwinds and rewinds, and, as he unwinds again, he feels in every fibre the perfection of the stroke – the mashie niblick, he also, both might have been made for this moment alone. Cheer-o,

Mayhew mutters – the three of them, the caddies and hangers-on too, are all floating away with the air ball, which mounts and mounts the pneumatic column for a long while, then poises, then drops. All anticipate the *hippertihop* on the green, the white *scut* of the invisible *coney* – yet there is nothing. It appears, Mayhew says as they go on, that you too have come a cropper. Arbuthnot smiles his lipless toady smile – *my anger amuses him!* And it all unfolds as Albert foresaw: the caddy wading in the mucky mere diverted from the stream, while Mayhew, increasingly intemperate, paces the bank, yelping commands. It isn't until Arbuthnot places a weighty hand on his shoulder that he settles down, accepts the two penalty strokes and the new ball. While the two of them play up to the green Albert stalks its hinterland, parting *quiff* after *quiff* of grass, each time seeing only what he expects: a straggle of old beech mast, a catkin, a strew-ing of *parched sheep shot* ... Albert disdains his own self-doubt, although it remains important that it be one of the others – although not necessarily Mayhew – who, on withdrawing the pin to retrieve his own ball, cries out in astonishment, Oh, I say! before stooping to pluck out the second that lies coddled in the cup and calling to Albert: Does yours have a mark that you recall? Albert calls back hoarsely, Three hearts! He hears not Arbuthnot's terse congratula-tion or Mayhew's feigned one – he ignores the ragged cheers of caddies and hangers-on, he strides on to the next tee, *releases the ratchet, swings the bipod forward, tightens the ratchet,* settles into his stance, grips the club, *flicks his eyes to the horizon, clicks the springloaded wheel to select the range, cranks the handle and lays down covering fire,* beneath which he can advance his reputation. Two birdies in succes-sion – an eagle at the 12th. If the first half of the match was distinguished by a terrible stasis as Albert's imposture held them all in check, now there is a delirious release into mobile warfare, as the trio quarter the remaining area of the course, then quarter it again. Pigeons hang in the hawthorn beside the 17th tee, their bodies *quite disgustingly plump* writhing amidst the thorns. It is *stand to*, and to the west the sun seeps through watery cloud, to the east all the Mary Annes and Mays in the villas of Castlebar Hill and Drayton Green poke the banked-down ranges with care: coal must be brought home by pram, a half-hundredweight at a time. Already the flow of commuters back from the station is choked off by death – while smoke rises from chimneypots and streams madder towards the next dawn. A sudden spring shower silvering slates – and on the 18th tee stands Mayhew, pushing away the brolly his cabby has taken from his bag and opened. – No, man, I cannot see from under it. There is the *pull* and then the *pull again* of mud on Albert's boots as they walk towards the clubhouse – clods of ire fall away and he is *inclined to leniency*. As they wait their turns to use the boot scraper, Mayhew and Arbuthnot pay off their caddies with the florins and half-crowns in their waistcoat pockets before withdrawing wallets from animal-damp tweed. Astonishing, Mayhew says as he hands over the pound note, what was it in the end – six, seven strokes? Albert is succinct: Fourteen. Mayhew flutes ruefully, And all achieved with two clubs – no driver, and no putter either . . . Still – he dabs his pantomime moustache – some might argue that only having two makes things easier, choosing the right club being part of the skill . . . of . . . the game . . . He falls silent. Albert accepts Arbuthnot's pound note and handshakes from both men – he leans on his spoon and mashie niblick *the Norwegian at the Pole*, while the hip flask is passed amongst them, then he uses the niblick's head to ease out the muddy slug trapped in the right-angle of heel and sole. I shall take the position at Woolwich, he says, each word *lightly slapping* Mayhew's rain-washed cheeks, the shell crisis needs must be addressed. *Incarnadined*, Mayhew's face is *a wound suffused with indignant hurt*: And you . . . you're the man for the task – you believe? Yes, Albert says, that's precisely what I believe. — He leaves them there, and, grabbing his jacket from the hook in the changing room, strides off to Hanwell Station, the shafts of the clubs grinding in his blistered hand. At Paddington he realises the weather has closed in in earnest, when, making his way along the platform, he has to dodge this way, then that, to avoid the tips of umbrella struts that *snipe* for his eyes – the enemy of the tall man in this *crowded stone trench*. Three ladies lurk by the ticket barrier – the youngest steps forward and stares at him boldly from the black-straw grotto of her hat. Albert notes her fashionably short skirt, she has slim ankles – *les attaches fines, the French would say* – she says, Shirker, which he affects not to hear. Shirker, she says again, struggling to contain herself as she is tossed from the hand of righteousness to that of decorum . . . *which drops the catch*. She drums her gloved hands on his chest. Now, now! Her older companion *a chinless drab* restrains her by the hips *and happily*. You've only to give it to him, Lucy. The third of their party *ashamed, possibly?* taps the platform to one side of her boots and then the other with the point of an umbrella Albert recognises as having been manufactured by the company with which his sister holds a position. This *sturdy body* is hatless – or rather her hair, worn in a Mikado tuck-up, is her hat. What's this! And this?! his assailant cries, but Albert, while perfectly aware of what is transpiring, remains powerless to intervene: he treads water some way off, looking back at the tall, limber young man, the golf clubs in one of his hands, the skirt of his cricketing pullover visible between the flaps of his jacket, and the

181

muddy spatter on his trews which are still tucked into his stockings. – Do you not see yourself, my fine fellow – d'you not? There are brave men dying at Ypres, while you – you ... Albert considers the third woman's movements to be mysterious, almost ritualised: the way her divided skirts sway as she taps the platform here, then there. Were this peacetime, someone might intervene, as it is he imagines that the passers-by – who hurry on, faces averted, cold grey gabardine shoulders *rain-shot* – have delegated this task, for they have more pressing ones: lager beers to be poured away into the gutter of Charlottenstrasse, cuckoo clocks torn from the walls of cafés and unceremoniously unwound, the complicated filigree of a Beethoven sonata *somehow picked apart* ... Miss ... Albert begins, he can feel the sharp corner of the Minister's letter in his breast pocket and wonders whether he should withdraw it with a flourish. However, he who is typically so attentive is lost for now in the steam and the smutty smoke that lies in a bank above them, *ill omened by the occasional gasolier* – up there rainwater cascades over the glass curves of the roof, alongside there is *the flesh-eating clank of buffers marrying*. Somehow a long white feather has flown into his hand. Propping the clubs against his belly, Albert takes his time examining it, running his fingertips along its *silkygrating* bars. Miss ... he begins again, but seeing this: her wild-eyed expression of triumph. He ceases and turns on his heel, the mashie niblick and the spoon raised in a lofty salute. As he does so he laughs full-throatedly, because from the expression on the third woman's face he believes she has deduced – it could be the influence of her coiffure – that it is Albert who is the Lord High Executioner. Missus Hedges will, he thinks, have ox tongue for supper, *lolling over the rim of the dish*, each papilla plainly visible from up here are the water tower and the campaniles of the first range of the hospital. He can't make out the second range – which, if his recollection is correct, only had a single storey – but whether this is because it's been demolished, or it is hidden by the first from this vantage, he cannot decide. — He got off the bus in Muswell Hill and stood for a long time looking in the window of an internet café, trying to make sense of it all: the plastic decals stuck on to the inside of the window advertised LEBARA with exaggeratedly joyous African faces, this being, he gathered from the listing of national flags and associated charges, a service that allowed you to call Swaziland, Rwanda and Gabon for mere pennies per minute. Who were these happy exiles, he wondered, yakking away for hour upon hour, their *verbigeration* wavering around the world? *I needn't've* because at that moment one had emerged in a *spiffy* maroon leather jacket, from the zippered pockets of which he took first one, then a second, then a third mobile phone – instruments of communication that he swapped from hand to hand, and when he had two in one, over and over. It bothered Busner, to whom it seemed the greatest profligacy: treating these artfully designed *jewels of micro-circuitry* as *worry beads*, then pausing to *tell* their *nodules*, then resuming once more shk-shk, clack-clack, over and under, back and forth. Now, from his peak perspective, he can scan entire sectors of northern London – from the *Parnassus of Totteridge* right round to *the Elysian Fields of Epping Forest* – not, of course, that he can identify all the bits in between, although where three grim multistorey blocks *riotously assemble* might be Edmonton. It would be a cliché and a lie to say that his nose had led him there, any more than his feet had taken him – feet that, swollen and complaining, have bullied him into removing his training shoes. — No, sitting on the bench, gazing across the vale of the North Circular to what used to be Friern Hospital, Busner reflects with some small satisfaction on his first morning as a penitent. He had set off from Kentish Town with no plan or preconceived route, yet at each point where the way divided, memory, that ever-present helpmeet, had showed him the right one. *Truth to tell* no matter how random his transit, Busner's *conscience could've reeled me in – my spore, my copro-lites, my coiled mess, is scattered that widely.* All offences are compounded, he realises belatedly, by the perpetrator not cleaning up afterwards – by first walking away, and then staying away. Behind him he senses the cavernous interior of the building, its acreages of rotten flooring, the tiles flaking away from the underside of its *lofty ceilings* . . . It is, Busner feels, an unloved and unlovely thing: Paris has Sacré-Cœur, Rio its cloud-cloaked Redeemer, but *what was on top of London – Ally Pally.* No doubt at its inception there had been boating, a switchback railway, the godly tootle of a record-breaking organ, massed brassy oompahing – all the busy relaxation of that Imperial era. Still, whenever he had ventured inside – no matter which decade – Busner had stumbled upon the same botched panto-graphs of municipality: a bamboo arras lost in a booming hall, freestanding screens of neon-indigo nylon ill-concealing gilded stacking chairs piled up to thrice head-height, grimly stained shafts tunnelling down into *kitchen mausoleums* . . . *Betja—, Betje—?* No, nobody could make out a case for the thing – yet here it still was. *It had burned – when?* A couple of times at least and no doubt *caught a packet* in the war, yet was simply *too big to be destroyed.* Busner grim-aced: fire was to it a form of agricultural technique, merely sweeping away the dead drifts of old catering trolleys so that *new shoots of the same old decrepitude could spring up.* You got troll feet, says a child who has arrived at his bench and stands sneering down at them. Busner smells salty breath and registers chewing that, despite its only this moment having claimed his attention, still seems incessant. The child – *a boy?* – wears some sort of smock with a cartoon face on it *that also gurns.* The child works its small jaws once, twice, three times, then *fly-catcher tongue: a tic-like flexion.* I am . . . Busner begins, and his fancy hardens into this conviction . . . a troll. The child's eyes widen pleasingly – but then along comes its mother, a regatta-striped buggy zigzagging from the ends of her fleeing arms. Predictably she's *anorexic – a common enough sequel to untreated post-partum depression.* He is delighted that she wrenches the child away and buckles it into the pushchair, yanking the strap up so that its smock bunches. Double bogies *skitterolving* on the smooth path, they are leaving nothing behind except this: the small face aimed back at him and still chewing, still *tongue-ticcing,* still *gobbling up the troll.* In seconds they are on the terrace below Busner *am I hungry?* then gone. Some epochal signal had been beamed from the roof of the Palace, this much he knew: a wooden puppet broken down into its constituent waveforms and then *reassembled a mile or two away by clever Scotsmen.* — With the mildly fungally infected big toenail of one foot Busner scratches the sole of the other – what was it he had said to Mimi? The Palace of Pain and the Palace of Pleasure facing one another across the slough of suburban despond. And what had she replied? Nothing. One, two, three . . . some years later, after he'd *walked away from the shit I'd done,* it occurred to Busner that she might have been paradoxically affected by all the hours she had spent encapsulating L-DOPA for him surrounded by those clouds of dopaminergic dust. By contrast with the sculpture court he had curated on Ward 20, she seemed with each successive encounter to be losing the power of voluntary movement more and more: standing forlorn by the bench, slight in her white coat, her hair-net bulging with her blonde curls, monkey-muzzled by her facemask, her forehead sweat-damp – *Carry on, Chemist!* He had joshed her – but there was no need to, her eyes were transfixed on her own hands as they *ticced about* the equipment, pouring, measuring, tapping, cranking and turning as she enacted the *very real pill-rolling necessary – or so I believed – to put a stop to its Parkinsonian mimicry.* Only when we touched did she unlock, did her synovial fluid flow, so that I felt her muscular rigidity liquefy into spasticity. We slow-danced around the lab, her face buried in my shoulder, *Bay-bee, bay-bee, sugar me,* she mumbling of this and that, an increasingly strident palilalia in which the names of colleagues, their malpractices and the leaden crassness of the administration became *tossed into a word salad.* With my lips to her neck, I felt her pulse speed up: one-twenty, one-thirty, one-forty, *gotta get my candy free, w'hey-hey –!* A bouncy little jig, punctuated by the *whip-crack-into-rice-pudding of the snare drum's rim shot.* There was no talk ever of fiancé or wife – such is the dark mirror of adultery, in which both parties elect to see nothing, instead, her letting drop an appointment at the FPA licensed everything — so, as the weeks and then the months passed, our lovemaking became characterised by bizarre notions and their attendant motions: a wheelchair left in a corridor would be commandeered to mechanise our coitus, while on another occasion we purloined the mobile hoist used to lower paraplegic patients into their baths. We braced ourselves in corners and against the undersides of shelves. *Dyspnoea . . .* She pants, this – *her thumb? – thrust whole into my anus is capricious . . .* her tongue, travelling *round and round my ear . . . compulsive.* Leaning back astride me, she's possessed by a mass of subhuman manias and still her pulse continues to accelerate: one-forty, one-fifty – if she were my patient *I'd administer a massive dose of parenteral barbiturates.* She blinks, she

186

grinds her teeth, her shoulders shake with a dreadful palsy as her pubic hair scratches frantically in mine, *One for you and one for me, Pardon me – comes to three!* Balanced impossibly, as a pin could never be on its point, to one side the abyss of frenzy, to the other that of stupor – with no warning there is *the inspiration of a leviathan!* she holds her breath for ten . . . twenty seconds . . . an agonising half-minute, during which he has to take in the Rembrandt lighting: her breasts heaving, flayed of their clothing, her dirty cherub's face, her unloosed hair a gilt sphere. And more: the pong of excess bleach caught on fraying linoleum, the mid-distant dissent of a distressed inmate terminated by doorslam, the drug dust that tickles his own nose, before: Paaaaaaaaahhh! Peanut breath is violently expelled and he is blown into a salt globe full of floaters, motes, spiralling animal-cules, fish oil, wallpaper paste, gentlemen's – relish. Soon enough he will have to *relearn once more the complex sequence of actions required to stand up* . . . What happened to Mary Quant? Max Factor. — It doesn't work for me, Enoch Mboya says, I just don't find it funny. Well, Busner chides, you're being obtuse as well as prudish – what're you, some sort of Mary Whitehouse? Mboya takes a pinch of oaken skin in thumb and forefinger, scrutinises it, then replies, Hardly. They laugh edgily – they are *deep in* now, the pair of them, *conspirators, really*. Whitcomb's authorisation was obtained for the purchase of the L-DOPA, but, beyond scanning the journal article Busner thrust before him, he has shown no interest in the trial – which is as well, because it's not a trial at all, *there being no control!* He titters, and Mboya who's sorting the latest batch of capsules into the compart-ments of a dispensary tray, looks at him reproachfully. Recently Busner has started to feel that his charge nurse is *reading my thoughts*, so engrafted have they become. Busner voices his next – What'd be the point of a control? – even though he's only reiterating what they've both said many times in the weeks leading up to giving the selected group of patients the drug, and many more in the anxiety-distended week since. Indeed, Mboya says, there'd be no point to a placebo: they don't know what we're giving to them, and nor do we for that matter. Both boldly going psychonauts have qualms: next-of-kin consent has been obtained at best haphazardly: a form which was composed by Busner has been Cyclostyled by Admin. and in vague terms it outlines the experiment. Mboya, Inglis, Vail and others charged with the care of the post-encephalitic patients have pressed these on the few relatives who still visit, and when called upon Busner has made himself available to answer their questions. In these encounters he makes use of a doctorly gambit he despises: talking down unless they up their game. To a very few of the few – only one or two – he admits: We know nothing much, L-DOPA has had some therapeutic results with ordinary Parkinsonian patients, however, this is a different form of the disease – if, indeed, it's the same disease at all. He forbore from adding: Besides, what've they – let alone you – got to lose? Nor did he point out that these *pecking, bobbing and stuffed bodies were barely human,* being to all intents and purposes *lame ducks* whose government subsidy might – altogether reasonably – have been withdrawn years or even decades before. *Why let 'em go on, the shitbuilders?* The enkies' children appeared to have suffered from the disease's fallout – prematurely aged, they limped on to the ward. In his mind's eye Busner always pictures them as wearing macs of pre-war neutrality, or else supporting themselves with duff umbrellas. Their bri-nylon shirts were damp through and mildewed – they were Harold Steptoes, orphaned children of parents who yet lived, biologically adult yet *balking at all the busyness of life*

– financial, emotional and sexual. Of course, he understood that such children and spouses who still visited had to be self-selecting for exactly these characteristics, after all. *How little would you have to have in your life in order to prioritise this thankless – and frankly useless –task?* Shall we? Mboya says, *the Coptic Bishop with his tray of wafers* – and so their round begins, since neither of them trusts anybody else to dole out the precious sacrament, especially now that they have chosen – Mboya being included in the clinical decision – to massively increase the dosage. One hundred, two hundred – up to five hundred milligrammes could be given by depot injection, but not entire grammes of the stuff. They had increased the dosage, and they had restricted its allocation to only six patients: four of the somnolent-opthalmoplegics, who were utterly extinct and sunk in the deepest catatonia – *Messers* Ostereich, Voss and McNeil, and the prodigious Leticia Gross – and two who, albeit stifled, still exhibited all the jerks, spasms and flurries of hyperkinesias – Helene Yudkin and Audrey Dearth. *Audrey Dearth* ... Busner feels no especial guilt about what is plainly favouritism, for her alternations between the dread entrancement of oculogyric crisis and the busy operation of her invisible lathe are peculiar, even for this most paradoxical of malaises. Seeing her now in the day-room, her tiny frail form enveloped in a chair, he feels she embodies a living past that forever eludes the most penetrating of thinkers – no veil of ignorance, or otherwise theoretically woven partition in the also theoretically woven fabric of the mind, but a real barrier, that he – *I!* – *will penetrate,* once, that is, *we actually touch,* for still it seems to him that they are forever approaching one another along all 1,884 feet and six inches of the lower corridor – *forever approaching, but yet to touch* ... Ready? Mboya asks. Busner nods – they have assumed their positions, Mboya opens

her jaws, then Busner slings in the two capsules, each of which contains a gramme *Brighton Aquarium – fishy treats for performing dolphins*. Audrey remains impassive, taken up by the Saturnian gravity and alien surface of a loose polystyrene tile some way above her head. Busner follows the L-DOPA with a slosh of water from a beaker, then falls to stroking her neck *chicken skin don't snag* as Mboya marries her gums. Audrey's dentures sink back down in the remaining water *the toy diver at Mark's bath time . . .* the distortions in the Perspex *bugsbunnying* the incisors. Do they, Busner muses aloud, ever put them in for her? Mboya shrugs. There is silence in the dayroom apart from her subtle gulp. Glancing towards west-facing windows, full of the risen sun, Busner is appalled by the alien white planet they all inhabit and the grossly etiolated forms that promenade its smooth surfaces, *oh, so slowly . . .*

Miss Dearth . . . Miss Dearth? She doesn't respond *but she hears, oh yes, she does*. They go on and repeat the same procedure for the three male guinea pigs, who are to be found becalmed in their backwater of the men's dormitory. Busner has charged Inglis with ensuring that all of them are got up every morning, cleaned, dressed and shaved. She was sarcasm itself: Ooh, par-don me, Doc-tor, but you want me to pre-tend dey goin' onna journey? Her hands on her hips, her breasts proud, a reddy flush in her cheeks. Busner thought bitterly, Was her go-slow ever called off? but only repaid her with sincerity, saying, Yes, yes, I want you pretend that – because they are going on a very strange journey and they can't very well do that smelling of urine – or with bed sores. This is, nurse, a hospital, not a concentration camp! Which is a conviction he simply doesn't feel: coercive institutions, he knows, only aggravate their inmates' sickness. What was it Marcus had said of his time at the Hatch? mere *trench warfare against mental disease* . . . Inglis is, Busner reflects, the sort who *knows my type . . . it is pointless to try* . . . And yet: sex begets more sex, and he is steeped in it, so it might be *worth a try* . . . Her sex *gapes darkly ahead of me . . . a tunnel – a corridor –*. Are we done here? Mboya says, and they go on with Busner's head aching with the effort of containing *the old booby hatch* as it was in its heyday, with its six miles of corridors, and its rigid segregation of male and female, a notionally self-supporting community with its own farm and orchard, its water supply, sewage-treatment works, gasworks – *gas!* – burial ground, brewery, laundry, tailoring shop, cobbling workshop, upholsterer and – *most crucially for the solution – railway spur* . . . He recovers his wits in the act of caressing Helene Yudkin's plump neck *same as when we had the labrador in Willesden and it needed worming*. Despite Mboya's skilled clamping of her jaws, Yudkin, who is at least seventy, has the vigour to grind her teeth in time with the flexing of her epiglottis. The noise drags him in its undertow *back to . . . Miriam* and her ridiculous machine for polishing beach-garnered pebbles that sits *slushscraping* by the back door. Busner marvels that she complains of there being no washing machine yet tends happily enough to this tumbling drum, the shiny products of which end up scattered all over the flat – on tables, down the back of seat cushions, a small shingle beach drifting across the kneehole desk Maurice gave him when they married. When Busner challenged her over the handicrafts avalanche, Miriam said, The boys love them, don't you boys? And Mark and Daniel chorused obediently, Yes, Mum, which was fast becoming a ritual – the way she expressed that *One for me and another one for me, Pardon me – comes to three!* Miss Yudkin's *foam rubber is fleshy to the touch*, on the Formica side table sits a gelid dish of *ying* stewed rhubarb and *yang* custard that no one has troubled to feed

191

her. On the arm of the chair her twisted hand dances *fingertrot, handango, thumba*, its digits *saucily entwining and scissoring, the nails high-flicking the worn nap*. It's a choreography that he knows he could resolve into quite distinct movements, if he could find the time to analyse it, and that these could in turn be broken down into different sorts of action. But what were they? Did Helene Yudkin recapitulate her own workaday repetitions – those as seamstress, or bakery assistant? Both positions he'd found out that she once filled. Or were these domestic digitations: the turning on and the turning off, the sweeping up and the dusting down? Or, again, maybe she saw them – if at all, so sunk was she in her Parkinsonian netherworld – as simply *divertimenti*. It didn't help him to hold this analogy at bay: that before the war the hospital received all the Jewish admissions in the London County Council region . . . *because?* Convenience, he supposed, keeping kosher, maintaining access to the *bearded weirdos* and the dubious spiritual benefit of their *legalistic mumbling* . . . Hergheraaaaghrrerrr, her nose – if it could only be abstracted from all the rest of her – was attractive, its wings dusted with powder, nostrils *porcelain fine* . . . Moving them may also have been of a piece with the exodus from the East End to the north-western suburbs – a wilderness on the way. Whatever the reason, the end result was this: that over a thousand of them had been concentrated here when the Luftwaffe's bombs fell on Poplar, Whitechapel, the Docks *and my own randomly selected people* . . . But what might be said of the Jewish enkies in relation to the rest? Did they manifest the same divergence as the English Jews from the general population – being *exactly the same, only much, much more so?* Herrrerrrg'herrr –. For a moment Miss Yudkin hesitates, her throat bobs, the L-DOPA begins its hopefully fantastic journey, then she resumes Hergheraaaaghrrerrr, and Mboya says, Shall we? So they stalk with great trepidation into the next embayment of the female dormitory, where a *manatee with a human face* lies on her iron-framed catafalque. You're worried, Mboya says as they stand regarding Leticia Gross, whose great flanks have quaked free of the covers. Naturally, Busner replies, look at her, she remains exactly the same: deafeningly inert. Mboya, as anxious as Busner and at least as exhausted – if not more – nevertheless gets it, understands the still greater mass that is packed into the woman-mountain, a violent compression – the stuff of her hammered mechanically into her casing – that necessarily implies its opposite: an equally violent explosion – *great blubbery chunks of her flung in our faces, our whites hosed down by blood spouts*, and this succeeded by *a tidal wave of noise louder than an H-bomb* . . . We can't go on like this, Busner goes on. It's not that I think the L-DOPA is toxic even at these high doses – although he knows nothing of the sort, says it only for their mutual reassurance – rather, it's that if Whitcomb does start poking his hooter in, without any results I'll be unable to justify the expense. Mboya sighs and adds, Then there's Inglis . . . The fall forward of Busner's chin is *cushioned, I'm getting chubby* . . . You can't, he laughs, get the staff nowadays . . . but he knows the reverse is the case: the staff they have don't get the patients – they resent the extra work involved in caring for the wholly incapacitated post-encephal-itics, preferring more tractable neurotics, bullyable depressives and eager-to-please psychotics. The nurses also resent the reorganisation of the ward required by the increased number of male patients – and all the upset this brings. But most of all they resent Busner, who, unlike most of his predecessors, rather than being content to rely on their greater familiarity with the patients, insists on imposing his own rubric, one that involves regular feeding, grooming and toilet assistance. In fairness to them it is a tall order: their pay has been frozen, their children's free milk has been taken away, the price of beer is rising so fast *they're obliged to brew their own* . . . and moreover there aren't enough of them: heavy and recalcitrant patients cannot be levitated to the ward's only WC, would that they could – he plunges into schoolboy reverie

. . . *a happy moment: the levitating game,* fingers prised into the ticklish armpits and legcrooks of the one chosen for this signal honour while the rest of us chanted *breathy balloon held squeaking* . . . then gently nudged him up effortlessly to the outstretch of their arms, awed by the *eclipse of the classroom light in its green metal coolie hat by his grey serge bottom* . . . They approach Leticia Gross's bed, Mboya tut-tutting at the dollops of her that squeeze between the sidebars. I don't know how she does it, he says – and indeed, it is a total mystery: she's incapable of raising a spoon to her rosebud lips, the nurses are more often culpable of innutrition rather than overfeeding, yet here she very much is, weighing in at *a couple of Henry Coopers or more* . . . Busner has long since cornered her funny little husband, who comes scurrying on to the ward most days, natty in a snap-brimmed hat with a loud paisley band – he has backchat for all the staff and patients, a stream of innuendo that Busner doubts he truly grasps, so innocent does he seem . . . *Confessions of a Dedicated Carer* . . . because then he settles down to ministering to this queen bee, fetching and carrying, straightening and laving – but when challenged he was aggrieved: I only give 'er the food she's given, Doc, he protested. I'm sure it 'as all the whatsits she needs – vitamins an' such. She was always, he sighed, such a dainty little fing, per-teet if you know what I mean, an' now juss look at 'er minced morsels! Busner wondered whether the innuendoes were a form of

194

compulsion as well, *a tic-of-humour rather than a sense of one?* But he said nothing of this to Simon Gross, just as he forbore from observing that it was over forty years since his wife had been anything much besides wholly inert – what would it be like if she were to come back? If this swollen grub were to split open – what might emerge? A dainty flapper, slim arms at her sides, *feet lifted in the Charleston?* Doubtful. – No, I don't understand it either, Enoch, but it's another of these things that convinces me that the very essence of this disease is paradox. Mboya grimaces: he too has seen others of the enkies who're eaten up by their malady – a morbid cachexia that leaves them newsreel starvelings whose lopsided heads have been threaded on to the barbed wire, so that they jerkily tabulate their own fast-approaching deaths. *Its own railway spur.* But, while there are those who're brutalised by the Nazi pathology, others such as Leticia are abusively pampered, fed up by it to a point where they can be *put on show for visiting Red Cross delegations – not that you'd want them to get too close to this!* They have let down the sidebars, her breast exhales towards them, a fleshslide releasing a pocket of fresh gas and another of stale sweat ruinous in its intensity . . . *It's frothy, man,* and this despite the reverent swabbing of her innermost grooves that Busner has seen her husband doing – much as another man might *clean his much loved car.* There is no neck for Busner to stroke in order to provoke her swallowing reflex, only Plasticine coils of fat, one upon the next but all *the colour of five-day-old brisket – there could be maggots in 'em* . . . he wafts away a fly. With Leticia they had thought to continue injecting the L-DOPA into her flesh – after all, she'd so much of it to spare. This was sheer prejudice, because it soon transpired that every square inch of her had its own susceptibilities: she howled when they pricked her, her skin inflamed around the puncture sites, her *ruptured veins wormed to the surface* . . . They had to find another way. Up by her mouth the smell is a worse compounding of food and tooth rot, her head is sunk deep in the folds of her neck, her still pretty face is sunk deep in the folds of her head. The precision of her features is at odds with the waywardness of the microphonic monologuing she softly lisps, fthuck this, fthuck that, fthucking cunt, fthucking arthole, fthuck it . . . fthuck it . . . a superficially chaotic series that Busner feels sure, if subjected to sustained deep-level analysis, would reveal the same complex regularities – arithmetical progressions, basal rhythms and sophisticated counterpoints – that he has detected in all the oscillations of his enkies, especially now that he's withdrawn them from their phenothiazide, their butyrophenone, their amantadine, and all the other muck that ensures they *keep the 4/4 beat ooh-ee, chirpy-chirpy cheep-cheep –. Enough!* Scouting around for a way into this petaline mouth with its foul scent while Mboya stands idly by, the embattled psychiatrist thinks of the nurses' station, which is well stocked with tin ashtrays and packets of Guards, No. 6, Kensitas, Peter Stuyvesant . . . a largesse of stinging smoke that often seems to him to have been savoured, then exhaled, simply in order to *inflame the patients*, since the main means of repression that the staff employ is to deprive them of their own fags. *I want one.* He had given up when he left Willesden – but not because of Doll. No, he associated the *mingling of smoke* with all those *other promiscuities: the messes of mung beans spooned from a common pot, the jazzy linkages of the loud wallpaper that swirled up the stairs, the entwining of the long hair of visiting psychiatrists who'd gone native with the filthy ponytails of the residents, the hooped scarves hula-hooping other hooped scarves* . . . And then there were conjunctions still more suspect – such as their refusal ever to link the men and women in their care to the term mad, or any of its synonyms – crazy, deranged, off-his-or-her-head – but only the uselessism: disturbed. The disturbed men and women copulated, and *fucked with the heads* of visiting psychoanalysts so that they became *engorged Looby Loos whose bellies split open and out tumbled all their passive-aggressive subpersonalities* . . . I'm going to bum a fag off Inglis when we're done here, Busner says, and Mboya says, Okay, fine, but how're we going to do this, I can't see her swallowing the capsules voluntarily, can you? And Busner says, I'm going to find a funnel and length of tubing that fits it, and you're going to open those caps and mix the powder with some water, and that's how we're going to get it down her. Mboya says disconsolately, It'll be like we're force-feeding her. No, Busner checks him, force-feeding her is exactly what we'll be doing. Off he goes, casting about scratched walls and worn-out floors for the items he needs. He passes Yudkin in her chair — passes *Miss Dearth in hers* . . . He stops, turns, enters the special little nook he has secured for her, which has an offcut of window and so an offcut of a view. She sits head up, shoulders back, her face – *that wrinkled void* – has *Kodachrome* and *definition*, gone is the *blurring* of the palsy that makes of so many of the post-encephalitics the restless subjects of long exposure. Instead, she looks right at him with focused blue eyes – *blue!* – and, speaking clearly and distinctly through the plates she must have put in herself, says, Ah, Doctor Busner, good of you to stop by, d'you think you could ask Nurse Inglis if I might have a cup of tea? Stanley does not hear this, for he stands with his back to the housemaid and entranced by all the comings and goings in a dovecote, a solid flint-knapped cylinder which is supported by stone brackets high up in *a traverse* of the kitchen garden's wall. Or perhaps, she adds, a glass of ale – there's a jug in the pantry? He hears this but flirts with the notion that it is one of the busy little doves that speaks, poking its pearly head from its nook, *ruffled up and coo-coo-concerned* . . . White splashes lumped grey and brown stain the brick path beneath his booted feet, the ammonia mixes with the freshness of the dog roses, Stanley hears the sluggish b'boom-b'boom-b'boom of his heart, a single feather falls revolving on the axis of its quill, *white, less so, white, less so.* At last he about-faces: she isn't pretty, her face is flat and wide, her hair *khaki* under her mob cap, her teeth a sort of obliquity in a disproportion- ately small mouth. Still, she is *young – and fresh*, and he senses *willing*, for she sees me upstanding, a hero with a corporal's stripe on my shoulder and my fine shanks well turned in my borrowed gaiters, my cap badge shined and my webbing blancoed this very morning, in the Albany, as Adeline looked on petulantly and said, What the devil're you bothering with that for? And Stanley, naked except for his cap, had grabbed his cock and, tugging back the foreskin so that the *pink umbrella* opened, brandished it at her, crying, Now don't chide me, my poppet, ain't I still your mutton lancer? Adeline had laughed – although not in a particularly nice way.

– Sir? Her coquettishness, such as it is, is all in the Oxfordshire burr and the hip she tilts with her own hand. They are alone in this far-flung sector of the extensive gardens – the others will be at tea and talk under the fruit trees on the far side of the house. Alone in a *cacophony* of cucumber frames, a *volley* of raspberry canes . . . over there will be *loads of eats, ham gashed open on a plate beside a loaf with a healed scar and a mess of stewed fruit brains*. Lording over the tea things will be the skull-head who, Adeline had told him, was indeed an earl. The housemaid isn't pretty and there are blackberry stains on the hand that holds the hip *Wallie, Wallie, Wall-flowers, Growing up so high – All these young ladies, Will all have to die*, but she is young and fresh and for once he does something simply because he can, and because he is angry with Adeline — boldly, he is upon her, her cry choked off by his mouth. There is a moment's resistance – time for him to taste the *tartness* on her teeth, smell the *purloined Pond's on her suet cheek* – then she yields, *We shall want you and miss you, But with all our might and main, We shall cheer you, thank you, kiss you, When you come back again* . . . This, Stanley thinks, I will take back with me: her dove's tongue darting timorously, her small hand finical, trapped in mine, the hollow of her back fitted to my forearm and *arch-ing* . . . *back*, layers upon layers of cloth sliding in all their secret ways. The housemaid accommodates her body to his, *nesting in, relaxing, going . . . all at once limp. Jack Johnson KO'ed in the 26th round* – there is no articulation to her limbs any more – all the tendon strings have been cut. Her tongue slops on his lip, and as he tastes, then gags, on the saltsplash of her blood he hears the unmistakable sound *whip-cracked-into-suet: a head-shot echoing around the flinty trench*. Her forehead and one eye are gone, her mob cap lies on the earthen pellets between the thorny stems of the roses, escaping from its tripe frills are hanks of her khaki hair, beneath which is the stewed fruit of her brains. Stanley lowers her down to the ground gently, *swaddled, she is – in death*. — I propose this, says the skull-head they all call Bertie, that when boys have attained the age of eighteen they should be sorted into three categories – quite arbitrarily . . . He speaks like this: in *perfectly ordered sentences, the words marching out from his bony hole in single file* . . . – Those in the first category should be put to death painlessly in a chamber filled with lethal gases, those in the second category should be deprived of a limb – or possibly an eye – while the unfortunates in the third category should be exposed both night and day to the most deafening noises conceivable. This must be continued, the Donner und Blitzen of shells falling, the mechanical turmoil of the machine guns, until they have all succumbed to nervous affliction – deafness, mental blindness, speechlessness, all the way unto madness . . . Bertie pauses long enough for Willis to put his oar in: And then? The skull-head's sockets swivel towards him dark with understanding – still, he takes his time to respond, carefully anointing a triangular slice of bread with butter, then blackberry jam, before tucking it under his top teeth. – Presently – he chews on the scrumptious irony – they shall be liberated to form the virile future manhood of the Britannic nation. This scheme of mine will, I think, be assented to by the great majority as being altogether more humane – and certainly œconomical – than the present mode of prosecuting the war. They sit opposite Stanley on an uncomfortable-looking high-backed wooden bench with asphodels carved into it: Bertie beside Adeline, Adeline beside Willis. Their heads are almost entangled in roses that twine themselves around a trellis. Their hostess – whose name Stanley caught, held momentarily, then lost – had excused herself a while since, saying, *I must go and lash those Jerry corpses together with wire so the farm-hands may drag them away to be rendered down into tallow* . . . He had thought her haughty in spite of the painted-over curse spot on her long top lip. Haughty and draped in yards of creamy chiffon – he was bemused as to what assistance the two odd hounds could give to her war work. Short-coated on their backs and heads, shaggy at their haunches, they bounded ahead of her as she swept through the orchard and disappeared behind the rounded end of a double-decker yew hedge.

– Mister . . . Corporal De'Ath? Stanley, hearing the rising note of Bertie's interrogative, looks at him, although he is not certain it is he who's being addressed. He enlisted at the Mitcham Road barracks as Death, the bruiser behind the counter telling the boy in front of him, Clear off – come back tomorrer an' see if you're nineteen. As Death he took his shilling and his one-and-ninepence ration money, and as Death he attested that he would fight for King and country. As Death he drilled with a dummy rifle and mimed fifteen rounds rapid fire – and no one thought it queer. He lay in the bell tent at night with the others' piss dribbling on his face, yet none of them said, I'm pissing on Death. As Death, 5665, private, Royal West Surreys, he marched to Aldershot – officers rode alongside, they wore stiff white collars and tan riding boots, and they dismounted from time to time to kick up the dust with their spurs and flash their monocles in the faces of the raw recruits. Private Death's father came up from Devon to see him, having finagled a pass in his usual way – and there was some confusion and not a little mirth when he introduced himself to the RSM as Samuel Deer, but that was soon submerged by many, many tin mugs of beer at tu'pence a mug – the grand spiflication continuing all that night, up and down the high street, with his new mates bellowing, He is a deer inall! for Rothschild had lost none of his easy charm. But it was as Death! that he awoke late and hung over, only to be accused of dumb insolence. And it was feeling like it that he did his jankers, took his pannikin up for his spoonful of bodge, choked it down – then chucked it up again. In the huts, at Sandling in Kent, Stanley lay in his bunk loathing the faint chinks in wooden shutters and waiting for the order to Stand to! *Now dress by the right boys and get in line, First by the numbers an' then by judgin' the time, For you whips 'em out an' you whips 'em in* . . . His cock is in his roughened hand, pulsing: she puts a cylindrical cushion on the high-canopied bed and puts her derriere on this and bades him *whip it in*

201

and let it bide a while . . . That's the way you fix yer bayonets in the *mornin'!* But when he told her what he had done, she clawed his neck and screamed at him, You're dead to me now! Sausages and mash, liver and bacon – all for fivepence. In barracks they lived like fighting cocks, but when they formed up and the GOC Aldershot came, together with Kitchener, to inspect them, it was as Death that he stood there, eyes front, and watching the baggily grey old men make their way along the line, taking sidelong glances at the gravestone faces. As Death he sneered when the MO lectured the company on the horrors of gon and syph, as Death he sat dulling his tunic buttons with acid, as Death he reported to the QM, who introduced him and six others to their new love – *Vicky*. Death and his section were taught to dash forward when the whistle blew, release the ratchet that secured her front legs so they could be swung open and then fixed by tightening it again. Sitting there, as Death, Stanley *removed* *the pins from her raven hair*, and the Number Two ran up and placed her body on top of her legs, her body – her death-dealing body, her 28-pound body. As Machine-Gunner Death he looked on while Number Two fiddled the first round of the belt into the feed block. As Death he flicked up her safety catch, as Death he *grasped her hips* *and, staring her full in her steely eye, gently touched her trigger.*

– Yes – yes . . . Bertie? Stanley has spoken too loudly and the skull-head's china jaw shatters, tea slops from the lip of his cup to the saucer below – a startled fly sways away and banks between the ham and the jam. – Corporal De'Ath – he steeples his *skeletal fingers* – I've no wish to insult you or in any way malign your patriotism, let alone call into question your volunteering – yet permit me to assume, from your presence here alone, that you share a few of our misgivings? There is a *crack* in the human warmth through which *the old house whistles languidly* – Stanley thinks it pretty enough, in its way, what with its mossy mortaring and the drowsy blink of the dark windows, and the nigger spiritual chorus of the yew hedge, *Oh, we do-on't want to loo-oose you, But we think you ought to go-o-o* . . . Yes, Stanley says eventually, yes, I do share your misgivings – this show with the Turks has got lots of us thinking. *The crack is sealed, the corkscrews screwed in, the wire strung, the duckboard put down, the sandbag heaved up – it takes five clear feet of hard-packed earth to stop a machine-gun bullet. The magic lantern clacks, the skull-head snaps* . . . – Well, Feydeau, with a few thousand like this young stalwart here, we'll be in with a chance when the Derby scheme gives way and the Dark Wizard promulgates his Act. Willis, yanking on his beard with both hands, tears a satisfied grin and says, I believe it also, Bertie, which is why the Fellowship would like you to put out a pamphlet of some sort right away. It's bound to attract considerable attention, and we could use it – if, that is, you're amenable – as the point of departure for a lecture tour either late this year or early in the new one. Adeline's strong white hand swaggers past the sugar bowl to fall upon Stanley's, the grievous twitching of which he only realises as she stills it, not with her pressure but the with the blatancy of this naked clasp. Her fingers stroke the powder-burnt backs of his, her thumb slides over the mound of his . . . — Stanley will never become accustomed to the seemingly casual acceptance of their liaison – not only by the likes of Willis, Bertie and the curse-spot-woman, but also by those in her family home. At Norr, where she had lured him after he had spent only a day with his people, her husband lauded Stanley's sacrifice, imposed a suit of good American cloth on him and turned upon them an eye not simply blind but indulgent. When Cameron had caught the boy's nursemaid *sucking on safety pins*, so indignant was

203

she to see them walking in the garden arm in arm, he threatened her with dismissal – and would have sacked her had Adeline not intervened. For all his polish Stanley knew Cameron's sort – his frank face hid a *gentleman's relish* that he shared with *the most appallingly coarse types*. The sergeant of the Buffs he'd burst in on at Bethune, and who simply kept on battering at the drab on the wooden ledge, the two patches of hair on his arse cheeks *thick as fur*. Having been tricked by a snide one into believing the queue of men snaking down the stairs was for loads of eats to which men fresh out from Blighty would have first dibs, Stanley havered between the grunting in the candle-light and the mockery of the Tommies behind the door. The sergeant took his time, *the suck out of her cunny* was his satisfied belch, then he pulled up his breeches by his braces and moved aside to reveal *gaping wet lips, hag hairs, brown-eyed teats* – a likeness of a raddled old woman's countenance that had nothing to do with the young girl whose body it was. The sergeant had turned to Stanley, his panting subsiding, his belly all shivery – he was neither annoyed nor discomfited and his hand said, *Your turn*. Three weeks later Stanley spotted his corpse in the no-man's-land of the Hohenzollern Redoubt – the sergeant had *done a somerset into the wire and sprawled there deadstock, all swole up – the maggots were having a terrific feed* . . . — Stanley frees his hand from hers and tongs a sugar lump from the bowl with his fingers. They say it's difficult to come by now – fivepence a pound. He puts the lump on his tongue

. . . *she is a sweet thing*, Adeline, in her suit of ash-coloured suede cloth and Russian squirrel embroidered in silk. On her shapely breast lies a redingote of lie-de-vin duvelyn and skunk. When she came into him at the Albany, dressed and ready to go out, Stanley made her say it several times over: red-ing-ote, du-ve-lyn, charmed by the sweet sounds. Now the skunk's small dead head nuzzles at her buttons, *she should find it a wet nurse* ... Steam rises in front of Stanley's eyes – *They've forgotten to fill'er up again, the water in Vicky's redingote is boiling! The steam'll give away our fucking position –!* Would you like another cup, sir? asks the maid he kissed in the kitchen garden – she has been resurrected with a heavy teapot in her hands. Oh, yes ... he says, thank you. She pours, then goes, disappearing like her mistress before her around the omnibus prow of the yew hedge. Adeline and the others are engrossed in talk of *some bugger pal, dead in Greece of a gnat bite* ... — they notice nothing, see not the London Omnibus Company 'B' Type, which might've been one of Rothschild's own, that was boarded by the quarante-deux hommes – the lucky ones, just disembarked at Boulogne from the packet boat Invicta – which then carried them gingerly towards Ypres, its soft tyres feeling the potholed road ahead. The 'bus as much its driver was aware that Death was among their passengers. At Poperinghe there's a change of plan and the machine gunners are turfed out. A staff officer with a dummy pack comes mincing up, followed by his batman struggling under a heavy valise. Stanley's section is turned south, to march the forty miles to Givenchy, where they are detailed to join the 6th Battalion of the Royal East Kents at Hohenzollern. It is the first time he hears the name of a Minnie and the first time he hears the crashing howl of one being fired. The canister, which is the size of a barrel and packed with explosive and grapeshot, is so very heavy that it *strains slowly up its funicular rail* into the late spring sky, appearing between two of the house's massive chimneystacks and hanging there for so long that *a couple of rooks flap in to perch on it* ... So long that, had he been inclined, Stanley could have suggested to his companions they draw lots in order to decide which

205

way they should run for cover. He says nothing, only watches, faintly bemused, as the Minnie at last *moans down* . . . – Will ye have a gasper, Stanley? – Yes, thank you, Willis, don't mind if I do . . . *and falls short* on the rockery, lifting all of its artfully arranged stones, stunted shrubs and winsome alpines almost as high as the parabola it has just described. The rockery is now suspended: an earthy cloud trailing filthy plumes that lazily rearranges itself into a rippling curtain of dirt that whips across their faces and the trellis behind them. Looking up from the lit tip of his cigarette, Stanley sees the deep funnel of the crater – the rockery has been obliterated, gone also is the housemaid, who, making her way along the brick path that runs between two stone soubrettes, liaised with the Minnie at the point of impact. The tray she was carrying – buckled and scorched – slams back down on to the table from which it was but lately removed, and a dark stain of tea, milk and water spreads through the damask – shattered crockery is smeared with jam, the skins of crushed grapes *slugupon* Adeline's bleeding hands. Of the maid nothing remains – her corpse, Stanley imagines, will have been subsumed into the yielding wall of the crater, where it will occupy its own neat cubby-hole, death and interment having been achieved simultaneously. – Would you mind passing the ashtray, Bertie? More vampiric rooks limp from the eaves of the house — and there is further bestial after-math, for, from where they have been crouching in the leopard-skin shadow of a silver birch, passing a fag from cupped hand to cupped hand, the other two members of the section come running – caddies, dragging between them the ammo box. The trestle table, the tea things, the cloth, the napkins and their silver rings – all are swept aside. With a virile vim Stanley *never guessed 'e 'ad innim*, Willis opens the legs, then, with equally astonishing zeal, Bertie attaches

206

the Vickers. Set beside the steadiness of the conchies, the machine gunners clearly have a case of the jitters – but is it any surprise they're nerve cases? While the others have been conversing and taking tea, they have had to withstand this drum fire: *Boom-boom! Boom-boom!* Always in fours, a bloodthirsty giant's timpani, *Fee-fi-fo-fum!* The 5.9s come soaring over the house, *Fosse 8*, trailing their smoky cloaks. Jack Johnson! Stanley cries to stiffen his men's resolve, An' we all know where ees bin! He throws himself prone and grasps the Vickers's grips, Willis feeds the belt into the block, and Stanley cranks the cocking lever. The black bastards keep on coming, their pulsating rush gaining inexorably in power and intensity, until, with a final vicious swipe, they impact on a potting shed, a five-bar gate, the lush meadow beyond it and the duck pond beyond that. Bertie bellows, Two francs says you can't get the fuckers on the mortar! as he pulls the tatty notes from his breast pocket. Willis shouts, I'll match 'im! Stanley calculates the range at around a hundred and thirty yards – he pulls on the trigger and the gun pushes back at him, a monotonous battering of recoil, ten rounds every second, so that his arms shake, and his fingers twitch and his teeth chatter. Slowly he takes the muzzle across a thirty-degree traverse, squinting through the sights as rounds nibble away at the corner of the house and clip the yew into shapelessness. Stanley is aware of a dangerous harmoni- ousness between the machine gun and him – he has an intimate knowledge of every nick and bump in its wooden grips, while above the roaring of the barrage he can still hear its *rat-a-tat-tat rag*. It's no use, though – his rounds are driving short into a grove of oak that is steadily being reduced to kindling. We'll have to reposition! he orders the section at the end of a long burst — and Adeline abandons the cover of the low wall to go forward and reconnoitre. *Look at her!* her skirts dragging through the muck, her proudly hatless head held high. There is no fear in her – she has the strange unfathomable conviction that *For aught the Parthian arrows fly, Swallows teeming against a pale-rose sky* she will come through the whole splendid show without so much as a scratch on her – only her abundance of dark curls looser and freer. As another Minnie comes barrelling over, she stands, and, pulling the pistol from her pretty hip, fires the Very light directly at it. A single rifle shot slices through the din – *she spins, tumbles, goes over-rowley* into the wire, which coils around her, cocooning her in its galvanised thorns, until all that can be seen of the sleeping beauty is *her blood-dimpled moonface – her jellied eels* lie on the garden wall. Stanley rises and floats back to the madness of the tea party . . . Bertie sits there – erect yet disjointed – a folded pad of muslin soaked with his own piss tied across the hole where his nose used to be. Willis, ignoring the mustard tongues that lick at the cups and saucers, presides over an engorged teapot. Crowdie? he asks, and, without waiting for Stanley's reply, tilts and pours out the thin brownish gruel so that it surges across the table carrying *dollops of mutton fat* . . . Y'know, Bertie observes, your country needs not you at the Front, it – she – needs you here. Stanley looks sharply at him: the anti-gas pad has gone and Bertie holds a cigarette *the way a southpaw holds a pen.* I must report, Stanley says curtly, to GOC Aldershot by stand-to tomorrow morning. If I don't report there, I'll be arrested, tried for desertion and shot. Willis, with an affecting casualness, has removed his *false teeth* – both sets – and now balances them *atop a splendid honeycomb.* He takes a biscuit and *dips it into his cup of crowdie.* We need someone, Bertie persists, who would be prepared to flout the authorities, who would take up the mantle of the early Christians. At the Front, we appreciate, such gestures are quite, um, inutile – but here, with the NCF's assistance, it seems to me that if the weight of public opinion were to be brought to bear effectively, this would militate against anything too beastly happening – these are still men, y'know, not monsters quite yet. Willis sucks and slobbers on his biscuit, Stanley bends to unbuckle the unfamiliar gaiters. – D'you mind, ol' man? Stanley nods in the direction of the tin of Fellner's whale oil and Willis passes the spermaceti across. Unlacing his boots, removing them and then stripping off his stockings, Stanley commences the salving of his rotten feet, which are *the colour of brisket five days old.* — Moving behind Adeline's face in such a way that their eyes no longer align, for a splinter of a second Audrey sees the corner of her visual field, and this makes her aware of how, while her cheeks rest in Adeline's, and her nose slots into Adeline's, the fit can never be exact – *there will always be these slippages.* That Adeline loves Stanley, Audrey does not doubt – she knows this from the inside, knows it by the frequency with which she darts looks at him, her eyes seeking his. Knows it also because when Willis or Bertie says anything she perceives as a threat to *her Mowgli,* Adeline *daggers* at them. Adeline loves Audrey's brother more than she understands, and in this regard Audrey has a relation with her closer even than this: her weary chest rising and falling inside the young woman's magnificent bosom, her slack skin sucking away from Adeline's taut. Audrey has always loved Stanley *more than I knew –* what was it Gilbert said, *A loaf of bread, a flask of wine, And thou beside me in the wilderness* . . . It is Stanley who is always beside her in this wilderness, *my bumps-a-daisy, my blue boy.* How Audrey would love to unbuckle his gaiters, take off his boots and stockings and rub the whale oil – which is what, they say, helps – into his poor feet. He sits there at the table sunk in his awful funk and overwhelmed by the tea things' inability to move of their own volition: the Dundee cake digging into its willow-pattern plate, the butter knives staking out the napery, the fine cups lined up – all have arrived here post-haste, rushing to outflank each other: teaspoon countering saucer, side plate checked by butter dish. From Nieuport to Ypres to Aubers to Arras, snaking through Picardy and across the River Somme, then looping past Soissons and on to Verdun. Whence came that epochal moment that everyone present – not only Audrey and her little brother – realised that this was how it would be *henceforth and forever*: this inexorable *grinding together* of the manslides of field grey, blue and brown? Whence arrived the apprehension that it is to this that they are fated: the taking of more tea, the exchange of Stottertante, the spreading of Heldenbutter, followed by the cramped movement into a reserve place at the table for a few days before *the entire bloody business* of the tea party without end *begins again* . . . On the Partie Réservée à la Correspondance of the card he had sent from Amiens before his only leave – a photographic card that showed Le Jardin Anglais de la Place Montplaisir, with massy crests of poplar, petrified fountains of willow fronds – he had scrawled, Tickler's jam, Tickler's jam, How I love old Tickler's jam, Plum and apple in a one-pound pot, Sent from Blighty in a ten-ton lot, *Every night when I'm asleep, I'm dreaming that I am, Forcing my way through the Dardanelles with a tin of Tickler's jam* . . . At present *a plump and studious Jew of the ginger type* has taken Feydeau's place at the tea table, while as for Bertie, in lieu of his *cracked-and-glued white face, there is a nigger's* – or, at any rate, the minstrel Audrey is aware of caring for her.

More tea, Miss Dearth? Busner asks. The old woman – *lady?* – has an erect bearing, sitting straight up in bed. She speaks with a peculiar accent as well – cockney *elocuted to death?* No, she says, I think not,

Doctor Busner, but may I ask – they dangle on her every clipped vowel, brown suede and black leather kicking in the dense atmosphere of the summertime ward – why it is that you refer to me as Miss Dearth, when my given name is Death, D-e-a-t-h, precisely so. I can conceive that such a name may seem not fit for a hospital – not encouraging . . . There've been times, I admit, when I've given ground to common superstition and styled myself De'Ath, but, so far as I'm aware, all my official documentation – at the Labour Exchange and suchlike, census forms and so forth – will have me registered as Death, Audrey. Busner and Mboya exchange looks – they hear what she says, they listen amazed to the way she is saying it: her small sharp chin is no longer digging into her sternum, her eyes are neither transfixed nor anomalously mobile in a masklike face – indeed, face and eyes synchronise together in the subtle interplay of normal expressiveness. Gone are the puckering, pursing and pouting of the Parkinsonian mouth, its compulsive grimacing, its incessant chewing. The presence of her dentures gives her jawline definition, plumps up her cheeks, and when she smiles – which she does – the prosthesis is *perfectly charming*. All this is, Busner thinks, still inadequate to the task of expressing the quality of her resipiscence – a return to good health of a miraculous nature. – I – I daresay Miss, ah, Death, that at least initially – upon your admission that is . . . he desires to chafe the backs of her hands, hold them palm-down and strum with his thumbs *vein, bone and tendon* . . . your details were taken down correctly, but that was a long time ago, you've been here at Friern Hospital . . . Busner's cadences are low and hesitant, the extreme oddness of it all is threatening to *gum me up* . . . his thoughts have *a jammy stickiness* . . . and he cannot drag his eyes up from below the bed, where a baby-blue plastic potty *loiters with obscene intent: the chambermaid has long gone – it remains . . .* a very long time. Audrey's face, *scored into innumerable long-playing grooves scratches . . . –* I know that, Doctor Busner – I am not a fool and nor have I been in a complete swoon these past years. If you wish to form some idea of the constitution of my mind, it may well aid you to think of me as a sort of soldier but recently returned from the Front, and afflicted with a very peculiar case of shell shock. Busner is caught and held, he realises, by the selenian serenity of her features. It's a shocker: she is a beautiful woman, and presumably always has been. Turned at last from the darkness, *she shines with self-possessed awareness of her own sex-appeal.* – Can I ask you, then, Miss Death – and please, I hope this doesn't offend you – what year this is? A cosmic anxiety disrupts the ancient's face – her fingers travel to her throat, her face. – I . . . I . . . Well, you can hardly expect – she ironises herself with mock-gentility – me to bother with such commonplaces. Busner, wishing to let her off the hook, pulls the sphygmomanometer from his coat pocket and Mboya rises to assist – but Audrey has pushed up the cuff of her nightie automatically, *it's a conditioned reflex.* While they make the routine observations – Pulse one-twenty, BP one-seventy over one hundred and . . . one-thirty over seventy-five – she attempts her own arithmetic: Is it nineteen-twen—, no, nineteen-thir—? She struggles to articulate the never-uttered decades, until her physician, despairing impulsively of making this in any way bearable, spots a copy of the Daily Mail left on a nearby bed and says, Grab that paper would you, Enoch. Taking it from him Audrey, unfolds its rattling skirting. She looks to her hands and stumbles, Wh-Whose are these . . . old hands, is – is this my morbid affliction? Then a photograph of the Lunar Roving Vehicle on the front page catches her eye. – What an otherworldly motor car, she says, the chauffeur appears to be wearing a diving apparatus – and the brolly they've mounted behind the dickey is . . . is upside down! She laughs, a jollily ascending lark the psychiatrist foresees shattering its skull on the transparent hardness of Now – but, recovering herself, Audrey becomes attentive to the paper's masthead and soundlessly shapes the syllables of the date. Slowly she refolds the paper and, passing it back to Mboya, says to Busner, Will you ask the blackie to fetch me my dressing gown? He looks to see how Mboya is taking it, but the charge nurse, whose long legs are casually crossed, only smiles sardonically and jiggles one foot so that it throws back its *flared cowl*. You do understand, Busner says, the situation – what year it is, how long you've been here? She composes herself before she replies, interleaving her fingers and arranging her laced-up hands on the turned-back sheet. He watches this intently, alive to her tremor – is it increasing in amplitude, in frequency? She *folds her Crimplene throat* and says, Er-hem, the situation – as you term it, Doctor Busner – is indeed quite extraordinary, but bear in mind that for me it has been quite, quite extraordinary for a very long time. If this specific or paregoric, or whatever it is you've dosed me with – what d'you call it by the by? He says: L-DOPA. She says, Eldoughpa, eh, – well, if this eldoughpa stuff continues to do its bit, then perhaps I will have the opportunity to tell you quite how extraordinary it has been for me. However, now is not the time, nor can we sit here all day twiddling our thumbs . . . The post-encephalitic is doing just that, the digits twirling with exceptional speed and suppleness. Busner gulps, riveted by the spinning thing, until along comes Enoch, stately enough and bearing a lime-green Terylene robe, its shapelessness emphasised by his modest headway. The garment is ugly, far too big for her and with a horrid fake-lacy collar – he expects her to reject it, and perhaps for the unaccountable resurrection to end right here, *throttled by its multitude of tiny nooses.* But no: Audrey takes the gown, holds it aloft, throws back the covers, slides her legs out, rises and *twirls the cape around her shoulders.* In profile: *the reworking of Annigoni's Queen* for whom the wonky bedside locker, the filmy-plastic water jug, the chipped green paint of the wall – all is folded into a backdrop, *a distant landscape of blue ruled-over hills.* Hands clasping the gown together, she advances perfectly steadily, – Excuse me, and Busner jumps up and pulls his chair from her progress – they watch, the nylon curtains clinging to them, as she proceeds the length of the dormitory and on into the rest of the ward. Stately, yes, and also legato, her hidden legs supplying the rhythm upon which her melody of movement is sustained, *Doo-d'doo, doo d'doo, doo-d'-dooo, doo-d'-dooo!* The two men are seized by the akinesia of others of the others whom she passes by – one paralysed by a pillar, a second arrested half risen from a chair – and whom she nods to, acknowledging these frozen subjects of her icy realm. *Doo-d'doo, doo d'doo, doo-d'-dooo, doo-d'-dooo!* On she lilts in her own netherworld – the ill-lit tunnel system of her affliction. Audrey has a word to describe her condition: I am unmusicked, she would whisper to herself – un-mu-sicked, but now she's *musicked again.* Another patient, not a post-encephalitic, sits at a table, a pencil in her hand its point inserted in a cogged Perspex disc that whirls in her fingers, throwing off graphite rings across the donated paper. Outside the windows it is early afternoon and a heavy summer downpour draws Spirograph patterns on the puddles spreading across the flat roof of Occupational Therapy. — What was it, Audrey reflects, that Gilbert had said – yes! A universe comesh when you shiver the mirror . . . shiver the mirror of what may appear to be – on the shuperficial level – the leasht of individual mindsh. *Doo-d'doo, doo d'doo, doo-d'-dooo, doo-d'-dooo . . . I am the piano – my memory the roll, my thoughts Doo-d'doo, doo d'doo, doo-d'-dooo, doo-d'-dooo . . .* The pane she leans her forehead against is hard and cool – that it is transparent doesn't mean it isn't there. He had said that thing and she was furious – furious! – that she had come all the way from Woolwich after a twelve-hour shift, braving the crowds in Beresford Square to struggle dangerously over the steering gear and ascend to the top deck by way of the stairway's rail, paid her ha'penny and then another tu'pence on the tube up from London Bridge – *escaping the thunderbolts underground together with thousands of others who lay there in mounds on the platforms* – only to have him smuggle her *like a common trollop* into his rooms above the colour shop on the Gray's Inn Road so that she might hear this – *this! the puffed-up little popinjay* declaiming these lines to her from his latest infantile fantasy, which lay there in light tinged greenish by the desk lamp's shade. Lay there, line below line of his girlishly rounded handwriting in green ink, in a quarto-sized manuscript book covered with green morocco that sat upon a similarly mounted blotter, handwriting that described – or so he had glossed it – his approbation of his own works, blinding him to the depredations exacted by hers – a society of the not too distant future in which the sprawling cities had been gathered up into pinnacles of glass, steel and concrete, of the sort lately found on Manhattan Island, leaving the countryside free not only for agricultural production – since, due to the chemistry of Herr Haber, this would require a fraction of the arable land employed heretofore – but a new Xanadu of pleasure gardens, and indeed entire tracts that could be allowed to revert to their autochthonous state, the greenwood providing for young men who would otherwise, perhaps, grow too softly effete – what with the ending of all wars through the institution of universal plenty – to practise the old chivalric arts of *queshting, joushting and sho forth* ... Audrey had been furious that she'd lent so much as an ear, let alone her intellect, to this lantern lecture, one that contradictorily diminished the magnitude of his pomposity and his conviction that it was his principles – rather than his weak lungs – that placed him on an upper storey of his own glassy moral pinnacle, one vastly elevated from the trenches where the Tommies choked to death on gas and blood, or the munitions factories where the Thomasinas lost their teeth and hair to quicksilver poisoning, or even yet the residents of a humble suburban villa near to Woking – three waif-like kiddies, a poor drab of a wife – who were lucky – according to Feydeau, whose general approval of his comrade's freedom from all convention balked at this – *if they clapped eyes on their father and husband more than once or twice a year.* It had been cold outside – along by Mount Pleasant there were banks of refrozen snowmelt pitted with the city's inexhaustible *filth*, and a special constable *picking at the rime on his tin hat.* At the hostel it would be colder still. Hating herself, Audrey had subsided on to the chaise-longue given to him by Venetia Stanley. Hating herself, she allowed him to unbutton, then undress her, in the smarting haze of his Logic smoke – and hating them both, she lay beneath him jerking not with pleasure provoked by his caresses but the repetitive motions of operating the lathe – twirling, cranking, pulling – that had been *dinned into every nerve-fibre* throughout the twelve-hour shift. Spent, in repose, there remained at least this charm clinging to Gilbert: his utter disregard of his pigeon chest or the scabrous pate that showed through his feathery hair in the steady illumination radiated by the large gas fire's white-hot coralline elements. He lay back in her arms and used the cork tip of his Logic to link with smoky ribbons the surrender at Kut, the battle of the Four Courts, the routing of Villa's desperadoes and Smuts's Kilimanjaro escapade, pinning these to an immaterial map that showed *the whole shtate of play*, and how it was that – despite all contrary indications – the *harmonioush reconshiliation* of capital and labour under the leadership of the scientifically enlightened and philosophically minded was *closhe at hand* . . . Audrey deprived him of his Logic and smoked to its *bitter end* . . . *His Dream*, the postcard is captioned, the photograph is a montage: a Tommy stands beside a bit of fence fringed with sweet william and marguerites. His rifle dangles from his shoulder, *lethal as a butterfly net*, his cap tips back at a bank-holiday-boater angle, and a stubby pipe is tucked in his hand. It's his wispy moustache and whimsical expression, as much as the ridiculous props and a painted backdrop of the setting sun cloudily encircled, that suggest the war is being fought near Epsom, and which make the peculiar womb that floats above and behind his head all the stranger: *is the baby-face in the womb His Dream?* Or does his sweetheart, in point of fact, bear no resemblance to this *winsome thing – her hair pinned up, her lips pricked red* – but is instead *a fat baggage of a fishwife, her bosom sagging, her tongue coarse in her broken mouth?* Gilbert snuggled further into Audrey, the featheriness polishing the side of her breast *is this my mind child?* He smelt of old flannel and fresh tobacco – she could scarcely contemplate the sordid business of rising, washing out her privy parts, then dressing for the fourth time that day: she had made ready in the dark at Plumstead, and when she arrived at the Arsenal changed into her rough ticken overall. At the end of the shift she had stripped it off, stuffed it in its bag and hung it on her hook in the shifting house before getting her incendiary hair down from its ugly net. *Shifting house* . . . Gilbert's rooms were a sort of shifting house, one in which she changed – as did he, although the skin he stepped into was always either too big or too small for him: at times he loomed large over the city, his words uncial type at the head of newspaper articles, his speeches calling forth turbulent crowds, his chubby face with its *dishrag of moustache* affording him this curious distinction: *a great weight of inoffensiveness*. Wealthy enough, for a so-called socialist, his suit coat slung over the back of his chair showed wartime privation, the collar and cuffs turned, the buttonholes worked over. A tin of Iron Jelloids shone greenish on the desk, proof, if any further were needed, of her lover's anaemic weakness. — There were six operations to be performed on Gilbert Cook – *six operations to cut his threads, internal and external, and to cut his recesses*. Audrey's arms moved in and out, her fingery bits pressed into him *here* and then *there* – Ah! No! No – No! He bucked and squirmed and his heels drummed on the chaise-longue – but, thinking of the soot-black buildings and monstrous *slapperti-slapperti-slapperti-bang!* of the overhead belts that powered the lathes, Audrey swung her headstock over him and continued her operations automatically, kissing him behind his ear, at the nape of his thick neck – she was tired but her desire to control him was on direct drive, she could not stop until the fitter came to regrind her cutter. She smoothed over the swarf on his lower belly and grasped the fifth piece to gauge it *and turn it upside down* . . . Gilbert gasped, Oh! In the soot-blackened buildings that house the New Fuse Factory, they never see the shell cases, only the fuse caps, and of those caps Audrey sees only their pins. – Aha-h'n-ha-ha! Adjusting her position so that his left buttock wound into the very threading of her, Audrey felt the complexity of glacé silk moving over and under. – Ha-ha-h'n-ha! There was Iron Jelloid breath in her nostrils – they never see the shell cases, only imagine their smoothly tapered brassy cones thrust into the breaches of the guns by Vesta Tilleys in rational dress. They *never see the shell cases* . . . Gilbert Cook has insinuated his hand behind his back and so he plays upon her while she works upon him, until with a clumsy Oof! he sits up, leans over and retrieves the latex prophylactic from where it lies beside the chaise-longue, rolls it back on and puts it inside her, not troubling with the tin of lubricant. The *cold rubber* smells in her mind, the headstock completes its six precision operations, the fuse pin drops down on to the tray below, *Vaseline spurts from the lathe* . . . They never see the shell cases and yet without the utmost assiduousness on their part they will remain just that: cases, inert sheaths full of nothing. *Doo-d'doo, doo d'doo, doo-d'-dooo, doo-d'-dooo*, the little melody that the autopiano salesman said was by Johannes Brahms infiltrates Audrey not as melody but as the subsiding rhythm of their *coitus* – a term gleaned from a booklet given her by Hilda Peabody and read by dwindling candlelight in the matchboard cubicle of the Plumstead hostel. The oil – the lubricating oil. They issue the lathe operators with aprons, but there's nothing done to protect their hands – the oil causes rashes, lividly pink corruptions of the skin that fill Audrey with funk, funk that in turn drives her on towards still more danger, past the Examining Shops, where defective caps and detonators are weeded out, down the muddy cobbled lane seamed by rails that runs between the new buildings, their tan brick as yet unbesmirched, surrounded by freshly seeded grassy plots upon which swank newly planted trees in June's green tulle. Beyond these lies the riverbank of reeds and sedge and marsh mallow, its white heads *crazed a little by the wind*. If she keeps her head level, Audrey can feel the last drops of astringent lotion cupped in their lower lids. Once every sixteen days they wash out the

canaries' eyes, and for the next five or six hours the world kaleido-
scopes, doubly so if Audrey looks into the oily waters of the ditches
dug around the Danger Buildings, which are connected to a larger
channel that debouches into the river, spreading rainbow swirls
within which stretch and curl the weird designs of those Futurists
whose own oils she had seen with Gilbert Cook at the Manor House
Gallery before the war. Was it this they had been attempting to
portray – *these spillages back into the past?* The Danger Buildings have
their own dirty-side canteens and on balmy days such as this the
doors are left open so that sparrows fidget in from the wider world
and peck at the crumbs that fall from the canaries' yellow hands.
Sitting at one of the long refectory tables, staring out through the
doors, her mouth gummed up with potted meat, Audrey is confused
by all the disruption: the ugly blare of a marching band hauling past
the British Grenadiers is accompanied by this solo shout: Eight-
five-seven-nine! Which also means *Or-dree!* Because for *that old lay,*
the Deputy Principal Overseer, there are no names. A motor car
pants past a chauffeuse at the wheel, and for a moment, framed by
the doorway, Audrey sees a short kinematograph of a familiar right-
angled triangle cleaving the sweetly choking engine fumes.

– 8579, Death? The DPO is right by her, staring down at the
remains of the munitionettes' tommy – crusts, crumpled-up wax
paper, tin mugs – with official gravity: for all her bulk *she's not the
hungry-gutted type.* – You are Death, aren't you? She pronounces the
name with relish, pleased by this exception to the rules. Yes, miss,
that's me. *Virile,* that's the word for the DPO – instead of gussying
herself up with key- and watchchains, *she should be playing a trouser
role.* She says, Mister De'Ath, the Controller of Artillery Production,
is here to do an inspection of the Danger Buildings – he isn't, by

some caprice of Jove, a relation of yours? Audrey is emphatic: No, miss, no relation at all that I'm aware of. The DPO hooks her thumbs in her broad leather belt. Capital! she says, in that case you shall help Mister Harris to show him round – come along now. She leads Audrey out of the canteen and then heads straight out through the shifting house. Audrey, still in her khaki overall, cap and Arsenal shoes, calls, Miss, I'm in my dirty-side togs, but the DPO doesn't break her stride, flinging back: Well, young lady, you can hardly give him an accurate impression of the work we do here if you're in your ball gown and pearls! Albert waits in the sunshine beside his official motor car: he is slender, youthful, so very tall in his top hat, emphasising cut-away coat and well-tailored striped waistcoat. The only marks of the burthen he bears are two comical smudges underneath his bulgy grey eyes *that might be greasepaint*. While he is introduced to her and Mister Harris, Audrey's brother doesn't show – as she knew he wouldn't – the least sign of having recognised her. The Prime Minister, or so they say, has engaged a suffragette driver – Audrey wonders if Bert has been compelled to a similar gesture, but the young woman – girl, really – behind the wheel has the silly painted face of a debutante, and wears her peaked cap and gauntlets with the affected, dégagé manner of someone at a promenade concert. Moving through the shifting house under the drear light that washes down from the high windows, Audrey doesn't hear the explanation of the safety procedures, but *Don't av any more, Missus Moore, Missus Moore, please don't av any more! The more you av, the more yull want, they say, An' enuff izzas good as a feast any day!* And sees Rothschild brandishing his moustache cup so that tea spatters across the oilcloth, and Olive with dull eyes and the imbecilic expression of *a calf soon to be poll-axed held to his cheesy cheek.* Auntie, who takes care of the shifting

221

house, shows the Controller the fillers' fireproofed gowns and explains how, while soft and pliable when new, they are now stiff with the impregnation of mercury and powder. If you please, Mister De'Ath, we had better get on, says the DPO, there is a lot to see and I'm certain your time is valuable. In her tone Audrey hears not contempt but the steely resistance of a social superior forced to bend to an inferior. Bert, she supposes, must hear this *off-key note* all the time, although he gives no sign of it as the DPO talks up and down to him of the shift system, and points out the regulations posted on the wall together with hortatory posters: HIS LIFE IN YOUR HANDS, A CLEAN WORKPLACE IS ESSENTIAL. From time to time he turns to his secretary – a ferret-faced young man who has the crabbed walk of the club-footed – to ensure he is taking notes *for form's sake*. – And over here, Mister De'Ath ... they troop across to the ambulance basket and the DPO hands Bert the inventory, which he runs his *Datas eye* down, committing immediately to memory lint dressings x 20, Germolene tubes x 20, hydroperoxide ointment x 20, etcetera ... Then the DPO, her frogging of key- and watchchains clinking, takes her leave: If you'll spare me, Mister De'Ath, I must give the shift absentee list to the Principal Foreman ... — Mister Harris pushes the swing doors to the Filling Shop and their rubber skirts drag in all the furious hubbub, the clatter of the chain hoists and the slap of the drive belts and underlying it all the relentless salvos of score upon score of wooden mallets, rising and falling and hammering a leaden rhythm into the Honeysuckle and the Rose. Moving towards the singing canaries, Audrey feels those other bodies carried between the shape of Bert and the shape of her: *casts, plaster-white and plaster-light of Vi and Olive ... and Stan ... Missus Moore, who lives next door, is such a dear old soul, Of children she 'as a*

222

score! Bert, Audrey knows, sends small but regular sums of money to Cheriton Bishop, sums that enable their parents to keep Olive at home rather than *sendin' her to the booby-hatch*. Vi is well situated at the GPO as a hello girl, her *empty head* filled with salutations, digits, valedictions, *over and over*. She is, Mary Jane writes, *walking out with a* —. – Miss Death? They have reached one of the benches where Trotyl and guncotton is wadded in alternate layers into the 50-pounders. It is clear that Mister Harris wishes Audrey to demonstrate, for he asks the canary to step aside – she does so, jaundiced hands fidgeting with the stuff of her tunic. The Trotyl's aroma has sweet rotten pears insistence, that of the guncotton is pervasively metallic and oily, and, for all the ventilation, it lies in the air just as the handfuls of fibrous lather lie on the bench, one of which, *heedless of his manicure!* Albert lifts to his pyramidal *hootah*. Strange to think of him leaning back in a shaving saloon, *guncotton covering his long face while the barber strops his razor* . . . Strange to think, the Controller says – and, despite his voice being raised, it is evident he soliloquises as much as he speaks to the others – that when this material is subjected to a further process, it becomes constituent of silver nitrate, which is used for the kinematographic film. Audrey thinks, at least the Tommies have steel helmets now: everyone has seen the kinematograph, seen the *umbrellas clustering in the muddy gutter, then lofted over the top into the buzzing rain* . . . The guncotton in the Filling Shop, Audrey imagines, is already impregnated with all these quicksilver scenes: it has the power to throw up spouts of dirt, shatter the limbers of gun carriages, the fetlocks of horses, the skulls of men – or only provide the means to show this: the *whirlwind reap'd for the dear, dear folks back home His dream* . . . Albert, the Controller, wishes to know the precise detail of the routine, and so Mister Harris gives him the overall picture: the numbers on each shift, the separation of tasks, the forming, pressing and filling machines, the division of the sexes with skilled male fitters kept back from the Board . . . *for now.* When the Foreman defers to Miss Death on the matter of the detail, saying, We would've preferred to keep this young miss in the Fuse Shop, she's a skilled lathe operator herself, Audrey interrupts, Pardon me, Mister Harris, I'm mostly concerned with the filling machines, but I do some manual work as well, as it pleases Mister Simmonds, besides it helps all concerned, we feel, to distribute the tasks a little more evenly . . . Everyone sees what she means, which is that the Trotyl should be distributed *a little more evenly.* The canaries who for twelve hours a day take the wads of guncotton and pack them into the shell cases, then sprinkle in the Trotyl, then tamp this violent-rending-asunder-in-waiting down still more with mallets, before packing in more guncotton, sprinkling in more Trotyl, until . . . *until no one in their right mind could conceive of all the mayhem* crammed into the smoothly tapering brass cylinders, with their *nipped waists and fetching bonnets.* The canaries, who are paid a supplement that they spend on gay ribbons with which to lace their boots, in defiance of their grim and unflattering uniforms, the canaries, whose hands, necks and faces bear the sickly taint of the explosives they handle all day, the canaries, who *trill cheep-cheep-cheep the home fires burn-ing* as their own eyes smart, the canaries, who are, Audrey thinks, the little sisters of the blue-gummed pieceworkers slathering on arsenic – *yes! a poisoned sisterhood, with their cheeks whited-out by Westray's,* no surprises, then, that they don't want to *av any more* . . . She is done and leans her hip hard against the bench, the mallet dangling from her hand, the filled 50-pounder cradled in her arms, her burning cheek pressed against the cold brass. The Controller says, Thank you, and, tucking his watch back in his pocket, turns to Mister Harris and Mister Simmonds the Overlooker, who has come scurrying up, *his moley nose questing for preferment.* – With four fillers per bench and forty-eight benches per building, and assuming this munitionette is exemplary – say a minute faster than the representative filler – that means only thirteen thousand, eight hundred and twenty-four filled per day, insufficient to keep up with the rate at which casings are being cast and braised or caps turned. You will show me, Mister Harris, where you're storing the unfilled backlog, a stockpile the men at the Front won't thank you for.

All cheeks are rouged but Audrey's – who is used since infancy to Albert's prodigious calculations . . . *Am I right, sir?* His skin has an unhealthy colour and his body, Stan thinks, is *twisted out of all decency.* His is a curious character, being at once *a gibbering wreck and a Tartar to boot.* He has scratched himself a sort of dugout behind a cattle bier built with the glossy-red bricks used in these parts. — Am I right, sir, Stan repeats, you're not able to go on? The officer cowers – he's lost his cap so there's no real way of establishing to whom he belongs, if anyone – he could even be a spy – there's talk of such characters: immaculately shined boots, in officers' uniforms but without regimental badges, members of *an international army of the higher orders.* The others of Stan's section are boiling the dixie for tea and propping opened tins of maconochie in the embers of the fire. He's a tall man, the officer, which makes his craven-baby posture each time one of the 4.7s that surround them fires a salvo all the more pathetic. But whenever the bombardment ceases, his voice resurges, building in timbre and volume until he speaks with parade-ground authority: You mustn't imagine, he says, that I've always been as you see me – I'm a regular, I was with the BEF at the beginning of the whole show

– you understand, Corporal? I was seconded to the French Fifth Army, but not for liaison – I'm NOT STAFF! – yelped above a salvo that rolls away to a serenely ignorant horizon. In its wake Lufty says, Steak, tripe and onion, and Feldman counters: Fried fish and fried taters . . . We were near Châlons on the Marne, the officer continues, it was a fine summer evening like this – except, he snorts, not like this at all because it was beautifully silent, YOU KNOW SUCH EVENINGS, CORPORAL, when the light begins to fade to the west and this becomes in some fashion mixed up with all that silence, A LARK CRYING OR A DOG barking in a farmyard sounds as peaceful as the breath of a sleeping babe . . . There is a longer lull in the firing and squatting down Stanley scrutinises the officer: the man is, he thinks, at least forty years of age and has the mobile wishy-washy face and buck teeth of a rabbit. His madness Stanley views compassionately only as this: a soiled and ill-fitting suit of clothes he wears on top of his uniform. *Kills all insane persons in fact? Yes, in mercy and in justice to themselves* . . . comes to him, an exchange between characters in a torn book recovered from a dugout after a direct hit, a novelette about a perfect New Amazonia of the far future, wherein stately Hermiones and Beryls do away with the feeble-minded . . . *by means of the black drop.* The smell of the heated maconochie has become in some fashion mixed up with the elemental cordite, and so Stanley considers this: might it be possible to eat a field piece? – We were sitting there watching the sunset – the officer sits hunched in his crazy billet, his moustache *scratching between his well-tailored knees* – the Frenchie and me both smoking our pipes, and the fading light was precisely, mark me, precisely like the silk chiffon sleeves of the dress my sweet young wife had worn to the Summer Exhibition at the Royal Academy, what . . .? Maybe only a month or so before the Boche invaded, when, without any warning at all, the WHOLE HORIZON BURST INTO FLAME ... All scenes of this nature are, Stanley believes, deathbed ones. All speeches of this type – halting, impassioned – are valedictions demanding mourning *right away.* He has heard *more than my fair share* at the Front, and come to believe that *they summon the bullet, the mortar and the shell* ... Fuck Widow Twankey 'ere, says Lufty, who's come up to the ruined bier and stands with his steaming mess tin in his hand, looking down at them. Lufty's nose has a bloody knob of cotton wool stuck to its end with plaster, his chestnut hair is all awry, his brown eyes *blink uncontrollably* ... Fuck Widow Twankey 'ere, he says again and kicks a toe-load of the parched earth on to the cowardly officer. Stanley relapses still more on to the resounding ground, NO, he shouts, BRING ME OVER MINE – I'll 'ear 'im out. Go on, he says to the officer, who, now it's been said, he recognises to be *more panto' dame than rabbit,* GO ON! It was ... the officer resumes in the aching silence after the concussion ... an artillery bombardment on a wide front – the first either of us had seen. Up until then – and this was August of '14 – no one had ever seen such a thing, you understand? Stanley nods and takes his own mess tin from Bobby, the Squad Number Five, who's shaking almost as badly as the officer. It is a measure of how far gone the man is that he does not respond to the smell of the food – he is beyond any sustenance, out there in the shadowland he *has captured and holds alone.* Horror gripped me, he says, like a bloody bastard ague – y'know, Corporal, that Frenchie and me, we were regulars, we'd seen war but it was war with hard blows and straight dealings – now we both knew, as we looked upon that curtain of fire, that everything had changed, that this ... thing – whatever it might be – had us in its grip, it was holding us tight in its grip, it would keep us in this grip SHAKING WITH THE EFFORT of holding us so tightly, gripping – and it would never let go its gripping. D'you see? All the shells, all the mines and the mortar rounds – your machine-gun ones too, they're only its shaking, d'you see? The shaking of that MONSTROUS HAND WHICH never moves, can never move.

The officer has extended his clenched fist: it shakes above Stanley's mess tin, but he goes on wielding his spoon, dipping for the blackish lumps of potato and flipping them aside. Each time the nearby battery fires another salvo, the officer's wrist jerks dramatically, *And whosoever will let him take the water of life freely* . . . Stanley rattles his teeth with the corner of the mess tin and the watery broth bleeds from the sides of his mouth. He rises up from his haunches too fast and the fuchsia sky and white gun smoke swirls about him, then he staggers, rights himself and kicks the dust from furrow to furrow of the fallow field, the mess tin dangling from the end of his arm, turnip flecks . . . *balling in the dirt.* A few paces from the smouldering fire Corbett and Feldman sit either side of the belt-filler. It pulls Feldman in by a length of pocketed canvas, and it rotates Corbett's arms with a turn of its hand-crank. It resembles, Stanley thinks, a giant apple-corer, but instead of peel there's this lumpy tongue of .50-calibre machine-gun rounds. *Pull, rotate, pull, rotate* . . . so the belt-filler makes use of its animal components: *pull, rotate . . . pull, rotate . . .* On the far side of the tumbled-down fence the jellyfish of camouflage netting rises and falls soundlessly . . . *in this ocean of noise* – the gunners, stripped to the waist, scamper about the heaving creature, their devil's tails of braces bouncing on their backsides. Up above an aircraft comes whining back from the lines – a Blériot Experimental – Stanley can see from five hundred feet below the black box of the camera clamped beside the cockpit, and the *delicate damsel flies* him back to the models he made before the war – how he had thrust himself *suddenly silver skyward* . . . there to stare directly down upon a broad green field across which surged flying wedges of blue-coated hussars, their cuirasses and helmets coruscating, a battle elegant and silent excepting *a piano accompaniment* . . . — When they came into the trenches at the Redoubt, the London Pals withdrew, leaving behind their hastily buried dead – rotting hands and feet punching and kicking from the parados – and their rubbish: a litter of tin cans that rattled in the night as the rats did their rounds under the singing wire, and their *stupid fucking signs: Leicester Square, Piccadilly – Fulham Road too* – painted with blanco on to bits of board that they'd stuck in the mud. They had thought, Stanley understood, that they were making of these corpse-heaps and grave-craters a landscape that neared home – with the fosses of Hampstead and Harrow and Crystal Palace lumping up in the distance, and the tidal flats of the Thames between them and the Fritzes. — He had seen it differently: London, the workshop of the world, with its cutlers, welders, carriage-makers, turners, pianola-assemblers, piecework cobblers chewing on brads *'til they spit blood* – London, with all its frenzied bending and shaping and fabricating this-out-of-that had really been an anticipation of *this*. Standing in the July field, his cock in his hand, piss *thick as soup* hosing the earth between his boots until it liquefies, Stanley Death feels his way towards a future he already occupies, a future in which annihilation will be assembled *piece by piece* – a bayonet thrust here, a trench mortar going off there, a shell arcing way over there where the Eindeckers strafe the trenches, but all of it under the same roof and part of the same process: the bantams and the big 'uns, the puling varsity boys and the hobbledehoys fed in

229

from the railheads, each one sheathed in buff, then fed on into the reserve trenches, then hand-cranked to the front line, then methodically taken apart. It was indeed as Bertie had said: they were of the third category, and so were to be subjected to the noise that went beyond noise, shaking bone in flesh and flesh in skin, until all that was left were maconochie in the mud and the rest in *streamers hanging on the old barbed wire*. Although *my Lord Skull* was wrong about the machine guns: their ceaseless hammering manufactured not turmoil but *a perfect system*, one that holds him in thrall, leaves him standing cock in hand. Many of the Tommies – half of Stanley's section included – believe as an article of faith that the war will go on forever, that having reached this state of absolute stasis – the armies evenly matched, their offence and defence cancelling to nought – that *it can never stop* . . . leastways until the last two men are poised, rifles parrying, bayonets pricking, and so topple forward into eviscerating extinction. Finally putting it away and strolling back to where the others lie, stunned by their feed and the barrage and a bottle of vino they pass from hand to hand, Stanley dissents: It is a matter of time, he thinks, of how you understand time: *Nisi agit non est*. The scientific adventurer pushes forward the crystal bar and the days zoetrope past and the housekeeper zips through the flickering laboratory again and again. He pulls up on the bar and she does it backwards, again and again. The drapes swish open and swish closed, the wind rises, falls, howls once more and the walls crumble away to leave him in his complicated cage of an apparatus, the weeds coiling up about its posts, struts and ribs . . . still Stanley is there, it is now – now and forever Feldman *lovingly oiling* Vicky, poking the rag into the grooves of her water jacket and running it along them dexterously. The others – Lufty, Bobby, Corbett and the Sergeant – are playing crown and anchor, laying the *mothsoft cards* down tenderly on an ammo box. They behave towards one another with elaborate and superstitious care. Luff may have stage fright, being the newest member of the cast, but the others have seen many performances – they cannot believe they will all make it through the forthcoming big show. But why not? *Now is forever, the jellyfish dances in the ocean of noise*, the shocked officer lies in spasm on his side, his hands and feet sketching possible trajectories in the dirt that follow some map or plan long since encrypted in his otherwise jumbled mind, Marcus must've come in by the main gates, turned right off the roundabout and puttered along the preposterously named Western Avenue, passing Blythe House, Villa No. 3 and the Upholstery Workshop, then manoeuvred his way between the spur and the Occupational Therapy Annexe, before finding a place to park. Busner watches him from above as he unloads his scaffolding-pole arms and legs from the car – *that it would be a Morris Traveller was predictable*, although not in fact a prediction the younger psychiatrist had made. What could be foreseen, he thinks, was that these portable biers would soon enough be dumped in the cabbage patch, their olde worlde bodywork – half timber, half sheet metal – rotting into compost. Marcus, his feet splayed, bends over to carefully lock the car's door before disappearing from view. He must know, Busner thinks, of some *secret tunnel into the castle keep* ... But surely, he says aloud, meeting Marcus at the ward's entrance, it wasn't still there after what, thirty years? The old man looks him up and down before replying – Marcus appears more intent and focused than Busner remembers him from the spring. He eyes Busner's white coat ... *he'd like it off my back.* On the contrary, he says at last, change at the Hatch was always a drawn-out affair, Shabbat without end – maybe it's why I remember the nights best. There was no requirement for me to be there, of course, but that awful . . . inertia was more bearable in the darkness. Some nurses patrolled from ward to ward – perambulators they were called – others just sat there by their nightlights, no reading . . . sitting there – another kind of catatonic, if you see what I mean. Walking with Marcus from the nurses' station into the day-room, then into the dormitories, Busner is grateful for at least *some bustle*: a cleaner mopping a glossy-brown coat on to dun lino, Hephzibah Inglis clopping by on her hard heels deigning to smile, Vail coaxing senile Mister Hedges to eat *none too gently* . . . Why, Busner puzzles, do I want the ghastly bloody place to look good? But he knows, it was always thus: each time he returned to Redington Road, his skinny legs bruised and his flabby tummy pinched, his trunk wadded with laundry often distempered by his own fearful piss, he'd soon enough be extolling the school's virtues to Uncle Maurice – how they'd won so many rugger matches, not that Zack had been playing – or put on a splendid As You Like It, not that Zack had been acting, although acting was what he did: nothing could be allowed to tarnish the lustre of the Founder's Trophy. And now – as then – Busner longs to run away and hide . . . Enoch emerges *prefectorial* from a curtained-off cubicle and, introducing them, Busner expects racialism from Marcus – but far from it, he *loves thy neighbour* and shakes his hand warmly while Busner explains, Mboya is my right-hand man, then launches into a little speech: I honestly feel we've achieved an amazing breakthrough here, Doctor Marcus. You said when we met that when you were here in the thirties it wasn't treatment you were engaged in but trench warfare against mental illness – just now you said that any change was a drawn-out business, well, I believe L-DOPA is our . . . our . . . tank – it's enabled us to break out of the trenches, to end the war of attrition and to make a rapid advance! Busner cannot take back the note of *stupid triumph*, or ignore the shadow of doubt that passes across Marcus's face. They have reached the first post-encephalitic patient, Reginald *call me Reggie* Voss. He came back to us, Busner says, last week – Monday, wasn't it, Enoch? Yes, Mboya says, Monday and on a comparatively low dosage of the drug. Marcus stoops down in his three well-made pieces of suit *despite the heat*, and brings his *duckbill* in to Reggie's soft and guileless face. They must be, Busner thinks, close contemporaries: the tall and short – yet what worlds separate them! Marcus ironised by his own imagined sufferings – and those of others – Voss just roused from slumbers innocent of napalm and Calley, spy planes and Apollo, *what dreams must he have?* May I ask you, Marcus says, what it is you're doing? Reggie, *outfitted by Oxfam*, sits in the chair by his bed, a stack of some sort of certificates on a tray across his knees. Each of the thick cards is impressed, in green, with the stylised silhouette of a tree, and as he speaks he continues uninterrupted the task of taking one, signing it with a Parker flourish, wafting it to dry the ink, then adding it to the pile of the already authenticated. These, Voss explains, are trees in Israel – I mean, he laughs, not the trees themselves, obviously, but the p-p-p- – desperate that his guinea pigs should perform well, Busner nearly intervenes, but Voss recovers licking spittle: shlupp-upp-p-paperwork for 'em. Y'see – he continues signing and speaking – I'm by way of being a Zionist, if you know what that is, and just about the time I was taken poorly there were grants and purchases of land being made. I'd plans to go out to Jaffa, y'know – yes, yes . . . and now I've discovered that all we dreamed of has come to pass! Then . . . he falters . . . I found out that both my parents had passed away – a terrible loss, yes, but when Cyril – Busner whispers:

His nephew – told me there was this sum of money that was mine in the Cooperative Society's bank, well, I knew pronto what I oughta . . . that is make for them – grow for them a memorial . . . in our homeland. Cyril – a treasure he is – looked into it all . . . the whole business, see . . . Busner anxiously notes the flapping of Voss's left hand, his breathing is rapid and shallow – the former, he hopes, is merely gestural, the latter not tachypnoea in the Parkinsonian sense but healthy excitement . . . now they'll have a forest of their own! Yes, the Charles and Hester Voss Forest! On the heights above Hebron, with cedars of Lebanon, yes, oaks and all sorts – yes! Voss's slippers thrum on the lino, ink spots dash across the candlewick bedspread. Marcus covers the dumpling hand with his large and bony one, It is marvellous, he says – but then as they leave the forester he turns snide: From Burnham Wood to Golders Green, eh . . . Busner ignores this – he's struggling with the resurgence of his own *palilalic verbigeration* as he tries to impress on Marcus the miraculous character of these . . . – Renaissances, rebirths – that's what they are. Really, you must understand, Reggie Voss there – he was manifesting the most extreme opisthotonos – bent back, right back – and ticcing all the time. He could barely speak – only grunt, barely feed himself let alone go to the lavatory – and now you see him, Marcus, d'you see him –. – Yes, yes. Marcus puts the same *dread hand* on Busner's arm. I do see it, Busner, and I'm of course familiar with the condition of post-encephalitic patients . . . their insensibility, their agitation . . . *Does he really remember, though?* Tormented by the idea that Marcus *takes me for a charlatan*, Busner bridles his enthusiasm, and, as the unusual ward round progresses, he attempts to give a calm clinical picture of the reborn. It's hard, though – what to say of Andrew McNeil, who, before being started on L-DOPA, was so hypotonic he couldn't be propped up in bed let alone maintain a seated posture, whose voice was a faint whisper, whose *face* was twisted into a grimace now anguished, now terrified, whose troubled sleep was indistinguishable from his waking nightmare, and who, upon resurfacing from the stagnant pond where he had floated face up for more than forty years, told the psychiatrist he had experienced it as a continuous present, *an awful and unchanging Now?* It occurs to me, Busner proposes as they stand watching McNeil – red-nosed and ruddy-cheeked, *a garden gnome*, happily engaged with a crossword – that it's movement that's essential for the formation of memories – that memory is a somatic phenomenon, and so if a mind can no longer manipulate its body in space, it loses the capacity to orientate within time . . . He tics with his tie, and would reach for a Biro to note this insight down were Marcus's expression not *so hopelessly sceptical* . . . The ward is hot, the angled casements seem not to vent the sodium hypochlorite vapours and urinous eddies, but only draw in the far-off shushing of traffic on the North Circular. — Busner is gripped by terrible doubts. Is it all a dream, my dream? Is it me who needs awakening? The elderly patients stirring for the first time in decades . . . turning to one another and speaking with such animation, not of their ordeal but of a universe of trivia regained: ballpoint pens and Nimble bread . . . might they be better off –? He can only press on: I'd like you to meet Mister Ostereich here . . . *De Gaulle standing tall*, back turned to his visitors, he does something to a photograph frame with a flannel . . . He's the most, ah, eloquent of the patients who've been given L-DOPA. Ostereich carries on wiping – so Busner persists with his own flannelling: He has described for me vividly what it's like to think of nothing – yes, thinking of nothing, he says, is not the same as thinking nothing, so, no Zen state of enlightenment at all but ... but a dreadful copybook sort of arithmetic, two-equals-two-equals-two, like that, over and over again. Or else, I am what I am what I am – like that, but this isn't an ex-is-tential question, it's only ... only an iter-iter- ... iteration of identity, its fact, nothing more, two-equals-two, I-am, d'you see? Marcus withers at him – Mboya appears anxious, Busner is saved by *Peter Cushing, re-emerging from the laboratory of his past* and including them all in a stare both accusatory and baleful. He says, For all this time I now realise that I was a sort of picture frame, you best believe it – quite like this one ... He fumbles with the clips, Mboya moves to assist him, but Ostereich wards him off ... No, no, no need for you – I have it, like this, see, tip-top ... Ostereich has freed the photograph, which shows uniformed bandsmen stiffly posed around the brassily silent cacophony of their instrumentation ... This is me ... he holds the frame in front of his face ... the framing of nothing, I had lost the general idea of what it was to have ... a general idea! His tongue comes out to moisten his lips and Busner wills it *back in! no fly-catching today, thank you very much* ... Ostereich's nose was broken, Busner imagines, in a Vienna playground in the early nineteen hundreds – he couldn't have served with that name, at least not in the British Army. Gratifyingly, Marcus is disposed to engage with Ostereich: And now, he asks, how do you feel now? The reborn one's Adam's apple bobs, his milky eyes well. – It is ... It is ... he chooses words from a child's lexicon ... altogether fab-u-lous, quite gorrrgeous! Germanic *r*'s are ironed in to his locutions ... I feel that Doctor Busner here must have transfused me ... He waves the flannel and the photograph ... taken my diseased blood and replaced it with champagne! As they leave the Viennese behind, Marcus says, You think yourself, what, a Christian

Barnard of the mind, is it? That it's as that confused old man says: you've transplanted their brains – or that it's as simple as apheresis? No, no, man, no drug could do this – no matter how revolutionary. You've seen results from pathology, I assume, you understand the histopathology, yes? You've seen the full extent of the lesions in these patients' brain stems, hmm? This is real observable organic damage, Busner, scrambled eggs – you get that, yes? What Busner appreciates is the *pecking* Missus Marcus must've been subjected to as for aeons she lay flayed on the plastic runners of the St John's Wood flat, together with cold cushions, the bony elements of old gas-fires, chopped liver ... *going off.* He can *taste* the despair. Marcus is, he reflects, the sort of man who, tiring of civilisation and all its discontents, wants to be alone – yet insists on someone else being alone with him: a hostage, the Geoffrey Jackson to his Tupamaros guerrillas. Still, there's no real harm in him – he cares. More than anything Busner desires the approval of this near-homonym of his uncle, so he holds his breath and counts *one, two, three* ... now that five of the post-encephalitic patients have begun to care for themselves the staff's workload has lightened – *their tigerish bitterness poured back into its tank.* I think ... he at last exhales, that you may be underestimating the brain's capacity for functional reorganisation, Doctor Marcus. It seems to me that science is not well advanced enough for us to assess the impact of a global dopamine deficit – you see ... these patients, living statues they were, and now see them: doing crosswords, signing certificates – speaking, like Mister Ostereich, with great insight about their condition, surely this proves that health goes deeper than any disease? Mboya continues to hang about nearby – Busner senses his mind churning down below, keeping him hovering on this wide smooth apron of the moment, while beyond there is *sea spray, the crude shapes of Channel freighters* . . . Where does he live? Tooting – and alone: a used tea mug set down on an *old laminated wireless* . . . a carpet cleaner, its brushes *furred with lint* . . . The long journey to Arnos Grove every day, his black hair brush drawn through the smutty flue – he says he doesn't mind – he reads. Busner knows this because his charge nurse is *more up to date than I am*, and talks over lunch in the canteen of the veil, and the master–

slave relationship, in the Lacanian sense. I shall, Busner thinks, suggest he consider analytic training – introduce him to some people at the Tavistock, *enough is . . . enough*. Which is what Miriam says: Enough is enough. She's no Missus Marcus and has drawn for him a final line to cross: Either we all go away on a proper holiday, together, or I'll take the children, with the firm expectation *very Miriam, that* that you will not be here in this flat when we return. Not there . . . with the fired-clay tiles and the thrownness of pottery lamps, not there . . . with the straw placemats . . . and the book with the headless, *legless woman-suit on the cover . . . handles at its hips* . . . An image it would doubtless be . . . *outrageous to admit* – even to himself – that he *finds . . . arousing*. His post-encephalitic patients, he knows, experience a strange *sleeeeewwwooooowing down of thought . . . the turntable dragging treble back to bass . . . a stickiness as oneinsightstrugglestodetachfrom . . . the next. A life in the day* – also its exact opposite: a pell-mell—onrush of the mind's stream that makes it impossible to grasp the shape of thoughts before they are . . . *torn apart.* Standing there with Marcus, he cannot tell which it is that afflicts him. Have they been like this for seconds . . . or hours? *I'm com-plete-ly craz-eee* – The thing I find most remarkable, Busner, Marcus remarks conversationally, is not the coming back to life of your enkies, but the mixed ward – I'd heard about 'em, of course, but it's still quite a revelation to see male and female patients together. Seems to me this is the thing that'll combat institutionalisation – at least until Mister Powell does away with the asylums altogether. Marcus strokes and pets his pot-belly in its tailored papoose – his expression as he looms over his younger colleague is kindly, at odds with what he says next: It'll all end badly, Busner, mark my words – what goes up . . . Well, I detect in you a need to make a big splash, be the big I-am. I've asked about and heard you were mixed up with that buffoon Laing – I daresay this L-DOPA represents another cure-all for you, that having failed to do away with schizophrenia, you're now set on abolishing another disease . . . One of G. C. Cook's aphorisms, isn't it: A universe comes to life when you shiver the mirror of the least of minds – but by the same token there's the mirror cracked, the mirror shattered . . . Well, ahem, possibly I express myself a little forcibly –. No, Busner says, no, it's fair enough, you must say what you think . . . *And crush me* . . . but please reserve your judgement until you've met some more of the patients, spoken with them. Marcus clears his throat, her-herg-h'herm, a lengthy and complacent gurgle. I came, he says glutinously, specifically to see my Miss Deerth, may we do that now? *For what we see is what we choose, What we keep or what we lose for-èver* . . . Sometimes, Busner thinks, the pop singers put it best, and to Marcus he is caustic: Death – she prefers her given name, now she's come back to life . . . *Don't – let – it – die, Don't let it die-ie-ie* . . . Why, Busner wonders, am I quite so plagued by these tapeworms spooling through my mind? Is it my unconscious ventriloquising through Hurricane Smith? And there's no thunder without lightning . . . — Is the figure dead? It's a male – for certain – and lies on its back, arms and legs flung up and apart, neck and head also elevated. Perhaps, he thinks, such violent deaths can only be visited – graphically at least – on the formerly stronger sex. Is there a suggestion of neckwear? He fondles his own unnoosed throat sympathetically. The black silhouette sprawls at the base of an orange triangle outlined in black, above it – and presumably to blame for its violent spasm – there is a single bold lightning strike. It reads DANGER OF DEATH along the base of the triangle – which strikes Busner as not commanding, rather laconic: Were you, old chap, to shin up the pitted concrete stanchion and, by poising on that bolt and swinging your other foot wide, circumvent the bunch of razor-wire, you'd be able to caress the porcelain, grasp the crackling hum . . . Would you, he wonders, in the last jolt of time before your heart short-circuited, and you were left dangling and jerking, with rotten smoke drifting from your ears, be able to feel, with fingertips questing for life, the steely filaments plaited into this hank of high tension? Busner pants, breathless from his rapid descent down from Alexandra Palace through the green nullity of the park, and, although there's no one about to witness his frailty, he disguises it as a sigh, Aaaaaah . . . Anyway, he decides, whatever my age, my weight . . . my training shoes would probably earth me. Between them on the *stale cake* of the path lies a single thick-cut chip – *how awful to have this menu description readily to hand!* Busner interrogates it with his gaze, tracking over the subtle tans of its fried glaze. Anything – fugue, or trance, or otherwise blind enslavement to the force of the subcortex, is better than this: the walk-in wardrobe labelled TREATMENT ROOM, the tight huddle of white coats and grey nylon tunics observing the niceties, Excuse me, d'you mind? While buckling restraints, checking the pulse, injecting the five mils of intravenous curare, and wiping the dried saliva of the last victim from the rubber mouth-guard. Aaaaaah . . . No one, he believes,

240

would know me: a slope-shouldered and knock-kneed moseyer through a dusty São Paolo square, *no evidence in my string shopping bag of the Nazi doctor I once was* . . . Mid-afternoon and there isn't a soul to see him as he makes his way through the Queen Anne wheelie-bin sheds and landscaped parking spaces of a, quote, prestigious housing development, unquote, *We were only obeying orders . . . It was a sort of group-think . . .* These Busner finds to be pathetic justifications, when the truth was: *We were making it up, improvising . . . using whatever there was to hand . . .* Before ECT they had put patients into comas with insulin, then resurrected them with glucose *sweet life ebbing in and out of them* . . . Or infected them with malaria, believing that the high fevers and hallucinations would drive out psychoses, a scorched-earth policy that was dignified: pyrotheraphy. Maybe these bizarre – and wholly unscientific – procedures had had some benefit, but only because of the fuss that was made over patients who otherwise were locked up on the ward and *imprisoned in their own screaming heads* . . . But really, the fuss was for the psychiatrists and the nurses, who dug holes in brain tissue and then filled them in – it was part job creation and part The Good Old Days: shticky plaster on the wounds, everyone involved a quick-change artist, rushing from unit to treatment room so they could *do their turn* . . . He had believed then – what? He hoped he'd been more honest than his older colleagues, who thought their manipulations were surgical, excising mad thoughts and the mad bits of the brain that thought them – whereas Zack knew that mental illnesses were creations quite as much as inflictions – worlds starker and simpler than those of health, but totalities for all that. This would have been back in *the seventies, a white-lined decade . . . along roads . . . around sports pitches, and white piping describing your ball sack in the blackout . . . Sheepily thick sideburns that needed shearing – my own included. George Best . . . the corrupt and booze-raddled face of Reggie . . . Maudsley – Maudlin – Maudling . . . Each era . . . new and old blended . . . the utterly familiar paintjob slapped on . . . Then . . . along the passage of the years, appears utterly alien and distempered once more. How could we have gone there/thought that/worn that/mouthed that/read those/taken part in such happenings, ma-an? Didn't we get it: Nothing comes of nothing.* Standing before a bow window crammed with tulle, behind it the ghosts of strangers' domesticity, Busner can no longer ask of himself, Where am I going? He knows – and understands also that using net curtains to guard your privacy is as futile, surely, as employing tenses to divide time? He sees the tubular-steel-legged beast of burden, smells the carbolic and hears the pathetic imploring of the Cordelia who's forgotten to learn her lines and so imagines – *I'd like to go back to the ward now, please, I'd – please . . . –* that hers is a voluntary role: *Nothing comes of nothing . . .* What was his name . . . the black chap? Mugabe? No, Mboya, that's it. He'd been far more pragmatic. It works, he'd said, we don't know why it works but it does – and he always said the whole disgusting thing, electro-con-vul-sive the-ra-py, not the sanitised initials we all took refuge in, so conflating it with its harmless and diagnostic cousin. Enoch said, Zack, I've seen men and women who were lost to the world come back after it – *It*. April radiation on the back of his neck as he moves on along the road, *Preposterous! It's not meant to be this way, the sun should shine in the past and in midsummer only, illuminating the tow-headed kids, hands clasped and swinging dizzily in just-threshed hayfields,* it beats down on the huge roundel of the ornamental bed which had been planted the previous year with rings of blue lobelias, white asylum and red begonias for the thirtieth anniversary of the Few. With this target plainly before him Busner can no longer pretend to aimlessness – from the ornamental bed on the roundabout *swings out all the rest of it:* the diverging roads, parked along them the odd Ford Anglia or Hillman Hunter. He sees the waxy banks of rhododendron screening off the Willow Shop, the Staff Club, Blythe House and Villa No. 3 – he sees the lawns, lush green where the gardeners' watering cans have wavered from the beds, otherwise parched tawny, in places scraped to grey by the repetitive circling of patients let out to be exercised by their demons. He cannot deny where he's going, only cavil that while he did tape on the electrodes on occasion, *I did pull the lever, pull the lever, pull the lever . . . but not at Friern, I never did it at Friern . . .* For there, in case meetings, he hung back and *made myself small . . .* shrinking away from what he saw as simply another demonstration: electricity as spectacle, Humphry Davy at the Royal Academy, with admiring ladies looking on, pulls the lever and the nurses and doctors pointedly ignore the contortions on the couch, the bucking, biting and jerking, and *the ozone smell and the singed-hair-smell . . .* The sun should shine down on childhood – on his own and those of his children. He can see them – all except Mark, who stands at the edge of the lawn in the shadowland, *already wearing at the age of seven . . . eight? his uncle's life-mask –.* The cars are tightly parked along Alexandra Park Road, with only an inch or two separating one rubber neoplasm from the next. So bulbous, the cars: vehicles in utero, in common with so much else in this timorous and ageing era, they've been shaped and smoothed so that their Thalidomide wing-mirrors and morbidly obese wheel arches can present no DANGER OF DEATH. Inside the steely cauls vestigial arms pull and push at levers, vestigial feet push pedals, the repetitive and compulsive motions damped down by *an amniotic fluid of new car smell* . . . They bounced when the current took them – a detail he had never heard spoken of: that their bodies were for long seconds vulcanised. If he glanced about the treatment room at that precise moment – whichever hospital it was in, the 'Bec or Napsbury – Busner would see the same studiously vacant faces bent to this strap or that button, or perhaps laying a *technically conciliatory* hand on the bound limb of the black silhouette that sprawled before them, Aaaaah . . . He's reached a main road – beyond it electronic signboards on poles, beige-painted steel bafflers, waxed redbrick – all the *gubbins* of a newly renovated overground station. Or is it a hospital – because, now he ponders it, all the city appears implanted with hospitals: small cottage ones in detached villas and terraced rows, large concrete ones dating from the sixties, seventies and eighties that now house multi-generational tribes of the economically paralysed – then there are the glass- and wood-slatted ones, more recent these – that act as sun-traps for convalescent bourgeois. *Not to mention* . . . the private ones, which are ranged around courtyards, their mock-Regency façades discreetly masking the moans of OxyContin addicts. He feels the talismanic shape of his Freedom Pass through the soft stuff of his tracksuit bottoms – *Freedom in what sense?* Only a monetary one, for, far from allowing him to do *whatever the hell I want, it's sharp corner spurs me on* . . . to train, tube or bus, where he must sit: conscious but completely powerless to influence the route taken by the vehicle – *as powerless as . . . its driver.* Hot grease spots Busner's throat as he marches across the road in time to the p'pop-pop-pop-p-p-p-p'popping. He shushes along the privet alley, mounts the bridge, bongs over the tracks and descends to the Station Road, where, beyond minicab madrasa and fret-worked Taj Mahal, he locates a

kiosk-sized café, in its window entrance gap-toothed lettering P E &
ASH, 2 GG, A ON,   USAGE, HIPS & EANS. There's a newsagent next
to the café – he might sit, the Guardian folded to a single column
and tucked underneath the lip of his plate, *as men of my age in all ages
do*, the eggy vapours condensing on the inside of his glasses, making
it quite impossible to read about the cardigans being worn on the
campaign trail. He is hungry – and the antidote for famine is well
known: white sacks stencilled UN F D A D P O AM. But what was
the antidote for chlorpromazine? Kemadrin? Kema- Kema-droll . . .?
Chemodoll? It is as he exercises his liberty and the barrier opens that
Busner realises: There can be no resistance any more – no GG or
USAGE, no procyclidine or orphenadrine, let alone mere diazepam,
can tranquillise the through train that blasts past, sending diesel
shockwaves dirtying over him . . . *Along comes Zachary*, trailing guilty
streamers and wondering only this: If *time, the March Hare, has got
there first* – time, lolloping along the gutters, yellow lines toothpast-
ing from its rear end, so that on the streets where this spoor has been
laid nothing can ever stop again: the traffic must course on, just as
the National Grid sparks through rail and brain. . . . *Along comes a
slow stopper*, from where he stands by a Plexiglas-fronted cabinet full
of these curiosities: berry-flavoured water, Skittles, *A Mars a day
makes you work, rest and* . . . Busner can see a few passengers gathered
by the doors, their bodies swaying, pathetic counterweights to the
train's mighty inertia. Gracie said this: that once, when she went see
her people at Reading, she changed trains at Windsor and people
were still speaking of it – how the Russian troops had come through
in the night. One train must've stopped for a while, and they got out,
walked up and down the platform, arm in arm, looking up at the
Castle keep, their soft fur-lined boots soundless on the flags. Anyroad,

the next morning all the slot machines had been jammed with rouble coins. Fancy that! Those daft Russkies trying to get out bars of Fry's and what-not an'juss loosin' all their brass, they must've been browned off. Rouble's probly a lot of money in Russiya . . . Audrey had only wondered: Do they really have slot machines on Windsor Station? but now she laughs good-humouredly at *dear Gracie*, who's done so much to make the painfully cramped cubicle they share bearable – pinning up grey silesia over the single windowpane because it's a trifle gayer than blackout cloth, although such fripperies risk the ire of the hostel's superintendent, Missus Varley, who, maddened by whatever tincture it is she keeps in her own room – or the lack of it – dresses down the girls, slaps and fines them. Gracie, sucking on her bottom lip with her skew-whiff teeth, leaves off her rearrangement of the mementos with which she's lined the single shelf above her black iron cot to say: Wotcher laughin' at, Ordree? then comes over to where Audrey sits on her own cot, lays a hand on her arm: Aw! Yer not laughin' at all, yer cryin', aincha? Wonderment in this, because Audrey Death is known to all the canaries to be *hard as nails*. — Audrey looks at the sulphurous hand on the embroidered sleeve of her best blouse and says, No, don't worry, dear, I'm not crying – or laughing at you – I'm only trying to stop . . . this . . . Her hands speak for her, scampering on her lap: fugitive creatures that, *tethered by my arms, can flee no further.* At first glance they appear seized by bumbling chance, only Audrey who experiences their darting and their digging from within knows it is not random at all, but a peculiar elaboration upon the repetitive motions they have been describing all day: the yanking of the levers and the turning of the hand-cranks that operate the filling machine, the hammering of the mallet she wields to pack down the last cupfuls of Trotyl and the final wads of guncotton

246

into the shell casings. Yes, an elaboration peculiar and subtle, because it is not these motions alone that her poor hands replicate, there are also – in the casting off of looped forefinger and thumb – those of the turret lathe she operated for six months in the New Fuse Factory, just as the sideways flicking of her right-hand little finger represents the fossilised trace of all those grosses of *p*'s struck during her three years as a typewriter for Thomas Ince & Coy, Manufacturers of Umbrellas, Fine Ladies' Walking Parasols, Garden Tents and Beach Pavilions, etcetera. More dreadful yet, the uncontrollable crooking of the thumb on the same hand reaches back still further to the hours of thimble drill at the National School in Fulham, as does the tweezering together of her left thumb and forefinger, a tic, Audrey realises, that occurs precisely once in every seven yanks on the invisible headstock lever, and which runs a hot wire through her nerve fibres from the needle drill that once accompanied it. – C'mon – come on! Gracie grasps the mad hands in hers and their energy runs up her arms, *shivering her timbers. Dear Gracie*, whose skin and hair now match, so that once she's pinned it up and stands before the glass putting on her paint for the concert party, to Audrey it seems she is creating her drooping lower lip, her small eager pink eyes and her ever-so-slightly sunken cheeks for the very first time. *Dear Gracie*, who preserves in her tin trunk the dried-out nosegay he bought her at Barnet Fair, together with all the Field Service postcards Gunner John Smith has sent her from the Front – two or three a week – making a pack as thick as it is wide, which, on the one occasion Gracie permitted her to hold, Audrey could not desist from riffling, so that, despite their sender's diligent crossings-out, they blurred into a single – and more sincere – incomprehension. *Jingling . . . jingling . . . jingoism . . .* Audrey hasn't shown her friend

247

the cards she receives from her own sweetheart – missives that in their own way are perfect complements to the Gunner's War Office effusions. I'm ready, she says, blowing out the candle. Gracie has opened the door and the gasoliers in the passage make of the photograph of *my own sweetheart on my own shelf an Ivory-light:* Stanley Death, Corporal, Machine-Gun Corps, whose image floats in the central panel of a leather-bound triple frame, flanked to the left by the Cheriton Bishop Deers, and to the right by Violet the Hello Girl, posing in her VAD uniform beside a Doric column on the capital of which sits a field telephone. Stanley, lolling in his oval of lost time, his hair combed straight back from his fine brow, his face unsullied as yet by war or any other carnality, his expression proud and puckish, while between his creamy flannel knees there is propped one of his own flying machines, its flimsy parallelograms, triangles and circlets of wood and wire covered in glacé silk. Albert has only half the picture, Audrey thinks, as she walks behind Gracie along the corridor of the hostel – a single-storey cage knocked up expressly to house the canaries – and what can Datas do if he doesn't have all the data? . . . *So you're wrong, sir!* Audrey knows the Arsenal's production not by statistics and calculations but by touch and feel. Of the thirteen thousand, eight hundred and twenty-four 50-pounder shell casings filled daily in the Danger Buildings, she adjudges a large percentage – perhaps as high as fifty – will be duds: the wadding too loose, the mixture of Trotyl and guncotton incorrect. Moreover, of the thousands of casings as yet unfilled and piled up under tarpaulins, in sheds and lean-tos, Audrey knows that many will have been imperfectly brazed and welded – *the tonic wine of rainfall drips through their torn seams* . . . Gracie, no more than the other girls whose boots rapper-ti-tap on the rough pine floorboards, should not be blamed

– she should be walking out with her young man beside a giggling brook, white linen skirts pressing upon nodding irises and perky primroses, not serving as a helot under the whip-eye of Missus Varley, who stands grudgingly counting them out into the summer evening. The hostel's superintendent, Audrey reckons, steals at least three shillings every week out of the ten the munitionettes hand over. Embezzles – and squanders still more on keeping the gas-jets lit solely to provide her with a pretext for barging unannounced into the girls' cubicles, on the lookout for the little bottles of Sanatogen so many of them have come to depend on. Bottles she confiscates – and drinks. *Dear Gracie* takes Audrey's arm and they follow behind the others as they scatter across the broken and uneven ground, raucous geese with russet and tawny plumage. Out here on the fringes of the city there are forlorn paddocks housing windy horses, the broken-down fences are kept standing by nettles – a jerry-built row of houses is unfinished, it simply stops short in a tumbledown of rabbit hutches and pigsties. Down towards Greenford a handful of factories up thrust their stubby chimney fingers, smearing sooty marks on the glowing sky, while from the unseen river comes the desolating t't't'toooooooooooot! of a tugboat. Long before the war and its blackout this region was, Audrey thinks, benighted – a dark penumbra around the London sun. The lych-gate of the mouldering church the girls wade past through meadow grass lies drunk on its perished hinges – the graveyard is *coiled with barbed blackberry wire*. Whence, Audrey fumes, will Gilbert's gleaming towers and motor-car highways come? What machine can thresh plenty out of this chaff? Light stripes the underside of drapes and doors, delineating the church hall, and Gertie, the *corker* in the lead, turns towards it, striding high-hipped and more manly than any man, the others in her train. They are living in that precise moment of the earthly revolution when colour fades, silver nitrate dusts the grass and the gravel surrounding the hall, and *gathers in drifts along the ditches – all is resolved into dark shapes and quaint silhouettes* . . . We 'ad t'do it, didn't we, Ordree? Gracie says out of the blue – and, despite the unexpectedness of this remark, Audrey knows of what she speaks, so, drawing Gracie tightly to her, close enough to feel the eccentric beat of her toxified heart, she replies, Yes, we 'ad t'do it, we 'ad t'do our bit, no matter what we thought about the sheer folly of it, and the dunderheaded vanity, we 'ad to set aside our own ambitions for the duration – we couldn't abandon 'em over there. *Dear Gracie* whimpers, An' . . . an' I'm awlright, ain't I, Ordree? Audrey recalls the *peachy young thing* in suffragette colours that she met at the WSPU meeting near Arnold Circus and is grateful that eventime has drained Gracie's skin so she can with conviction say –. I say, says a one-legged boy with officer's crowns on his collar and a comical fez on his head, who leans against the wall of the hall, you gels have a confounded cheek! The others have clattered inside and now the Honeysuckle and the Rose blooms out from the open door. – We've an absolutely spiffing feed all set out, and you're loitering out here gassing. The boy's jaunty air, the flash of the monocle across his breast as he swings round on his crutch to usher them in – are the false notes plucked upon his broken body. The cold black barrels of his pupils bore into his ghostly face . . . *Chu Chin Chow.* There is indeed a spiffing feed: bottles of ale and ginger beer, pots of meat paste, four large cottage loaves and a tin basin full of éclairs. We scrounged 'em from a baker's in Sidcup, the boy explains, juggling himself between his crutch and a laughable pipe *he should 'ave a rattle* . . . Chappie said we were robbing him out of house and home, but when I marched the whole squad on to the premises, well, he could hardly refuse us – sacrifice an' all that argy-bargy . . . He falls silent as the singing lulls to an end, its short-lived harmony supplanted by the ceaseless monotony of the anti-aircraft batteries at Eltham Palace. In here Audrey sees there is colour: the blacked-out windows have been dressed with red, white and blue bunting, as have a framed photograph of Queen Alexandra and a framed text of the Lord's Prayer. There are poesies of summer wild-flowers tied with ribbon to the chair backs – it's *as gay as all get out*, apart from *the vellum faces of the poor cows*, and the broken and band-aged bodies of the British bulldogs – whose hair shocks from tightly wound crêpe, their faces are masked by it, their arms are slung in it, and, as Audrey travels from wound to wound, the Tommies commence their own miserable rondeau: We're 'ere because we're 'ere because we're 'ere! to the accompaniment of Jews' harps, mouth organs improvised from combs and tissue paper, and the grim drub-bing of an upright long past tunefulness: Rainin', rainin', rainin', always bloomin' well rainin', Rainin' all the mornin', Rainin' all the night . . . is seamlessly joined, then smoothly gives ground to: Where are our uniforms? Far, far a-waay, When will our rifles come, p'raps, p'raps one da-aay –. Why, asks Gertie the corker, do they still sing these songs? They're home now . . . A chubby-faced sergeant hangs on her words but cannot answer – has he not noticed the orange tint to her exuberant locks, or wondered why she wears white cotton gloves to nosh on an éclair? He sweats copiously, labouring over his next breath, H'herrr, h'herrr, spittle greenish and blood-flecked gath-ering at the corners of his mouth. B'herrr, he manages, b'herrr – then fights his way through the tangles of tobacco smoke to the door and is gone, heaving, into the night air. Audrey ignores Gertie's question – because surely it's obvious: they sing the songs of over there, because from now on and forever they will remain *over there – this is no quick turn, the chairman will never hammer them off. There's no escaping it – lying in flooded shell hole or bloodied dugout, the sleepers can never awake! Every faltering trump must surely be their last – yet still another h'herrr comes, there's no gassing – they're all gas cases . . .* The Welsbach mantle in its wire globe flares brighter than the sun, Missus Varley, her face caricatured by Bass – *Insist on Seeing the Label!* – stares through the cracked pane of forced gaiety at Audrey, who sinks down on to a providential chair and discovers herself eye-level with the groin of the boy-amputee. He – or a draper's assistant – has pinned the trouser leg up under the skirts of his tunic so that it appears that half his leg remains, but now, from the way the cloth lies flat, Audrey can tell it's all gone. Behind the complexities of his button fly she knows of this: the aimless target of traumatised flesh and sawn bone, his poor little *ding-dong a'donging down there in the dark, boneless, never able to support him* . . . She leans forward, hugging her nausea to her breast, seeing amputees hung about with false legs: the pleats of an irrational dress that hides where they are divided. Her breath catches, then curdles in her throat – the hands that Gracie stilled go to work again, finding a plastic wheel and *twisting* this, seeking out a moulded handle and *yanking* that. The tabletop tips water into a lap that's ceased to exist — for she's lying flat on her back with the young officer saying, Are you all right, Miss Death? She thinks: How does he know my name? She thinks: there was smoke from his pipe and the fags of the others, smoke *caught and combed in and over and pulled through*, and now there filters through the disinfection of the ward this litany: Guards, No. 6, No. 10, Peter Stuyvesant, Kensitas, Senior . . . Senior . . . and again: Guards, No. 6, No. 10, Peter Stuyvesant, Kensitas, Senior . . . Senior . . . Busner is strongly inclined to supply the Service, what harm can there be in it? It's so very sad to hear this plaint of longing from the next bed, as he bends to the handle and cranks this one upright. Since he's resumed smoking Busner sees smoke *everywhere* – although the patients are forbidden to in the dormitories, he sees it here as well, bluey-grey and strained by the white bars of the bedsteads, curling up brownish to *satirise* the fire-resistant ceiling tiles – above this hypocritical ceiling *what?* the original Victorian plasterwork, egg-and-dart, scrolls and scallops . . . *petrified smoke.* Her paper-thin eyelids crinkle – but don't retract. Marcus has been enthroned on an easy chair dragged in from the day-room, and Busner bows to him, saying, She's extremely elderly now, as you can see. Marcus holds a mug – Tottenham Hotspur's cockerel prances around it. *He deigns,* Yes, well . . . obviously. I mean, she was well advanced in middle age before the war. Well preserved, though, had a head still – full head . . . of striking red hair. She'll need some consoling for its loss. Busner is grateful the older man is talking to him at all, *I need consoling for my loss.* Biddable patients are rewarded by the nurses with cigarettes – latterly they've had to reward him as well. Dazedly, Busner examines her: blood pressure, pulse, instead of an intrusive thermometer a damp hand against her dry forehead. Eyes shut, Audrey listens to his huffing – smells it *smoky and sour.* She has no patience for his air of perpetual bumptiousness – already she understands that he expects a lot of her, and if she struggles to make sense of this strange new world it is only in order to deny him . . . *everything.* I do believe she's awake, Busner, says the other one . . . *Marcus? Another Jew-boy,* but she remembers him as *upright, handsome, correct . . . dapper,* moreover, *always willing to speak to me as if I were a sensible person,* notwithstanding that *I couldn't reply.* Until now. Marcus puts the cockerel down on the adjustable table that Busner has levelled and leans forward. It is not, Busner thinks, a face I'd like to be confronted with immediately upon waking from a half-century's nap – that duckbill and those gaping nostrils would hardly console me for the loss of my hair, my life, the world-that-was and *everything . . . east of Aden*. Still, Marcus can at least perform this senior service: to act as a time chamber within which Audrey can rest a while as she's decompressed by his chat – *all that heavy Victoriana, the lead-glass domes sealing off stuffed and supercilious dodos that must stand about on the dusty tallboys and dirtied doilies of her mind*. Marcus can sort out all this bric-a-brac and in its place *tell her about . . . about . . . polystyrene – yes, that. And PVC too. He can introduce her to the ringing emptiness of inflatable plastic chairs and Habitat lampshades – and to nets clinking with glass floats strung along the walls of trendy bistros. He can bring her up to speed on the flatulence induced by home-brewed –*. Oh, good heavens! Audrey cries, eyes wide open, Who on earth is this old man! Busner, worried that he's about to get the giggles, abandons himself to his craving: I think I'll leave the two of you alone for a while so that you can get . . . reacquainted. He strolls away down the dormitory, looking in on the right *at a Rodin draped in sheets and left in storage:* Missus Gross. In sympathy with his overworked staff, Busner's disappointed to note that her *niblet of a husband* isn't about this afternoon — since awakening, Gross's voracity has become still more excessive: she bullies the nurses, compelling them to bring her whatever they can scrounge, and, terrified that *she might . . . perhaps, roll over and crush them*, they do: *worker termites in the service of a tyrannical queen*. Outsized plates of chips from the staff canteen, steel basins jumbled with stale éclairs and the big mixing bowls shivering with the jelly she particularly favours – jelly she incorporates into her own wobbly Tupperware with loud slurps and percussive lip-smacks. As a practitioner Busner is disappointed *the proper Charlie isn't about to fetch and carry and cadge*, thus taking the pressure of her monstrousness off his staff, – but as a civilised man he is glad: no one person should have to deal with *this*. Good afternoon, Leticia, he says, attempting a breezy neutrality. She looks up from the mirror of a powder compact with which she's been examining her face in many tiny eyefuls. I'm delighted, he continues, *Angel Delighted* to see you take an interest in your appearance – it's been a long time since you've cared . . . The indefinite nature of this long time is deliberate on Busner's part, although of all the post-encephalitics Leticia Gross is the least affected by her time-travel – from hot jazz to teeny bop she hasn't missed a beat, and the velocity of her internal metronome is immediately evident: she drops the compact into the mess of screwed-up sweet wrappers and gnawed lolly sticks that Busner now notices is shoved between the sheet and her slab thigh. As two flies wobble aloft, she puts her disconcerting sky-blue eyes on him and, splitting her baby pout, buzzes a speech, Idon'tknowabouthatDoctorBusner IonlyknowwhatIdoesrightnowwhenwe'retalkingtogetherwhenI'mth inkingaboutthewaryou'venonotiontherewasnothingtoeatatallnonoth ingtheydidn'tgiveussomuchastherationwhichwewererightfullyentitle dtoshockingehifCharliehadn't'vecomeupmostdaysIshould'vestarved hegavemebreadofftherationthat'swhatitwashetellsmenow'courseIdid n'tknowatthetimehalfgoneIwasothersin'eretheygavesomemuckto'em andtheygotawfulsicktheirhairfelloutandeverythingb'lievemeonthis- oneit'strueIswear . . . that he is able to understand – with difficulty – only because he's taken the time to sit with her, concentrate and measure the prodigious speed and accuracy of her diction with stop- watch and tape recorder, so discovering that she can reach five hundred words per minute without missing so much as a single syllable. From deep in the core of Leticia Gross – I'dliketoknow exactlywhatitwastheywerefeedingthosepoorsoulssomesortagruelrem indedmeofburgoonotthatIhadsuchbutmyfatherservedintheGreat Warandhesaidtheygave'emasortaporridgeofcrackedwheatbutthiswas n'twheatCharliesaysitwascorntheygotfromtheYanks – these waves of healthfulness vigorously radiate, penetrating all the fatty lagging, and in the ten days since the L-DOPA has winched this colossus up Busner has spent as many hours alone with her, entranced by the exactitude of her recollection, *If only Marcus could be bothered to pay attention to this*: HewentdowntoCarswellStreetwherethey'dopened uparecruitin'officebuttheysent'imback'omesayin'therewasnocalljustth enformarriedmenbesides'isjobwhichwasasafiremanatthattimeonas mallPortAutoritylighterwaswhatd'yousayessentialthat'sithewaswell paidmindweallus'adshoesan'nicethings, *perhaps he would change his tune – after all, could the organic damage really be that extensive if it left this much intact?* Moreover, the forced quality of her reminiscence was a phenomenon Leticia Gross was perfectly well aware of: thereIgoagainDocrabbitin'on, so that to follow the insightful thread paid out by this ever-wakeful Penelope was to enter the labyrinthine night-without-end before L-DOPA, so as to experience alongside her its narcolepsies, sleep paralyses and daymares of premature burial. Leticia revealed to him the lowering underworld of the post-encephalitic, wherein the myriad tics, jerks and spasms acted to bore the tunnels and hollow out the burrows required by a multitude of subpersonalities – selflets, which were at once regressively primitive and highly organised. The revolting urges of the aggressive woman-mountain – her hoarding of crumpled rubbish, crusts of bread, her own faeces! were in his eyes only the behavioural counterbalance to her astonishingly lucid overview – it was Leticia who told Busner how she had to match everything, whether in the phenomenal world – one teaspoon aligned with a second, two hairclips with two more – or that of ideas, for, she said, she could not think of anything without picturing it mirrored, yoghurt pot-with-yoghurt pot, pain-with-pain. Alerted to it, Busner then found evidence of this tendency to symmetrise in all the others – although Leticia's own coinage for it, arithomania, seemed more apt, conjuring up as it did the past she had been torn out of, its newsreels of single figures surging together in *Chaplinesque festination* to form *a silent murmuration of people* . . . On the third day Busner had given Leticia a Biro and a large stiff-backed exercise book that she could prop against her sugarloaf belly. He had done so – he now accepts – in expectation of some redemption: her purging herself through clarity of expression, eloquence – *all the usual rot.* Now, opening the marbled covers, he's overwhelmed to discover the impetuosity of her thought has been replicated in her script. The first few pages are patterned with a dense and incised cuneiform that presses *Brailleishly* into the verso, the next recto and several more besides – but from leaf-to-leaf *this convolvulus throws out suckers*, at first to the lines above and below, then further afield. Ten pages on an entry headed with yesterday's date consists of only four and a half words, Imusthaveanenem — – the Latin absence of spacing corresponding to her *splutterance* – that take up an entire page, which, when he turns it expecting confirmation of her paranoia, is followed by a perfectly formed *a* stretching top to bottom and side to side, *Giotto's circle* . . . He isn't altogether surprised, because the bizarre – and shameless – anal fixation that Leticia Gross's journal reveals has already been relayed to him by the appalled nurses, and at that precise moment is echoed by her hoarsely bellowing, Imusthaveanenema! Imusthaveanenema! Imusthaveanenema! the imprecation following him – blushing, shamed – as he beats a hasty retreat from her nook, turns tail and speeds towards the nurses' office. Wits are collected into two lots as Busner fiddles filter-tip from foiled sachet. 1. I could, he thinks, alter her dosage of L-DOPA and maybe try her out on some amantadine to see if this has any impact on these . . . these . . . side effects. 2. The perfection of that *a* is surely, he hypothesises, another facet of the symmetrising – it is diagrammatic of a smaller *a* – or a larger one. Mister Ostereich – *if he'd stayed in Vienna he could've been part of its School* . . . had told Busner there were times when for him any symbols – words, numerals, pictorial – were experienced as a sort of map, one that if concentrated on became a map of a map that was itself a map of a further map. This strikes the psychiatrist – sucking in, holding, eyes pricking with teary relief – as possibly the phenomenological correlate of the post-encephalitic mind physically mapping the manifold under- and overlays of its own hellish pathology. Immured in glass, Paaaah! the substantial cloud of dun smoke releases him: a tubbyish genie in his early thirties wearing a wrinkled white coat who props on the corner of a steel desk painted institutional grey-green in the distant reaches of a North London mental hospital while Evonne Goolagong thrills the Centre Court crowd by *flashing her frilly knickers* –. Hephzibah Inglis snaps open the door and bustles inside in a flurry of annoyance. – 'Oo say you can take me fags like dat, Doc-tor – go buy yer own! I spec' you earn what? Four mebbe five times my pay – you should feel shame with yersel', and she snatches up the pack of cigarettes and tucks it away in his tunic pocket, For fuck's sake d'you want a number-bloody-one? In the kissing pink of dawn Stanley sees a lipstick smear of privation bow across Bobby's white face. To cheer him up as they make their way into the eerie woodland of splintered trunks and fractured boughs, Stanley puts on the toffee nose of Grahame-White and says, I say, old fellow, what a splendid show! But only Feldman, who's hefting along Vicky, manages a laugh. Stanley knows why: laughter can be nothing but *a cackle around the Devil's cauldron* – the smoke from lachrymatory shells clings to the shredded foliage, while at treetop height *woolly bears* detonate with flatly malevolent crumps, shedding shrapnel and *dirty black fur.* — The section had come up through Naours and Saint-Gratien, stopping from time to time to consult the field-issue maps that were, Stanley thought, maps of maps that were themselves only the maps of all this ... *fucking confusion.* They'd swung along the chalky road to Albert, where they'd been issued with steel helmets and side arms. Now, as he stumbles over roots and tears himself from brambly embraces – dragged down by the deadweight of his pack, Vicky's spare barrels and the Colt .45 – Stanley marvels at the sentimental feelings he harbours for the Redoubt – the almost leisurely stand-tos, with such homely noises as the cheeping of baby rats, the breezy rattle of tin cans caught on the wire, and the very occasional dull whiplash of a Jerry sniper's bullet. At Crucifix Corner, where the bulk of the infantry were wheeled left towards Thiepval, the section had tended right in the direction of Fricourt, then slowed, picking its way between the *locust masses of men feeding upon the land* ... The barrage is due to be lifted any minute now, and, although the machine gunners will hang back, the fear stirs in their guts, churning them, so that one after another Stanley's comrades fall out to puke their burgoo and the *sweet ghost* of their rum ration. Stanley alone remains free from nausea – true, he feels its accompanist fingering his throat with great sensitivity, and so is able to scent the difference between the shells as they shriek overhead towards the German lines. He sniffs judiciously at the *pitch-pine vapours* that drift down from every second or third one, and which he identifies as . . . *eau de dud*. Not that it'll make any difference – *we all know, they all know, even the fucking top brass know by now that artillery fire, no matter how accurate, can never breach wire.* The projectiles plunge down and the wiry embroidery hoicks up lazily to expose for long and salacious moments *earth-soiled bloomers*, then tumbles just as lazily back into place, only a little disordered by the violence of the assault. He feels fear – *I'm no Enigmarelle, no automaton.* He feels fear, and in the din that jumbles up his works – the cogs, gears and springs that keep him moving relentlessly forward – he rummages for the sureties of childhood: *If you 'ave any more, Missus Moore, I dunno what we'll do, I'm sure! Our cemetery's so small, There'll be no room fer 'em all! Don't 'ave any more, Missus Moore –!* The Long Toms and howitzers firing from miles back have stopped. The curved and delicate eggshell of light fractures with the reedy pee-eeet! of officers' whistles. They drop down into a sunken lane, passing the heavy ammo boxes from hand to hand. *One we did earlier:* a staff officer lies back against the bank, his dead face quite composed, his ridiculous cockade embellished naturally by fronds of bracken. There's nothing but *Tickler's jam, Tickler's jam! where his bottom half oughta be* – nearby lies his enormous Percheron horse, quite still but without a mark on it – which is some sort of relief, because now the barrage has lifted they can all hear the screaming of horses and mules hit by the premature bursts of . . . *those fucking duds*. Stanley feels fear as he quick-steps carefully between the cloddish hooves – he conjures up the Old Man taking the lead along the lane, the skirts of his rabbit-skin coat flapping, the friendly smoke from his seegar chucking jolly little clouds over his shoulder that sport in the steadily strengthening sunlight. Corbett, who has the mastery of map work, consults the small square of *where-we-are* and they mount the bank again, back up into the rotten-egg stench of the gassed wood. Stanley feels fear – he knows fear: the breathless terror of numbly pulling on the flannel bag, becoming enshrouded in chemical reek, the *where-we-were* reduced to a small square of mica that frames popping eyes and gaping mouths, while diaphragm heaves, chest shudders, *head spins with the . . . effort . . . not . . . to . . . breathe –! Paaaah!* and the world disappears into his own mist. Stanley feels fear – but he feels hunger more. The worst thing about this entire fucking war, he thinks as they skulk towards the light and the relentless chattering of the enemy Maxims, is the lousy fucking poverty – the eleven measly bob a week, the hard biscuit teeming with weevils, the piss-green tea, the chatting along the seams of shit-browned long johns, the bully beef – and the rats, cleverer than the men, crawling on their heads while they slept to get food bags hung from joists. Had it been a dream, or was it when he'd served briefly as a batman? The *piss-yellow champagne foaming in real glass goblets, bloody big bowls of rhubarb, cold meats fanned out on plates, or else quivering in aspic. A phonograph set up, triplets of piano notes d'doo-doo-dooing from its flaring muzzle. An entire salmon – naked, boned and laid out on cucumber petticoats –!* Ha! He laughs aloud at his own idiotic maundering – for no officer, no matter how well supplied with cigars from Fox's, cocaine pep pills from Harrods and the latest Rudyard Kipling or G. C. Cook from Hatchard's, could lay his lily-white hands on a whole salmon! No, they'd partaken of mutton chops, right enough, with new potatoes, peas and string-fucking-beans . . . – Some more, sir? As he manipulated a pair of spoons, in their eyes the least of individual minds . . . *a wop waiter at Simpson's*, Stanley had prayed devoutly for a Jack Johnson to *KO them there and then, silence the scratching tune and their daft banter*. He had been born to soar aloft, yet here he was *dishing it up to these pink-faced shavers. – More beans, old bean? Ha-ha! – underground, in a tomb-in-waiting*. One side of Stanley's pack drags heavier. Down at the bottom of it, stuffed under the shit-stained long johns and the scrounged bully, is a pair of Luger pistols wrapped in a German officer's greyback and shoved in a pickelhaube. Pausing to catch his breath, his hand laid tenderly on a deep and *evilly jagged gash in thou, gentle hornbeam*, Stanley identifies the helmet's blunt spike digging into his kidneys *thru'pence, frying in their own blood and piss* . . . His comrades hang on to such things as souvenirs – but these aren't: they're *arms for a future rising*. He sees himself still in uniform but wearing the pickelhaube – he stands on the front steps while the parlour maid, distressed by this apparition, trips away to find the master of the house, who comes to the door with a sheaf of official papers in one hand and a horsehair flyswatter in the other. Well, what d'you want my man? asks Albert De'Ath, feigning not to recognise his brother. Stan raises the Luger and holds its barrel against Bert's *raw oyster*. Four million rifles, Stan says matter-of-factly, two hundred and fifty thousand machine guns, fifty-two thousand aeroplanes, twenty-five thousand artillery pieces and one hundred and seventy million shells, *Am I right, sir?* Albert for once takes no umbrage, only bows meekly to the inevitable. Stepping over his surprisingly corpulent dead body, Stan strolls along the hallway to what he supposes is a breakfast room. Here a potted palm cascades on a stand, and rack of freshly made toast steams on an oval mahogany table. Stan takes a piece, butters it with an ivory-handled knife, then *pushes it whole into my dry mouth – the corners stabbin' the insides of me cheeks* ... It tastes of boot blacking – and cordite, beyond any shadow of doubt he is scared – terror is the ground *vibrating beneath my feet*, ground that heaves a hundred yards in front of where the section has taken cover, *its piecrust buckles, earth-juice spurts flashing tastily* into the cacophonous four-beat b'-b'-b'-boom! that should have preceded it. Stanley is scared – and his fear is a hungering: he could *eat the hornbeam for a joint*, the tangle of undergrowth at its roots *for a salad*. He could *crunch up* Vicky's three spare barrels in their webbing bundle – and *shovel down a box of ammo for puddin'*. He could eat and eat and eat – no one, he wagers, has ever before experienced such a *shameless voracity*. He will consume the dead Mutton Lancers and the straggling back Scots Guards, he will *help myself* to the ruins of a small farmhouse and its shattered outbuildings despite their already having been feasted upon by the Hun's artillery. He will feed his way across the broad and churned valley, then munch his way up the chalky rise, snaffling the bodies of the fallen, using their bayonets to pick his teeth, until he reaches the wire, *rolls into it and kips the kip of the stuffed. Then* ... *later* ... *no enemies any more, only the sweet* ... *sweet enema of putrefaction: Bliss!* Ah, well lads! Corbett shouts the second the barrage lifts. S'pose we better get forward and put up the ol' um-ber-ella! And forward they go, inching their way snail-like around giant clods and raw gouges until they reach the cover of the remaining brick walls — *a lovely situation for Vicky*, what with a smooth bit of tiling to set her legs on, and the bottom half of a window to poke her muzzle through. Dark burgundy dapples on broken red pantiles, there's a botheration of greenbottles around some two-days-since dead thing – and, for all that, miraculous damsons still whole on the one remaining branch of a scythed orchard, and Vicky *rat-a-tat-tat-trilling* with pleasure between his hands as Feldman, legs spread and top-to-tail, feeds her the belt. It would be pretty cushy were it not that even with his pack off Stanley cannot help but wrench his head up and around to the left, where some invisible object compels his attention. As they reach the end of each belt, back goes his shoulder, round and up swings his head. Now, now, Stan, says Corbett, keep steady at that range – and he crawls forward to check it. Stanley understands wherefrom comes his compulsion: for hours and days now, *weeks slotting into the canvas pockets of months* – so that the entire year and a half trails across the foreign field – he has lain on his belly listening to the incoming sing over the machine gun's drumming, and his spasmodic assessments of whether – and if so which way – he should go for cover have left him with this permanent crick, this, and his *magnificent powers of espial*: the Tommies' queer superstition is also Stanley's addiction to count-ing by threes – three fags, three shells, three lots of food, three nights, three days, three brass, three rats, three cups of vino, three tots of rum, *with three of any-bloody-thing it's always the third that's got your number*, so watch out for it, *keep counting*, always keep counting. They fire continuously for hour upon hour, the bullets spitting in a jet low across the valley. Every fourth round is a tracer to help them keep the range – but the day is so bright these are barely visible. They change one barrel and then the second – they run out of water for *Vicky's redingote* by about ten thirty and, with no source readily available, take it in turns to piss in her reservoir. The smell of hot urine intensi-fies *the Devil's fart* of the cordite, the sweetly rotting *flesh* of *fruit* – and *men*. Terror *gathers* in the gun's grips and *shudders* through him with the recoil – it might be safer, he thinks, if he were to flit back through the wood with Luftie on the ammo run – although the truth is that for Stanley there can be no DANGER OF DEATH, no dark patch spreading across the tiles. His asinine moniker has put paid to that – each new man who joins the Death squad has this impressed upon him: 'E's a fucking 'uman rabbit's foot, the Lance 'ere, or a Cornish pixie – go on, lay yer 'and on 'im, 'e won't mind . . . There can be no DANGER OF DEATH when it's DEATH WHO'S THE DANGER, a transposition that sets Stanley off on another futile train of thought: Why is it that he has this overpowering need to match things up, to put a box of matches in one pocket if there's a box in the other, to ensure there are the same number of rifle cartridges in each of his pouches, to wind on his puttees with an equal number of turns? And it isn't only things – ideas, fleeting apprehensions, the ghosts of formerly finer feelings that flit across the waste land of his terror, all must be married up so that they precisely match: *two-equals-two-equals-two*, an iteration of equivalence that he fervently believes will cancel out the lethal threes. Vicky giggles about this: rat-a-tat-tat, rat-a-tat-tat, and she sings also: *We're 'ere because we're 'ere because we're 'ere*, as she tickles the backs of Stanley's hands with her trigger guards. And, despite the absence of the land ironclads and the presence to the west of a river lazing through its bends, there is a similar neat vee in the chalky bluffs against which the machine gun cries out, and so he is enabled to make the necessary pairing between *Norr and . . . here*. Three years have passed since he stood by the window of the empee's country house and *Wallie, Wallie, Wall-flowers, Growing up so high – All these young ladies, Will all have to die* . . . The men in their creamy-linen uniforms spoke, as he recalls it, of *Bulgaria and certain alliances and the Irish – it was always the poor fucking Irish, dying for a post office or a sessions* – and here is Stanley *Death raining down death* on a Daimler he cannot see but which he is busily disassembling, his bullets methodically shearing off one mudguard, then the next, drilling out the spokes from the wheels, unbolting those wheels from their axles, hammering the chassis into scrap, and finally pulverising its engine into all its component parts.

They've been at it for nigh on four hours when on the stroke of twelve Jerry's Maxims stop. Immediately after this Luftie comes back with the order to cease fire themselves – watch hand *slim-stroking butterfly feeler*, silence – *hateful*. How many rounds have they loosed? Two-hundred-and-fifty per box, eight boxes each run back from the forward depot, an ammo run every quarter-hour making for thirty-two thousand ... *Am I right, sir?* The silence is hateful: Vicky's nose tilts to the ground – the men swoon as smoke pools, then flows from the battlefield, they are listening to the *thud-thud-* pumping of their young hearts, hearing all their component parts. They are *licking* ... *kissing* the tarnished casing of lockets, *hissing out* their own smoke as the blood *rush-ush-ushes* through their battered ears. The vanguard of defeat has already invaded them *fucked-up francs-tireurs who straggle ahead limping, crawling, dragging themselves back into the battle of life* ... One little Scots gamecock bob-flits-whirrs from shell hole to ditch to tree stump for a couple of hours, before arriving at their position with his kilt in tatters. He collapses against the remains of the scullery wall and lying there lifts his remaining hand to his black cracked lips over and over again *miming* ... *what?* Is it a request for the water they cannot spare – or the valiant urge to *tootle his bugle?* With superhuman toughness he'd managed to strap a tourniquet around the stump of his blown-to-bits hand *or else he'd've gone long since* ... Feldman, spooked by the Jock's sightless eyes and his dirge of amansamansamans ... wants to: Finish 'im off – in kindness – but Corbett says, In justice any man who's come through that has earned the right to take his chances. So

266

the disagreement nags between them as the greenbottles give up on the other thing to trickle across to the Scotsman's nostrils, to pour over his mouth and eyes ... — A long time of this, until Feldman puts the bins to his eyes and, seeing two or three Union flags jerking about part-way up the ridge, says, We've taken their frontline, lads, p'raps the support 'as ... then trails off, the bins dropping on their lanyard. He lifts them again, shakes his head disbelieving – and they fall again. He lifts them –. For fuck's sake! Corbett cries, Now you an' 'im both! – because they're in time, Feldman and the Jock, lifting and dropping their arms. Corbett snatches the bins and the lanyard rucks up the front of Feldman's tunic – *He looks like a kid getting ragged. Wiv 'is blond curls and periwinkle eyes you'd never peg 'im for a Jew boy* – took all he got with *remarkable pluck* ... Eldest son of a schneider from up the Mile End Road – *tho' you'd never guess that either:* made of himself a well-spoken coke and oil merchant in Shadwell *selling direct to the public – but the dandiprat took it personal when the Contemptible points his old white-gloved hand, so up he goes for his shilling ... His daddy? Mortimerfied oy-yoy-yoy! Rocking back and forth on his bum, forgetting his thimble drill. And now where's the hand that wore the glove? Feeding fishies wiv its bleedin' manicure* – and here's Solly, such a face on 'im that Luftie's stopped filling Vicky with the piss-pan to laugh at him. Corbett ain't laughing, tho', Oh my sainted fucking aunt diddlin' 'erself with a cruci-fucking-fix, he says *by way of comfort – that being the way of it with him* ... Tenderly he untangles the lanyard from Feldman's buttons and lifts the bins from around his neck. The section don't speak as they pass the bins from hand to hand. Later, Stanley remembers *amansamanferall ... amansamanferall* ... and the whistling of the stretcher parties emerging from the wood. To begin with it is impossible to take it all in – probably just as well. The eyepieces are the viewfinder of a handheld stereoscope: it should therefore be possible to change the card, or remove them from his powder-stung eyes altogether to reveal the parlour at Waldemar Avenue, Gladstone's plaster noggin, the Solar lamp on the table with its dangling prisms, the cottage piano and his sisters' samplers – anything should be possible, not this: the figures elbow to elbow so closely are they packed, on their knees, *praying maybe to the womanly breast of the hillside*. The boys concertinaed in their khaki sacks at the end of this *spiffing company sports day – will there be prizes? Fifty francs and a silver cup for the bull's eye?* The bins take Stanley's bugged eyes probing into hollows, roving over spurs, and everywhere they go they discover more and more bodies – not hanging on the wire but reclining into it, so very dense are the coils those methodical Teutons have laid down. Amansamanferall . . . Amansamanferall . . . grates the dying Scotsman, Amansamanferall . . . Luftie, when it's his turn with the bins, begins to weep, and Stanley says: They put this one on to take the pressure offa Frenchie down the line, but Frenchie – he has the right idea: when they ordered 'im back into the line 'e shot 'is own fucking officers – and Corbett says, Now, now . . . and there might have been some bother if the first of the stretcher parties hadn't come along at that point, and a second lieutenant who was with them – and who seemed *the very soul of decency* – said that Fritz had very decently stopped firing so they could go and bring in the wounded – which is how Stanley comes to be tearing up a stretch of duckboard on to which he thinks they might be able to roll a tubby private of the Second Royal Welsh who's taken a couple of rounds in the thigh – but no bones broken or arteries busted, so all things being well he's a chance of making it if they get him back. A fighting chance if Feldman will only stop larking about

– not that there is any joy to it, it's more that the set-up of the Jerry trench has pushed him over the edge. Look at this, Lance! he cries. And this – and that! calling Stanley's attention to the electrical wiring running from neat porcelain to neat porcelain along the trench wall. We know about it already, you daft bugger! Stanley cries. Don't you remember the deep dugout? — The deep dugout, splendidly dry and with only the faintest odour of mouse droppings. Stanley had found a real china plate piled with slices of black bread and white onions, and set beside this a clear glass bottle – on the label a bunch of cherries *lusty* in the pulsing light still being generated by an unseen and thrumming generator. Heedless as yet of Feldman's crack-up, Stanley had seated himself at the table and crammed down the coarse food with little sips of the cherry brandy . . . *kleine Boche stands on me tongue wielding 'is Kleinflammenwerfer* . . . Solly wouldn't keep still, kept diving into adjoining burrows to rummage in the bedding. – Feather quilts! he cried. Pillows! and returned with a single-page newssheet he said he could read on account of German not being that different from the Yiddisher lingo, *Yes, yes, it revealed to him – sweethearts under linden trees, that spanking-hot summer . . . freshly brewed lager-beer with cloves . . . snatches of these simple boys' souls, who, from Bavaria and Franconia, had got themselves planted here in the soil that clung to the roses of Picardy . . .* There were pistols and rifles still in the dugout – and plenty of their brand-new Stahlhelms, such had been the frenzy of their retreat. Stanley had not been interested in these, although he took a couple of their potato-mashers, the superiority of which . . . *everyone knows.* In the dugout he had felt a bowel-loosening apprehension – the dense, cool air pressing in on him – and when, despite the ceasefire, there came the soft crump! of a falling shell, fear infiltrated his mind . . . *a dirty plume*. He'd rolled a cigarette with a corner of the newssheet and some coal-black tobacco, then *availed myself of the facilities* that, outrageously, had been plumbed in, so that, rising from the shapely seat, he was able rejoice in the *fly away, little brown bird* as he carefully wiped his arse with more of the Gothic type, discovering it to be unexpectedly kind to his piles. — Up top Solly has come upon the Welshman – who screams as Stan kicks the board in under him. Come and give me a hand, you daft fucker! Stan cries, knowing there's little point because Solly's all the way over now, *dog-faced, gnashing . . . paws a blur as he scampers this way and that* along the trench, from traverse to traverse, climbing up on to the neatly carpentered fire step to yap about their craftsmanship: You can always rely on a German, he howls, to d-d-d-doo-doo-doo the b-b-best he c-c-can with the t-t-tools available. Stanley's hands tic to his wire cutters and the grenades in his belt – in that instant he resolves to ditch the Welshman and if necessary lay Solly out, if that's what it'll take to get him back . . . *Too late!* because Solly has mounted the fire step and pulls himself from arms to knees, gibbering upright, low-angled afternoon sunlight striking him together with twenty or so 7.92-millimetre rounds from a Maschinengewehr 08 that must have loitered behind in a reserve trench, its craftsmen resolved to *bide their time and do the best they could with the tools available.* Leisurely – Solly Feldman's death, *so very slow* . . . While Stanley has never been one of those machine-gunners who enjoy comparing the attractions of the Vickers .303 with those of her *kissing cousin*, the enfilade that buzzes over the trench, then burrs back to capture Solly and hold him in its kinetic embrace, leads him to consider – even as his comrade's arms windmill crazily – that Jerry's may be the better weapon. *See, see!* how it clasps him to its *leaden bosom*, reluctant to let him fall, although there's hardly anything left but a *tattered red rag*. In the stretched moments as Solomon Feldman flaps into extinction, Stanley dwells upon this: that never before in his interminable nineteen months of service at the Front has he witnessed the impact of machine-gun fire. His fingers clenched on the trigger, Vicky *trembling in my grasp, spitting and gasping inches in front of my face* – yet theirs was never *an exclusive relation*, there were always these *others* with whom they were *joined by the bullets*. Solomon Feldman *has his Heimatschuss an' 'e's gone west*. Pointless to think of getting the Welshman back now – Stanley has seen enough to know . . . *his time approaches*. Instead, he turns and legs it along the trench, hoping there's just the one Maschinengewehr covering this section. Where the trench makes a sharp right-angle a sap runs back towards the British lines, and he takes this bend for home, potato-mashers bouncing on his hips – rifle butt one side, Colt the other, both *goading my withers, I'm Rothschild's pair, trotting down Brook Green Road and turning into the Broadway* . . . He sees the well-crafted step that leads up into the bramble patch, he sees old Hammersmith Town Hall soberly clad in red sandstone, gas-jets atop fluted iron pillars burning either side of its stolid portico. He hears the first salvo of the resumed barrage quite some time after registering the shell's scream, and so he dithers: is the noise more piercing in his right or his left ear? He twists in the sap, compelled to turn first up, back and to the left, then up, back and to the right – it's pointless anyway, because as it homes in on him the rising Eeeeeeeeee! bores into the absolute core of his brain *spores glow dried-out dandelion head* and he knows he would have to go over the top to evade the shell that stops precisely where his gaze locks . . . *Umbrellas Re-covered and Repaired on the Premises, Umbrellas*

Re-covered in One Hour, 2/6, King Street opposite the Temperance Hotel . . . If only he had availed himself of this service, because *when all was said and done you should never go out without one.* Nevertheless, he acquiesces to this: that the shell *one of ours* will fall between him and *Jerry's Maxim* — such dull matters are *a mere flapdoodle* – what's significant is that Stanley can see inside the brass casing of the 50-pounder, make out not only the discrete layers of Trotyl, guncotton and tri-nitro-toluene but what put them there: the sprinkling, wadding and pounding of those yellow hands. He sees those hands also *fritillaries fluttering* above the dingy wooden bench, he hears the *peevish whine* of the lathe, the *hissing contempt* of the oxy-acetylene torch, the *rheumatic complaint* of the overhead hoist, and he hearkens to the lusty voices raised in song, *Where are the girls of the Arsenal? Working night and day, Wearing the roses off their cheeks for precious little pay, Some style us canaries but we're working the same as the lads across the sea, If it wasn't for us, the munitions girls, where would the Empire be –?* The arrested shell sings a hundred feet above the trench *in a cloud of penny novelettes*, and the turning of its fuse cap and detonator plug, the brazing of its smoothly seductive haunches – all the scores and hundreds of repetitive motions that led to its triumphantly short-lived embodiment are there, plain to his exophthalmic eye. And Stanley Death understands, even as the rest is over, and the angelic feet begin once more to pump the pedals, the perforations are engaged by the ebony pegs, and the pianola resumes its plummet *Doo-d'doo, doo d'doo, doo-d'-dooo, doo-d'-dooooooooooooooo* . . . that upon impact all of its strings, hammers, levers, cogs and screws will blast across the shattered terrain in wave upon wave of tics, jerks, yawns, spasms, blinks, gasps, quivers, pursing, bobbing, pouts, chews, grindings, palsies, tremors and twitches, sending them dancing from mind to mind, so animating body after body to perform choreography that will stand in for civilisation unprompted, matinee upon matinee – evenings as well – *a merry dance* ... However, this is all he thinks – the moment is over, the shell detonates, thrusting up an obscenely wobbling earthen breaker that curls over the sap – over Stanley, where he claws at its wall of sweet-smelling loam. Reddy-dark and then maroon-to-black, it pushes his eyes back into their sockets, it rushes silence beating into his eardrums, it packs around arms, legs, trunk, neck, head – hammering down cottony paralysis into every join and crevice – if, that is, these bits are between anything at all, for there is no feeling any more – none after that final and extreme myoclonic jerk: the arms flung backwards, the spine bowed by the shockwave. There is no information, no current, no resistance, no up or down or back-to-front – only this that worms through the mind, a thought that sucks upon its own tail even as it is reborn, disappearing into one hole, re-emerging from another, expressing only this nightmarishly symmetrical identity: *I-am I-am I-am I-am*, which is simultaneously expressed numerically, *one-equals-one-equals-one-equals-one*, over and over again, its maddening equivalence allowing for no purchase, nothing to be gripped upon, so that the *I* that *am* might be assisted to *sit up* – which is what Gracie does, and, although Audrey feels her friend's arm behind her back, smells the broth, sees its *floury steam sift through my hair* and sees also her own top half, propped up now on a bolster, two cushions and a pillow, while above her tousled head hangs a dear little watercolour of a windmill backed by clouds that Gracie found in the bric-a-brac shop on Coldharbour Lane – *still I am not in Flat G, 309 Clapham Road* but remain in that other place, where, naked, she thrusts out her behind and kicks out her legs as she *impiously struts* the boards before an audience she can

273

only dimly perceive, although – from the shape of its noses, the strength of its chins – she knows it to be composed *entirely of Doctor Trevelyans who smile and with folded eyeglasses tap the backs of their copies of Married Love in time,* as she sings over and over and over again, *Don't 'av any more, Missus Moore, Don't 'av any more, Missus Moore, Don't 'av any more, Missus Moore* – a futilely contradictory ditty, because how can you avoid having more when your name is Moore, and therefore the very demand defeats itself, as there are more and more Moores the more this imprisoned part of Audrey descants, *Don't 'av any more, Missus Moore* – more Moores and more Trevelyans as well, the rat-a-tat-tapping of their tortoiseshell spectacle frames on the book covers *a hideous chaffering* – if only she could get past this bulky womanish obstruction! On to: *Too many double gins, Give the ladies double chins, Too many double gins, Give the ladies double chins* – gins and chins proliferating now, chins doubling up as mouths yawn so more and more gins may be poured down, stray teeth in a magenta juniper haze, torn bodices . . . – *No!* Not there, on further: *Our cemetery's so small, There'll be no room fer 'em all, Our cemetery's so small there'll be no room fer 'em* – *no!* Not there either, so the bed of the lathe *that's me* ratchets back to *Don't 'av any more, Missus Moore,* while Gracie holds her around the shoulders, shouting it all down with the gentle entreaty, Can't you at least take some of this broth, Aud'? There's some brawn left inall if you'd fancy that – I'll go an' get it straightways . . . It has been two weeks since Audrey has lain in this swoon, two weeks during which Gracie has had to rouse her up for the lavatory and feeding. To Gracie's untutored eye there is nothing mysterious about her friend's affliction: illness is all around them in the long, low block of flats, it lingers in the dim stairwells, then either mounts the stairs to the three storeys above, or descends to the one below, where it slouches along the ill-lit passageways, a bad nurse bearing jugs full of microbes and bowls brimming with bacteria, who makes of this place a dying-in hospital. The building is only a couple of years old and there is still the foul sweat of distemper on the walls, and the nosey tickle of sawdust in the tiny angular bay windows. Illness is all around them – twitching the chintz back and opening the casement, Gracie hears Audrey mutter, Poor man they 'ung 'im, while from outside come the chants of urchins playing in the front yard: She open ve winder an' in-flew-enza! She open ve winder an' in-flew-enza! In the flat above them a returned Tommy has run a fever of a hundred and four for seven straight days. Audrey managed to whisper an address – Gracie took a precious sixpence and went to the office, where she painfully composed the telegram: MISS DEATH ILL STOP SEND HELP PLEASE STOP, at a loss to know what to do with her *five spare words*. The doctor who finally comes from Kennington – paid for, Gracie assumes, by Audrey's lover – speaks of this poor soul and many others. The isolation wards and fever hospitals are all full, he says, and, being a staunch progressive who believes in speaking the truth, whispers: the morgues and cemeteries also, I've been at Mortlake and seen bodies laid out in a potting shed . . . *Our cemetery's so small, There'll be no room fer 'em all, Our cemetery's so small there'll be no –*. He examines Audrey with enough care, exerting himself to lift her with an arm behind her shoulders so he may sound her with the *cold collation* of his stethoscope *aspic shivery lies between my blancmanges, fish slice on my neck . . . dill tickles my nostrils . . .* He is much taken by Gracie, and when she brings him a bowl of warm water to wash his hands in, he takes hers and, examining their backs, says, Oleum? She concedes as much with eyes downcast on the brown burn speckles. The doctor is not much more than thirty, very earnest and sandy, with a narrow skull and hazel eyes. When he tucks his stethoscope up inside his hat brim, it lies against his sparse hair *black crêpe on a photograph frame*. I've seen, he says, Thomasinas who've worked with tri-nitro-toluene, cordite and Trotyl, and who're gravely ill now – how d'you fare? Gracie looks away to where her old overall dress, her jacket and her trousers hang on the hook behind the door, the stiffness of the material giving them ... *body*. I miss ... she is hesitant ... t'be honest I miss the wages, sir, an' the other girls. No work t'be 'ad juss now, no matter 'ow far you goes paddin' the 'oof. An' since they done turfed us straight out of the settlement 'ouse – rent 'ere's eatin' up our savings, an' what with Ordree not workin' ... She falls silent, wondering if she should add that she begrudges her friend nothing – but it isn't moral hygiene that interests the doctor. Headaches? he queries. Any, ah, hysterical seizures – fits? The ether, y'know, in the cordite – it's been known to be productive of epilepsy. *No paint or powder* but he examines her face critically. It's, she says, as you see, sir, I've only the jaundice to show fer me three years – an' that's fadin'. Gracie wants to ask about Audrey, whose head is cast down in the pillows, while her knees are *Mother Brown!* an unnatural posture she maintains as she murmurs, Dunavanymaw, dunavanymaw – and soon enough, Gracie knows, her friend will start to sob, she will keen and writhe, ravaged by grief. It is not, Lord knows, that there isn't enough to sadden her – the loss of her younger brother, the estrangement from her family, and the near-total abandonment by *fancy-pants Mister Cook, the swine* ... *that's as may be*, there is still more grief in Audrey's wasted frame than it can contain: *a world of it*. The doctor – whose name is Vowles – sighs. – We-ell ... I've read a warning put out by the Medical Association concerning a strange sort of brain fever – strikes people down who're

276

in the finest of fettle, strikes 'em down in a trice. Your friend ... well, her symptoms would seem to indicate that she does have this ... this sleepy sickness, however, the malady is so, ah, curious that I cannot diagnose it with any certainty ... He pauses – the cramped quarters are on the lower-ground floor, a dugout that forces its occupants to stare up at a pictorial space *wherein the most abbreviated things have become ... elongated.* A telegram boy halts alongside the top panes of the snub bay window and bends to pull up his stocking – Doctor Vowles thinks of the skull in Holbein's Ambassadors, *its disturbing anamorphosis* ... I've seen two or three others who're as difficult to bestir – who cannot do anything for themselves ... The oppression of the half-buried room, the two ailing young women, his own exhaustion – it all bears down on him, and he steps to the window to breathe deeply. Gracie waits, her yellow hands twisting inside the pockets of her paler yellow apron. Vowles recovers: ... and who, when they're able to speak of it at all, report strange hallucinations and violent headaches, but then ... the sickroom camphor and the stench of sweat-saturated sheets is as nauseating to him as *Wilson's claim that the war almost justified itself* ... I have another patient, a lady in Pimlico, who's afflicted with the exact same unreasonable anxieties, these flushes and sweats, but who, far from languishing, can gain no repose at all – she's been pacing and fretting for five days now, I've never seen the like: the strongest drugs make no impression on her, salts of salicylic won't touch her fever, I greatly fear –. He stops, looks round, sees his Gladstone – acts upon this by crossing the room with two long strides, withdrawing a pad, taking a fountain pen from his breast pocket, scrawling upon a sheet, hunching up to tear it free and handing it to Gracie. He queries: Have you sufficient funds? not knowing what he will do if she doesn't – for, while Cook cabled to him that he would accommodate Vowles's bill, *he said nothing of further subventions.* — When he is gone, his boot heels ringing up the bare stairs to the front hall, Gracie reads the note to the chemist: Salicyclic prep. Asprin x 20 grns. Two weeks now and no sign of change: Audrey bellows, her knees fall down and her *back bends . . . bends . . .* the cushions and the pillow roll down under her back and she arches over them, her eyes all bloodshot sclera, their lids quivery. What is it that she sees, Gracie wonders, up there inside 'er own 'ead? Audrey arches still more, lifting her torso clear of the covers – her arms are flung back and her nails pick at the wallpaper, fingers scrabbling up to discover the picture frame, *I-am I-am I-am . . .* and then there is sensation – the answering pressure of fingers that make his fingers exist once more, and once they are, so are his wrists, his forearms, his elbows, *all me benders . . .* It is touch, Stanley thinks, the movement of touch that makes us be in time – for time had fled me also. *Nisi agit non est . . .* He thinks all this as first one arm, then the other, is freed from its interment in this citadel shaped so exactly like himself. Next there is further loosening of the hard-packed earth – it squeezes, then releases him, compelling a slithery second birth as the final backward dive he made when the shockwave hit still continues *hours . . . days?* later. Small clods, agitated, *tickle away* and his own face is exposed – whose other faces will he see, *Fritzes'? Frenchies'? Our own? Will they be soldiers or stretcher-bearers?* He strains for voices – there is only panting h-h-h-h-huh, thumping, and the falling away of the dug earth. Stanley calmly awaits the reddening-to-orange as daylight impresses his eyelids – it does not come. His rescuers must have hollowed out a cavity beneath his bent back because all at once he tumbles painfully on to the till, sees only the fencing of erratic wands – electric torch

beams that magic up a dirty leg, a dirtier shirt-tail. His emergence is
haled in various tongues: Veranstalten Sie ihn! Tirez-le libre! C'mon
now, men –! Then he is being dragged bodily along a Russian sap
that descends steadily down, its chalky walls beautifully ridged by
the mattock strokes that hacked it out – here and there sardine tin
lamps glimmer in little niches. Stunned by joy in living at all, to
begin with Stanley is inured to scrape and dunt – soon enough,
though, he bridles, legs bicycle, grip, propel him standing ... The
rescue party halts. Stanley's bare head scrapes against the tunnel roof
– his steel helmet has gone. He reaches for the lanyard – the Colt is
lost as well, webbing, ammo pouches, belt, potato-mashers, haversack ... the entire battle order *gone*. His rescuers' breathing rasps
harsh, flutters *bully beef* on his face. Wh-what waar woo? he numbles.
A lithening potht? From far overhead the noise of the barrage
declines into innocence, *a carpet beaten on a clothesline*. One of the
rescuers – whose wide face, *combed yellow* in the lamplight, Stanley is
surprised to see *thickly carpeted* by beard – reaches out to take the
insignia on Stanley's collar between his blackened nails. Death,
Lance-Corporal, 32nd Machine-Gun Company, 5665, Stanley says
– he cannot stand to attention but attempts a salute that ... *flops*. The
bearded man laughs, and it is then Stanley notices that he, like the
others, is naked apart from a shirt – his isn't a greyback but a fancy
cambric thing *more like a woman's blouse*, with pleats on the bodice,
puffed sleeves and a patterning of embroidered flowers *planted in the
dirt*. The bearded man laughs again and, leaving go Stanley's miniature crossed Vickerses, takes the floppy hand gently in his, tugging it
down so that they stand there in the subterranean passage holding
hands ... *like kids*. Tush, the bearded man says softly, there's no call
for sooch talk down 'ere, chappie. He has long North Country vowels

and is oddly courteous. You moost've 'ad a 'elluv a shock from that there blast – lookie-thar, yer kecks're all blow t'bits. Stanley peers down into the fawnlight – it's true, his trousers are in tatters, his drawers as well. His boots have *deserted me* and his tunic is in filthy ribbons. Even set beside this strange crew he's a *sorry ragamuffin*. The bearded man resumes, Ahm called Michael and this 'ere – he indicates a slim, curly-haired figure with a fleecy beard and round, wire-rimmed spectacles – is Winfried, boot we call 'im, Winnie fer convenience. Thass Jean-François – a sallow-faced giant of man, bowed under the weight of his heavy, swallowtail moustaches – boot Johnnie t'uz, an' this wun 'ere is Mohan. The Hindoo is clean-shaven in comparison with his mates, with only a thin braiding of black hairs on his full brown cheeks. Nah then, says Michael, having effected these peculiar introductions, try again t'givuz yer 'andle. Stanley says, It's Stan, my name is Stan. Michael squeezes his wrist. Good, he says, you're getting the 'ang of it beauty, Stan. Without relinquishing his grip, Michael draws Stanley on behind him. Mind yer 'ead, he says, it's no better fer a lanky wun doon 'ere than oop top –. Laughing, he corrects himself: Savin' that 'ere the worst azall 'appen is yer brains being bashed rather than blown t'smithereens. The gradient steepens and steepens, the tunnel doubles-back on itself and back again as it corkscrews into the earth, around corners worn smooth by the rubbing of shoulders . . . It's no Russian sap, Stanley realises: not this deep – and these men are no black hand gang sent out to do the business before the big push, nor sappers either – for where's their tackle? *Curiouser and curiouser* . . . The party shuffles by a narrow gallery lit by electric bulbs strung from a wire in the bright light of which casualties are being treated. Stanley hangs back to see field dressings torn apart, the bandage tossed aside, the ampoule of iodine broken into the wound – he sees morphia injected into *tallowy* flesh. We don't keep 'em, Michael explains. Leastways, not oonless it's a scratch. We taykem back oop, lissen fer the ebbin' an' flowin' uvvit, an' when we joodge it right nibble oor way through t'oonderbits inta a shell crater or a trench an' leave 'em there fer t'oopsiders t'find. Stanley has absolutely no idea what Michael is talking about – although he grasps that the Northerner knows this and speaks only as he does to calm him, as he might have done a restive horse spooked by the cacophony of war. The long shaft termin- ates in a chalky grotto some twenty feet across, its roof high enough to allow all of them – Stanley and Jean-François included – to stand erect. Oor deepest point in this partuv t'line, Michael says, and Winfried plays his torch beam over the galvanised iron walls *seeped- upon brown*, writing into legibility the familiar mock street signs. Michael points to one that reads Unter den Linden and says, Over- yonder to the Jerries . . . then to the Champs-Élysées, saying, South-west to the Frenchies . . . and finally to the Tottenham Court Road: An' back there to the British lines, see, we moost know oor way round better than t'belligerents – fer them it's joost back an' forth a few paces, fer uz it's scootlin' all abaht. Stanley revolves and in this murky-go-round sees the faint rings cast by the torchlight trav- elling along these man-made gullets *like a . . . sort of pulse, I s'pose you'd say*. Michael says, Now, laddie, Ah reckon yoove earned yer tommy, cummere, and, flinging an arm around the taller man's shoul- ders, he encourages him under a low lintel, through hangings of sackcloth and canvas, to where there's a rich, homely glow of firelight and a *Catholic blaze* of candles. The cool mustiness of the tunnel is replaced by fat frying – the saliva gushes into Stanley's dry mouth. Men are packed into the well-lit chamber: Britons of all shapes, sizes, classes – Germans and French ditto, some *plucky little* Belgians, a scattering of coolies, several more Hindoos, also Negroes from the colonies – many are altogether naked, others wear bits and pieces of military-issue kit, others still oddments of civilian clothing, including ladies' walking cloaks, boudoir bonnets and even – adapted with blade and twine – the occasional corset. The men lounge on blanket-covered divans hewn from the sides of the burrow – they all seem to be simultaneously smoking pipes, mopping greasy plates with hunks of black bread and reading. The studied silence of their concentration is undisturbed by the arrival of Michael's party, the members of which distribute themselves here, there – *wherever we can . . . mingling not with laughing comrades.* Stanley finds himself wedged between *a hook-nosed Levantine and a flat-faced Finn*, at his feet lies an etiolated and languid figure, *not a stitch on 'im*, with the most singularly *sticking-out ears*, who absent-mindedly rearranges his genitals, pulling the pinched sac of his scrotum from between hairless thighs, then sets down his Everyman edition of Pater's Appreciations and calls over to the big blackamoor who's cooking on a pot-bellied iron stove, I say, spear me another banger or two, will you, ol' man? The blackamoor calls back, Two zeppelins anna cloud cummin' up! And in due course the plate does come, hand to hand, on it two sausages and a lump of mashed potato. To Stanley the forceful impression of a domesticity long cultivated is unutterably sad: *Where is dopey Olive, chirpy Vi? We sit no more at the familiar table of home . . .* He hunches over, weeping not because of the pain from his strained back or bruised arms and legs, but unashamedly as his sensibility quickens. — The barrage, so muted now it resounds only as memories of *summer rainfall on the roof of a bandstand . . .* Michael squeezes in beside Stan, gloves his hands with his own thickly callused ones and says, Y'know biggest problem we 'av is wi t'smoke. See, we can mekk t'cunningest of chimbleys – he points to where a contrivance of soldered tin snakes up from the stove's flue to wander across the uneven roof of the burrow – boot we still ass t'vent it soomwhere. Means we can only 'av cooking an' 'eating by night . . . *They've no part in the labour of the day-time* . . . Not so bad now, but coom winter it gets right parky down 'ere. The naked officer at their feet drawls up from his resumed Pater, Yaas, deuced fucking cold. The newcomers have all found perches, and now their food comes – the plates are all in use, so they are furnished with platters fashioned from the lids of ammo boxes and other scrap. Nestling in his lap, scorching his thighs, Stanley's platter supports greenish gravy, a potato splodge . . . *England's foam*, a single sausage that oozes grubbily from its split charcoal skin and some slices of what looks . . . *like polony*. A tin mug of tea is pressed into his free hand – he takes a sip *strong, sweet* . . . That's good, he says, and, apart from name, rank, number, these are the first words he has spoken since his rescue. A skinny Irishman, naked except for a purple feather boa, says, Ah, yes, when Mboya makes tay, he makes tay . . . Stanley picks up the sausage and reveals the letters MARMAL on his makeshift plate – MARMAL, what might that mean? Surely it can only be marmalade missing its ADE? Why, then, do all these other possibilities press in on her claiming her aching attention: MARMALOUS DISPLAY OF RAGTIME FLYING, MARMA-LARCHING THROUGH PLUCKY BELGIUM A VICTORY REVUE, AT THE STEPNEY PARAGON THE JAILBIRDS AND THEIR BLACK MARMARIA – this last cannot be true, for there would be no room for it on the hoarding, which is only a board covering one of the hotel's windows. The Alexandra is up for sale, a fact attested to by the estate agents' names – Knight, Frank & Rutley – on another slab. It is they, she thinks, who will endure – and quite possibly longer than the buildings they sell, which seems preposterous, looking up at the Mameluke bulk of the establishment: its four storeys of windows – each one shuttered and wrought about with iron, its Saracen's helmet dome covered in scales of lead flashing and surmounted by a coronet of iron railings. Tarrying, she thinks, that's what I am: *tarrying . . .* and so detaches her eye from the hoarding and its mysterious MARMAL, its timelessness of new poster peeling away from old bill booming Rowntree's Elect Cocoa, to take in the smaller Saracen's helmet capping the stairs down into the Underground station — then, and only then, does Audrey remember *whence I came.* Standing in the ill-lit culvert with the thunderbolt plunging towards her, trying desperately to judge *where it might fall,* she had become so agitated that she reeled away from the parapet edge to cower under the tiled curve of the parados, wanting to scream over the roar at all the other typewriters, clerks and shop girls that *this'll be a direct hit!* Boarding the train automatically, grateful only that it had not exploded, it was not until the second stop that she realised it was going the wrong way – not towards Old Street and the sooty tramp down through weavers' alleys to the Bishopsgate garret, but south. At Clapham Common, tormented by the weight of the earth above her head – *or in it, together with gasbags and pisspipes* – she unlatched the carriage door, *treadmilled up the escalator so fast* and emerged yawning uncontrollably into windy daylight and the mawkish cries of two piker heather sellers, who, flanking the station entrance, bullied all comers and goers with their vicious little sprigs. — Surfaced to this dilemma: should she attempt to fasten the Ince's Ladies Walking Umbrella that had been a gift from Mister Thomas when she resumed her position at the firm – the ribs and struts of which flexed, unsettlingly alive, as the breeze tugged at their glacé silk webbing? She could not, she felt, rely on the liveliness of her fingers to pull the cloth band around and manoeuvre its button through the wiry eyelet – *this thimble drill is beyond me.* The alternative – to open the umbrella and rest its post casually against her shoulder – was a possibility that appeared equally remote. Her fingers were far off – her *hands farther still and missing in action.* Screws of newspaper and heather flowers shimmied across the pavement, starlings blew backwards overhead – Audrey could not assess the power of the wind, nor comprehend how it was that it managed to come first from this quarter, then from that, whistling through her *unceasingly*, fluting in her mouth, her nostrils, her ears, her vagina. — Waking that very morning, Audrey found the world was *barred to me:* she could hear Gracie already up and moving about, the rap! as she knocked the old leaves from the slops basin, the compelling raaaasp as she unscrewed the caddy. Audrey had felt a dreadful apprehension – something was *about to happen, a momentous – no, calamitous event . . .* Two pimples on her top lip, big, beneath her tentative tongue. This was not the revolution – the two hundred thousand strikers rising up and following the Spartacus League's example – but an oppressive alteration to the most fundamental terms of her being: the way she sees and breathes, moves and dreams. She clutched at the sidebars of the bedstead, iron smarting her twisting hands, she arched backwards into the water-colour from the bric-a-brac shop and stood there beneath the windmill's sails and they . . . *turned.* She moaned and Gracie came to her, her cool touch breaking the enchantment of Audrey's febrile swoon. She held the cup to Audrey's lips . . . *strong, sweet . . .* That's good, she said. Gracie helped her to rise and dress. – Returned to Ince's only three weeks since and already the tedium of

285

the endeavour bore down on Audrey without mercy: Appleby's sententiousness – which, before the war, if not exactly agreeable, could still be endured – was now insupportable. The lost boys were still rotting in the mud – their comrades, having chased Jerry back to his own corner, were *a rash of khaki on the bare autumnal earth* ... Appleby's mean-spirited carping and his harping upon the traditions of the firm – *the flitch of his neck with its piggish bristles ... why isn't he dead?* He had installed a capacious umbrella stand while she was at the Arsenal – his sole effort to be up to date, and he promoted this to her relentlessly – for the messenger boys had already *addenuff* – pulling out first one, then another model, opening an original Paragon so she might admire its sturdy yet resilient baleen ribs – *disgusting, this whale's mouth opening and closing again: a leviathan feeding on the rotten core of the City, thrashin' about atop its stinking dust heap of high and low finance.* Appleby took out a prototype lopsided umbrella, its post set obliquely so that when held at an angle it would still provide total coverage. As he did a crotchety turn about the attic, bowing beneath the trusses, Audrey stared very fixedly at the anciently adzed beam that ran above her brand-new Underwood – only her eyes could inch along, tapping in the small nicks and notches, then return and inch along again, *remaking the small nicks and notches* ... The rest of her was unbearably heavy, *so heavy* ... she knew not why the floor did not give way under her, sending her tumbling down to lie among the stacked boxes in the storeroom of the Treadwell Boot Company *Makes Life's Walk Easier* ... Gracie had said to her, I fink you better stop 'ome, but Audrey was determined: We cannot afford it. Appleby withdrew more prototypes – an umbrella with a mica panel in its cover, through which a small square of the soused world might be glimpsed. The

Paragon Optimus with its patented Automaton frame – pull a lever and the tightly wound silken bundle telescoped out. Compact, Appleby observed, untangling the ribs one by one, but sadly inefficient. He next erected the square umbrella and, setting it on the floor, expanded on its architectural qualities, its fittingness for the modern city, being as it was only a smaller and more portable example of the tiled roof. Then there were various umbrellas equipped with drip protectors – spongy guttering that edged the cover, and that connected to a drainpipe running down the post, capillary action drawing up, then squirting out, the water . . . *which EVERY LADY SHOULD KNOW, the compressed towels being only 2⅓ inches long and available in tiny silver packets that could be slotted into Southall's Protective Apron and then fired! Because it was blood, blood . . . all about blood.* — The previous week Audrey had languished, too lethargic to attend the memorial service held for the munitionettes at St Paul's – and since then the malaise had come upon her relentlessly, in mounting *heavy, earthy* waves, until this morning she had feared she might *never dig myself out from under it.* Now, in Clapham High Street, her eyes scoot along the oriental roofline to *a seraglio of bakers, where plump and eunuch loaves are squeezed and rubbed by houris in mob caps.* In the midst of her *accelerated cerebration* Audrey catches hold of this: it is not the Ladies Walking Umbrella that cannot be furled, strapped and closed – *it is me, I've got the wind up me.* It is Audrey's arms that, beyond her control, fly up and away, struts jerkily unfolding from ribs, then bending back on themselves, so that the riveted pivots bend and pop – her skirts blow up, and, caught by the strengthening wind, the canopy of cloth drags her backwards, her stockings are half unrolled on her stiff posts, her handles in their worn leather boots rattle across a cellar grating. Through the mica panel in her skirts she sees a jeweller's with its display of NOTED LUCKY WEDDING RINGS – then, caught in her coat buttons, the cloth begins to rip – she thuds into the roadway and is wrenched this way and that across it, mercifully avoiding the bow of a tram, a gig, a grocer's boy on a tricycle ... Audrey feels the jumbling of her skeletal limbs as she is blown *over-rowley* past the Temperance Fountain and towards the chestnuts screening the railings of Holy Trinity — through the eye of this whirligig, the woman-contrivance receives this reminiscence: *comin' up 'ere with Mary Jane one Christmas to see Gus Elen an' 'is old woman 'anding out gifts from their spankin' new motor car.* Not that Audrey's mother counted on getting one, it was the gaiety of it all she craved: the band playing marches on the bandstand dressed with holly and ivy, a paper cone of sweetly greasy hot nuts. Mary Jane, out on the grassy plain streaked with melting and dirtied snow, the ice wind parting around her bombazine prow, an expression of the profoundest concentration on her face, the hint of *steam an' old cabbage water as she takes a stance* ... Only now, *spiralling to pieces*, her own skirts lifted to show *all I've got*, does Audrey realise what her mother was doing, *She never got inter the wayuv bloomers* ... another privy thing vouchsafed to her daughter. — *That is that:* the umbrella is turned right inside out. It lies in the grass by the railings, a mess of buckled steel rods and shredded silk – a redundant thing no longer capable of any effort, war or otherwise. And so it remains there, a thing taken up only to be forgotten for a long while I have expected you to come and call on me. Adeline pauses on a half-landing – situation and pose, both, Audrey imagines, have been contrived for effect. She had been kept waiting by the mistress of Norr House – the housekeeper, treating her dismissively, had placed Audrey on an oakenly uncomfortable chair in the hall, the strong suggestion being that she should stay put. As soon as the woman had fussed off, Audrey got up and wandered about, chafing the piercing tingle of her chilblains and poking into a strangely sparse drawing room, where there was a lustre of polish – the smooth secretion of all those workers' rubbings – that shone from wood, wood, more wood. There was a dying log fire, and above its mantelpiece a tapestry woven with the figure of a medieval damsel armed with a spindle – a child's board game was set out on a large, low settle. Going forward, Audrey saw printed the legend Willie's Walk to Grandmamma. Players' coloured counters were scattered along the trail, winding across the linen-backed paper, and a teetotum lay keeled over beside a pictorial ravine. Audrey wondered: Was Adeline's little boy called Willie? She had never asked Stan, and he – alive to his older sister's disapproval – had never ventured anything concerning Missus Cameron's domestic circumstances. It had been a long, cold tramp from Carshalton Station – Audrey thought about five miles. She did not mind, though – it would have been self-murder to have asked in her note to Adeline that she be met. Besides, Audrey needed all the fresh air she could get on her half-days away from the Danger Buildings – simply to be *rid of the mustard smell, the burnt-garlic reek, the ground horserad- ishes* ... Not that these were any more than approximations: the odour of the Buildings was indefinable, you had to be there — not here, where paper flowers tickle your nose and where Adeline is: raised up on the fresh white beech of her stair, her hemline high enough to show plenty of fresh white silk stocking, and her neckline low enough to reveal the whiteness of her bosom. Between these whitenesses there floats a Japanese kimono, its pattern of heavy blue and magenta lotus flowers *nodding her head* ... At least she has the decency not to affect mourning – the only black thing hung about

Adeline is the velvet ribbon – *dévoré?* – criss-crossing into the beaver's tail of dark hair that rests upon her too-wan neck. She resumes her descent and her speech: I–I was unsure about contacting you, Miss De'Ath . . . In truth, I didn't know precisely where to find you . . . Audrey supposes another might locate in Adeline's hesitancy the sincerity she has precisely placed there – however, Audrey is not to be seduced. Death, she says plainly, as Adeline is led across the hall by her own outstretched hand. Death, she says again, rising from the absurd chair. Free from personal vanity as she tries to be, Audrey cannot help seeing herself in the kohl-edged cameo of Adeline's eyes, floating there . . . *Nobody's dream*, her grey alpaca skirt's brush braid adjusted several times over, the dyed straw of her hat retouched with a sixpenny bottle from Woolworth's, the faded raptures and plushette roses on her jacket collar crushed by the rain, her boots oft-mended on a Sunday – the only religious rite ever observed in the Death household. To forestall any pity, to compel this moneyed sensualist's attention to the true nature of things, Audrey strips off her glove so that they meet skin to skin, chipped nails sliding past manicured ones. The back of Audrey's hand is uppermost, a freckled and oleum-pitted garnet in the fine lady's clasp. Adeline's palm is passionately hot, and beneath the brittle pad of her thumb Audrey detects a strong and rapid pulse. Ah, yes, Death, says Adeline. I knew, of course, that Stanley had enlisted under that name. Audrey, wishing within the confines of manners to be without pity, says, It is our name – when I went for factory work it was the name I had to give. She requires that this coldness between them be retained – that the chatelaine of Norr's class position be sharply defined. Adeline frustrates this by refusing to let go of Audrey's hand, drawing her instead towards another door off the hall, then through this into a cosy chamber – the walls brightly papered, many-branched candelabras set either end of a mantelpiece, below which *honeycombs incandesce* . . . Pine cones, Adeline says, a silly affectation, I daresay, but I collect them every year to burn – the candlelight is also perhaps an affectation, but I find it more aesthetical than the electric, besides, we think it incumbent on us to save fuel oil for . . . she falters . . . for the effort, and so do not have the generator except when people are down at the weekend. Adeline has manoeuvred them on to a small settee, where they are perfectly snug and still linked – she must have rung the bell because a very young girl enters, not in uniform but in a simple blue cotton frock gathered at her waist, and with her ash-blonde hair loose about her shoulders. Another affectation? Audrey says tartly once Adeline has given an order for tea, tea cakes and some of that fruit cake if Cook has any left? Yes, I suppose it is one, she replies easily, but I don't see why they should have to be in black at all times. I give them an allowance – a generous one I believe – and they're at liberty to get such clothes as are suitable. My own dressmaker will run them something up – like that, and almost at no profit to herself. Of course, Adeline sighs, at weekends it needs to be different – my husband takes the conventional view on staff. Audrey is unimpressed by *Marie Antoinette playing with her domestics* – more so by her casualness in speaking of *the cuckold*. She would like to look down on Adeline – her hostess has forestalled this by *hanging on to me:* they remain intimate in the complexity of their bones, the stretched coverings of their skins' overlay.

Adeline sops up Audrey's face – her eyes swell, cheeks plump up, lips thicken, as she absorbs pert nose, trowel chin, flaming auburn hair. An Ophelia, she thinks, of a Pre-Raph' sort, lying on her back not in water – but in the effluvium of manufacture, her madness – a sort of palsy – obscured by this murk. She says, I confess, I cannot see much of Stanley in you, my dear – nor of your elder brother. Audrey is dismayed – a reagent that converts most of her ire to raging curiosity, and she effervesces: Have you met him? Adeline smiles and says, No, though I've read enough about the phenomenon that is Albert De'Ath in the newspapers to feel as if I have –. The girl returns with a trestle that she kicks open beside them, then goes out and comes back again with a laden tray of tea things that she sets down on it, Chinese or Indian, Miss? she asks, but Adeline says: That won't be necessary, Flossie, we can manage for ourselves. Once the girl has gone, Audrey, rubbing freed hand with gloved one, says caustically, It'd be no affectation at all, Missus Cameron, if you were to ask Flossie to take some tea with us – I hardly think she's any more socially inferior than I. Adeline laughs unaffectedly – nor does she commit the crime of saying anything at all. Settling back in the settee, Audrey feels her wet petticoat chafe against her calves. Adeline inquires after preferences: Milk, lemon, sugar? – The tea has a perfumed aroma and a mildly brackish taste: Oolong, Audrey observes, Gilbert used to have it all the time before the war. Now he blames the Kaiser's submariners for upsetting his beverage habits. Adeline raises one perfectly plucked eyebrow. Is that all he blames them for? she says, and this is evidence of a sympathy that has flared up between them, here, beside a tall vase of late-flowering hydrangeas, here, where a volume is laid casually on a window seat, The Forsyte Saga on its spine, here, next to diamond panes rattled by the October storm. — Night has arrived expectedly, and Adeline rises to draw the curtains – which are cambric and decorated with diamond patterns of tiny yellow flowers to match the yellow-grained wallpaper. I might roll my dampness across them, Audrey thinks, impress myself upon them – repeat the pattern of me: I-am, I-am, I-am. Adeline says, I thought that I'd enjoy the house far more than I have. I take the blame for all the wood panelling, the shutters and the frankly rather . . . asinine furnishings. I'd thought – well, what? I suppose that by allowing the medieval inclinations of our celebrated architect full reign he'd create for us a paradisical setting within which the old ways might be re-established . . . old honesties . . . the barriers between man and woman, mistress and servant, might . . . dissolve –. She interrupts herself with more laughter: Utter bosh, naturally – worse than bosh, a species of cant. Two years ago I had a local joiner come and cover the panelling in here, then I had it papered as you see. It's here that I spend almost all my time – it's a pleasant enough room, gay and bright, yet no sooner did your brother go to France that it became . . . well, a sort of tomb for me. Oh, a flowery enough bower round it – she stabs with her teacake to the right, the left – I'll grant you, but still a tomb and moreover one that's inside of this tomb of a house, which in turn is lodged inside another sort of grave altogether. Please – please don't think I ask for your sympathy, M-Miss D-Death – Audrey? *Still, she has it: the squirming of her on the settee, the grabbing and twisting of a small cushion in her strong hands, is far from refined – not pretty at all.* The pine cones spit a resinous scent that should be pleasing – especially when mingled with the fresh flowers and the butter liquefying on Audrey's teacake. It matters, Audrey sees, that as Adeline manipulates so is she manipulated by those vast and impersonal forces that hold all small beings in thrall. She has not only Audrey's sympathy but her pity as well – *which would surely push her further down into the bloody mud. Poor, poor privilege that availeth you nought . . . Such good causes . . . the clamour of which presumably once filled your echoing time, are now those that augment the power that has robbed you of your lover – a loss that has, if it is possible, parted you still further from your kowtowing husband, who sits in the echoing House, raising his topper when instinct moves him to baaa more platitudes – while you . . . you are like Gilman, with time enough on your soft hands to be tormented by your wallpaper . . .* Adeline is convulsed by the giant's fingers pressing into her breasts, her sides, the softly vulnerable pit of her – they poke her unfeelingly – she is nothing, Audrey thinks, but an instrument with which to communicate the trivial nature of human sentiment, a telegraph key repetitively jabbed dot-dot-dot, dash-dash-dash, or a Hello Girl's switchboard into which are thrust the hard points of connection, when all the giant wishes to convey is *goodbye-goodbye-goodbye . . .* You must, Adeline sobs, forgive me, I do miss him so awfully badly . . . She takes a handkerchief from her sleeve, presses it to one coon eye, then the other, staunching her uselessness, her passivity. Audrey, whose own hands fret with the myriad shocks following on from her work, has at least this consolation: that she is a part of the giant – an infinitesimally small part, *perhaps a hair twisting on the muscled expanse of his back,* but, for all that, a part – whereas *this fine lady is nothing at all.* Audrey bites into her teacake, savours its warmth and delicacy – bread is at tenpence a loaf, and its price rises more and more, leavened by the blockade of Canadian wheat. Her hostess should be out there in the wind and the rain and the darkness withal, *sowing the winter seed and clad in travesty: a kirtle gathered at the waist by a plaited cord of sisal.* There – not in here, in her *gay tomb,* bemoaning the days when the goings on of the SPR or the anti-vivisectionists were enough to *fill her empty life with meaning . . .* Did you, Adeline asks plaintively, have much news from him – any letters? Audrey is angrily piteous – not dishonest. No, she says, Stan was never a writer – a reader, yes, when we were kids we all read, but before we little ones could he went to the library, read the latest scientific romances, then told 'em to us – that's me and our sisters –. She stops, then resumes: But not writing, not even when he fell under the sway of your friend Willis, no ... especially not then. And you, Adeline, did he write to you?

They sit there watching the fresh batch of pine cones Adeline has thrown on the fire go up in smoke, and Audrey muses, Are we parties to the same eldritch vision? A Zeppelin downed by the guns that subsides, all its fiery cathedral of buttresses, arches and beams burning in the night sky – then: the dull ashy corpse of it scattered across the furrows of an Essex field, the ruination of flight – *Icarus, raped and defiled for the readers of the much attenuated pages of the picture papers* ... I have, Adeline says, one or two of the models that he made – of flying machines. Willie wants very desperately to play with them but I shan't allow it. I have these too. She rises abruptly, crosses her candlelit tomb. Opening the lid of a writing case, she withdraws a package of postcards tied up with black ribbons *like her hair that he loosed*. Audrey knows what they are – she does not bother to feign interest when Adeline unties the bundle and passes them across, only flips through them as she might a novelty flicker book, engineering not movement but this stasis: I-am, I-am, I-am, I-am — for what Stanley Death had done with these Field Service postcards was the same as he had with those sent to his sister, and doubtless to Samuel and Mary Jane Deer as well. Whereas the authorities had enjoined the writer to cross out one phrase or the other to create the semblance of a missive, Stanley had scored them all through except for this essential declaration: I am ~~quite well, I have been admitted to the hospital sick/wounded, and am going on~~

~~well/and hope to be discharged soon,~~ I am ~~being sent down to the base, I have received your letter dated/telegram/parcel, Letter follows at first opportunity, I have received no letter from you lately/for a long time.~~ The command ~~Signature Only~~ had been deleted as well, as had the stentorian ~~If You Make Any Other Mark on this Card it will be Destroyed.~~ When Audrey received the first of many such as these, she had wondered at the response of the military censor to her brother's furious effacements of all but the fact of his existence. Packet after packet full of men dispatched across the Channel, wave upon wave of them sent over the top, bag after bag of these pathetic cards posted back to Blighty, it was all, surely, a product of the same narrow-mindedness: no order had been disobeyed, so Stanley's cards might be passed. Or perhaps the censor – who Audrey envisaged sat in a safe bureau, miles from the Front, beside a warm stove, a glass of something to hand and a Froggy doxy too – was amused by initial-ling these crazy ragtime communiqués, so scrawled PFL – it was always the same man – laughingly. I-am, I-am, I-am, – two I-ams per card, scores of them sent to her, to Adeline – and no other words from him in the ten interminably lengthening months since he had returned to France. I-am, I-am, I-am – a magic spell, chanted by a terrified child in the drained-out nothingness before dawn, I-am, I-am, I-am – Audrey sighs dispiritedly, aware suddenly of her own flickering existence and deathly fatigue. They both know that only one product derives from these formulae: that . . . *he is not.* – You don't imagine –. Adeline cannot continue. She tries again: They say missing and presumed . . . so you don't think –. And once more fails. Neither of them is a believer – in Jesus or Pan. *All hope is abandoned – all vitality drained away* . . . the rain that drives against the window is no more than . . . *evaporation, condensation, caused by fluctuations in* temperature, air pressure . . . *all eminently, tediously discoverable . . .* no mystery: *he is not.* Adeline binds the wound, returns it to the writing case. She pulls the plaited cord of sisal and, when Flossie enters, asks for whisky, soda and the cigarette box. When they have come Audrey sips fire and smoke, then rises from the settee to flick brimstone on to the fire and lifts her skirt to dry her petticoat. Adeline says, Forgive me, I should've proposed a hot bath and a change of clothes when you arrived, most remiss –. – Thass orlright, Addyline – she slurs and cockneyfies deliberately – you 'as made the hoffer now, an' I 'umbly accepts. — The bath is over six feet long, with sides so high that as she lies in the puddle of hot water at the bottom of it the enamelled rim gravemouths above her *I fell inter a box of eggs, All the yeller run down me legs, All the white run up me shirt, I fell inter a box of eggs . . .* She and Adeline are lodged together in the amber effervescence of the whisky and soda. Looking through steamy zephyrs at the imprint of green willow leaves upon the creamy drapes, Audrey quietly sing-songs, Is it girt or is it sere? Should you be thee and me be thy, or thy be you and me be thee? They had laughed, Gilbert and her, at the daft mummery of the guild socialists, with their *shprat shuppers held to raishe fundsh for their minishcule editionsh of hand-printed booksh* – they had been certain, Cook and Death, that the future belonged solely to those who could not only control the existing engines of production but make new ones. And here she was, utterly *fagged out* in a rich woman's bathtub, looking up at the motto some *floppy-tied aesthetical craftsman* had chiselled into the wood panelling: When Adam Delved and Eve Span Who was then the Gentleman? In the adjoining dressing room she can hear Adeline *playing at being my maid* – and no doubt *looking out something serviceable that had been obtained ready-made from Liberty's, worn once for a country walk, mothballed, and is now hatching out again after its long hibernation* . . . When, however, she is dressed in Adeline's fine linen underthings and her own dried-out alpaca, when she is seated back down in Adeline's tomb with another glass of her husband's whisky and soda, and another of his cigarettes, when she hears the motor car being brought around from the stables, its engine snarling through the storm, Audrey can no longer maintain such disagreeableness in the face of Adeline's overwhelming grief: she sobs, she laughs hysterically, she makes as if to tear her clothes – for wont of any other course, Audrey takes the other woman in her arms, strokes the hair *that he did* . . . — In the gale, under the crazed lamplight, Flossie stands with several parcels in a net. Please do not refuse me, Adeline says, they're only a few comforts – some brandy and fruitcake, a box of cigarettes . . . My pride, Audrey tells her, runs still and cold and deeper than any patronage. She takes the net from Flossie, who says, Excuse me, miss, but ma'am says that you're at the Arsenal – is it true, that you're a munitionette? The girl's frank face, *yellowed only by the lamplight*, slides away into that of her mistress, *addled and blotched*. They are not, Audrey says succinctly, hiring – then she allows the chauffeur to hand her up. Everything slides away: the peculiar old–young house, its chatelaine's teary goodbyes, the sweet-smelling stillness of her flowery tomb. As soon as the motor car picks up speed, Audrey's ticcing resurges, at first it is only a fidgeting at the stuff of her skirt, soon enough she is typing invisible orders in her lap, and by the time she is handed down on to the rainswept forecourt of the station it is all Audrey can manage not to *circle the wheel, pull the lever and rotate the headstock* . . . *circle the wheel, pull the lever and rotate the headstock* . . . She allows the chauffeur to hand her up and she settles in the seat immediately behind the one she supposes

298

he will sit in – it's the first vehicle of any description she has been in for half a century but she recognises most of the controls – gear and brake levers, the steering wheel. She wonders – if her recovery continues – whether she'll be allowed to drive – or at least pretend to do so, *a rusty old Enigmarelle, prompted by pokes in its back to do the trick for the cockney crowd* . . . Not that there's much of one, only *the two shonk doctors, Long nose, ugly face, oughta be put under a glass case* . . . *their two favourite blackies, and four or five of my fellow sleepy-heads.* The fat one has been left upstairs, beached, *her crabby little husband scuttling around her* . . . Helene, who Audrey has always *quite warmed to*, is there, and also the three old *monkey men*, who have to be pushed and pulled up *into the charabanc* . . . Busner, standing beside Doctor Marcus, watches as Mboya and Inglis coax the enkies into the Ford Strachan, which is parked on the back road alongside the Upholstery Workshop. It's good of you, he says, to come along. Marcus laughs: The sun has got his hat on, so I've come out to play! I mean, an outing – wouldn't miss it for the world! Busner looks askance at his retired colleague. Marcus is sporting an unexpectedly snazzy short-sleeved shirt, which is vertically striped chocolate and ultramarine, *Granddad takes a trip* . . . his trendy appearance compromised, though, by *soup stains?* He wonders whether Marcus's myopia precludes him from seeing the full extent of his ironic stain – irony that's within irony, which in turn is stranded, this ironic citadel, *rusting in a desert of dryness.* It took, Busner tells him, an awful lot of pressuring on my part before Whitcomb would allow me to take them out of the hospital at all –. Marcus snorts, Ah, Whitcomb, your bête noire – the Professor Moriarty to your Sherlock Holmes. What d'you imagine, Busner, he's going to do to frustrate your investigations, when you don't really know what it is you're investigating?

Busner wants to say something about the micro- and macro-quantal character of the post-encephalitics' ticcing, about his analyses of their metronomic states, about how he believes the dissolution – and now the reintegration – of their physical wholeness suggests an order within their chaos – wants to, but is leery of Marcus's contempt – and besides, there's *plenty of time for that*. For assertiveness, he calls over to Dunphy – the heavyset porter who's approved to drive the minibus – Are they all aboard? Dunphy sweeps his cap from his *Milo O'Shea* head, gives a mock-bow and twirls his free hand, inviting them to *roll up for the mystery tour* ... Bring me sunshine in your smile, Dunphy sing-songs in an undertone, Bring me laugh-ter, all the while ... The minibus isn't mini enough, the tiny congregation from Ward 20 is lost in its angled pews – Ostereich sits to attention in the middle row to the left, behind him cluster Voss and McNeil, *scared bunnies*. At the very back Mboya and Inglis are kept apart by a wall of sound: the irrepressible volubility of Helene Yudkin, who, as Busner oofs aboard, is saying, Look at these, what would you call 'em? Sort of nozzle thingies – but nozzles for what, they aren't going to squirt us with water, are they –? Of all the awakened enkies she's the least shocked by now – back up on the ward she'll stand for hours flicking the light switches on and off, unremittingly delighted by the photons' discharge. It's magic! she crows, I do honestly believe it to be magic! Everywhere she goes novelty entrances her – now she runs her hands over the electrified checks of the seat cover, Lovely, she coos, such a beautiful fabric ... Busner sits down beside Miss Death, who perches behind the driver's seat, and they are joined by Marcus, who, awkwardly folding his drop-leaf body, slots it in behind them. Well, he hales her, good morning to you, madam, and how're you feeling –. Perfectly all right, she chops him off, and remains with her face averted to the window. Busner thinks: What does she see there, up and to the left? Or is it the onset of an oculogyric crisis? It's one-two-three . . . ten days since her reawakening, but – he counts on – sixteen since her last, so one is due! Then, as they rock over a pothole, it strikes him: We're moving, and she sees a vista that's utterly novel – the long façade of the hospital contracting, the brick-work beneath its dulled windows *streaked by dried tears and going away from her* . . . Busner requires of Audrey Death what any physician does of his star patient – that she should damn her former one by *telling him calmly and coherently how excellently she's doing on her daily two grammes of eldoughpa, still, there's plenty of time for that as well* . . . – So – Marcus pushes his pitted nose between their seat-backs – where're we headed on this daytrip, the British Museum perhaps? Busner is flummoxed: I'm sorry? And Marcus brays, expos-ing big and ivoried tusks – *He is the walrus* – then comes out with *the wheeze he's probably been rehearsing since he left St John's Wood:* Busner, if you've disinterred some mummies, surely the proper thing to do is take 'em to see some of their own kind. Audrey murmurs, Howard Carter . . . Marcus is shocked by his own crassness at having spoken as if she weren't there, Busner by this time bomb. – What did you say, Miss Death? He speaks loudly – Dunphy is riding the clutch, revving the minibus out from between the gatehouses and on to Friern Barnet Road. – I said Howard Carter, he was the fellow who dug up the supposedly accursed tomb – I remember that. All the orderlies were talking about it. Biggest flap since the Brides in the Bath, sold a packet of penny papers they did when he died – sheer superstition, of course . . . pouce à l'oreille . . . I wonder what happened to . . . *who's she speaking to?* that nincompoop Feydeau – long dead, I s'pose . . . long gone . . . Ignoring the consternation she's provoked, Audrey relapses into her seat and silence as the minibus prowls past the awnings of the Rosemount Guest House. Or Kew Gardens, Marcus bumbles on, Kew Gardens are always awfully jolly. Busner corrects him: No, Kew'd be too far for their first trip out, I've settled on somewhere local – the Alexandra Palace. Marcus bleats, Ally-Pally! What the hell is there to do or see there? Place is pretty much derelict nowadays, surely. Busner gets out his notebook and, selecting the red Biro from the row in his breast pocket, awkwardly jots down the insight which, although taking form in him for some time, only crystallizes now, in the telling of it. – Not do – see, it's what they've been looking at for years – decades now. It's – it's the horizon of their world – the outer limit. By going there and looking back at Friern, we'll be breaking the spell for them – setting them free. It's these words he's scrawled: *setting them free,* underlined twice, wonkily. Marcus receives them in silence, only the *chopped-liverish air* he emits from his tightened lips suggests that lodged inside him is a *balloon full of bilious cynicism.* When he does at length speak, his tone is confidential: You do understand, the functional integrity of the cerebral cortex is an absolute – mark me – absolute prerequisite for anything resembling homeostasis . . . Busner knows *what he's driving at . . . that none of this can last . . . because in my heart of hearts I know: there are no such things as miracle drugs.* It's a conclusion that Busner had arrived at three years before, when, peering horrified into the scrap of mirror above the sink in the poky downstairs lavatory of the Willesden Concept House, he had seen his nose detach from above his lip and commence a halting – but for all that, undeniably real – circuit of his face. Besides, Marcus *bangs on,* how much is this stuff costing? And when Busner admits that it's in the region of four hundred pounds per pound, he laughs long before forcing out, Well, that's hardly

302

going to help the balance-of-bloody-payments! *And yet . . . And yet . . .* as Dunphy grinds the gears and the minibus hops-skips-jumps across the North Circular, Busner finds *I'm not put out at all*, because: Look, he says to Marcus, look at them – look at the joy they're taking in each other. The old alienist turns to observe the three elderly men: Voss, Ostereich, McNeil, who for so many years have been bounded not simply by the man-made but the mad-made – chairs upholstered by maniacs, broom handles wonkily turned by hebephrenics – and whose first few minutes on board the bus were spent rearing away from the undulating asphalt tongue they feared would lash through the windscreen and slurp them from their seats, but who are now relaxing at the sight of summer gardens. The puce droop of a laden rosebush, the lofty and fierily crowned sunflowers, the blazing crenulations of potted germaniums – these, the jolly bastions of Englishness, they remember well enough. They're lulled by the miniaturised farmland of allotments and sheds, then aroused by plants and flowers that are strange to them – the kinky shock of some pampas grass excites them, then a buddleia thrusting from the pier of a railway bridge *really gets them going*, and so they begin to *natter away.* — My old dad kept a whelk stall on Dover front, says McNeil, but he hated the things with a passion! Lumps of fishy rubber, he used to say, give me an 'andful of fresh spring onions any day, Alf – 'eads down in the earth, feet up in the fresh air, way your mother ought t'be! A clap of laughter is followed by Ostereich's confession that, You know, when I was a boy in Vienna we lived in an apartment – but my uncle, he had a Schrebergarten – an allotment you would say – and he grew the most marvellous currants, I do so love the currants! Oh, he continues, why is it that I feel so bloody marvellous today! Whereupon Voss chimes in: I know just what you mean – the last time I felt this way was in a dentist's parlour when he'd given me the funny stuff –! You were lucky, McNeil breaks in, we only ever 'ad sixpence for the puller – so no gas! Once again the three old men laugh and Marcus says to Busner, You don't think there's a certain morbidity in such, ah, ebullience? Tightening the arm he's thrown around the back of Audrey's seat, Busner says, Can't you manage to go with the flow just a little, Doctor Marcus? Don't you get it: they're on holiday – the holiday of a lifetime? — Which is what, he ruminates miserably, Miriam wants – not an ordinary seaside jaunt to some Cornish cove where the boys can make sand-castles and the baby eat them. Nor will a potter along Brittany lanes in the Austin do – they are to jet away from Heathrow in a fort-night's time. I'll make all the arrangements, she had said, pulling the rim of the Lazy Susan so that the sweet-and-sour pork balls were drawn towards her *hardly kosher*. Moodily he had listened to the muted sproing and yawp of the Chinese background music, murkily he considered the flakes of fish food that flip-flopped down into the tank from the same hand with which the waiter had just laid out their plates – although why this should matter he did not know. The boys in their green-and-gold barred ties and grey Aertex shirts had sat subdued by this: the strangeness of this meal out, en famille, the sole point of which was to arrange still more strangeness: a family holiday that, should he decide not to accompany them, would be the start of *a permanent vacation – from me*. Zack had read somewhere that white was the Chinese colour for mourning, why then were the tablecloths in the Jade Garden not pink, or purple – or black, yes, black would, he had thought, be best, for with his acquiescence to this perfectly reasonable request – *I am dying* . . . Yes, of course, he had said – and: The Alhambra, that'll be sensational, I've always wanted to go. Honest? Miriam said. Honest, her duplicitous husband replied, taking her hand and rubbing his thumb over the fretwork of bone and tendon and artery . . . *I have died.* And he was buried in a grave *the same shape as I am,* right down to the extra half-whorl on his ears, the slight webbing between the third and fourth toes of his right foot, and the protuberance of his navel, which was all that remained of the linkage to the mother *I cannot remember,* – despite being certain that her eyes – wary, as those of the dead must be – were staring out at him through Miriam's, the lids of which she had anointed for this special occasion with white mascara, making her look suitably close to extinction – *like Chi Chi.* Sitting there, putrefying, Zack had realised that the earth so densely packed around his body must be of a special sort, or how else could it fit him so well? Much of it was the translucent atmosphere of the Jade Garden, some was his own cotton, flannel and wool – but there was still more of this magic clay modelled into his wife's living hand, and this pulsed, squeezing *my cold dead one,* while Miriam's voice resounded still: *Pliz remembah ve gro'o, onlee wunce a year* . . . He turns to Audrey Death and says, This year, this . . . usually . . . He hunkers round to face Mboya, who sits *Byzantine at the back of the bus, the sun filigreeing his almost-Afro.* – Enoch – she, you . . . What did you call the little structure Miss Death made under her bed? Mboya shakes puppyish to attention. Her shrine, he calls back, we called it her shrine . . . Hephzibah Inglis frowns *sensing blasphemy?* and Busner says, Yes, your shrine, Miss Death – every year, for as long as Mister Mboya has been caring for you, you've made an odd little shrine or grotto under your bed, can you remember this at all? Audrey smiles, her twiggy fingers go to her temples and scratch at the dried-out nest of white hair. Audrey's grisly habit is a sore trial to Busner, these pathetic cast-offs of human vermin sent for fumigation – he wishes her clad in . . . What? A twin set – or a long tweed skirt, a blouse with a lacy collar clasped by a cameo? Anything – but not this brown velour bag of a dress, far too large for her, and over it a robin-red, zip-up cardigan that's far too small. The nurses have found her cara-mel-coloured slip-on shoes of exceptional ugliness, and the darned heel of a thick wool sock bulges carbuncular on her emaciated calf . . . Yet a sneer fissures her top lip and slashes her battered cheek, *and this, I love her for, because it's proof that she remains above it all.* She says, We called them grottoes, Doctor Busner – lots of children made 'em when I was a girl in Fulham. No one, as I recall, ever hazarded an explanation – it was just something we did, a folk custom . . . maybe t'do with the seasons, 'cause we'd dress 'em with spring flowers – dandelions, buttercups, pansies maybe, lifted from gardens a street or two away . . . She laughs, a dry rasp. – Respectable types hated grottoing for that reason, but they'd still give us coppers – out've superstition, I s'pose . . . The minibus has silenced her, its engine whining hysterically as they lurch up Muswell Hill Broadway in a queue of traffic. Her puritanical gaze falls on a gaggle of schoolboys with collar- and even shoulder-length hair outside a sweetshop . . . *And when did you last see your father?* And then rises over the parade to where tiled roofs *pagoda* up to the apex of the hill – she cannot believe this: that the skin prison within which she has been sewn for all these years *or so they say* . . . has turned out to be so flimsy. In the depths of her sopor she had dreamed this: the hospital grow-ing out of her mortal shell, its whitewashed and bare walls *stretching . . . creasing . . . folding into nacre.* Always she remained *on the inside . . . trapped*, the heavy girders arched within her bent back, their rivets *my vertebrae* . . . Cut through the dimpled plasterwork of her skull, dirty skylights illuminated . . . *nothing*. The floors – wood-block, asphalt, flagged – rose and fell as she walked, *so cemented were they to my feet*, and, as she shambled the long galleries, staggered the longer corridors, wheeled about the airing courts again and again, howled in the improved padded rooms, then flung her own bony cage against the locked fireguards, so she spat in the faces of these phthistical fellows – her mutinous other selves, hundreds upon thousands of them, their rough ticken overalls of a piece with the hospital's fabric, *their unravelling forestalled – for now – by its vicious selvedge. Presently* . . . there is this hand pressed on hot glass, this hand through which the sunlight glows, illuminating *a schoolroom map of Imperial possessions* – childhood freckles and oleum burns from the Arsenal have merged their territories into these liver-spotted *protectorates and dominions. Now* . . . there is this hand, swooping angelically past well-to-do house fronts – *newly built yet already frighteningly aged* – each with its unkempt garden and motor car garishly painted red, blue, or green. Audrey whispers to the forlorn fingers, We've got 'ere at last to Muswell Hill – we must visit Uncle Henry, discover if it's true about the General. She whispers again: Move – and they do, feebly tracing the contours of *a great monstrous absurd place* that stands out on the skyline – *a burlesque block with huge truncated pyramids at either corner* . . . The minibus rounds the final bend from Duke's Avenue and Dunphy responds to the shabby grandeur of the Alexandra Palace – or so it seems to Busner – by pulling up sharply in front of its bombastic portico. Too sharply: the patients and their carers rock and roll in their seats beneath the sunken stare of its cyclopean oculus, and the high-hat of its baseless pediment. Have a care! Busner cries, and Dunphy pulls parodically on his forelock. – Sorry, sorr . . . It's always, Busner thinks, the fucking Irish. He doesn't have time to bother with this – he's up and assisting his prize enkies down from the vehicle, watching them emerge tottering into the daylight, living dead only recently risen from their graves, whose dentures couldn't manage human flesh . . . *unless it was puréed for them*. Marcus was right

there's nothing doing at Ally-Pally. Under the colossal biscuit-barrel vaulting of the roof the immense building is hollowed out, empty except for a café and roller-skating rink of varnished pine upon which leotarded teenage girls scour around and around. The excursion party from Friern wanders this way, then that, smelling the mustiness of a different kind of institution. They stop to marvel at the enormous organ, with its three-storey-high pipes – Busner doesn't mind, he's only concerned to point out to the doubting Marcus how very normal the enkies are – they do not tic or jerk, their footsteps are halting, true, yet only to the same degree as any others of the elderly who have been long confined. Marcus, unimpressed, turns away from him, devotes his attentions to Voss, Ostereich and McNeil, taking them by the arm in turns, gently guiding them through the echoing chambers, speaking to each of them of the great changes wrought upon the world since their immurement. Always he's careful to relate these momentous external events to those smaller alterations in their own regime that may have trickled down to their buried awareness. Do they recall, he asks, some of their fellow inmates going out to work on London County Council farms? This, he tells McNeil, would've been in the late twenties, after the great convulsion of the General Strike, when it was believed – in the wider world as much as the restricted one of Colney Hatch – that energetic employment prevented the diseased mind from dwelling on its fantasies – lascivious or socialistic. Or how about the red and yellow cards that some of their fellows used to wear about their necks – did they remember this practice? Did they register its falling away? They might be pleased to learn that this was but the bureaucratic evidence of a revolution in hygiene, sanitation and the elimination of the diseases that had decimated their peers. — Observing Marcus, so doltish in his interactions with the fully socialised, yet capable of assisting these post-encephalitics with such delicacy and finesse, Busner reflects yet again that the psy professions are *in and of themselves mental pathologies*. He thinks of the neurotic psychoanalysts he knows, for whom anal-retention is the rule rather than the exception, of how they are scarcely able to function outside their consulting rooms – where all is static for year after year, and such human contact that they must have is conducted neutrally with the back of a head. *Why did I offer up mine for this botched execution, les quatre cents coups of Mmm . . . How does that make you feel? and always – always! – Mummy.* He ponders again the laboratory psychologists, with their clipboards and galvanometers, measuring the skin that *they've set crawling* with their own bloodless reduction of wayward contingency to the stifling, the statistical. As for psychiatrists such as Marcus, who've spent their entire working lives attempting – in many cases sincerely – to empathise with patients who're *so far out as to be otherworldly*, surely what success they may've had can only be because they're *nothing but a stranger in this world, I'm nothing but a stranger in this world . . .* — Rusting, pitted and eccentric ballbearings, the ageing patients wobble from one tarry ramp to the next as they debouche from this Babylonian bagatelle. Mboya and Inglis steer Audrey Death and Helene Yudkin to a bench that faces out from the Acropolis and has an unobstructed view of the city below, Busner and Marcus settle the male patients alongside, and Dunphy, with jobsworth's reluctance, goes back to the café to fetch teas and sandwiches. *State of emergency is a profound misnomer when it comes to describing the situation here* – there's no ambulance clangour or tinkle of broken glass, only orderly processions of houses that mount up the hillsides, while overhead sail flotillas of clouds, perfectly intact, and towards Eltham mares' tails flick at the Kentish downs. No, no state of emergency – only the pathos of a closed children's zoo, a drained boating lake, a crazy-golf course padlocked in chain restraints – *there's nothing for the Rip Van Winkles to do but survey this city as strange to them as Peking or Padua* ... Survey it, and, if it could be arranged, *eat good old-fashioned fish and chips all wrapped up in the Pentagon Papers* ... Spotting the concrete ack-ack mounts mushrooming in the defunct boating lake, Helene Yudkin says, What on earth? undoing Marcus's cat's cradle of integrative gestalt. That ... he says wearily, and Busner sees in the old psychiatrist's eyes Chamberlain, with the useless rearmament of his umbrella. Panzer divisions bucket across Marcus's high forehead, Pearl Harbor seethes in one hairy ear, Nagasaki in the other, the railway spurs end in the region of his pot-belly, and he pants asthmatically, unable to expel *the good news of the Holocaust she's slept through* ... Audrey, *blown plastic shell warm* with the tea of life, thinks only of Gilbert and his pinnacles of glass and steel – towers she sees rising from the centre of London, and which are surmounted by the comical silhouettes of *oil lamps, coal scuttles and hatboxes!* Gilbert had prophesised green fields and sylvan groves in between his phalansteries, but Audrey can make out only this: that the orderly city she remembers from her youth – its huckaback woven from street, square and crescent – has rucked up and torn ... *worse, been put away damp, so that mildew spreads across it* ... And to spare her own distress at this neglect of civic good form, she lets her head fall back so the mighty drapes of sky-blue chiffon may sweep into her. Up there a white needle – sharp, unwavering – draws a fraying thread through the heavens, *a godly thimble drill* that culminates in *an unholy boom!* followed by the trickling down of earth dislodged from between trusses and falling against galvanised iron, a sound that more than any other Stanley has come to associate with his new Morlock's existence. There is no longer fearful apprehension of the shells homing in, nor frenzied calculations to be made of their point of impact, for the final blow has already been struck: *All are dead – all are buried.* The party pauses in the tunnel, the lights – electrical in this section that passes below the German lines – have flickered and then died . . . *Why don't you feel fear?* The question flaps around them all in the darkness – *touches them, surely, with its leathery wings?* At Stan's side crouches Michael, who smells wholesomely of hay and horses – there is a frankness to his very sweat. The others Stan isn't so sure about: before they left their burrow for this raid on the surface, these men all donned Adrian helmets – the modified sort, from Verdun, with attached masks of thin steel strips and noseguards. These they had still further adjusted, by gluing bits of fur to them and soldering on brass buttons, until they resembled the headdresses of tribal savages. Still more savage were the bandoliers worn about their naked shoulders, the entrenching tools and saw-toothed bayonets hung from the leather belts slung low on their bare hips. Up until this moment Stan had been growing – yes, that was it, growing – in the deep dugout, just as before that he must have been growing alone beneath the earth: *a tuber . . . or a human in embryo?* He had slept in the burrow and woken again – eaten and dozed off once more. How many times this had been repeated he could not have said: men came and went in this cavern hollowed out from the darkness, but there seemed no pattern to their movements, no sense of their having been ordered to do so. The shameless bookworm was joined by a young Prussian, equally nude, whose head was shaven apart from a suede divot on the very top – duelling scars barred his hollow cheeks, and on his bare arm he sported a death's head armlet. Ja ja, danke, he said when passed a banger speared on a toasting fork. The only constant in this flickery hollow was *the big nigger who did the cooking, Jack Johnson – now we know where e's bin . . .* His frame may have been as massive as a boxer's, but his expression was studious, his lips quite thin. His hair had grown out into *the woolly ball of his forefathers . . .* He was always there – and, although the others came and went, they proved their own constancy through the touches they bestowed, for the underground men had no more propriety than they did modesty, rubbing skin on skin, groping, pinching and bussing one another – they even nipped, *puppies inna sack . . .* They– they bin all broke doon, Michael said of his comrades, so thissus is 'ow they poot themsel together again – wi this pantomime. But iss allus a pantomime, ain't it, Stan – the brass wi' their braid an swaggerin' sticks, ministers wi' shiny toppers – t'King inall . . . — Now, in the blacked-out tunnel, with the last blast still reverberating, Michael answers him: Fear, aye, fear's a foony thing. I coom down through one of them big craters in the redoubt, durin' t'second shindy at Wipers – whole boonch more coom down through Messines – thass 'ow it is: t'bigger t'charge, t'more as gets buried –. Another ferocious crump! and this time the electric bulbs swell back to life so that the party can resume its shuffle up the tunnel, towards the surface. Ewe might say, Michael continues, his words mixed up with the dust, that all that time we spent oop top was by way of bein' trainin' – trainin' fer down 'ere. Oop there t'Lawd could see uz – t'brass could see uz, t' daisy cutters cood cüt uz all about. Oop there t'toonels 'ave no roofs, an' death, like, it rains down from t'sky. But down 'ere the lid's poot back on, see – down 'ere there's no orderin' any soul over t'top. We voloonteer t'go oop, Stan – free men. The droom fire is oor thunder, an' the gun smoke, why, that's oor clouds – see, clouds . . . not men, mebbe angels, aye, angels, Stan – floatin' oop . . . Stand to: the *bugles nightjarring from the British lines.* What was it Luftie the country boy had said: *suck on your John Thomas if they couldn't get a cow's bubbies . . .* The squad of Ally Slopers crouches twenty feet back from where the tunnel, unpropped, droops into *a rheumy eyeful of evening sky . . . We cannot march, we cannot fight, What fucking good are we?* What might Willis or his friend Bertie make of this, Stanley wonders, for it's surely all they've ever dreamed of – men of all classes, hues, tongues, gathered together in free association, and *brazen in their lack of shame . . . they rest,* arms about each other's shoulders, hand to hand, *holy palmers of . . . a fag,* quietly conversing in their odd lingo – *a crowdie of tongues, full of bits . . .* The barrage dies away, the night creeps from shell hole to shell hole, insinuates itself snakily through the wire . . . Tonight will be no Crystal Palace firework show – nein aschpotten: *the 180s have fallen silent . . .* and they squint at only the occasional Very light crazing up, then plunging down to *burn its own tail . . .* Above ground they set to: following the night from muddy slough to ditch, taking a field dressing from one dead man's haversack and attaching it to the wounds of his comrade who still lives. Triage, or so it would seem, comes naturally to Stan – *haven't I already been making these judgements for months?* Of Feldman, of the Welshman, of the officer who grovelled in the bier two nights before the offensive . . . back and back to Aldershot, where the epileptic lurched out of the makeshift ring *blowin' Palmolive bubbles,* then dropped stone-dead at the RSM's feet. Stan had had a half-sov' on that bout – but here the most ardent weather-telegraphers got cured of the habit, for there was nothing to foretell, saving conflict without end. Cooling steel and drying blood – they orientate by these smells, not by the stars. They drag the seriously injured as close to the wire of either side as they dare, irrespective of which army paybook they carry – after all, *the only allegiance worth bearing is to life* ... Others they dispatch below – they don't know it yet, but at long last they've caught a Blighty one that will make them at home ... *in France*. The troglodytes carry morphia with them, and when a man is too far gone they give him a dose sufficient unto the end. Michael – *an arch-angel, and the last presence they see floating before them* ... *Warmer, realer, than that of Mons: no churchy phantom, conjured out of hunger, pain, thirst and fear – but a live man whose warm hand grasps torn wrists, rolls back blood-soaked cuffs, lets the needle in* ... Once or twice as they go about their business in the short and moonless night, Stan thinks of his section, short two men – maybe more – withdrawn to a reserve trench, their umbrella neatly folded, there to lick their wounds, *swollen tongues clammy on bully beef* ... No reflection – in this tortured realm of shadows and shades the underground men needs must be as alert as any raiding party – and some of these they do encounter, whispering: 'Re you the FANY? The topsiders are halt-ing, insensible, hair-trigger alert, bruised, raw, all at once. Observing them, Stanley wonders, Was I like that, shifting in an eye-blink from petrified terror to furious agitation? He watches them go by, feeling their way over the broken ground while fixed on this one prospect: their own deaths, under cover of which they mend their wire and drag back one of their wounded: a junior officer, hung about with stale whisky breath, a grim whiff of things to come – gas gangrene at the dressing station, the stench of his necrotic flesh. The topsiders have only one language at their disposal: the infuriated muttering of the compelled – whereas the troglodytes twist whichever tongue may be required: reassuring whimpering Frontsoldaten that they will not be schaden, calming Tommies with cock-er-ney cheer and *fucking oaths* . . . From the Germans' salients on the ridge to the British forward trenches down in the valley, the troglodytes slip back and forth – they recover side arms and rifles, pull potato-mashers from belts, unfired Stokes ones from the very mouths of the newfangled trench mortars: all are spirited down into the underworld and cached in its caverns. Long before dawn flushes the underside of the thick cloud to the east, they have withdrawn, none of the topsiders any the wiser. The tunnel descends from this chaos into an orderly innards of galvanised iron, pit props and efficiently wired lighting – as they are being swallowed up, Michael sticks in the earthen gullet: They muss not know of uz – not now, not ever. Think on't, Stan, iffen they knew they'd turn their goons on uz, winkle uz aht, drag uz oop. And when they'd every lass wunnuvuz they'd begin again wi' their slaughter. No . . . he turns and on they go, and they have regained the underground circus and dived inside their burrow before he resumes . . . No, there's only wun way t'coom dahn: by sheer blüdy chance, like wot you did . . . There is the blackamoor waiting for them with hot tea, and most of the subterraneans cast off their motley kit: the drawling former-subaltern resumes the pomp of his nudity, the ottoman of his groundsheet and the solace of his Pater. I once met –. Stanley stops himself there, for the young man at his feet is looking down at him from below *Schnauzkrampf.* Up above the barrage resumes – one-eighty-league steel-toecaps tramping across the former fields. The electric surges, dims, surges again and goes out. It takes a while for the cook to find his matches and light a lamp – in the utter darkness the sandy trickles, the woody creaks, metallic ticks, all are amplified: the whisper and groan of premature burial. Stanley fears he may lose his sangfroid, but the others simply chatter away: *Worked for a provision merchant 'fore I got the chuck . . . Si vous soulevez un jupon vous ne devez jamais exprimer la surprise à ce que vous trouverez sous ce . . . Went up from Saint-Denis to the Hotel de Ville and she was waiting for me . . . My oooold Dutch . . .* Stanley's eardrums, pummelled and stretched by blast after blast, have acquired a traumatised sensitivity, and as he turns his head this way, then that, these voices tickle across them, bristles on bare skin, mixed up with brass-band discordancies *Ooo-eee oom-pah-pah!* speech squeezing into and out of comprehensibility as the needle passes through its arc, sweeping over Luxembourg, Hilversum, Bremen, black bars in the sky that *cut across the puce clouds bleeding mauve rain . . .* The aesthete on the burrow's floor has kept ahold of watch and seals. He positions them carelessly around his lower belly, dumpy alpinists chained together for *the ascent of Mount Cock.* The idle yet systematic play of his fingers is *immensely appealing* she thinks as her own twist the dial, her ear pressed against the mesh grille. Erhem! Busner clears his throat, releases Uncle Maurice's red silk tie, which unfurls over the curve of his belly. Erhem – *Heath as it is spoken* – and he states again: Miss Death, would you like some help with the radio – I could . . . tune it for you? He wants to probe her relentlessly: What does she think of it? Had she been aware of Marconi's experiments? Could she then – with her Arts & Crafts imagination – have conceived of this hence: the world woven into a tight basketry of voice and music? Desires to – but is wary of her scorn. Besides, she has spotted her visitor, who havers beside Busner, his desert boots and fawn corduroys surely an academic exercise in informality, given his Wilfrid Hyde-White top half: the black suit jacket and *wedge of blacker – what? What's that garment they wear, a vest . . . A singlet . . . a sleeveless pullover? It seems always to've been polyester, but that can't've been true of the Warden-of-bloody-Barchester.* Anyway, it isn't this that matters, thinks Busner: it's the dog collar, which, although a simple enough hoop of white celluloid, is yet linked to a leash we all strain against. The Hospital Chaplain is young enough to be a trendy vicar – *and dishonest to God.* He's tall enough to have had *extra meat off the ration,* his long thin nose, mild brown eyes and still milky curls suggest the drinking of a lot of weak Nescafé and the leisurely patter-cake of Anglican platitudes – but his hands clutch spasmodically at the front flaps of his jacket to *tug them down . . .* while the flakes of dead white scalp on his shoulders imply *awful things about his underwear –.* Who's this fellow? Audrey prompts, then countermands herself: Let him step forward and say. Busner admires her: *Ooh, she's fierce!* as the Chaplain sidles in and, grasping the back of a chair, says, D'you mind? Audrey replies, Not at all. She has half risen from her own and juts out her hand – a strong gesture brutally undermined by the frailty of all the rest: the weedy hair and the cadaverous face, the insult to her ideals of Little Red Riding Hood's cast-off cardigan. Still, frail as she may be, and with a fearful asymmetry, she's managed to bring the old wireless across to this table – *she's interested in what lies beyond, if not above.* Poised on the plastic laminate: a plastic water jug, a plastic beaker, an aluminium kettle. The radio whistles until Busner turns it off. Thank you, croaks an effaced figure hidden in one of the chairs facing the television, and now they can all hear the raucous singing inside the simulacrum of the Moulin Rouge, inside the Warner Brothers' lot, inside the set – and this Busner finds obscurely cheering: Nostalgia, he thinks, more and more of it will be needed to tranquillise the collective psychosis of a steadily ageing population. And he would've reached for the appropriate Biro were he not having such *a bad day*. A cavity *big enough to stuff my tongue inside* has appeared magically overnight, together with its twingeing sequel: a note from Whitcomb stuffed in his pigeonhole requesting a meeting fairly urgently, *to talk some matters over . . . matters – that'll make martyrs . . . martyrs/schmatte* which is what Busner wants of the Chaplain: just possibly he can discover more about Audrey's family where all the other staff have failed? Busner thinks it unlikely she's a believer, yet a woman of her era will, he suspects, retain a certain respect for *a man of the nylon*. Without funds Busner cannot get Miss Death anything better to wear than this rubbish bag of a dress, but where there are relatives there may be funds – or a nest egg, put aside by her and swelled by compounding interest into a Roc's one: an Arabian fortune. Besides, Busner wonders, what are the clergy for if not the conjuring up of blood out of tepid institutional tea? Not that it was he who called for spiritual assistance, he'd scarcely been aware there was a hospital chaplain. A rabbi came alternate Saturdays: *Grossman*. Busner had seen the *big pallid gingernut* laying tefelin on some of the twitchers – binding their palsy with the leather bands – or muttering a prayer over a schizoid, the slushy regurgitation of Hebrew – *chicken shoup with bitsh in it* – mingling with the psychotic drone. No: the Chaplain had *trumped himself* – he had, he said, heard certain rumours of extraordinary awakenings among the catatonic patients in Busner's care, and resurrection being – as it were – his business, he'd come to visit the Gethsemane of Ward 20. — So the psychiatrist leaves them together in the day-room with its soiled floral-pattern curtains, surrounded by its undergrowth of easy chairs and right next to *a stony radiator* that no christly superstar – however omnipotent – could roll away since it was *locked inside a fucking cage!* He abandons the odd couple sitting either side of the silenced radio *news from nowhere*, and, as he tacks his way *chubby Chay Blyth* through the reefs of tables and iron-pillar narrows, sees only this: the ashy smears left after bodies have been vaporised by a flash *brighter than ten thousand suns . . . All my life . . . crouching under desks . . . only the klaxon's wail cannot fail . . .* He is bitterly aware that no matter how diligently he and his ilk peruse the New Left Review, they will never put a stop to it: *no happening could ever prevent it from . . . happening.* The hospital flattened – surrounding it, stretching away over the low Middlesex hills and down into the re-exposed valleys, a burnt tracery of closes, avenues and cul-de-sacs lined with neat, ashy plots, within each of which sits a semi-detached pile of rubble accessible via a cinder pathway. *And what is left standing?* Helene Yudkin with a hairdryer in one shaky hand, its flex scribbling up from a socket – he watches *more than her I long for a simple past . . .* as she toggles the switch and basks in its warm whirring, turning her shrunken girl's head this way and that as it shoots over her ski-jump nose. Lovely, she says, and then, marvellous – isn't it, Doctor, isn't it marvellous – so lulling . . . snug as a . . . woolly hat – a tam, a tam that haint there, no, it haint, a phantom tam, a phantam . . . She giggles – Busner, intent on the nurses' cigarettes *where have they hidden them?* and the view they'll afford through prettifying swirls at the tangle of his emotional life – Mimi has dropped her own bombshell – stops: *a phantam!* Witty-ticcy Yudkin is three weeks into the new regime and receiving two grammes of L-DOPA a day – as he wishes it, she's an exemplary picture of improved wellbeing and energy, her voice stronger, her movements fluid, and with only the occasional jamming, she walks stably and without assistance – and she feels *marvellous*. That she will stand for hour upon hour at light switch, kettle, hairdryer – any appliance she can lay her *hot little hands on* – is, he has decided, only *a reasonable response* to the electro-age she finds zapping around her. He chooses to ignore the forced reminiscences she reports – the past driving a coach and four through the present. According to Helene *rag-and-bone men get onter the ward quite regular an' gallop up and down whippin' their nags up, stopping to water 'em in the lav-a-tory bowl . . . Drunk summat terrible they is on gin at fourpence-ha'penny . . .* She retains the entire retail price index, circa 1919 – so what? Surely this is a corrective of sorts – her mind assimilating all that lost time by hanging on still more firmly to what she has? What he won't confront is the renewed chewing, the dimple worming in her cheek as she *eats herself up from within* . . . What's through the graph-paper window today? Same as yesterday: a plump shrink wrestling with a semi-clad blonde pharmacist *who's got a zone of erogeneity deep in her throat* . . . he thrusts her aside into a puff of dopaminergic dust – he'll force out his own short-term reminiscence: Mimi's shaky announcement *rattling beneath me* that she has called off her engagement to her soldier – *he'd have to be a fucking soldier!* Busner anticipates this: bare-knuckled boxing in the airing court *for the benefit of Mister Kike*, the starveling patients in their donated clothing chanting in a ring, cheering and clapping the man on – *Edwardianly moustachioed, he is, and in tight white breeches* – as he *beats me to mush and slush.* Crowded together with the rest of the sports fans: Miriam and Mimi, waving their hands rhapsodically in the air, happy to attend this *Concert for Busnerflesh* . . . This too he thrusts aside: the hospital is a degenerate city, the jargon of the staff – our diagnoses, our pathological labels and bogus practices – all obscure this: the gossipy reality, *the talk of the gutter* . . . the purloined cigarette rests in the notch of the tin ashtray and from its cellulose stopper *mustard gas leaks* . . . — On Saturday he'd taken Mark to the ABC Muswell Hill. Zack had looked only cursorily at the airily contrived monumentalism of the zeppelin, the choking spume of the night-time gas attack, the erect posture of the goggle-sporting Hun with the Iron Cross stamped on his leather breast. No, what caught, then held the professional observer was the boy's unblinking and *grating* fixation upon the screen that floated up above them, pinioned between long insets of brassy rods and stylised laurel leaves – the forlorn Deco interior of the cinema *dragging along A . . . B . . . C . . .* behind the streamlining of history. This, Zack had thought, is the whole of the twentieth century thus far: a white sheet thrown over our heady hopes, our disturbed dreams, our fleshly desires – with no sense of smell *we touch only plush skin, rub it in, gargle the mucal ice cream deep in our throats, but without pleasure* . . . This is our crisis of fixed regard: the zeppelin crashes to the cold earth again and again, a cathedral of rumpled buttresses, flaming arches, burning beams. They returned blinking into the egregious daylight to discover kiddie karts circling the roundabout and dropping off the hill down towards Crouch End – his hand in Mark's *was strange to me*. This, Zack had thought, is my awakening and it's always been thus, when I was his age, coming out of the Everyman, I'd experience the same estrangement from my shoes *cow, folded and sewn*. And he'd had this intimation: it'll only accelerate from here on in, I shall emerge from the darkness into the light faster and faster, a rollier and pollier silent comedian, double-, triple-, septuple-taking on doors, window screens, the cosmic fatuity of style –. Dad, Mark had said, Dad, you're hurting me – because, of course, it was the child's hand that had been clutched in his – and such a beautiful child, *his skin ivoried by ... neglect?* The boy's fixity had seemed to persist – he too was estranged from Wimpy Bar, 104A bus, all the rolling stones of old London town – a bad future was, Zack thought, tucked into the turn-ups of his dungarees and proclaimed its dominion across the Esso roundel of his promotional T-shirt.

Stubbing out the cigarette after a valedictory drag *the taste is flat,* Busner meets the Chaplain on his way out of the ward. What? he says. That was quick. And meanly persists: Y'know, Reverend, there're plenty more in here in need of some, ah, Christian comfort. The man is not to be guyed, nor is he apologetic: I'll be back, he says, but right now I have to take the Salvation Army visitors round – they come up weekly to check the acute wards for missing persons, but you probably knew that, Doctor? *Touché.* The Chaplain's brown eyes may be mild – but they're insistent and unblinking, *better to drown in their tepid tea than bite down on this fucking cavity full of poisonous smoke and die in my Nuremberg cell.* I thought you might like to know, the Chaplain continues, that Miss Death was really quite chatty – a remarkable lady, bears no resentment or rancour, one would say saintly if it weren't such a damn cliché. Busner resurges: Family – did she mention any? The Chaplain resumes satisfiedly: She told me of two brothers, one she thinks will have kept the, um, unusual family name – the other, Albert, she says Frenchified it – her expression – to De'Ath. Busner, appalled by this conscientious – if waspish – pastoralism, aims a jibe: In point of fact, Reverend, Death is fairly common –. Patrick, please, the Chaplain says, and motors on: Miss Death told me Stanley was reported missing in action on the Somme in 1916, so there's probably not much point in trying to track him down, or the other brother, Albert, who, if he were alive, would be in his

322

mid-eighties by now ... The cavity *big enough to fit the Chaplain inside, he could preach to the exposed nerve-ending, Rock of ages cleft for thee* ... however, he was a prominent civil servant, and married with at least one child. It shouldn't be difficult to find the family and who knows – the Chaplain smiles, steeples his fingers *an allusion to prayer?* – they may have Christian comfort to give and welcome the opportunity to help out their poor old auntie –. – Okay, good. Thank you. Busner hopes his abruptness conveys his own spiritual inclinations: *holy speed, in mens sano, shit off a shovel* ... – Okay, good. Thank you, he says again, backing away towards the day-room. — At the hastily convened press conference Mimi and Miriam are placed centre stage in drag of dull suit with clip-on sideburns – Whitcomb with them, *the eggheaded Professor who wears an explosive string vest.* Phallic microphones probe at their unyielding mouths as they announce the mainland bombing campaign, but *the real supremo, the diabolic mastermind, sits to one side lost in a donkey jacket too large for him, his small head shrunken still more beneath that ice bag of a tweed cap.* Busner knows that look, has seen that wary look, *fears that look* –. He had a house in the Paragon, the Chaplain calls after Busner. D'you know it – at Blackheath? Frightfully pretty – of course, that would've been a very long time ago – before she fell ill. Busner calls back: Okay, good. Thank you – I'll look into it and, wrenching round at last, succeeds in unbolting himself from the Chaplain's *mild steel threads.* — Every Wednesday, together with the Guardian, a comic is delivered for Mark: The Beezer. Miriam beats up a soft-boiled egg in a teacup and feeds it to the baby – the egginess is unbearable to Zack: *all-in-one human and chicken ovulation* ... *Chicks eatin' eggs* and this is what you get, Aaaargh! Whoopee! Cripes! P'yong! Antics the seven-year-old scans with tremendous seriousness, his eyes entrapped *in just the way*

323

they were when we left the ABC ... Ho-ho! Phew! Tum-ti-tum! LOOK
AT THESE SUPER PRIZES! PEN AND PENCIL SET – TENNIS
RACKET – ROLLER SKATES – CRICKET SET – RECORD TOKEN
– FLYING MODEL AEROPLANE. The winner of the Star Prize – a
Record Token and a 50p Postal Order – is Mark Busner, South
Grove, Highgate N6, for this: Man (in psychiatrist's office) – 'Please
help me – I think I'm a pair of curtains.' Psychiatrist – 'Now, now,
pull yourself together!' Shadowing the Ooh-err! bum, or Oi! bonce,
there are invariably a few black strokes to provide a sense of movement – movement, and so time within which a small boy may be
alarmed, happy, fearful, overjoyed? In the toasted atmosphere
surrounding his eldest son's small face there are no black strokes,
beneath it there's no inscription. Aren't you pleased? his father asked
him, but the boy only shrugged, and now Busner thinks bitterly, I am
Colonel Blink the Short-Sighted Gink not to've grasped that there
was something seriously wrong – I'm a buffoon in Barney's Barmy
Army with a hastily inked-in moustache who's been fooled by Jerry's
equally ill-conceived disguise. Still, if I hurry I can turn the tables on
them by rolling the barrel full of explosives into their camp, so: DER
BOMB, DER BOMB, DER BARREL IS RIGHT BESIDE YOU!
and BOOM! A sight to gladden Freddy Ayer's hooded eyes: the
block letters surrounded with a yellow flash and the tannish cedillas
of flying staves. Poor, fat, badly drawn Jerry, *so much for his mainland
bombing campaign* ... Maurice, his homburg looking as tall as Tom
Mix's Stetson, pulls back one curtain and then the other, the cold
light surges into the empty room with its lumped-up dust sheets and
stacks of pre-war newspapers – *the worms' casts of the real family that
hadn't been cut in two* ... — I stood there then, Busner thinks, as I
stand here now on the twelve thirty-nine from Moorgate to Welwyn

Garden City, on the eighth of April 2010: despite my closest living relative having been right beside me *I was still alone* ... a boy blown in half when the road was mined yet again at Le Sars had been taken down by some over-enthusiastic poilus up from the south, Michael happened to be there and heard his dying words – *the usual sad guff, sweetheart, mother, sarsap-a-fucking-rilla* – but also that he'd miss a concert party that evening at which – or so it had been rumoured – Miss Dorothy Ward would be singing. They went up into a curtain of drizzle some way behind Guedecourt: Michael, Stanley and five others in tankers' uniforms that were clean enough to withstand scrutiny being *fresh out of a Mark 1 tin* that had ditched some way short of Le Transloy. It wasn't so unusual for them to surface behind the reserve trenches – happened all the time, although mostly inadvertently when an unanticipated advance by one side or the other left the underground men marooned. With their German-improved Greathead shields, their powerful digging and boring machines, and their advanced Edisonian listening equipment – courtesy of the Byng boys – the troglodytes could outpace any topsiders' tunnelling, achieving three times their velocity: chuffing through the earth as a train comes along a straight branch line, of an evening ... *Jack the Ripper stole a kipper, Jack the Ripper stole a kipper* ... the chucking back of the till sounding, beneath the ground, uncannily like the rhythm of wheels-on-bogies ... *ch-k' ch-kunk ch-k' ch-kunk ch-k' –*. Extensions had been dug deep into the combatants' territories – east to intersect with the mines of the Sambre-et-Meuse Valley, west to infiltrate those of the Pas-de-Calais. With so much more coal now available, a turning circuit was under construction beneath Ypres, in anticipation of bringing rolling stock down. Surfacing behind the lines, one or two of the troglodytes might take their chances, hoping

325

they would be seized by their former enemies and so suffer no worse fate than imprisonment. But if a man were suddenly to come amongst former comrades – well he would either to've assumed another man's identity, or else explain how it was he had survived – prospered seemingly – during his prolonged absence from his unit. It was strongly rumoured that the returnees of all armies were summarily shot – but this was not what kept them in their amenable Hades, bent to their boring, a shadowy force creeping under an advance, nipping at the heels of a retreat, burrowing far down below the shell holes of the new no-man's-land and so re-establishing their subterranean liberty. No, Stanley understood *the new law of threes* operating in the sod: esprit de corps, a sense of justness, and this strange dialectic: There was one group of men here, a second over there, antipathetic to them in every way – and in the middle there was this third and better part, *a combination of the two no longer trammelled by rank, king-emperor, kaiser or patrie in any shape – a hotchpotch, a linguistic stew, that, should a man partake of it, soon rose unbidden to his own lips: their happy argot.* Grecian love also. It was Phelps – the resplendently naked subaltern who instructed Stanley in the latest principles of political economy – who had introduced him to this gentle comfort – in the dark, the holding of hands and the rasping of a bearded cheek upon its brother's. Stanley was shocked only by his own perfunctory acceptance: *This was the way you unfixed your bayonet in the eternal eventime . . .* 'tho, thinking upon it, he realised what the conflict had done to him: rubbed away at all the corns of convention, so that once the abrasion of the barrage ceased to operate upon him *the dead hard skin sloughed off,* leaving behind pale naked forms entwined together in the bowels of the earth . . . *quite natural, tubers, mandrake roots . . .* Whether it be Tommy and Frontschwein, poilu and pointu, or a mountainous

Senegalese twinned with a tiny Chinese coolie. Stanley wished Feydeau could have seen it – they coupled so casually, the underground men, and no one – or so it seemed – thought anything much of it at all, it was merely the promiscuous instinct for life: the only distinctions that they made between the topsiders was whether they could be saved, the sole ones amongst themselves, *whether he could be loved* –. Where the blazes did you spring from? says the muffled-up shape of an officer stood pissing against *the oiled cotton that stretches high over the twisted ribs and spars which used to be Mametz Wood.* The day is an elegant parasol tasselled with clouds, the night an umbrella with starry holes torn in its cover. Got ditched up by Le Sars two days since, Stanley says jollily, moving in closer so that the man can see the crowns on his purloined uniform and the crossed machine guns. – Oh, I say – the officer's features are *teddy bear* in their woolly surroundings – you tank-wallahs're bloody lucky to've come through that show, is that your whole crew? Stanley concedes that it is, concurs in their good fortune, asks of the officer if he knows where the heavy bunch are stationed. Oh no, he says, if'n I did I still wouldn't flap my mouth . . . he picks at his mitts . . . best be gettin' back to Division – they'll set you arights. Down there's Montauban, sunken lane from there goes back up the line – y'll be happy in it . . . *as etappenschwein in shit* . . . Slogging along, Stan chides himself for not making the best of it: the night sky and the crescent nailed up on this – *up there are moon-men holed up in its cheesy canyons, crash-landed balloonists prob'ly huntin' 'em down with fowling pieces – the duffers! They should know their powder won't ignite in a vacuum* . . . Behind the party the Materialschlacht goes on: *dips, hooter, fusees, Very lights – the whole bang-shoot topped off by Jerry's Big Berthas firing from below the horizon. Such illuminations! Gas-jets behind frosted glass – the world's a pub, so set up the Dewar's!* He ought to enjoy it – but he can't, so accustomed is Stan to the embrace of Mother Earth that with each step they take towards the rear the red man *saws a little further around my scalp with his rusty bayonet*, and he feels the chill night air on bare bone – which is *the sky dome through which thoughts trail phosphorescent . . . Shuttlecock, shuttlecock, if you don't spin, I'll break your bones and bury your skin . . .* Released from their clayey restraint, Stan's arms begin to twitch, his shoulders to heave – he is compelled to swivel round so he can search the sky above and to the right. — At Division there is only an encampment of huddling Amiens huts and a big marquee that must have been pitched especially for the show. Lit from within, its barber's pole stripes wriggle to the tinkle of ragtime piano played by a cheeky chappie, who, as the troglodytes enter, pulls off his boot and runs his heel along the keys t'-t'-t'-t'-t'-t'-t'-t'-t'-ting-a-ling-dring-drang-ra-drong-gong! *He's the spit of Fred D'Albert – maybe it is he? Wouldn't you like to ride in my aer-o-plane!* The stage has been knocked up from duckboards and props with mud still on them – there's no limelight only a row of hissing Tilleys. The men sit staring at the painted back-drop of a balustrade, on it a statue of an armless Greek goddess, and behind this a great crudely rendered mass of nasturtiums and sweet peas. The men – who are *a mess o' rice puddin'* after the chinks, Hindoos and blackamoors below ground – have imposed their own hierarchy on this entertainment, with the brass at the front: a stout and red-faced colonel sits on a wicker chair dragged in from some fallow farmhouse that should be supporting a bent old back – *not this fat arse, should be creaking as Vieux MacDonald washes his ivories in a glass of pear brandy – not screeching reedy as Colonel-fucking-Blink squints through the Tilleys and takes a sip from his hip flask . . .* Behind the officer, falling away, tier upon tier of bull-necked RSMs and military police, stoical sergeants and crapulent corporals ranged on benches – then, cross-legged on the bare earth, are the rows of lousy cropped mops and filthy gorblimeys, smaller and smaller, pipe-puffing Old Bills and waifish little Alphies, their heads bowed, shoulders hunched, hands cupped to protect the precious embers – all the way to the back flaps, where the bantams sit, their necks wet, their eyes dully regarding *the splendid show of all these khaki backs*. The Tommies mutter, groan, and shuffle to make room for the troglodytes, while the awed whisper goes round, Tankers . . . Tankers . . . the heavy bunch . . . In a way, Stan thinks, it isn't too unfair an imposture – for aren't we tankers of a sort? Behind their steel shield they too push forward inexorably, albeit rolling under all obstacles – rather than over. In the few minutes that they all sit watching Fred D'Albert rinky-dinky-plinky-plonking, Stanley eavesdrops on a drawling lieutenant of the Greys: Eeee-nor-mously foreshortened, blighter was only identified by his cigarette case – from Asprey's, or so I'm weliably informed . . . And picks up other tit-bits: *Wilson re-elected, the Welsh Wizard in Number Ten, old Franny-Joe dead in 'is bed, Nastyputin shoved under the Russiyan ice* . . . He listens, but is more absorbed in his own posture: holding still, clasping his own shaking hands – so absorbed that at first he doesn't register the auburn bombshell who explodes on to the stage. She wears a patriotic dress: red bodice, white waist, blue skirts that froth up from the makeshift footlights to reveal *lovely calves*. We're fuckin' dead already, moans the man next to Stanley, because a woman is usually the last thing you see at the dressing station *when the shit from your punctured guts has poisoned your blood*. This, Stanley thinks, this is why X-rays were invented, to see through all that silk and linen, to reveal the clean white limbs and blushing cunny of Miss Dorothy Ward, who makes a low bow *so we all hang on her neckline*, then *lets fly with a blast of soft shrapnel that caresses us all.* I should love to see my best girl, Cuddling up again we soon should be, Whoa! – the men all chorus and continue: Tiddly-iddly-ighty, Hurry me home to Blighty, Blighty, is the place for me! Back and forth across the narrow stage she promenades, pushing up her derrière, flinging out her long legs, – and, despite the fug of wet wool and fag smoke, the beer-soaked breath and leering sweat, the hyacinth, the jasmine and the sharp urinous tang of her own sweet perfume falls gently on all of them – and now Stan hears the lines that came before, *Jack Dunn, son of a gun, over in France today, Keeps fit doing his bit up to his eyes in clay* . . . That winter had seen skin left behind on the steel hafts of mattocks and spades, – it was too cold to melt the diesel oil in the engines they had rigged up to edge their Greathead shields forward, so the trogs sat tight in the frozen ground, deep in their burrows behind layer upon layer of canvas, a Rattenkönig biding its time, sallying forth only for food or fuel . . . *Each night after a fight to pass the time along, He's got a little gramophone that plays this song* . . . Come the spring some went on up to Arras, marching by night along the winding strip of no-man's-land, and by day taking cover underground – telegraph and telephone wires had been strung between the discontinuous tunnel systems, so that everywhere they arrived they found loving arms, warm soup, a dry straw palliasse on which to lay their heads . . . *Take me back to dear old Blighty! Put me on the train for London town! Take me over there, Drop me anywhere, Liverpool, Leeds or Birmingham, well, I don't care!* Stanley had been sorry to bid farewell to Michael, who felt it incumbent on him to aim south, to the Hindenburg Line, not believing that Nivelle's offensive would be any sort of coup – let alone le dernier. There's a duty my duck, he said. Frenchie is a proud fellow, and more lads coom down to uz at Vairdoon than anywhere else along the Front – it'll be the same now: they've a stomach for a different fight, though! . . . *Tiddly-iddly-ighty, Hurry me home to Blighty, Blighty is the place for me!* — Squelching in the mud below Vimy Ridge, Stanley remembered Michael's words. The tunnels here were deep and well secured – scores of generators had been brought down from the overrun German trenches, and some Jerry engineers had come down with them who were like the Wizard of Menlow Park when it came to knocking up pumps and other contraptions. Still, no pump could suck up this evil slurry, which churned into whirlpools that sucked in men trussed up in their greatcoats, entire field pieces, and on one momentous occasion a tank that wallowed into the tortured morass as the U-boats did beneath the seas . . . *Bill Spry, started to fly, up in an aeroplane, In France, taking a chance, wish'd he was down again, Poor Bill, feeling so ill, yell'd out to Pilot Brown: Steady a bit, yer fool! We're turning upside down!* The world be turned that way, said a burly pilot officer, come down fléchette-fast, parting company from his spinning Camel two hundred feet up – or so he said – plummeting away from its twin Vickers, which went on firing lead arabesques, then slithering from the lip-into-the-cup, where the trogs had just opened an entry point. One minute I was up above, sculpting the very clouds and bein' the very flower of chivalry – he was en route to return a dropped map case to a worthy foe – the next I'm down here in the depths with you mudlarks! Dinnae fash yersel'! cried the ex-drummer boy who first tried to restrain the aviator – then laid him out cold. From Huggins, the pilot, Stanley learned of the Petrograd rising. You lot're bolshier than the Bolshies, he said, once they had taken him deep below and *shown 'im the ropes* – and he spoke of his

331

wee terrier, Boinkum, left behind at Roclincourt. They lay there in the subterranean gallery, on their galvanised-iron platforms, looking up at the dripping earthen sky – and Huggins spoke of how Boinkum would howl when he wasn't allowed to go up to the dogfights with his master. Fast friends they became – beneath Wancourt, Monchy and Thélus. Huggins grew fanciful, saying he could see clouds boiling in the mud and smell the wind of change in the miasmas of their tunnels and burrows. He had nightmares, waking terror-struck in the impenetrable darkness, *Thousands of tire-Boches!* he had seen, *Thousands, thrustin' down at us* –! And of course, the world being turned that way, they were all hurled skywards and impaled on this fakir's bed. Stan stroked Huggins's rough curls and encircled the former pilot's heavy chest with his wiry arms, cooing to him, *Take me back to dear old Blighty! Put me on the train for London town! Take me over there, Drop me anywhere, Liverpool, Leeds or Birmingham, well, I don't care!* — More than a year later they were still together, having been squeezed further north along the lubricated chute between the maddened masses – past Lens, Neuve-Chapelle and Fromelles, they arrived in time to experience the merciless bombardment of Passchendaele from below. It was around that time that the first doughboys joined them through the Messines craters, and, seeing these big western farm boys, filthy and demoralised, Stanley laid bare for them the state of affairs: The khaki cattle are on this side, see, and the field-grey ones gettin' a taste of their own marmeladeneimer are over there. The wire separates these two breeds just as it does your livestock on the range – but that's a bit thick, see, and one day, when the time's right, the fences'll be cut and all these chaps'll mingle together, just as we do here – and then they'll all go home. I'm . . . I'm as sure you're like me as – damnit –! He and Huggins sang to the doughboys,

I should love to see my best girl, Cuddling up again we soon should be, Whoa!
Tiddly-iddly-ighty, Hurry me home to Blighty, Blighty is the place for me!
In those doomdripped days they thought often of the London sewers
– not as deep as the underground tunnels, right enough, but then: Not
even bombs want to drop in the shit, said Stanley, who many of them
had taken to calling Henry Morton, on account of his exploratory turn
of mind. Greengage, a onetime sapper who had worked in them as a
lad, spoke of their remarkable taint, how poking towheads down or
pulling up dead dogs he would near-savour the blending of detergent
and excreta, while the waters roared on through the glistening tiled
culvert and over a subterranean precipice big enough to swaller a 'bus!
The sewers, Greengage contended, are a place in their own right, not
juss the love tunnels of rats an' turds, but the bowels of the very metropolis, and as such necessary to the functioning of its monumental body:
there could be no pretty faces promenading through Mayfair without
the shitty business underneath . . . *Jack Lee, 'aving his tea, says to his pal*
MacFayne, Look, chum, it's apple and plum! It's apple and plum again!
Same stuff, isn't it rough? fed up with it I am! Oh for a pot of Aunt Eliza's
raspb'ry jam! The troglodytes debated the wisdom of devoting their
energies to making of their own shafts and culverts a drainage system,
for the topsiders were drowning in the standing water now that the
Flanders dykes and ditches had been destroyed.

Up above three thousand British guns fired four million shells.
Below in their burrows the trogs smoked Lucky Strike cigarettes and
studied Sidgwick on ethics. They read the poetry of Robert Browning,
learnt Arabic script from Ali the Zouave, or refined their understanding of surplus value and the public utility of social-credit unions.
All those *phases of development* Stanley had found it so hard to
concentrate on, he now he understood and could expound upon.

Feydeau's Discussion Club and its association with the Socialist League had all been minuted by him – so it was that in his underground reclusion he recalled the words of Morris and Kropotkin, the papers given by Missus Marx Aveling and Miss Schreiner. Those who descended had scant interest in the International Alliance of Women or the International League for Peace and Freedom – but Stan did. He sent his own emissaries aloft, and they came back with copies of the Ardent and The Freewoman, and with books by Miss Dix and Missus Perkins Gilman. Stanley explained to his comrades that: The future belongs to the feminised man, he who is capable of wearing cambric with pleasure – as we do – and of loving – as we do – and of regarding the fairer sex to be our own, and women to be to be not helpmeets but authorities on the blood-law of biology. So as to align still more completely with the emergent world-consciousness, Stanley obtained Southall's Sanitary Towels and wore them one week a month – then he would not lie with Huggins. He sewed a fillet in his blouse and filled it with increasing amounts of sand, a half-pound per month, while encouraging the others to join in his couvade. And the troglodytes listened – and they approved, and many followed his lead, with the exception of Mohan, who, having been with Stanley since he first came down, felt free to chide him: Blighty, you should know this, Henry Morton, this is a Hindi word, bilyati – meaning foreign, you see. Now, taken up by the Britishers to mean their home, it will point back at them – a bilyati gun. And every time you say it, sing it, scream it, you fire the bilyati gun in your own face! ... *Take me back to dear old bilyati! Put me on the train for London town! Take me over there, Drop me anywhere, Liverpool, Leeds or Birmingham, well, I don't care!* It was not until many months later – after the collapse of the Italian Front, the Bolsheviks' rising and the taking of the Holy City, that a fellow called Cummins, who'd been a shop steward in Greenock, came down to them. He talked heatedly of Henderson's constitution, and Stan said, Well and good – your catechism. Yet it's so here already: what little there is belongs to us all in kind, there's no sugar – so we're never bitter. No man would think to lug one of the great shields into his own little pit! As for administration, what of it? A tunnel needs pumping and it's all hands to the levers, a new one wants electrification and the men with know-how are parcelled up the line without any ado – these things simply happen. But, Cummins said, this is anarchism, man – there's no system, no method, no means of carryin' it forward as a programme for the nation –. To drown him out they all sang: *I should love to see my best girl, Cuddling up again we soon should be, Whoa!* And to inflame the doughty Scot still more, Stan planted a smacker on his dirty forehead ... *Tiddly-iddly-ighty, Hurry me home to Blighty, Blighty is the place for me!* When Ludo broke through at Arras, Cummins – who had a stubborn sense of his own socialistic amour proper – said that this'd teach the trogs – who were in considerable disarray. Stanley and Huggins laughed at him. We'll sail a lighter up the Scheldt! they cried. Don't you see, it matters not a fig to us who's victorious – there're strikes aplenty in Germany, they've no more belly for it than the rest, it ain't the Russkies who've capitulated at Brest–Litovsk, it's Ludo, Fuckenhayn and Kaiser-bloody-Bill! — And Schmidt, from Köln, who had a lusty tenor, a nose that could smell a bottle of Moselle through sixty feet of cold dead mud, and a genius for organising chorales, led them into the verse, *One day Mickey O'Shea stood in a trench somewhere, So brave, having a shave, and trying to part his hair. Mick yells, dodging the shells and lumps of dynamite: Talk of the Crystal Palace on a Firework night –!* To vex the Scot further, Stan took the just-boiled dixie, and, making him a cup of George, handed it over, saying, The fucking Irish, they've got the right idea: no work – that's the soup ticket! And Cummins smiled in a doubly-deboshed way. — It had grown quiet on this section of the line, and they'd been there so long the trogs had set the place up all snug: brought down glassware, a horsehair settee, two big old paintings of civic dignitaries from the remains of a Stadhuis, and a model of the pre-war coal mines that recalled to the troglodytes' minds their own extensive tunnel system made awfully small. There was also a sheep dog who did gamely enough in his treadmill on a diet of Victoria's Houndmeal that Stan ordered from Spillers of Cardiff and had delivered poste-restante to Boulogne. Brass quoits, a fifteen-inch-long crystal dolphin, a glass case full of stuffed hummingbirds arranged in a fleur-de-lis, a Chinese vase that held a variety of different parasols and ladies walking umbrellas – dressing cases, valises, portmanteaus, collar and bonnet boxes. Goin' on a journey, are ye, Cummins grumbled, and Stan said, I rather think we will be soon enough. — The summer waned up above, and the febrile Tommies chased the feverish Jerries east – the subterraneans, unaffected by the pandemic, came boiling up

out of das Grab – so many of them! Lice! Silverfish! They had not known of their own numbers, had not appreciated the greatness of the deliverance afforded beneath no-man's-land. Up they came from the pits, soak holes, and deep-bore tunnels shaped by their fugitive bodies – the resurrected, the reborn ... And then the polyglot pack divided, weeping farewell on one another's shoulders, lovers parted, brothers separated – and away they went: the Germans tiptoeing behind the vanquished Kaiserliches Heer, the British, French and Belgians behind the demobilising allies. It was a game of grandmamma's footsteps played along a three-hundred-mile front: when the topsiders turned round, haunted by this prickling sensation that a multitude of someones thronged at their backs, the underground men stood stock still, counting off the minutes before they could safely move again, while silently singing, *Take me back to dear old Blighty! Put me on the train for London town! Take me over there, Drop me anywhere, Liverpool, Leeds or Birmingham, well, I don't care!* They commandeered a fishing boat they'd found hauled up for caulking on a shingle bank a few miles down the coast from Nieuport. In that great space of wind, salt spray and the grey-green wave backs, the men were stunned – they stripped off and rolled over and over again across the hot pebbles. Stanley, Huggins, Cummins and Mohan were in the vanguard of the returnees, together with thirteen coolies they brought with them from the bowels of the earth. Already, at the railheads and in the seething tent encampments that flapped across the land, the trogs had sewn their revolutionary seed. It needed no broadcasting: they were the war's bumper crop, implanted for long years in the ploughed earth of Flanders, Artois, Picardy and Champagne, they had sprung up, white-green from their long inhumation, the inspiring refutation of all the stifling aims promulgated by the cracked brass. So many of them, the arisen, adding soda to the spirits of their war-weary comrades, so that, once merged, the entire moving mass became giddy with a sense of its own transformative power. — They landed in Broadstairs bay and went straight up the hill to the station. The narrow streets of the town were full of newspaper boys crying the latest headlines: THOUSANDS GIVEN UP FOR DEAD FOUND TO BE LIVING IN EXTENSIVE TUNNELLING BENEATH NO-MAN'S-LAND, but far more germaine were: MARY ALLEN ASSUMES COMMAND OF RESURGENT WSPU and:

LAID-OFF MUNITIONETTES ANGRY DEMONSTRATIONS. Stanley prevailed upon the ticket-office clerk to give them all passes by appealing to his egalitarian nature – and this the clerk did, while looking askance at those he believed to be white slavers, and those he considered to be sickeningly effeminate, what with their blouses, their long hair and their Augustus John hats. Stanley addressed the clerk and his own comrades thus: There're a million women in this land of ours who've been subjected to both the disciplines and the privations of industrial work, work for which they have nothing to show but the loss of their health and the deaths of their loved ones. These, then, are our natural allies, lads – we've no need of the broken Tommies, nor of Cummins's lot – excusing your presence, Horace ... — In Woolwich, Sidcup, Eltham and Plumstead they went from hostel to hostel, and at all locations they found the green-and-red-striped banners already flying: red for the revolution and green for that scientific cultivation of the land they believed would allow for a New Britain, its well-fed and healthy folk freed from material want not by the machines – which had been engines only for the maceration of bodies and the grinding up of souls – but by the Ardent Spirit of natural increase, chemically assisted. The old order has been buried, Stanley told these rough girls from Silvertown and Mile End, beneath the soil of France and Belgium! And he promised them that from now on their lives would be like hopping or a fruit-picking holiday – albeit without the necessity to fill such and such a number of bushels. The rough girls teased him, saying, My, my, ain't 'e grown – a bang-up-to-date Burlington Bertie – so that he rejoined: Us all, dallying in the fields, kipping in the haystacks, wandering orchards that belong to us, our aprons filled with ripe pears ... The trams were so overwhelmed by the revolutionists that they crept along at walking pace, palpitating with the close-packed bodies of young women and men – liberties were undoubtedly taken, yet they were given as well: a paroxysm of free love that sent clergymen scuttling from the streets, convinced the last trumpet had been sounded, when it was only the joyous tootling of ten thousand bugles. And everywhere that Stanley went, while he spoke with all, he sought only one: *I should love to see my best girl, Cuddling up again we soon should be, WHOA!* — From the Queen Mary Hostel in Plumstead he was directed – by a vicious old sot – to the Ministry's Resettlement House in Pimlico. When he arrived the place was empty but for two dashing young ladies covered in paint and smoking cigarettes in extravagantly long onyx holders. They stood at the open drawers of the steel cabinets and flipped through hundreds of filing cards before finding the correct address. — The centre of the city was in a state of foment, news flew out from the telegraph offices and telephone exchanges of more and more echelons going over to the Red-and-Greens: all forty thousand women of the VAD, a further eighteen from the Land Army, a topping twenty-odd from Queen Mary's Corps – detachments of Territorials that had arrived double-quick in order to guard Whitehall and Parliament against the insurrectionaries formed up, but then refused to fire upon them, casting aside their weapons and uniting in the giddying dawn of the New Age. With all the excitement – the singing, the chanting, and the motor cars racing through the streets with their horns blaring – he yet saw no real violence. On the embankment by Millbank a few flappers twitted an old gentleman – pulling his swallow-tails, snatching his cigar, *the flash of the monocle across his breast as he swings round and around until it flies off into the river* ... No transport to be had, so Stan walks over Vauxhall Bridge and then up the South Lambeth Road: the north side may've been in an uproar, but here a nurse strolls behind a perambulator, each tightly laced boot exactly framed by a paving stone – a grocer's boy wheels a bicycle top-heavy with rhubarb beneath the blue-and-cream-striped awnings of a row of shops, and the horse droppings scattered on the warm setts give off ineffably sweet smells of *hay and happily digested oats*, the flies curling up from them *a healthy part of the whole* that settles once more as soon as Stan has passed by. The London suburbs are, he thinks, far too widespread and full of their own bricky solidity to be blown up by any mere human impact: towards Croydon and Sydenham Hill the revolutionary wave will be dying away in plashes of over-familiarity and small perturbations of unconventionality, such as *the wearing of a cap at a rakish angle* . . . In the front yard of the long, four-storey apartment building there are piles of sand and broken tiles left behind by the contractors, above these range windows sunk in mock-Tudor half-timbering, while in the very centre of the building a Neoclassical pediment has been placed with a roundel instead of a lunette – the roundel has these figures set into it: 1916. *Apple tree, pear tree, plum tree pie, How many children before I die? One, two, three* — at least five of them, barefoot, in dirty knickerbockers and, despite the September sunshine, all with thick mufflers around their stalk-necks – he supposes to ward off the influenza that must still be hovering here, among the gold medallions scattered between the chestnut boughs. And so they chant: She open ve winder an' in-flew-enza! She open ve winder an' in-flew-enza! which draws him towards a raised casement in the sub-basement. That's it. He understands now: no matter what enlightenment comes with the New Dawn, even when the fever hospitals, gaols and asylums are turned over to the revolutionists to become beacons of free-association and communal living, *still*

no acts of women or men can ever raise the soil from my back, Our ceme-
tery's so small there'll be no room fer 'em all, Our cemetery's so small there'll
be no room fer 'em all . . . The insupportable weight and density of the
mud, packed by the pounding of the shells into every nook and
cranny of his form – the steel, and the steel that's made that steel – of
all this there will be more: more milled and turned and drilled, the
component parts stretching out into the future on a ceaselessly
revolving conveyor belt that has no end. He need never have resur-
faced at all – his hands shake and twitch, his *back bends . . . bends . . .* he
is seized by impulsiveness in fingers, hands, feet, toes, and in his
inclinations also, an irresistible urge to point, poke, touch, lick, want
– *this, that, all others . . .* and yet he cannot, of his own volition, move
at all, *Tiddly-iddly-ighty, Hurry me home to Blighty, Blighty is the place*
for me! – the bilyati gun *goes off in my face . . .* The milieu intérieur, a
sepulchral Scots voice intones, as described by Claude Bernard – it is,
I would say, best understood as a landscape of its own – a habitable
terrain, why not? Possessing hills, rivers, lochs – fields and meadows
too . . . However, if you take a closer look, you'll see that the significant features are, aye, well, broad fairways, sand traps and beautiful
– mark me, bea-u-tiful – greens. A second voice – weedy, querulous
– intervenes: You make it sound like a golf course. SEPULCHRAL:
Well, indeed – that is its problem in a nutshell. I mean, in so far as
the milieu intérieur is a place that can be mapped out within the
catatonic's mind, it's also most assuredly incapable of sustaining life.
It cannot feed its creator – while those others who play round it are
ghosts . . . shades –. WEEDY: Ghostly fours –. SEPULCHRAL: Fours,
pairs – she, the catatonic you see before you, she waves them through
– that's precisely what she's doing right now, waving them through.
She cannot play with them because they don't, rightly speaking, exist,

and so she gives them precedence –. WEEDY: And what about the treatment, how does that alter things? SEPULCHRAL: What we do here? Why, blow it all to smithereens of course – I mean, ideally it would, but perhaps only plough it over for a season or so. The important thing is the dramatics of the procedure – we cannot, at present, know the precise effects on the brain, but the induced coma state, the intensity of the shock itself, and then: hey presto! the reawakening with a jab of glucose. I suppose a fancy way of putting it would be to say that she'll reach a new psycho-physical accommodation, but I'm a plain-speaking Renfrewshire man, no truck with scientific jargon of any sort – nor am I in thrall to the kirk, still, I've seen absolutely astonishing resurrections . . . Nurse Greengage, would you be so good as to shut the door and bolt it? GREENGAGE: Certainly, Doctor Cummins. WEEDY: What're they for? CUMMINS: The restraints? Surely they took you through the whole drill at Claybury, young man, absolutely standard procedure. WEEDY: Oh, I don't know – can you be certain that –? I mean, I've read through her notes quite thoroughly, it doesn't appear on the face of it that this is schizophrenic catatonia per se – . CUMMINS (laughing, a dreadful grating sound): Per se! Oh, do give it a rest, Marcus – it doesn't matter a fig what's caused the catatonia, could be syphilis or bloody socialism for that matter . . . (he hums) . . . The more we are to-gether the merrier we shall be –! Oh, come on, man, I'm only joshing you, you take everything too damn seriously – it's not as if I'm advocating the good old English fist, do I look like a New Party man? Y'know, what we damn well do need is some sort of an atom-smasher like they have in Cambridge, smash all the madness to pieces, eh? As things stand we throw the switch on this apparatus here and we short-circuit half the hospital – you must've noticed? MARCUS: Yes . . . I have, and it's an eerie sight – if the fuses don't blow, the bulbs all along the lower corridor go dim, one after another, travelling down that enormous length . . . like a sort of pulse, I s'pose you'd say. CUMMINS: Spare us the piety – pass me that kidney dish, Nurse . . . Thankee . . . a-ha. Have you see the plans for the new Underground station, Marcus? MARCUS: No, I haven't as yet. CUMMINS: Queerest thing – shaped like a sort of hatbox, can't say I care for it, I'm old enough to remember when, in the waiting rooms of London suburban stations, you'd get a couple of oils of some civic dignitaries or other hung up on the wall and a stuffed bird or two in a glass case! *He lies, the torturer, he is Albert's creature . . .* — They had been happy and sustained a functioning community. There had been – so far as she was aware – additional production, although this was by no means demanded of them after the suffering they had endured performing the Imperialists' war work, and the stresses of the revolution. Some brushes, clothes pegs and baskets – simple artefacts they were happy to turn out. Stanley had said: You and your comrades take the old booby-hatch up in Friern Barnet – we've no use for it now the greater part of the inmates have been discharged to the care of their families or their local cooperatives. And there'll be a form of justice, I believe, in free women and men of a rational cast ruling the roost where but lately the poor and deluded were confined against their will. (CUMMINS: *Some of this electrolytic cream spread on the temples will ensure closer contact and improve connectivity . . .*) They had retained their overalls from the munitions factories as a badge of pride – besides, what could be more supremely rational dress than these rough ticken clothes? Tunics, divided skirts and heavy jackets that protected them from the cold and damp of the old buildings, warding off an ague that seemed present in their very bricks and mortar.

343

This was during the early days – later on, when things had been more organised, clothes were donated by the London fieldworkers, nothing too fancy but perfectly serviceable and freely given. A thousand female comrades took up their quarters on the western side of the former asylum, and a thousand male ones to the east. Mingling among both sexes and assigned to their living units were a proportion of malefactors and counter-revolutionists distinguishable by their dark and drab uniforms. These women and men were charged with the mundane and trivial tasks: the locking and unlocking of doors, the changing of soiled sheets and garments, the administration of medicines, and the assistance of those who requested peace and quiet to special reclusion units. The notion was that they were to be re-educated by their close association with these women of high ideals, whose long and arduous labours had dinned into them a mortal legacy of diseases: tuberculosis, typhoid, dysentery and venereal infections transmitted via sexual congress with males of the exploitative class. (CUMMINS: *If you'd all please ensure that you're standing with both feet on the rubber matting . . .*) Theirs was not the only phalanstery to be established by the Central Cooperative under the chairmanship of Stanley Death. The communalists chose not to discuss such mundane matters, but over the years I learned – by earwigging on the resentful detainees – that there were others at Hanwell, Napsbury, Claybury, Sheffield, Banstead and Tooting Bec – a ring of them surrounding the site of the former metropolis, wherein the same experiments in communal living, and the same practices of the freest thought, were pursued. The wildest and the freest of thoughts – and speech! A'stutterin' anna mutterin' . . . she's seen a fellow in a picture on the wall, and he's stepped out of it and had her away, into the family way, she's given birth! To an

344

automaton! A little Enigmarelle of her own! (CUMMINS: *Interestingly, there is some evidence that menstruation may adversely effect the therapy – not an issue in this patient's case, nor those of most of the other female inmates, whose menses are . . . How'd'you put it, Nurse?* GREENGAGE: *Well, I don't know, Doctor –.* CUMMINS: *Disrupted? Suppressed?* GREENGAGE: *Well, they doesn't 'ave their monthlies, if that's what you mean . . .* CUMMINS: *Oh, indeed, si vous soulevez un jupon vous ne devez jamais exprimer la surprise . . .*) Spirit-rapping, table-turning – it was scarcely to be marvelled at that they would entertain such things – the communal areas crackled with talk of travelling to other worlds, humans vivisected into being from the bound forms of animals. Some were certain that death-rays were being beamed at them from the People's Palace across the vale, and that these emissions caused them to hear the voices of their loved ones who had passed over – they spent hours, days, setting down these communiqués in the penny jotters obtainable from the commissary. Yet this was understandable, surely? Forgivable in the light of the percipient discussions that were also held regarding universal provision of family planning, infant welfare, education and social security – discussions I myself minuted, then presented in report form to the commissioners of Stanley's Board of Control, who inspected the phalanstery on an annual basis. (MARCUS: *She seems completely inert now – marked hypotonia.* CUMMINS: *That's entirely as it should be, the curare means even if you boink 'em they don't react – see?*) Not that they paid these much attention – but, then, that too was understandable . . . forgivable – didn't they have their own work cut out for them: demolishing the centuries-old unsanitary housing and stony bombast that the foolish capitalists and warmongers had formerly believed the greatest city on earth? Then raising in its stead a few slim and tapering steel-and-glass towers, while establishing on its shattered remains the raised field systems determined by the new agriculture – fields for wheat, of course, but also orchards and water meadows, vineyards too – for why shouldn't the ordinary folk also have Hock and seltzer? (CUMMINS: *And ... on!*) — It was Gracie who first noticed the changes under way: the infiltration of BoC spies among those sent for re-education, the alteration of the regime from voluntary retreat, to one of ... confinement. The introduction of electrification to the phalanstery, and other forms of mechanisation that were precisely the regimentations and oppressions of the human spirit and the human body that the revolution had been against! Next came the punishments – which were presented, derangingly, as ... treatments, but which left these once-proud women and men ... gibbering, wholly broken down ... in pieces. I told her: This is Albert's doing. He has won out finally. *Death-rays of Stanley, death-rays of Albert playing, each on the other brother's blank face ...* and Albert the winner, as always, reimposing his own cruel regime on the but recently liberated land. Soon enough they came: the redbrick serpents snaking over Muswell Hill and coiling across the valley towards the phalanstery, *civilisssation* they hissed. Dear Gracie – she had never fully adjusted to life at Colney Hatch. She said ... she said to me, that to look along the lower corridor, to allow your eyeball to shoot along its third-of-a-mile barrel was ... to give in to ... a sort of ... madness: the blinding white flash *skronks* into the negative images of feathery weeds agitating along the trackside. The train sways away and he stands on the platform looking up at the steep sides of the cutting and thinking: For this, I am ... not ready. And so, after stomping laboriously up the steel staircase he turns east along Friern Barnet Lane, intending ... *what?* He checks his watch (a sixteen-year-old petrol station giveaway, the face of which I have looked upon thousands of times yet never seen): One thirty – the pubs will be serving *grapeshot peas, gassy lager, offensive chip weaponry, battering cod . . . I'm hungry . . . but not for THAT!* He plods on, intending, he thinks, simply to take a look at Arnos Grove tube station, the Modernist hatbox design of which he has strangely *fond memories* . . . Take a look – or perhaps enter, *exercise my Freedom and board a train that will take me home.* Home. It has come to him unbidden: the notion that the flat on Fortess Road, with its tatty furnishings and ambient sound of insurance brokers . . . *Female, fifty-three, ten years no-claims – one for John at Aviva?* was his home, more than the Redington Road house had ever been – or any of his other habitations, which, now he came to think of it, were really *dens . . . and I, a fox . . .* an interloper into the husbandry of fence, flowerbed and shed who scratched out his own smelly shelter for a year or ten, raised a few cubs who needed National Health glasses, then skulked away again –. What's your dick like, homey, what're you into –? is slung from the open window of car that spurts past, together with the cat's-piss-smell of contemporary marijuana – *a hot hatch, isn't that what they're called?* Why fight it? Busner thinks, Why delay or drag my feet when the past is inexorably creeping up behind? Which is – he goes on at himself – the essence, surely, of all talking therapies, and something that Ronnie nailed perfectly adequately in that silly chapbook of his – what did he call them? The whirligogs and fankles that beset our emotions. — On he goes, reflecting ruefully on the vogue for such things in the seventies, including his own inquire-within tool: *The Riddle!* He barks with laughter, then chuckles more sincerely in acknowledgement of his own follies . . . *after all, perhaps at last I'm solving it?* The road grumbles between nondescript

347

residential blocks and postwar houses, then beetles over the brow of the hill and smooths down to a *fistulous roundabout* from which spin off shopping parades. *It's the same sequencing of consumer DNA* that he had left behind not twenty minutes since: Y Beauty & Hair (*Why indeed?*), Monarch Dental Services (*The teeth of kings?*), a fried-chicken joint, a newsagent plastered with phonecard decals, a betting shop ... *and again, once more – with feeling* ... His feet are aching and sodden in their age-inappropriate footwear, although, he considers: In an earlier era I'd've been crippled by now with lumbago or gout – maladies that have *an honestly Anglo-Saxon ring, Falstaffian almost* ... He pulls himself together with the steel bar surrounding a waist-high freestanding hoarding, upon the metal sheet of which a young woman enjoys herself with a Magnum ice cream. In through the half-open door of the bookie he sees the bruising after-images of horse races: roan threads spooling through Haydock Park, digital threads cantering beneath them, the *glabellar tap that causes blinking cursors* ... The binary storm rages around him, a blizzard of ones and noughts – *why fight it?* I am, Busner thinks, no Falstaff, only a maddened Lear out on the toughened-glass heath, where *nothing comes of nothing. And yet* ... *and yet* ... there is something: the cursor blinking on and off, *one or nought, should or ought?* It strikes him that: It must've been at exactly that time – to the very year – that they were developing the first microprocessors, writing new program-ming languages and creating operating systems that pushed them together *soft into hard* ... Not that we – I – was aware of it, comput-ers were Toltec pyramids, stepped down into the basements of corporate HQs, and ministered to by priestly Morlocks in white coats. I do remember an early computer game – Ping? Pong? – at any rate, two white bars either side of a blackened television screen,

348

batting between them a white cursor which on impact made a synthesised tongue-popping noise. It was absurdly unimpressive – as a visualisation of table tennis cruder than a child's stick drawing of a real live man, *but Mark loved it . . . so for hour after hour we'd played it in amusement arcades: pulling the levers, twisting the dials, our heads hanging there in all the ring-a-ding-dinging and the reek of melting sugar . . .* He sighs, Aaaaah, – Mark had given him a novelty ballpoint pen, inside its fat belly were six ink cartridges: *green, blue, black, red . . . I forget the other two . . .* He had explained his note-taking system to the boy and this was his thoughtful response. Mark showed his father how you could push down two of the coloured ballpoints at once, and so write duochrome. Busner had long since ceased to take any sort of notes at all – *let alone such pretentious ones!* Yet he feels the want of that pen now, imagines wielding it with all six nibs out, so as to fuse colour and symbology in this realisation being compounded within him from *images, memories, recent ideas and long-since-made clinical observations . . .* A mother and small child exit the newsagents – they wear matching scarlet puffa jackets so bright they could be *spotted floundering on a glacier from a helicopter . . .* The child tears the cellophane from a lollipop, the mother the cellophane from a packet of cigarettes, *the breeze choreographs their filmy discards . . .* Aaaah, he turns abruptly away to see that the memories have indeed crept right up behind him, and that they *aren't so much as bothering to play the game!* for when he turns towards them they wiggle their limbs shamelessly in the bright spring sunlight: Miriam: *who gave me that digital watch,* and *that bastard Whitcomb – he had one of the first pocket calculators and was mucking about with it the day I went to see him and he told me they were thinking of pulling the plug* from a socket hidden behind a grotesque coat tree, its nine upturned

349

branches ending in animal horns of some sort that have been mounted into the wood. The parlour maid gets to her feet all tangled up in her full skirts and the cabling of the machine, which is, Audrey thinks, as ugly as the coat tree, being confected out of broom, bagpipes and an electrical fan. Its whine whirrs away into silence, and the housekeeper who has opened the door – *a grim-faced harridan* with her face scraped back into her hair and her hair scraped back into a *frightening bun* – calls back: That'll do for now, Rose, before giving her attention once more to this unanticipated visitor. Is it Mister or Missus De'Ath that you wishes to see? No title is bestowed on Audrey *maybe if I had a visiting card?* who replies, I don't suppose my brother will be at home, so if you could kindly tell my sister-in-law that Audrey De'Ath desires a word I'd be most obliged. She believes this well done, and that she is also well got up to pay this call in a new pleated skirt, linen for best, belted mackintosh and cloche hat. She has also borrowed a slim parasol with a porcelain handle from Appleby's collection that *must cost a month of this one's wages – poor old mare, back in harness again!* The housekeeper runs a sceptical eye from the top to the bottom of Audrey, while behind her the parlour maid continues her battle with the lashing tail of the vacuuming machine. The housekeeper is on the point of shutting the door in Audrey's face while she goes to speak to her mistress, when two doors open simultaneously on to the hallway – one at the very back, through which Albert emerges, treading gingerly, a large china tankard in his hand – and one to the left, whence comes in *a crisp cloud of white organdie* a lady of Audrey's own age, who, although she has only clapped eyes on her once, briefly, and six years previously, she nevertheless immediately recognises. Albert pads towards the door, saying, What's this, then, Missus Egremont – then sees who it is and for a moment his

350

broad, smooth face is seized by an unaccountable expression: *Albert . . . shocked?* before he moves to his wife's side and takes her arm. Rosalind, my dear, he says, this is my sister Audrey. And to Audrey there is a curt: You'd better step in here. They all three go into the drawing room, which is *as uglily done out as the hall.* Surveying the heavy old pieces of oak and mahogany furniture that have been pressed into service for telephone tables, wireless and phonograph cabinets, Audrey surmises that this a domesticated battle of the sexes, one, moreover, in which the amiable and doughy blonde has already capitulated. The three of them move in and out, round and between overstuffed armchairs – a formal dance of awkwardness, until Albert says, Won't you sit down, Audrey? No fanks, Bert, Audrey replies, cockneyfying purely to see its effect on the two of them. Then she takes up a paper knife that lies on the mantelpiece and ting-tings it along a row of china dogs, china sheep, china shepherdesses in hooped skirts with china crooks, until it clanks against a brass box fashioned from the casing of a 50-pounder shell. On the domed lid of this is inscribed: In Grateful Acknowledgement of the Service Given by Albert De'Ath –. Which is all Audrey wishes to know, so she prises open the lid with the paper knife, revealing the *little white cartridges*, and says, D'you mind? then without waiting for an answer withdraws a cigarette. Both De'Aths start forward, speaking over one another, The matches are –/Can I get you a –? and laughing she is pleased to take receipt of both boxes, deftly remove a match from each one, strike both and suck fire from one flamelet, then the other, funnelling the smoke out at them – the dead matches she drops in the grate. You're all done at the Arsenal, then? she says presently, and Albert concedes this with a nod, before continuing, so as to forestall the looming oddity of the situation, May I introduce you to my wife,

351

Rosalind? Audrey grimaces. – Charmed, I'm sure, and, taking the *baby-soft* hand she's offered, continues: I expect you miss your gauntlets and your racy peaked cap. Rosalind blushes. – I'm – I'm . . . Well, frankly, I'm amazed you remember –. Well, I do, Audrey states baldly, and leaves go the hand, but it seems that you do too. Tell me, what did my brother say to you that day at the Danger Buildings? If he didn't speak of me on that occasion, he must've since – told you something of my way of carrying on, eh? My scandalous amours and incendiary opinions? Rosalind is *struck dumber* – she shares with her husband an air of ponderous containment, and, while pretty enough, Audrey detects within her overripe skin *fleshiness about to ooze grubbily out.* We all, Albert declares, did our bit. *As if this is what's at issue between us!* Audrey laughs bitterly, flings herself down in one of the chairs, boldly crosses her legs, takes a pull on her gasper and rejoins: Maybe so, Bert, although some of us sacrificed more than others, and some of us . . . She looks pointedly to the crystal dolphin that leaps beside a Chinese vase . . . gained. Turning to the *silly thing in her shepherdess's dress*, she raises her voice: Did he ever speak to you of our brother, my dear? Did he so much as tell you he 'ad one? Well, 'e weren't as clever as Bert – not a born 'ustler like your ever so upstandin' 'usband! Stan wasn't one to black the King's boots, oh no, couldn't turn three tricks at once for the same master – but 'e was our flesh an' blood –! A cry drops down into the drawing room from high up in the house, piped here through a speaking tube Albert has had installed. Baby! Rosalind exclaims, then, spying an Old English sheepdog that lies on its back by the hearth with rigid straw-filled limbs upthrust, he chortles indulgently: Oh, the silly thing's left his doggie here, I shall have to take Darsing up to him . . . You will excuse –. And she is gone, the stuffed dog tucked awkwardly under her fleecy arm.

Well, Audrey persists once Rosalind has left the room, did you – did you ever speak of him to your well-bred wife? Can you so much as bear to think of him, remember him? You may be a great computer, Bert, but there're some things that can never be accounted for. Albert simply regards her, his pregnant eyes full of . . . *hatred, no, that's too passionate for him – he never hates, only kills all insane persons in fact? Yes, in mercy and in justice to themselves* . . . At length he says, There is the matter of Collins and the Free State, some might consider it a war – a civil war indeed. Audrey says: Is that your view, Bert? Do you think the poor bloody Irish a sufficient cause of your coldness? Is it this that makes you such a white man? Albert blanches, his tone dulls and flattens still more *lead flushing.* I am not, he says, at the office this morning because this afternoon I shall be taking the boat train from Waterloo – there are cemeteries to be surveyed, sites for the monument and so forth –. He stops, seeing not his sister – her fiery auburn hair constrained, he has noted, to a fashionable bob – but the churned Flanders mud, sutured by white wooden crosses – and he hears not her but the silly ass of an architect he has to deal with, a dishevelled fellow who makes puns both excruciating and dishonourable – *the Gate of Messiness is what he calls his own design!* What's in the mug? Audrey asks. Mug? he queries. Yes, the mug you had in your hand when I came in. *He's losing his hair, the brassy nob of his head shines through – losing his hair and gaining the weight of influence . . . but he's still tough . . . still dangerous . . .* Albert picks up the tankard from the table where he'd placed it among a slew of his tools: metal rulers, propelling pencils, slide rules, dividers . . . Audrey thinks: She hasn't got the measure of him, he does as he pleases

– always has. He's taken this lovely house and started to clutter it up – she'll go first, then he'll fill it to the rafters with his jumble. Not that it's confusing to him: he knows where ev-ery-thing is . . . *Am I right, sir?* It's a sort of tonic, Albert says gingerly, of my own, ah, devising. Audrey laughs. – Give over, Bert, what d'you mean by that? He peers into the tankard, then tilts it towards her so she can see the thick brown liquid it contains. It's the black drop! she cries delightedly, and Albert says, Hardly, it's a mixture of Bemax, molasses and some extracts of these new vit-a-mines together with my own, ah, solvent. She cackles again. – Solvent! Whass that when it's at 'ome? Before answering her, he takes a long draught from the tankard – it leaves a sewerage mark around his shaved-beige lips: *mercurochrome-brown with a cream foam rim.* Milk stout, he says, wiping this off with his handkerchief, Huggins' for preference – but Guinness if it isn't to be had. Audrey splutters: You – You, you're turnin' inter the old man after all! For a time both are silent in contemplation of the Cheriton Bishop Deers, Samuel's decline has been precipitate . . . *a downhill stampede – brakes on the 'bus failed, the heavy vehicle running down its own team . . . shafts, then legs shattered . . . rabbit-skin coat all torn and bloody . . . horses squealereaming . . . Only terminus likely: the knackers.* Whatever else you may be, Bert, Audrey says presently, I never pegged you for a crank — and that word alone, crank, springs the lever from the cog, so that the balls of the horizontal pendulum begin to rotate beneath the glass dome of the clock on the mantel. A melodious chiming, d'ding-ding-ding, d'ding-ding-dong, summons Audrey to her feet – it had been growing within her these past few weeks, seizing at first a single hand or foot, clenching, then releasing it with the viciousness of an old . . . *enemy.* To the model lighthouse, given to Albert

354

De'Ath in his capacity as a Fellow of Trinity House, she charlestons, her legs propellering, and grasps the top of the tinplate tower. Aha! as she suspected: another cigarette case. She nips one from the hole directly into her mouth, then a second, then a third – fourth – fifth – sixth – all flung and lip-caught unerringly, *Sorta fing the Brothers Luck did at Karno's Fun Factory – there was six of 'em inall!* She turns to show off her white fangs to her big brother, who backs towards the door *so's to give me more room* – space that allows her to windmill her arms as well as her legs, to pluck up cushions from the sofas and chairs so that she may juggle with them, to take up handfuls of Albert's pointed implements so that she may drum with them – *such a turn! he ain't about to stop me – and I can't help meself!* This wilfulness has been growing alongside the t-t-t-t-ticcing of her hands and the j-j-j-j-jerking of her neck – and now it occurs to her that this trip to Blackheath – unanticipated by her quite as much as by them – may be another instance of an action beyond her control that will be repeated *again and again annagain.* That she will find herself walking up Montpelier Row from the station, skirting the grassy edge of the heath, trotting up the stairs of the imposing house *over and over anover*, until the spring winds down and the penny peepshow snaps shut – except that this cannot happen, because, in the midst of all the fluttering, clawing and pecking of *the intrepid birdwoman*, other more sinister rhythms have begun to be imposed: the rotation of an historic flywheel, the pulling of an eternal lever, the lowering of that *perspicacious thinker*, the headstock. And this is no fun at all, these long-buried motions *tearing through my skin.* Audrey hears machine guns roaring and sees Rosalind coming back into the room, *silly moo*, judging from her expression, *she's never seen a good old-fashioned cock-ney clog dance before!* – while as for the creature in her arms: *thass no baby! 'e oughta be in trousies* ... Oh, says Rosalind, Oh, Albert! She lays her hand across the little boy's eyes to hide this sight: not a woman – *a puppet heaving rocks*, and then, when the thing begins to scream, Don't av any more, Missus Moore, Don't av any more, Missus Moore, Rosalind presses his tousled head to her breast and claps her hand to his other ear. *Oh, Albert!* resonates into the child's mind followed by *Poor Peterkins!* – which is him, or some other little boy with the same name who sits inside his mother's *soft bits* more closely held, more deeply loved.

Tactically, the De'Aths withdraw to the hallway, where Rose the parlour maid stands with handfuls of apron and jaw dropping – others of the domestics have, equally tactically, made themselves scarce. Alone in the tumult of her thoughts and limbs, as she turns this, the most vital fuse cap of the entire never-ending war, Audrey hears these sounds above the screeching of her lathe: a man crying Fre-esh fi-ish! again and again from the road outside, the gentle whinny of his horse, the lifting of the earpiece, the sinisterly abrasive return of the sprung dial, the menacing conformity of her brother's voice saying, Hello, would you kindly connect me to the R Division station at Blackheath Road? I think you'll find that the number is two-one-six-nought *availeth me*, Busner thinks, and then: Mis-understood visions and the faces of clocks. He had left the car at the park gates, intending to take a walk to *clear my mind*. In August the city emptied out a little – but the drive all the way from Friern Barnet through the tail-end of the rush hour was still gruelling – all those *mental patients sitting silently howling in their foam-padded cells*. He had locked his own *a practitioner's privilege* and, pocketing the keys, escorted its discharged inmate down the avenue that leads to the Observatory, while rolling his head around on his neck, loosening his shoulders and swinging his arms – all of which was what passed for exercise, now that his liaisons with Mimi had been abruptly terminated. *Mi-mi! Mi-mi! Mi-miiii ...!* The siren of an ambulance whipping across the heath behind him is, he realises, what has called this car crash to mind: It wasn't only her engagement to the squaddy she had wrenched away from, she was *cutting herself free from all bodywork ...* At the Observatory, Busner stands, letting his eyeballs shoot down the green slope to the Naval College, volley through the Cutty Sark's rigging, spin through the tightly packed terraces of Millwall and Cubitt Town – swerving around the pegs of three newish multi-storey council blocks – before cannoning away across Mile End, Hackney, Highbury, Finsbury Park and Crouch End *back to whence I came ...* In the mid-distance the dust of demolition lies in filthy rags on the broken bones of dead houses in Limehouse and Poplar. He wonders if the Observatory is still in use – did star-struck boffins sit beneath its cloven copper dome *firing their eyes at the distant past of other worlds?* The city, Busner realises, tires him – already he has no patience with its affectations, its attitudinising, which take on such *permanent and concrete forms.* He sees Mimi *blown thistledown,* rising up from the embankment beside the Isle of Dogs foot tunnel, her body gently clapping inside the gleaming bell of her transparent plastic umbrella. She is, he thinks, a child of the future, not a miserably authoritarian nanny of the past, her bare legs *reaching out ...* It is precisely at this moment that he crosses his own *prime meridian* and understands: *My youth is over – and with it any blame that attaches to ... who, the Luftwaffe? Or to them for trusting to the Anderson and not bothering to take the three hundred and twenty-nine steps down into the underground?* His youth is over, and, while he may go on turning Ronnie's whirligogs, repeating the same mistakes

357

while expecting different results, *because that's what people do*, he will not compound these errors any further by typing his patients. Henceforth there will be only *me* and *you*, never again the fraudulence of either *us* or *them*. He'd like to celebrate this by cutting a caper, picking a flower, embracing a child – instead he sinks his hands deeper in his pockets, smells the sticky sap of the limes, and listens as the first heavy drops of rain splatter on their foliage. If I was that dapper chap on the telly, he thinks, I'd've brought my umbrella with me. But he is none of these things: dapper, a chap, on the telly – and so arrives jogging back at the Austin, hunched over, his sports coat sodden, his grey flannel trousers greyer. — Standing on the pavement, looking up at the elegant curve of the grand development, with its beautifully four-square brick beads strung along colonnades, Busner notes that for every property that is well maintained there are two more that have tripped up into neglect: jigsaw chunks of stucco have dropped from their entablatures, and behind the elegant pillars are coal sacks and clothes-drying racks, pigeon-manured shrubs have taken root on ledges and in the crooks of walls, television aerials lurch from the chopped-off polyhedrons of their roofs. The address given for Sir Albert De'Ath, KG, KBE, in the 1955 edition of Who's Who Busner had found in the hospital library – and subsequently confirmed as still being his residence in a current A–D phonebook – is the most rundown of all. *No paragon* . . . what with its curtained and shuttered windows, and its overgrown front garden wherein the weeds have sprung up around a feature that looks to be a crudely fashioned pair of . . . *Indian clubs?* He wonders if he's made a mistake and the huge old pile is being squatted – the single bell push *a nipple, inverted in its plaster aureole* calls forth a disorderly chorus of chimes, buzzes, bongs and rings that sounds away into the distant recesses of

358

the house, and, while Busner is puzzling over the nature of someone who could rig up such a fantastical system, *presumably he's deaf* – he's startled by the premature cracking open of the door and the emergence of a sagging and heavily powdered face surrounded by a shockingly luxuriant blue-rinsed perm . . . *almost an Afro!* Doctor Busner? the woman whistles through goofy teeth – and as he confirms this she swings the door right open and ushers him in. I'm Missus Haines, we spoke on the telephone yesterday morning, she says. There's a hefty Birman cat stalking round and around between her stubby legs, its thick furry tail lashing up her tweed skirt – she pays this no attention. Sir Albert, she continues, is expecting you. Then she does nothing. They stand there facing each other in the hallway, and, as Busner's eyes adjust to the gloom, he begins to see *how very weird it all is:* not one or two but seven coat trees all hung about with old mackintoshes, mufflers and even Edwardian duster coats are marching along the hallway towards the back of the house. The slope-shoulders of these *headless giants* brush against epidermal Anaglypta that's sloughing off in strips and patches – the hall runner, of good quality, exhibits the same *punctuation of time*, dashes and commas of wear exposing its underlay. His eyes escape the Birman's empty, narcissistic ones by rising to take in the hanks of wiring and the thin copper tubing of old gas pipes running along the picture rail, together with a thicker pipe . . . *a speaking tube?* There's far less dust than Busner would've expected – whatever irregular things go on here, hoovering is daily – it's only that nothing has ever been removed or replaced, simply added to or adapted. From the ceiling hang three different light fitments from three different eras – gas-brackets still crook from the walls, *this must've been going on since* – Nineteen eighteen, Missus Haines says, Mister and Missus De'Ath – as they were then – moved in here in the summer of nineteen eighteen, shortly after they were married. I joined the establishment in nineteen twenty, and one of my first tasks was the vacuum cleaning – they'd a machine already, you see, Sir Albert was always bang up to date with such things. At a loss as to where he should go with this information – a perfect synthesis of telepathy and the mundane – Busner asks: Have you always been employed by Sir Albert? She laughs, Oh, no, bless you – I went off, did all sorts . . . married a railway man – we were at Orpington up until the war . . . No, Sir Albert always kept in touch, and when Lady De'Ath passed away three years ago, he wrote asking me to come back and housekeep for him. Well, I'd not long lost my Rodney, so I jumped at the idea . . . It seems most unlikely to Busner that Missus Haines has been able to jump at much for *decades, but her tongue leaps about enough* . . . He stands there *letting it all lap over me*, while his own tongue circles the *ice rink* of silver amalgam that Missus Uren, the dentist in East Finchley, has implanted in his molar . . . We don't, as it 'appens, get much in the way of callers, she's saying when this *vestibular interlude* is abruptly terminated by the unmistakable sound of a saucepan boiling over – and, now he comes to think of it, the pong of fish cooking in milk has been steadily building all this while. – Oh, oh –! Missus Haines does indeed *jump to it*, the cat scats, and Busner is left alone to consider how it's Albert De'Ath's way, apparently, *to always keep in touch* – this, and how useful one of the tent-sized macs would've been when he was getting soaked in Greenwich Park. When she returns Missus Haines is wrapped up in an apron printed with photographs of the front doors and fanlights of Georgian houses. They're all from Dublin, she says, pretty, ain't they? I'll see to some tea, she goes on, you'll find Sir Albert in the front room to your left there, and mind –.

She stops, and in her expression Busner sees mingled protectiveness and *a sort of outrage?* He waits for her to complete the sentence but she doesn't, only leaves him to go through the door indicated with the admonition, mind, hanging in his own. It rapidly transpires that *mind is spot on* – as warning, as description, as mantra, motto and injunction. Emanating from the tall old man seated in the wing armchair in the red-velvet-curtained bay window of the large and fiendishly cluttered room is such a strong sensation of a brain churning through calculations, evaluations, judgements, deductions, inductions and assays, that Busner near-staggers under the impact of this furious concentration: mental activity that's beamed through large, limpid, protuberant grey eyes either side of a *Palaeolithic flint axe* of a nose, and focused directly on him. *It doesn't help matters* ... that Sir Albert is *Mekon* bald, or that a number of pairs of wire-rimmed spectacles are pushed up on his soaring forehead, their oval lenses shining in the downlight of a standard lamp positioned by his chair. Busner thinks: A shaven and mummified big cat that yet lives! For Sir Albert is wound up to his armpits in a bright red-and-yellow tartan rug, above which rises the corpse-like skin of yet another mackintosh buttoned up high on his columnar neck. *It doesn't help matters* ... that there is nowhere Busner can look to for repose: every surface is piled with books, papers, leather-covered boxes, scientific instruments – he recognises a primitive centrifuge, gramme scales and an astrolabe – framed photographs of power stations and models of electricity generators, Gestetner machines and old upright typewriters, rubber-stamp stands and blotters cluttered with dipping-nib pens, clocks, vases and china figurines, silver trays and salvers piled with foxed visiting cards and golf-tees, presentation model aircraft cast in steel and mounted on wooden plinths – he identifies a Mosquito fighter-bomber – rococo golf trophies with miniature players immortalised on their lids in mid-swing. *It doesn't help matters . . .* that all this stuff spreads across a terrain of heavy old Edwardian furniture – settees and tables, desks and revolving bookcases – so that, rather than appearing as inert, it seethes and undulates threateningly. The wall above the fireplace is tiled with framed certificates and photographs of a younger Sir Albert rearing over diminutive delegations of Japanese civil servants, or else intimidating political leaders with his already-bare cranium – registering some satisfaction, Busner spots one in which he's bearing down on an uneasy-looking John Foster Dulles. However, this *doesn't help matters much . . .* because there are further oddities, such as a globular rattan chair dangling from a chain attached to the ceiling, and a new-model colour television set plumped on a leather pouffe, which is switched on with the volume mercifully turned down, but displaying the Black and White Minstrels in lavender tailcoats and top hats *hoofing it . . .* All of these things, in their various ways, refer Busner back to the supervening factor of Sir Albert's mind, and *nor does it help matters . . .* that on the tray-table set across the arms of the old man's chair are ranged a number of hearing aids, the wires of which are belayed up the slopes of his eminence to where two or three disappear into the confusing outcroppings of his *Gautama ears* . . . And most of all, *it doesn't help matters . . .* that the first words Sir Albert says are, Are you a Jew? then he rearranges the spectacles so as to align the lenses of three pairs, through which his eyes swell alarmingly. Yes, he says eventually, I see that you are one. Busner is at a loss – he thinks back to his first encounter with Marcus six months before. He had thought that a tricky encounter, and the St John's Wood flat a bizarre habitation – *but now this!* Clearing his throat, he offers a shameful exculpation: Erhem, yes, well . . . but not at all an observant one. If Sir Albert had had any eyebrows he might have been raising them, but as it is his spectacles coruscate from the corrugating of his iron brow, then he continues blithely: People often claim that their friends are Jews, as if this were in some way meritorious . . . He pauses, giving Busner time to savour the accentless quality of his voice and its lack of resonance or timbre . . . None of my friends, he resumes, were ever Jews – to my knowledge, some members of your tribe can pass exceptionally well. However, I have had many Jewish colleagues, subordinates and some superiors throughout my career, and on the whole I've found them to be markedly more efficient than gentiles. If, Doctor Busner, we can maintain a professional demeanour in our dealings with one another, I see no reason why there should be any unpleasantness – d'you smoke? Wrong-footed, Busner blurts: Y-Yes, I'm afraid I do. Sir Albert smiles encouragingly – a worrying sight. If, he says, you lift the top of that model lighthouse you'll find it is, in point of fact, a cigarette box – the lighter is beside it in the guise of a rickshaw. While Busner flips up the rickshaw-wallah's head, the ancient Mandarin fiddles with one of the hearing aids on his tray-table, so that for the remainder of their interview a high-pitched electronic whistling ebbs and flows in unnerving accompaniment. Do you know much about the application of the transistor to the amplification of sound? Sir Albert asks once Busner's cigarette – a bone-dry Senior Service – has been lit, and he stands puffing on it with what he hopes is a semblance of relaxation: one elbow propped on the mantelpiece in among its welter of knick-knacks – clearly, he is not going to be offered a seat. Um, no, he answers, I'm afraid I don't know a great deal about deafness generally, it's not my special –. No, the old man interrupts him,

363

it isn't necessary for you to raise your voice – I know a great deal about it, and these devices are the latest and most efficient models. As to your specialism, Missus Haines told me that you are a psychiatric practitioner, on the staff of the Colney Hatch asylum I believe? Yes, Busner agrees, unwilling to correct the Mind *on a point of fact* . . . Where, or so I'm informed, you are responsible for the supervision of various lunatics, among them my sister, Audrey Death. Again, Busner assents, although this was a flat statement – but then, full of acrid seniority, he at last *finds the balls* to cavil: Your sister, Sir Albert, is not remotely insane – indeed, she's very possibly one of the sanest people I've ever met, especially considering the ordeal she's been through these past fifty years. Stunned by his own bravado, he wonders distractedly whether the ashtray is in the guise of a pottery tortoise. Next, he ponders the grate, which is piled with neatly arranged coals. Don't, Sir Albert says perfunctorily, the fire is coal-effect – far more efficient, there'll scarcely be a coal-mining industry left in this country in twenty years' time – not that this will affect the domestic-pricing structure . . . For a moment it appears that Mind may be exhibiting the very human vagaries of age, and wandering, but then: You'll find that the tortoise you suspect is indeed – if you raise its shell – a viable receptacle. I'm surprised by what you tell me regarding my sister – the last time I saw her she attempted to assault my wife and young son, and had to be removed from this house by the police. She had suffered, it seemed, a complete mental collapse. I discovered soon after that that she'd been confined at Colney Hatch – as next of kin they sent me a questionnaire they wished me to fill out, it concerned her health, her habits, her moods, mode of life and so forth – I was ill-equipped to assist, having had virtually no contact with her for some years preceding this. It is scarcely any business of

yours, Doctor Busner, but I suppose *Alea iacta est*, so I may as well
tell you that her morals were loose and her politics, frankly, extreme.
It seems to Busner that Sir Albert has timed this speech to coincide
with Missus Haines's entrance: she comes through the door bearing . . . *a Teasmade?* Busner moves to intercept and so help her, but
she evades him by slipping behind the wooden cabinet of a twenties
vintage foldaway bed. – I have . . . Sir Albert says as the elderly
woman kneels to plug the Teasmade into a socket hidden by the
skirts of the velvet curtains . . . a conviction that tea should be drunk
as soon as possible after it has been made – both for reasons of taste
and health. He flashes his compound eyes at Busner, clearly wishing
to solicit a *Why?*, but Busner sticks to his own professional agenda:
You did see her during the First War, though – I've read your entry
in Who's Who, sir, and I know from Miss Death that she worked at
the Arsenal as well –. True enough, Sir Albert's flat tone hacks in, but
I assure you I didn't see her more than once or twice – we were at
polar opposites to one another, she a cog, so to speak, in the machine,
while I was concerned with the administration of all shell production
– and latterly the entire Arsenal –. He is interrupted by the alarm
going off on the Teasmade, and they wait in silence while Missus
Haines concocts two cups of tea, adding a large slop of milk to both
together with *one, two, three . . . four!* lumps of sugar. Busner doesn't
object – he's grateful to be getting any refreshment at all, and wonders
if *he'll have her disinfect the cup when I've gone* . . . The teas distributed,
Missus Haines unplugs the device and retreats with it – both men
suck on our tooth rot, Sir Albert noisily so. Once cup and saucer are
reunited, he says, *apropos of everything!* I owe my longevity to my
messery. Pardon? Busner says, nonplussed. Mind motors on serenely:
My messsery, it's an adjuvant of my own devising, a mixture of raw

365

cane molasses, Bemax, vitamins and milk stout – although this last ingredient has become problematical, with only Mackeson's to be had. Of course, when I first hit on it – during the Great War as it happens – I wasn't yet aware of what is was an adjuvant for, I thought it simply an efficacious stimulant-cum-dietary supplement – but in recent years, prescribed really quite toxic compounds for my blood pressure and so forth, I've come to understand that it also functions to boost their therapeutic effects while also reducing their side ones. Sclerosis . . . he remarks sententiously . . . being endemic in the males of my line, I should've been dead long ago without it – and, if not dead, my mental capacities would undoubtedly be in decline. If, Doctor Busner, you had a more practically useful specialisation, you might find it profitable to research my messery's pharmacological properties –. Well, Busner puts in, sensing a possible source of merit, there's no reason why I shouldn't run some preliminary tests on your, um, messery – we have a basic laboratory at Friern, and a . . . um, reasonably biddable pharmacist. Mind considers this from on top of his gabardine mountain, then he says: Yes, Friern Barnet Road to here, assuming you took the most direct route and came under the river via the Rotherhithe Tunnel – what motor car do you have? Busner replies bemusedly: An . . . Austin. Yes, yes, Mind raps back, but what model? Busner dutifully offers up: A Maxi, the new five-door hatchback. Mind pauses, and Busner braces himself for a swerve into the follies of government policy, the farrago of British Leyland . . . *and who knows what else!* But Mind takes an unforeseen turn: In that case your wheels are sixty-nine point eight inches in circumference, resulting in thirteen thousand, two hundred and eighty-nine point three six three nought five seven three two four eight four nought seven six four three three one two one nought one nine one six eight three revolutions of them throughout the journey – approximately. Marvelling at his own sangfroid, Busner says: Why only approximately? Mind ruffles: Well, obviously I can know neither your exact route, nor how conscientious you are regarding tyre pressures – they might be variable. If I knew how variable I could give you different results for each wheel – quite possibly to greater than twenty-seven places. It is markedly stuffy in the big room, so full is it of everything that Sir Albert *retains, but where on earth could he have seen a technical-specifications manual for an Austin Maxi?* Trapped behind the closed curtains, it's impossible to tell if the rain has stopped – Busner wishes to believe it has, and that a summery evening will ensue, featuring wine poured on a damp, cooling terrace, and small but witty talk among good friends. These are not desiderata that he, personally, pursues – but in a voyeuristic fashion *I want them to be going on* ... with the understanding that at some unspecified time in the future ... *I'll make the effort needed to have them in my own life*, rather than ... *this weirdness*. His hand twitches to the row of Biros along his breast pocket, and the old man scythes in: Not much of a display handkerchief, eh, colour-coded according to subject matter, I assume? Green for poetical tropes, blue for reminiscences, black for your own insights – and the aperçus of others – red for observations picked up in the exercise of your medical duties, am I right? Busner says, You're right – although I'm at a loss to understand how you knew –. Come, come, Mind chides him, you knew it, and it isn't that complex a system. Busner says, The other thing – calculating the car-wheel revolutions, that's not too unusual an example of eidetic memory, you being, Sir Albert, what's termed in the literature, a savant –. So, the red pen? Mind offers up. The psychiatrist laughs: No, I might use the red one if your messery were responsible for your calculating ability, but I don't think you believe that any more than I do. No, the blue pen, Sir Albert, for my memories of a superior mnemonist – not the only one in your immediate family either – Miss Death, is, I'm convinced, similarly gifted, and perhaps has an advantage over you, given that for the past fifty years there has been scarcely any new data –. Explain, Mind utters, and if it will aid your concentration help yourself to another cigarette. Busner says, I'd rather sit down, Sir Albert, and as the old man raises no objection, he does, after removing a stiff-legged and mouldering stuffed dog from a wooden swivel office chair. Your sister . . . he begins, and then . . . lays it all out for him: the encephalitis lethargica epidemic, the characteristic form of Audrey Death's collapse, her hospitalisation and long, long period of effective misdiagnosis and mistreatment. He glosses his own arrival at Friern, then moves swiftly on to the discovery that L-DOPA could have a therapeutic application for these long-since-abandoned patients. Busner has no idea what to expect from Sir Albert when he has finished speaking. Viciously erect in his wing armchair, his lenses shining forth from his oppressive cranium, his expression presumably unchanged from when he *last carpeted this, that or however many other merely human subordinates*, the old man still manages to confound him by offering up a single word: And? Busner, forgetting to be intimidated, shoots back: And what? A cappuccino machine froths in the region of Sir Albert's larynx, and Busner realises with amazement that . . . *he's sighing*: Khhhherrr . . . then he says *with just a soupçon of warmth*, And what d'you want me to do about any of it? Busner creaks forward to get a better view of this emotionality before he replies, Do? Um, well, I suppose I assumed you might like to see your sister, or, at the very least, offer assistance of some kind. The allowances for long-stay

368

mental hospital patients are worse than paltry – in the region of forty pounds a week is spent to feed, house and clothe them, probably not much more – allowing for inflation – than was allocated during the Edwardian era. He had hoped that this appeal to the fiscal question would engage the old civil servant – instead Sir Albert indulges in another hiatus, during which Busner scrutinises the many, many degree certificates that he now sees framed on the walls – so many that they constitute a sort of *wallpapering of autodidacticism*. There are degrees in German, divinity, economics, philosophy, law, modern history, comparative religion, mathematics, several different languages, ancient history, physics, politics, geography, and so on *ad tedium*. Obviously, Busner thinks, he has suffered for his learning – and it's now our turn. Sir Albert says: I only ever had forty-two minutes a day to study. Busner starts: I'm sorry –? Sir Albert has regained his colourless composure and continues: Twenty-one minutes each morning on the train from Blackheath to Charing Cross, then a second twenty-one minutes during the evening commute – this was all I had available to me for study – so you see, all of 'em are extramural degrees from London University. In my day it was, of course, quite unthinkable for a young man of my class background to read for an ordinary degree – I joined the civil service when I was eighteen, but you knew that. I was supporting both my parents and a younger imbecilic sister by the time I was twenty-two – I was in charge of Shell Production at the Arsenal eight years subsequent to that. After my notably feckless sister had her nervous collapse – in this very room, as it happens – I cannot say that I made any great moves to assist her. She blamed me, y'know, for the death of our brother, she took the – in my view doubly indefensible – position that, as the official responsible for manufacturing the ordnance

369

used during the offensive in which he died, I should've both been aware of the high proportion of dud shells being sent to the Front, and moved to rectify this. As it was, many of them either exploded prematurely, inflicting casualties among the attacking British forces, or failed to detonate on impact and thus proved inutile when it came to the destruction of the German's *Drahtverhau* –. Pardon? Busner interjects. Sir Albert sighs again: Khhhherrr . . . their barbed-wire entanglements, young man, as a Jew of German extraction I'd've expected you to have at least a rudimentary vocabulary. Anyway, you haven't interrupted my flow, that is all there is to say on the matter. Busner does some of his own cogitating before he speaks, then he adopts his most professionally conciliatory tone: Surely, Sir Albert, after so many years have passed, you can find it in you to forgive her? This was a young woman, who, whatever she may've said at the time, was almost certainly beginning to be affected by the pathological inflammation of her brain tissue – and besides . . . after so very long . . . He falters and then stops altogether, for Sir Albert's colour is deepening to an angry choler, *You'll have an apoplexy, guv'nor . . .* rings down the decades into the old man's ears, together with the tintinnabulation of his own self-improved hearing aid. You have not been listening to me, Doctor Busner! he barks, I said that I found my sister's position doubly indefensible. It is not that I cannot forgive her for her outrageous slandering of my public service: on the contrary, I was perfectly well aware at the time of the defectiveness of much of the ordnance, aware also of its almost complete ineffectiveness when it was used in the bombardment of well-established and deeply entrenched positions. Doctor Busner, I did not study law, or philosophy, or indeed comparative religion for all those three hundred and seventy-two thousand, nine hundred and sixty minutes without coming to a fine understanding of the nature of moral responsibility and blame. I have made my peace with myself – and am prepared also to make it with my Maker – and when it comes to my conduct during those years I may be allowed many things: my obvious youth, the temper of the times, the war frenzy that gripped the general populace and that amounted to – an apposite expression from your own usually fuzzy professional terminology – group-think. Although, let me be clear: I do not forgive my younger self on the basis of any specious relativism – regardless of place or time, before God some acts will always be wrong – but there was much mitigation. Whether such mitigation can be applied to my sister's own conduct, I very much doubt: a self-professed pacifist, she willingly became a vital component in the engine of war. A socialistic collectivist, she yet felt free to deliver the damning judgements that only behove an individual. A violent advocate of women's rights and suffrage, she nonetheless chose, quixotically, to set aside her convictions in the belief that Omnia vincit amor. As to your argument that she was already suffering with encephalitis lethargica at the time of our brother's death, this is simply not borne out by the facts. I have read Constantin von Economo's original paper on the disease – something that you, with your limited capacity for languages, cannot have done – and while he first identified the pathology in Vienna in 1916, cases were not recognised in England until early 1918 – indeed, the paper published in the Lancet that first drew the attention of the authorities to the potential wastage of manpower implied by this epidemic appeared only in April – the twentieth, if my memory still serves me. No, when my sister was working at the Arsenal, turning the fuse caps of shells, then filling and packing those shells, she was as physically sound as any of her fellow workers, workers who, it may please you to learn, had significantly better occupational health than those in comparable peacetime industries – a matter on which the statistics, should you care to consult the relevant papers, will certainly bear me out. No, Audrey's attitude was doubly indefensible, Doctor Busner, because if anyone could be said to be to blame for Lance-Corporal Stanley Death's death – which, so far as we can judge, was indeed the result of a premature shell detonation, given the location in which his remains were eventually discovered, in 1928 – then it was she and her fellow munitions workers, whose lackadaisical and generally inefficient approach to their duties at times bordered on criminal negligence. So, you perceive the impasse, Doctor Busner: it is not that I cannot forgive her for blaming me – a resentment that, given her long period of mental inanition, I daresay has been significantly attenuated – but rather that it is I, remaining in complete and continuous possession of all my faculties, who have blamed her for every single one of the intervening twenty thousand and ninety-three days since our brother was killed – including this one. Therefore, whatever the circumstances under which she is currently detained, it is unthinkable that I should have any contact with her, while as to visiting her at the hospital, that is absolutely out of the question. And now, Doctor Busner, I believe what professional business we have with one another is concluded. I might, were yours a social visit, ask you remain a while and take another cup of tea. It is – he gestures towards the set – mine and Missus Haines's usual practice to watch a television programme at this time – this evening we are both looking forward to the Two Ronnies. However, for reasons I've already made crystal clear, yours is not – nor could ever be – a social visit, and therefore you would oblige me by leaving post-haste.

But he did come. Standing on the pavement, looking up at the *most insane thing I've seen all day*, a hoarding upon which is inscribed the slogan LIVE YOUR LIFE IN LUXURY AT PRINCESS PARK MANOR, beside the further selling point: HEALTH CLUB OPEN TO NON-RESIDENTS, Busner recalls the afternoon in August 1971 when Sir Albert De'Ath walked unannounced on to Ward 20 of Friern Hospital. Busner didn't think to ask the old man what had had changed his massive and inertial Mind, because at the time, with his own departure for Spain only days away, the psychiatrist was alto-gether preoccupied by the increasing instability of his small cohort of post-encephalitics. — The hoarding is separated by wavy lines into three sections, the right-hand one features a luridly blue-and-green photograph cropped so as to include only the tree-fringed central section of the façade: its disproportionately elongated dome, a single campanile, and the arched portico, make of the former lunatic asylum *a plausible manor, if, that is you have no memory* ... In the second section a young man in a shiny black singlet stares determinedly ahead, his muscular arms cocked so that his clenched fists repose by his bulging pectorals. From his earphones and their bridle of cable, as much as the blurry young woman in the background in shorts and on an exercise machine, Busner deduces that this must be the health club open to non-residents – while the third section, which features, shot from above, the top half of a lunging swim-suited figure dappled by a leprosy of chlorinated water, must, he assumes, be an image of the fully equipped indoor swimming pool. He continues to stand, caught in *a crisis of fixed regard* by the hoarding, its marketing buzz-line, *Award-winning individually designed quality apartments set in 30 acres of stunning parkland*, sawing into his skull, along with: *Live your life in luxury at Princess Park Manor* ... *Princess Park!* The Park bit, he concedes, has a blunt topographic plausibility, but Princess? What

373

could possibly account for this renaming other than an impulse to mythologise of Hitlerian proportions – *did they have no idea of what went on here!* Princess evokes, he supposes, sleeping beauties, snuggled up in their quality apartments beneath clean duvets, awaiting only the kiss of a handsome prince in a shiny black singlet to awaken them to another day in the fitness suite, with its wide variety of studio classes and personal training – *not forgetting the health and beauty spa!* — There had been no beauty and precious little health that day. As Busner had led Sir Albert through the grotty day-room and into the female dormitory, Mboya, Inglis, Vail – the names came back to him now – had waylaid him one after another: Mister Ostereich was having another respiratory crisis, should they give him a further twenty milligrammes of intravenous Benadryl? Helene Yudkin's opisthotonos had recurred – if she could stand at all, she bent back and back so far that she fell over, should they administer Symmetrel as a partial agonist to the L-DOPA? And Leticia Gross – they had whispered her name, although the bellowing of the woman-mountain resounded lustily through the ward – is terrified, would he give her an injection of some kind? Largactil – or Valium? Sir Albert had been altogether unaffected by the tumult: erect and severe in an unlikely suit of black-and-white houndstooth cheque, he was wearing just the one pair of spectacles and a single hearing aid. I have come to visit my sister, he had said to Busner when they encountered one another by the nurses' station – *and that was that.* All Busner had hoped for was that his sister would be as unaffected by the trouble as he was – for that's what Busner chose to think of it as: *a little trouble*, nothing to be concerned about – simply side-effects of the L-DOPA that could be managed with the right complementary drugs. They would titrate the doses differently, use phenothiazine

374

and butyrophenone as buffers – *put up the umbrella* as much as the nurses required, but at all costs keep on with the trial *that's nothing of the sort* . . . — Glancing back to make sure that the old man is still following him, Busner looks into first one embayment, then the next, worried at what he may see: the bluing face of a post-encephalitic holding his breath . . . *'til he bursts*, or the tongue of another poking out uncontrollably to catch *flies that for once aren't there* . . . the eyes of a third battened on to a corner of the ward, *entranced by a cobweb* . . . In his growling guts Busner knows that things are going badly wrong – has known it since shortly after the outing to Alexandra Palace: together with Mboya he has already tried cutting the enkies' L-DOPA, increasing it, administering it in smaller doses – but whatever they do the ghastly symptoms of the malady re-emerge . . . *bones ploughed up from a battlefield.* And in his calmer, more analytic moments he understands this: that these are no side-effects at all, but simply the total refutation of what he has fervently wanted to believe: that far from orderly health being fundamental to the human condition, it is chaotic disease that howls through the enkies' cellular caverns, and screeches between the manifold branches of their brain-stems. He blames Whitcomb for this – if only *the bloody man* wasn't so fixated on what he terms the Bottom Line – a penny-pinching and mercenary limitation that Busner envisions as a limbo-dancer's pole, beneath which the consultant *bends back . . . and back . . .* the flaps of his white coat dragging in the . . . *dirt of his own fucking making!* Staff numbers have been cut throughout the hospital, the Occupational Therapy Department half closed – and the effects on all the patients are already evident, but especially on the chronic ones: they slump about the rundown wards with still more of nothing to do, their state-underfunded skins sagging into their donated

375

clothing, their sad eyes filmed with two parts of chlorpromazine to one of . . . *neglect.*

In his wake Sir Albert keeps on coming. Mind, Busner suspects, cannot possibly assimilate all this confusion – repels it in fact: a bow-wave of psychic distortion that moves ahead of Mind's relentless cerebration, or, if it becomes too choppy, is cleaved by Mind's prow of a nose. Halting, Busner asks Sir Albert to wait for a moment: It might be a little shocking for her if you were to arrive completely unannounced – and leaves Mind to meditate on the flat roof of the laid-off Occupational Therapy Annexe. Peeking into Audrey's niche, Busner is delighted to find her her unusual self: tart, self-contained, and intent upon the Financial Times, items from which she insists on reading out to him: the dividends being paid to shareholders by Rio Tinto Zinc and Allied British Securities, fluctuations in the currency exchanges, the precise amount of the balance-of-payments deficit. Busner, putting on his Panglossian spectacles, chooses to see this as nothing more than a benign extension of her interest in the world and, squatting down in front of her chair, looks upon her *love lies bleeding* hair and the heroic cast of her long-suffering beauty . . . *with a lover's eyes.* It's at this moment he *drops my own bombshell* . . . saying: By the way, Miss Death, your brother is here to see you — and then, fearing that he might prejudice the encounter by letting slip some of his own banked-up antipathy, he rises abruptly and goes to fetch Sir Albert. He could not know . . . / *How could I have known?* — It's the stately whoosh past of a bus with NOW YOU CAN CHANGE YOUR PACKET EVERY MONTH WITH FLEXIBLE BOOSTERS plastered across its side that determines him: I shall say, he thinks, that I want to have a look at one of these Last Few Remaining Apartments, with a view to my retirement – then they'll show me round, and gladly! A security guard slumps in a yellow fluorescent tabard on a chair outside the gatehouse *looking exactly like a long-stay mental patient* ... and beyond him Busner sees that the old Friend's Shop has been converted into a sales office for the Princess Park, with an ecologically hopeful armature of ... *I once had a* ... Norwegian wood. Standing, looking through the wide windows at the dinky leaseholds dotted across a scale model of the development that's spread along a vast tabletop, Busner is gripped by remorse and castigates himself: Isn't this the way you've always regarded the world, you cold bastard, as a readily apprehensible – no reducible! – object that you could look down upon from your peak perspective? But then he gives himself succour too, for, inasmuch as the new inmates of Friern Hospital have the blurry features and disproportionate limbs of all diminutions, *so I, the omniscient God, am always kept apart from them by a Plexiglas cover* ... And moreover: *How could I've known?* — That Audrey sits, the Financial Times crumpled in her lap, waiting with calm, firm conviction for Stanley to come. He will be much aged – she accepts that: he is seventy-nine. She thinks he will probably be one of those men who put on a lot of weight in middle age, and so, in those few seconds before he arrives, she rubs at the outlines of her memory of him, smudging the neat pencil strokes of his youthful form into a believable corpulence ... *And he will be jolly*, she thinks: a jolly man, who always remembers his deliverance from the hell of the battlefield ... *lifted up by the Archangel Michael, borne home with his cushy one* ... *to Blighty*. Of his life after the war she can form no picture except this: *He will have had children – many children, he will have had all the children I never did, and they too will be beautiful* ... And she sees the children, with young Stan's tall willowy form, and young Adeline's strong, handsome features.

This is as clear and present to her as the old liver-spotted hands that lie unwrapping themselves from the pink sheets ... *with their twitching* – so much clearer than the tower covered with thousands upon thousands of tiny black windows that rears over her, a tower topped off with an ugly advertisement hoarding that bears her brother Albert's agèd face, through the bulgy grey eyes of which beam down at her ... *deff-rays.*

A short time later Sir Albert De'Ath and Doctor Zachary Busner sit either side of the utilitarian desk in the nurses' station of Ward 20. Busner smokes one of his own cigarettes – filterless Gauloises Caporal that none of the nurses can bear. Sir Albert has accepted a cup of tea, and now he adds demerara sugar from a rumpled cellophane packet with quick digging movements of a spoon that remind Busner of ... *someone hurriedly filling in a grave.* I have been researching further on encephalitis lethargica, Sir Albert says. Oh, really ... Busner isn't exactly distracted, however he is quietly enjoying the way that Mind seems so much pettier when prised from its strange reef of impedimenta and set down in this workaday context, with a tatty staff roster framing its bald cranium. Ye-es, Sir Albert continues, as I said when we first met, I was aware of the epidemic at the time and had retained this data – the Lancet article, the HMSO report put out later in 1918, and a few other bits and pieces – but learning of my sister's condition led me to investigate the matter more thoroughly and from a historical perspective. The old man, hunched up in his *spiffy togs,* sups his tea, and Busner mentally *rubs at his outline,* sees him *smudged into senescence* and so becoming *eminently suitable for admission.* – I wonder if you were aware that – insofar as these things can be established from fragmentary contemporary records and long after the fact – there seem to've been a number of other outbreaks. Really, Busner dreamily exhales. Sir Albert grows pettish: Yes, really, Doctor Busner: in London in the 1670s, in Manchester in the 1840s – in Vienna at the turn of the century, as we know, – and then quite possibly in the Nazi's concentration camp at Theresienstadt during the Second War . . . This does get through the tabac brun to the psychiatrist, who leans forward and stubs out his cigarette. Sir Albert continues in his usual robotic tone: Of course, on the face of it, there are perfectly obvious reasons – common to any of the epidemiological studies – why a brain fever should've affected people in these cities at these times: density of population, insufficiency of diet, etcetera, etcetera . . . Yet something about the possible outbreak at Theresienstadt made me look at the question in a less analytical and more . . . in a more . . . It is strange indeed to see *Mind lost for words* . . . yes, a more symbolic way – perhaps that's your influence, Busner, or at least the influence of your professional expertise. To wipe away the bad taste of his sarcasm, Sir Albert gets out a heavily wadded and stained handkerchief from his breast pocket and rubs it around his mouth, then he resumes: I'm not sure if you're familiar with Theresienstadt . . . *Where is this going? Does he want me put in there, long after the fact?* but even by German standards it was a model of efficient administration and planning – albeit put to rather, ahem, inhumane ends. Perhaps as many twenty thousand Jews and other undesirables were crowded within the old town walls, which were not much more than half a mile square. Inside there were workshops of all sorts – upholstery, shoemaking, etcetera – a bakery, and a brewery, they even had a machine shop and an electricity-generating plant, and at one time, I believe, a small chamber orchestra and a theatre. Sir Albert takes a gulping tea break, then, with a sweet and tannic sigh, begins again: Ahhh, the aim, of course, was not to in any way improve the lot of the inmates, but rather to create a version of a Potemkin village that could be shown off to visiting Red Cross delegations – they made a rather grisly film of it, the Nazis, although unfortunately I've been unable to see a copy ... It would've been interesting ... he muses, long and *disturbingly elegant* fingers *fondling his empty cup* ... because it might've helped me to confirm the outline of my theory –. Which is? Busner breaks in, fully expecting some anti-Semitic nastiness. Surely, Sir Albert continues unruffled, you see the similarities here: all these cities had the high populations needed to support the disease vector at the time the epidemics occurred – indeed, they had all recently undergone considerable population explosions – but Theresienstadt is a case apart. If we look for the factor it has in common with the others – London on the brink of the first Industrial Revolution, Manchester in the throes of the second, Vienna caught up in a frenzy of wartime armaments production – we might hypothesise that it is not the numbers or density of humans that was the decider, but the density of mechanisation, of ... technology. Anyway ... abruptly for such an elderly man, Sir Albert rises to his full, looming height ... it is, as I say, merely the outline of a theory, I offer it to you by way of a valediction. And then Busner remembers: But, Sir Albert, I haven't asked you ... I mean ... how did it go with your sister? Mind looks down on him with ill-concealed contempt, and says: Go? It didn't go with my sister at all, Doctor Busner – she is, as I suspected, quite catatonic, altogether unreachable – didn't register my presence at all so far as I could make out, and looked to be stricken by a terrible sadness, Melancholica attonica, I believe it's called ... You see, I hope, that I'm not entirely the brute you take me for, I've explained it to your assistant –. – Assistant? Busner is on his feet as well, and the two of them edge round the desk in their respective crannies. Ye-es, Sir Albert says, African gentleman – Mboya, is it? Seemed very capable, I told him I'd make all the arrangements necessary for an annuity to be paid to Audrey for the rest of her life – paid even in the event of my predeceasing her. I was able to tell him this – and here Mind is unable to repress a smirk of conceit – in his own language, with which I have a little familiarity.

They are on the ward, and Sir Albert is pushing open the double doors to the corridor. His own language? Busner says, You mean ... Kikuyu? Sir Albert stops to beam contempt down at him, then answers: Good heavens, no, Dholuo – Mboya is a Luo, not a Kikuyu, which probably explains why he's here and not in Kenya, eh? I'm not surprised your career is failing to advance beyond this institution, Busner, given your lack of interest in your colleagues. And with this parting knock-out blow, *our professional association clearly being at an end, Sir Albert, for all his apparent solidity – dematerialised* ... — Can I help you? she says. The woman is in her late thirties, idiosyncratically plump in places – the undersides of her arms, the top of her hips and ribcage – that imply the wearing of restrictive undergarments beneath her stretchy black top and stretchy black slacks. *Self-defeating* ... *really.* She has a handsome, hawkish face – *Greek?* – unloosed dark hair, and a prepossessing lack of make-up. *Not what you expect from an estate agent.* – I ... ah, well ... They are standing beside the large tabletop model of the hospital-turned-luxury development, and, feeling the beginnings of a swoon, Busner puts his old hand on to it to *help myself* ... I – I used to work here! The statement comes out as a weird exultation – he had been fully intending to stick with his imposture of being a prospective buyer for one of these Last Few Remaining Apartments, right up until it popped out of his mouth. The woman seems altogether unfazed. Really, she says, and what was it you did here – her eye tracks over his grubby clothing, rests on the crumpled and sweat-rimmed hat – did you used to work in the Upholstery Workshop, or the Occupational Therapy Unit, possibly? He laughs. – No, no, I really did work here – I was a psychiatrist. Around them in the former Friends' Shop her own colleagues are tap-tap-tappety-tapping at their keyboards, twitch-twitch-twitchety-twitching at their computer mice, their eyes ticcing back and forth across a few fractions of inches, and *in these acts alone crossing continents, journeying to alien worlds, or penetrating the psyches of others* . . . Shouldn't be such a snob, he admonishes himself, after all, why's it any different to poring over an atlas while listening to a radio – which I did plenty as a child? The woman has folded her arms to create more . . . *novel lumps – shouldn't be judgemental about that either, not at my age* . . . and she says, I'm sorry, it's just that we get a fair number of old patients coming back to look at the place. Busner starts to say: I'm surpri—, but then stops, realising that he isn't surprised in the least. I suppose, he continues instead, that they are looking for some kind of . . . then trails off. The woman looks at him critically and vocalises his thought: Security? Yes, I know they are, because they often tell me it was here they felt most secure – many, of course, are not at all happy, some are terribly distressed. It's Busner's turn to look at her critically, he can detect no irony in her tone, her expression is open . . . *sincere.* She seems a most unaccountably *therapeutic estate agent* . . . He smiles, and says, Am I right in thinking that you too feel a sense of security here? The woman laughs, a pleasingly rich and chocolatey chuckle, Ha-ha, well, ha, yes . . . She puts out a hand, the maintenance of which, he imagines, costs her considerable effort, since each nail has been individually painted . . . *with crescent moons, rainbows, a dove, ten little scenes of rather mawkish . . . security* . . . I'm Athena Dukakis, she says as they shake – and Busner searches quickly through many silver bands *including one on her thumb!* for the gold one on her marriage finger: *mere force of habit* . . . Busner, he offers up, Doctor Zack Busner – I was here for a couple of years in the early seventies. Releasing his hand, *Missus* Dukakis turns to the model and gestures. – Well, as you see, there've been a lot of changes. I suppose I know the place as well as anyone – I almost grew up here: my father bought the buildings when the hospital was shut down in 1992. Busner again searches her handsome face and warm tone for any irony, any *doubling or subterfuge . . . a trapdoor beneath which the oubliette yawns, full of pain and despair* . . . He says judiciously, It must've been pretty strange for a young girl, I mean – it was a mental hospital. Dukakis *makes things intelligible for me* . . . by running her crescent-moon-tipped finger along the Plexiglas lid of the model while saying, As you can see, the first thing he did was to demolish the entire second range of the hospital, leaving the first-range front-age intact – which is really the finer, original architecture, together with the spurs built off it in the 1860s. But you're right, it was strange – she flips from realtor to reminiscent – I was in my teens, and he'd bring me up here on site visits and let me wander about. The last handful of patients had left in a hurry – their toothbrushes were still in the bathroom recesses, a few rather pitiful belongings in their bedside cabinets. The medical staff had abandoned all sorts of . . . strange equipment – and there were the padded cells, of course, they pretty much freaked me out! Silently, their eyes travel over the simulacrum of *the booby-hatch* . . . and Busner remembers the strange atmosphere of the old asylums in the late 1980s and early 1990s, how,

383

as they were wound down, with each patient discharged a bed would be removed and not replaced, until there were only these small mattress islands in the great echoing wards – islands squatted on by hairy geriatrics *Barbary apes . . .* It was, he thinks, akin to some process of decolonisation, with the far-flung possessions of the therapeutic empire being successively ceded, given up to the wrecker's ball, and to . . . *luxury flats.*

There are a number of rigid paper bags standing on the desks, plan chests and the model's table – regal purple bags decorated with the development's logo: the elongated dome of the former hospital and its two flanking campaniles . . . *fake, sucking the stench of madness into the suburban skies, what do they suck up now, potpourri, freshly ground coffee?* Athena Dukakis says, We've got a sort of presentation-thingy on tomorrow, if you're wondering about the bags – they're goodie ones, give-aways, a CD-ROM with a virtual tour of the development, a scented candle, bath salts . . . that sort of thing . . . She falls silent, then, *perking up again,* says, Look, to be frank, it's pretty quiet just now – what with the credit crunch and all that our sales aren't exactly . . . booming. Would you like me to show you round? This is said impulsively, *but with a decided warmth . . .* As he follows her down the drive towards the roundabout with its ornamental flowerbed – which is far more refulgent than he remembers it, a blaze of pink, mauve and scarlet – Busner wonders *why has she warmed to me?* For he's altogether conscious of his gracelessness, stumbling along, footsore in his training shoes *Addenough . . .* and topped off by his dosser's hat, the very image of a returning patient in search of security – *or an Unknown Pauper Lunatic, what happened to him?* And, more to the point, Busner thinks, what happened to the old alienist, Marcus, whom I deceived – as if he needed protecting! – about the statue? If he were alive now, he'd be – what? over a hundred – still, it was quite possible to imagine him hanging on in his St John's Wood flat, and persecuting *the little wife who comes crackling across the plastic with her liverish offerings . . .* They reach the main doors, and as Busner turns to trudge obediently past, he's shocked to see that they have swung soundlessly open of their own accord, while behind them a further set of glass doors schuss apart: *the magical entrance to Sleeping Beauty's castle . . . The mountainside, the flower grows, The riverside where the water flows for-èver . . .* Athena Dukakis laughs. – I see you're confused by the doors – it was the second thing my dad did: open them up, after all, you could hardly have the keep-fit crew skulking round the side, now could you? Where the cantilevered landing once reared above the dead theatrical space – and he remembers now, a hyperactive Cordelia babbled, *N-N-N-Nothing c-c-c-comes of n-n-nothing –* there are instead *lots of things,* the high hall having been sliced in three, horizontally, these compartments to be viewed through a rood screen of blond wood and glassy panels. At their feet these windows disclose the sunken swimming pool, through the azure fluid of which a swimmer stretches photo-opportunistically – while at their chest-height a broad floor of quarry tiling supports seating areas of round-backed armchairs, a zinc-fronted bar, and all the other silent clamour of a coffee bar in full afternoon swing: *one or two muffin-heads eating sweetbreads the same shape.* And up above this, a further platform hovers under the old beams and trusses of the original roof, a platform upon which, behind a glass balustrade, can be seen thronging the shiny racks of running machines. Busner sees several pairs of legs going back and forth, back and forth . . . *but going nowhere. Festination . . .* comes to him, and then he spots the shiny steer-horns of rowing machines, and of other lifting, stretching and yanking devices, some of which are being repetitively hauled up and down, up and down, to raise no other masses than . . . *bigger triceps, biceps and deltoids* . . . From the same mental recess comes . . . *a mobile spasm of athetosis and myoclonic jerking* . . . Busner looks up at the eyes of one of the runners-on-the-spot above his head, and notes that these are fixed unwaveringly on a mid-distance towards which her festinating feet will *never carry her* and he thinks: She's having an oculogyric crisis. Next he concentrates hard and can separate from the gargling of the espresso machine and the wind-chiming of the Muzak the mounting chuffer-chuff-chuff of her breathing, and so diagnoses the onset of . . . *a respiratory crisis!* The young man in the photograph on the hoarding by the main gates, *or his twin*, brushes past the gawping Busner, who looks down at his sports bag and is gone from the fitness centre back into *a hot hangover . . . which has to be the worst kind there is* . . . — How long, he wonders despairingly, will I have to stand in this fucking queue? What makes it worse is that there's nothing to look at but the stone floor scattered with the crumpled-up results of scores of tiny financial transactions, the window *which hurts my eyes,* or the thing he wishes to avoid: the man who's at the counter in front of him, and who bends to address the cashier through the metal grille, speaking so croakily that it's altogether impossible for Busner to decide what language he's using. *He is me* . . . the fifty-peseta clipper-cut intended to impose respectability – this being a representative monarchy in which, should they choose to, the shaven-headed, shiny-origami-hat-wearing agents loyal to the Caudillo might well *shear you in public* . . . – the filthy-blue BOAC flight bag full of empty wine bottles, and *that tremor,* the insistent shaking of a nervous system habituated to *regular*

386

sedation with ethyl alcohol ... Busner has no doubt that the old remittance man is a Brit – even if he can't tell what language he's speaking, the loud mangling of it remains indisputably *YouKay* ... There seems to be some sort of dispute going on concerning the dirty little scrap of paper the remittance man keeps thrusting under the grille, and with a sickening jolt Busner realises that this is a Thomas Cook traveller's cheque exactly like the ones he needs to cash. The Spanish holiday, he thinks, has been broadly a success: they have looked, eaten, talked, driven, done it all over again. There has been no great intimacy between him and Miriam, but that's *only to be expected* ... it's exhausting enough keeping the baby cool, making sure all the children are hydrated with expensive bottled water. No, the holiday has been a success, and there are only a few more days before they fly home – it's not exactly been *The jungle life of mystery* ... but, arguably, it's been a perfectly acceptable chapter of ... *The wide and graceful history of life* ... He probably shouldn't have drunk quite so much last night, but that too *is only to be expected* ... If only it weren't so hot in this pestilential bank – if only the restive queue behind him didn't twitch so – each time Busner looks back at them, he sees an upsetting agitation of hands, flicking hair, brushing lips, licking tongues. And the old remittance man *with his dreadful palsy!* The confrontation has reached some sort of climax, because here into the bank comes a jack-booted Guardia Civil who must have been summoned by *some ulterior buzzer* ... Despairingly, Busner watches as the old remittance man is hauled off by the strap of his bag, his empties clinking, his eyes *blinking with tears* ... *I ought to do something, help him* ... but all Busner does is to take his place at the grille, and begin the laborious signing once, twice, flicking to the next, signing once, twice, flicking to the next – a *thumbah*, or possibly a *handango*, that recalls to his mind the repetitive ticcing of Helene Yudkin — and all at once he knows what a foul and irretrievable mistake he has made: *I should never have left them – never!* For the last four days of the holiday Busner is present in body only, he can barely rouse himself to speak *to my three waif-like kiddies and my poor drab of a wife.* When the cab drops them at the Grove, he goes into the flat only to dig out the keys to the Austin, and then he pushes past Miriam, who's struggling in with the suitcases. She says nothing: there is nothing to be said – *nothing comes of nothing, but neglect is something – and divorce came of that* . . . — When he reached Ward 20, it was late afternoon, and the sunbeams struck down through the lancet windows at precise forty-five degree angles, *I thought of castles then – specifically their dungeons, the stone-flagged cells housing Medieval inmates, their matted and filthy hair poking from between the struts and ribs of complicated fetters and cages . . . something out of Grimmelshausen . . .* He could see none of the medical staff in the day-room and the nurses' station was empty but for . . . *smoke, the acrid ghost of all our concern.* When Busner had left for Spain, Audrey Death had still been the most stable of the post-encephalitics – her stuporous state when her older brother had made his once-in-a-century visit had been: Partly shock, Doctor Busner, she told him. It would, I think, have been courteous to've at least told me that you had been to see him, as it was I was quite severely shocked – and besides, I've nothing to say to Albert De'Ath, we don't so much as share a given name – the only thing we have in common is the accident of our parentage. If you've spent any time with him you have, I daresay, been exposed to his formidable powers of reasoning – capabilities sadly unmatched by any real compassion, let alone warmth. He is the most fearful reactionary. Too much messery, Busner had muttered, and Audrey said: Speak up, young fellow, and Busner said again: I expect he's had too much of his messery – whereupon the elderly lady *laughed, she laughed – a delightful laugh: warm and seductive* ... This was the memory he took away with him: of a very thin, hunched and frail patient – that was true – but one in full possession of her senses, perfectly lucid ... *and engaged.* I do so enjoy, she had said to him, going up to see the musical woman – Missus Down, is it? – she plays, quite coincidentally, an air I remember from girlhood, Brahms's intermezzo, in A, d'you know it? Busner said, Not off the top of –. And she hummed *she hummed,* Doo-d'doo, doo d'doo, doo-d'-dooo, doo-d'-dooo, triplets of notes lilting up and down, and he had left her there – *a little twitchy, un peu rackety, true, but that was only to be expected* ... — He returned to find the most complete disharmony. *In the first cell I came to, on the men's dormitory* ... The three old men, Messrs Voss, Ostereich and McNeil, were as inert as when Busner had first seen them: they seemed no longer men at all but ... *derelict houses, burnt out and decaying* ... their faces rigidly masked, their heads lolling on their necks, their entire musculatures eroding from their frames, *so that every part of them slid away.* He had attempted, futilely, to arouse them – pulling up an eyelid, calling into the dark and sadly unwashed cavern of an ear. Nothing. Worse than nothing: a sense of a profound absence – not only that there was no sentience in any of the three, *but there never had been* ... *it'd been my dream, perhaps, as much as theirs* ... He went into the women's dormitory and discovered the colossal frame of Leticia Gross still lumped on her reinforced catafalque – but whereas when he had left she had been a troubling presence, what with her bullying and commanding of the nursing staff, now she was a twenty-five-stone absence, a mound of inanition, her petite features seemingly in the process of being reabsorbed by her rolls and dewlaps of flesh . . . *in a heavy and sluggish wave of rolling dystonia.* There was no sign of her cheeky-chappie husband – none of the medical staff were in evidence at all. He went next to Helene Yudkin's bed, and found there at least some signs of life, but only . . . *signing once, twice, flicking to the next, signing once, twice again, flicking to the next* . . . the thumbah and handango of her compulsive traveller's-cheque-ticcing . . . *she could not speak, she couldn't say anything was marvellous any more . . . she was lost to me* . . . At last Busner had met with Hephzibah Inglis hurrying along. What has happened to my enkies? he had challenged her, without any other greeting or pleasantry . . . *and she looked at me as simply another puffed-up doctor, engorged with my own professional status, rolling over the little people and so spared me nothing*: – Your enkies, Doc-tor Busner? Why, all dat foolishness was done put a stop to second you skipped off a-broad. Doctor Whitcomb, he see de dread-ful state of dese poor folk so he took 'em off dat damn fool drug of yours – he took de drugs inall –. He had wrenched himself away from Inglis's complacent smirk and headed at last for the little niche he had secured for her, with its scrap of view – headed at last towards Audrey Death, cursing himself . . . *for having ever forgotten her for an instant, for having chosen to ignore my responsibilities as her physician* . . . and arrived to find that it was all far, far worse than he had feared: she was not only wrenched halfway round in her chair, her eyes fixated on an invisible object above and behind her, but those eyes had flies clustered in them, while her arms and legs had been strapped to that chair. He went straight to the buckles of these straps and began unfastening them. I shouldn't do dat if I was you,

Doc-tor, said Inglis coming up behind him. You don't know de half of it, when she be freed she go flat-out crazy –. Then he had lost his temper, and begun shouting at her: Don't you know that the proud boast of this fucking miserable bloody place was that *no hand or foot will be bound here . . .* — Shall we go on, Doctor Busner? Athena Dukakis asks, and he says, Of course, of course, do forgive me, I was only struck by how . . . well, how strange this all is – I mean, you've kept the original foundation stone. They stand looking at the white plaque, scanning its incised lettering: THIS FOUNDATION STONE WAS LAID BY FIELD MARSHAL HIS ROYAL HIGHNESS PRINCE ALBERT . . . followed by the list of Commissioners for Lunacy and assorted beneficent dignitaries, at the bottom of which surrounded by scrollwork there is this motto: NO HAND OR FOOT WILL BE BOUND HERE. Some people, Busner says as they leave the fitness centre, might find it rather, well, rather disturbing to be living enclosed by these walls – which in their time have witnessed so much mental distress. Dukakis looks at him critically. Surely, she says, that's a little hippy-dippy for a psychiatrist, I mean, don't tell me you're one of those people who thinks old buildings can have psychic auras. Anyway, they're lovely buildings now – you can see that. They are strolling between a bushy hedge and the façade of the first range, the brickwork of which has been returned to its original honey colour. The windows are beautifully pristine, and every few yards a cast-iron lamp standard containing an electric bulb has been erected. This is meant to instil in the residents, Busner supposes, a pleasing sense of Victorian civic pride with *none of the accompanying low wattage.* Hippy-dippy we were, he thinks – and those of us who didn't float off back to nature, or take to the barricades, took a sort of solace in our own nostalgic Victoriana. He smiles, thinking of the sartorial fripperies of the period – the long white silk scarves, and original tailcoats picked up at flea markets, and the bandsmen's scarlet coats that could be spotted weaving their way through the crowds at the Isle of Wight festival, gold frogging leaping about in time to Hendrix's axe-work. Miriam insisted on William Morris floral-patterned wallpaper – while Busner had his own brief flirtation with a handlebar moustache and a velvet smoking jacket . . . *It must've been strange for them, the reawakened, to have swum back to consciousness in a world done up in a travesty of their own childhood, complete with a soundtrack of oompah psychedelia* . . . As Inglis claimed, the restraints had been necessary, for, when the sixteen hours of Audrey Death's oculogyric crisis drew to an end, she did not relapse into akinesia but became animated by the most extreme ticcing Busner had ever seen – a Saint Vitus Dance of every part of her: her fingers flicked, her hands spasmed, her arms, legs and neck jerked about wildly – if not prevented from standing she would leap to her feet unsteadily, then canter up and down the ward until she knocked into a wall or a piece of furniture and spun to the floor. It was with the entirely humane aim of preventing her from breaking her brittle bones that she had been restrained. Safely strapped down, she still came out with these . . . *strange cries, spontaneous jactitations* . . . Buy! Buy! she had cried, and: Sell! Sell! Disjointed numerical commands had also spilled from her mouth: Give me fourteen-eighty! I'll take nine! Try seventy-one! Hold four thousand and twenty-two! Go to them for a hundred and nine – Now! And all of this frightening gibberish had been mixed in with a chaotic choreography of tics that, try as he might, the psychiatrist could subject to no analysis, nor perceive any congruence in. He and Mboya had pleaded with Whitcomb to allow them, in Audrey Death's case at least, to restart the L-DOPA. Given the old woman's state of extreme agrypnia – a sleeplessness that would not respond to any sedative dose short of a toxic one – the consultant relented. However, even back on the drug, she continued her erratic course, flipping between this extreme rapidity of thought and movement, and periods of increasingly deep catatonia. Over the course of a fortnight or so Busner battled to save his favourite patient, to somehow keep her balanced on this knife-edge of stability . . . *The tiger's free, the kangaroo, It's up to me and up to you* . . . A miserable and forlorn hope: it had been Mboya who finally insisted that they stop the treatment altogether . . . *In mercy and justice he said – and he was right* . . . The final words Audrey Death had spoken before relapsing into a merciful swoon were a string of nonsensical fractions – eighteen over four-point-two, ninety-four over thirteen-point-seven, sixty-six-point-three over thirty-three-point-three recurring – that, even as he accepted the futility of the exercise, Busner had tried to fit into some conceptual framework. Were they, perhaps, the numerical analogue of her brain chemistry's intro-conversions between the discrete and the continuous, the quantifiable and the relativistic?

Having reached the far end of the first range, they're walking along the grassy strip where the second range used to be. Unbounded by its lowering bulk, the old airing courts between the spurs are jolly sunlit patches of *grassy sanity* . . . What happened, Busner asks the developer's daughter, to the long corridor in the sub-basement? She snorts: Well, amazing as it was, we could hardly preserve all 1,884 feet and six inches of it – it's not really the sort of thing our potential residents are looking for . . . No, if you come over here . . . She trips down an incline towards the back of the building . . . you can see that it's been chopped up into a series of vestibules that run along behind each residential block. If you look through the window here you can still get an idea of it. He looks as she tells him to, and gets no idea of that *human linear-particle accelerator* at all – is only dazzled by the reflections of the glass and underwhelmed by what he suspects are pegs on the white-painted wall hung with a couple of Barbour jackets and a woolly hat or two. Beyond these prosaic things: a second window, and beyond that another window, behind which, doubtless, *hangs more rainwear . . .* A cartoonish and synthesised diddle-um-pom-quack! comes from somewhere about Dukakis's person, and continues to diddle-um-pom-quack! as she pats herself down with her pictorial manicure until she locates her mobile phone. Busner backs off to give her the fifteen feet of mandated public privacy. Along comes Zachary, he thinks, and then: *I'm an ape man . . . I'm an ape-ape man . . .* returns to him, complete with steel drums and jangling guitars. I'm afraid that was the Sales Centre, she says, tucking the phone away, it seems we do have a prospect after all – sorry, but I'll have to go back and give 'em the spiel. She smiles *winningly*, and continues: Do feel free to carry on looking around – there's a show flat at the other end of the main building if you want to get an idea of what it's like inside, and if you've got any questions come and track me down. She's backing away, *pantherish* in her Lycra . . . *I should've liked to press that flesh again . . .* he voices his thanks, and then she is gone, leaving him in the former airing court, breathing too heavily – panting almost. He leans against the window of the chopped-up corridor, and the dark starship of the old hospital turns on this axis about his ageing head. I'm having, Busner realises, a panic attack – and he tries to laugh it off: Well, I suppose there has to be a first time for everything . . . *What we see is what we choose, What we keep or what we lose for-èver . . .* Then he hauls himself upright, takes off his hat, massages his temples, shakes his head and thinks: So long as I'm plagued by these ancient ditties I can't be dead yet! He takes a critical and evaluative look round at the airing court again, and finds to his surprise that he's fully orientated within the shell of Friern Hospital as it was four decades before. With a mixture of shock and satisfaction Busner realises that he's standing . . . *exactly at the point where I was when I first saw her, the saliva gathering on her fine cheekbone and then looping down to that floor unbroken, her small foot in its child's slipper kicking against the lip of linoleum tile* . . . He turns back to the window and leans his forehead against it. It has taken a very long while, but he's arrived at last: *I forgot them* . . . he concedes in weariness, in desolation . . . *I stayed on at Friern for a month or two after that, but then I walked away, as I've walked away from everything in my life: marriages, jobs, colleagues, commitments, patients – I forgot them all* . . . *The world is ours to tear apart, But what if it's too late to start again? And it is too late* . . . Because, thinking back to those last few weeks of the trial-that-never-was-a-trial, he understands: *it all had to do with time.* He recalls the films he made of the post-encephalitic patients, specifically the one of Audrey Death operating her invisible lathe . . . *I saw it! I saw that it was out of sequence* . . . *that through her ticcing she was travelling in time* . . . But it had been too radical a hypothesis to entertain: that embodied in these poor sufferers' shaking frames was the entire mechanical age – that just as the schizophrenics' delusions partook of modish anxieties, so the post-encephalitics' akinesia and festination had been the stop/ start, the on/off, the o/1, of a two-step with technology . . . *and she, Audrey, anticipated it!* In her last frenzied weeks before she finally collapsed, she had given him a preview of what was to come: the binary blizzard that would blow through humanity's consciousness

— Perhaps if there had been the right scans available . . . Later, in the 1980s, I could've looked inside her brain – seen it . . . But, even as he thinks this, Busner knows how impossible that would have been . . . *because I lacked the feeling . . . the artistry . . .* The pop ditties that had infested his mind had been, he now understands, continuous reminders not only of this unfinished and abandoned travail, but of all the other crimes of forgetting he had committed: *Don't let it die, Don't let it die . . .* Hurricane Smith had groaned these melodic truisms – but simply because they were truisms, it didn't mean they weren't . . . *true.* Busner presses his face to the cold glass, he cups his hands around his face to block out the sunlight. Colonel Blink sees clearly the vestibule fashioned from a mere fifteen feet of the old hospital corridor: those aren't Barbour jackets hanging from the pegs but . . . *bodies . . .* the corpse of his schizophrenic brother, Henry, who committed suicide at fifty-two, after thirty years as an inmate of psychiatric hospitals. He hangs there, looking much as he must have . . . *before they cut him down . . .* the collar of his dirty lumberjack's shirt caught on the varnished wooden prong, one of his polythene-and-coat hanger blooms poking from the pocket of his cruelly hiked-up jeans . . . *I visited him – but never enough, I was swayed by Ronnie's madness about madness into believing that it was me that had caused his illness . . .* And beside his dead brother twitches the still-living body of Busner's eldest son, Mark . . . *his poor face!* who, although not doomed to the soul-aching gloom of the strip-lit wards, remains the unwilling, tempestuous and tortured recipient of . . . *care in the community . . .* and who has to wait a very long time in his Stanmore bedsit for a visit from his psychiatrist father to . . . *check he's taking his medication, so that Hey, Presto! no mental illness – all gone . . .* And beyond these discards, what is it that Busner sees

propped up in the corner, her thin metal ribs and struts all furled in the stained folds of her old silken skin? His very own ... *Sleeping Beauty* ... her neck, gripped in the kyphotic vice of her extreme old age, curves up and over into a hook, so that levelled at him is its very blunt and accusatory end.

The text of this book is set in Adobe Caslon, named after the English punch-cutter and type-founder William Caslon I (1692–1766). Caslon's rather old-fashioned types were modelled on seventeenth-century Dutch designs, but found wide acceptance throughout the English-speaking world for much of the eighteenth century until being replaced by newer types towards the end of the century. Used in 1776 to print the Declaration of Independence, they were revived in the nineteenth century, and have been popular ever since, particularly amongst fine printers. There are several digital versions, of which Carol Twombly's Adobe Caslon is one.